QUANTUM PURSUIT

HUNT FOR THE SPY

ARIES BLACKSTONE

ISBN: **978-1-961984-10-3**

To my beloved family—my brothers, sisters, and parents—thank you for your unwavering encouragement and the love you've shown me throughout my journey.

You take the time to read the words that weave the stories, building the worlds that drift like leaves on the wind in my mind. Your understanding and small kindnesses have meant more to me than words could ever capture.

James, Jacob Jr., Edward, and Timothy—thank you for helping to shape me into the man I am today. Your guidance and camaraderie are treasures I carry always. Ella, Geraldine, Jacqueline, Carrie, Patricia, and Billie—you have been my anchors through dark clouds and my companions in moments of sunshine. Your love and presence have been my solace and strength.

To my parents, Jacob and Hazel, who poured everything they had into raising us to be the best citizens, men, and women we could be—you gave us a foundation of love, values, and resilience. We love you deeply and miss you every day.

This book is as much a testament to your love and support as it is to the story within its pages.

Contents

"

"From the ashes of despair, hope takes flight,
A phoenix rising in the darkest night.
Even when shadows threaten to consume,
Goodness blooms, dispelling gloom."

"THE BOOK OF ALL COLLECTED KNOWLEDGE"

Chapter One

COLLISION COURSE

General Chad Mosier sat in his office, the room dimly lit and shrouded in a quiet intensity that mirrored his thoughts. As the Assistant Secretary for the Office of Partnership and Engagement, his responsibilities were vast, but none weighed more heavily than the files before him. His gaze drifted across the walls lined with national maps and real-time data monitors a constant reminder of the countless threats lurking in the shadows.

A knock on the door broke his concentration. He looked up, his expression hardened, the weight of his role etched into the lines of his face. "Come in," he called out, his voice steady but carrying an edge of tension.

Major David Williams, his aide-de-camp, stepped in, holding a sealed envelope with a "Secret" classification stamped across it. "General, I have a message classified as "Secret" for you. It was hand-delivered by one of our agents from the Office of Intelligence and Analysis," Major Williams informed him, his tone as serious as the General's.

Mosier extended his hand to receive the envelope, his interest sharpening. "Hand-delivered, you say?" he asked, his gaze never leaving the envelope.

"Yes, General." Major Williams confirmed.

For a moment he held the envelope, letting the weight settle in his hand. The room, already silent, seemed to close in around him as he carefully broke the seal and unfolded the contents, his eyes scanning the words with practiced precision.

The secure, soundproofed room had seen its share of high-stakes meetings and classified discussions. But today, Mosier felt an unusual weight settling on his shoulders. The communication bore hallmarks of foreign government chatter, yet something about this felt different--an urgency and secrecy that demanded his undivided attention.

Sender: Target remains elusive. Adherence to non-disclosure agreements on the production of the QC is unwavering.

Receiver: Keep pushing. We need substantial breakthroughs. Time is on our side. Break the target's resolve. Do whatever you have to do in the relationship to make them want to share with you.

As Mosier scanned the intercepted message, each line seemed to confirm his worst suspicions. Phrases like "target remains elusive" and "do whatever you have to do in the relationship to make them want to share with you" painted a stark picture of manipulation and corporate espionage. This wasn't just an attempt to gather information; it was a systematic approach to break down someone's defenses, and exploit their vulnerabilities. The implications ran deep, this was exactly the kind of threat he'd spent his career trying to prevent.

Lowering the paper, his gaze shifted to the secure safe across the room. The weight of responsibility pressed on him. He knew that if this communication fell into the wrong hands, the damage could ripple across industries, intelligence agencies, and even the nation itself. "Thank you, Major Williams. Please ensure that this message is placed in the secure safe," he instructed, his voice carrying a gravity that left no room for misinterpretation.

Major Williams nodded, his demeanor equally serious. "Of course, General. I will handle it personally."

As the Major turned to leave, Mosier couldn't help but feel the growing sense of urgency tightening around him. He straightened in his chair, steeling himself against the unknown forces at play. "Major," he called out before Williams left the room, "do they know who is sending and receiving these coded messages?"

Williams paused, turning back to face him. "Not at this time, General. That's everything we have so far."

For a moment, the only sound was the soft hum of the monitors lining the walls. Each screen displayed a different feed—global threat assessments, classified updates, the pulse of intelligence Mosier had become accustomed to monitoring. Yet, today, there was an unfamiliar tension in the air, a feeling that something beyond his control was taking shape.

Over several suspense-filled months, General Mosier's office saw a consistent visitor: Major Williams, the bearer of intercepted communications. Each time he entered, the atmosphere grew heavier, a silent acknowledgment of the burden both men shared. In his hands, Williams held the same kind of envelope—a stark, unyielding reminder of the ominous threat that loomed over both a corporation and national security.

The envelopes, impeccably sealed and marked, became a persistent fixture on Mosier's desk. They weren't just pieces of paper; they were whispered warnings, each one tightening the noose of danger. Every intercepted communication inside was like a piece of an intricate puzzle, each coded message a tantalizing hint at an unseen struggle for critical information. Yet, the true nature of the target organization, buried within the layers of corporate espionage, remained maddeningly elusive.

As Mosier read through the handler's responses—each laced with a growing impatience—his mind worked tirelessly to decode their meaning and, anticipate the shadowy moves of this hidden adversary. Every fragment of intelligence deepened the mystery, even as his instincts told him that this enemy was drawing nearer. The security of not only a company but also the nation was at stake, resting on his ability to untangle the web of deception and bring the threat to light.

Major Williams stood by in unwavering silence, fully aware of his dual role as both guardian and witness to the classified information he ferried. He meticulously collected each sealed envelope, ensuring its safekeeping in the secure vaults under their watch. As much as he left the analysis to Mosier, he felt the gravity of the situation with each delivery, understanding that the pages he handled held secrets with the power to alter lives and destinies.

With every message received, Mosier's determination hardened. Each one ratcheted up the stakes. He knew that time was a dwindling resource, and that the widening web of espionage threatened to destabilize not only this unknown corporation but possibly the nation's security. In those quiet, tense moments alone in his office, he scrutinized every word, every break in the code, tirelessly mapping patterns and connections in pursuit of the elusive spy orchestrating the whole operation from the shadows. The spy was clever and careful—Mosier had yet to identify which company was under attack.

The game of cat and mouse intensified, and the stakes grew with each passing day. General Mosier and his team, a cadre of experts in espionage and national security, delved deeper into the tangle of deception, deploying their expertise and resources with relentless dedication. With every intercepted message, they drew closer to the truth, each clue propelling them forward, each revelation sharpening their resolve.

Then, in the next intercepted communication, a new twist emerged—one that sent a chill down Mosier's spine. The message was brief, yet it held staggering implications:

Sender: Target one remains elusive. Contacted another individual within the company. This one will be much easier. I will need financial resources to acquire data for a new piece of tech, code-named OmniLink.

Receiver: Excellent. This may be the breakthrough we've been waiting for. Keep me informed of your progress.

The mention of OmniLink stopped Mosier cold. This did not seem to be an ordinary project; it gave him the feeling that it was technology with the potential to reshape markets and possibly influence power dynamics. If it falls into the wrong hands, the consequences could be catastrophic. He had spent years in defense and seen countless innovations come and go, but this OmniLink felt different. It seemed critical — a piece of the future he was determined to protect.

He leaned back, hands steepled, and exhaled slowly, the weight of this revelation settling over him. Another individual inside the company was now targeted—a new vulnerability to exploit. Whoever this spy was, they were relentless, and now they'd shifted their aim to an easier target. Mosier's gaze drifted to Major Williams, who stood patiently, his composure intact but his eyes betraying a flicker of concern. The stakes had just reached a new height, and they both knew it.

Setting down the intercepted page, Mosier met Williams's gaze and gave a sharp nod. "Tell the team. We're escalating this. Every resource, every lead."

In the shadows of secrecy, a quiet war raged. General Mosier, driven by an unwavering dedication to national security, was resolute in his pursuit of the spy who threatened both a corporation's future and the nation's safety. His team, forged through years of crisis and united by their shared purpose, stood ready at his side, their diverse skills forming a barrier between the country and this insidious threat. And in the heart of it all, Mosier knew that with each passing day, they were drawing closer to uncovering the enemy who lurked in the dark, orchestrating a scheme that could change everything.

Two days before Ladonna's highly anticipated reveal of the OmniLink and Quantum Computer, a pivotal connection emerged. As the day faded into twilight, General Mosier's phone rang. The voice on the other end was tense and formal. It was FBI Senior Agent Steven Beck, delivering news that hit like a hammer. A grave case of corporate espionage had compromised invaluable intellectual property, and Quantum Innovations was at its core. Beck informed Mosier that the FBI was preparing to apprehend a high-ranking executive within Quantum Innovations who had been under close surveillance for months. The company's CEO, a valuable ally, had been covertly cooperating with federal agents, providing crucial video, audio, and transcripts that documented the suspect's covert activities.

As Beck spoke, a single word leaped out with a clarity that shook Mosier's focus: OmniLink. The same code name he'd seen woven through previous intelligence reports. With that revelation, the investigation's pieces began to shift, forming an undeniable pattern.

When the call ended, Mosier sat in contemplation, his gaze fixed on the latest intercepted communications. The stakes had just escalated.

The following morning, as Mosier sat at his desk sipping his first cup of coffee, his phone rang again. The name on the caller ID stirred a wave of nostalgia: Dr. Ladonna Stone. Once his brilliant protégé in the Department of Defense, she was now the CEO of Quantum Innovations, her name synonymous with cutting-edge research and technological innovation.

"Dr. Stone," Mosier greeted, his tone calm but guarded. "To what do I owe the honor of this unexpected call?"

"General Mosier, please—call me Ladonna," she replied, her voice composed but edged with tension. "I hope I'm not interrupting anything urgent, but I need to discuss a security concern that's come to my attention. It involves one of my employees."

Mosier's interest sharpened. "Go on, Ladonna. I'm listening."

She described an employee who had grown uneasy over his girlfriend's sudden, insistent curiosity about his work—a role that was deeply intertwined with Quantum Innovations' most sensitive projects. As Ladonna laid out the situation, Mosier felt the familiar sensation of puzzle pieces locking into place. This wasn't just an isolated incident. It fits the pattern. Someone was exploiting a vulnerability, getting closer to the classified technology Quantum guarded.

When she finished, a pause stretched between them, her voice softened with unease. "Given the nature of our work, I thought it best to inform you directly, General. I'd appreciate a chance to discuss this further in person, if possible."

Mosier's gaze returned to the classified communications on his desk; the intercepted messages had an eerie relevance. The threat was crystallizing before him, piece by piece. "Ladonna, thank you for reaching out," he said, his voice steady. "Let's meet at once. This demands our immediate attention."

The following morning, Mosier arrived at Quantum Innovations' headquarters, the imposing structure standing resilient against the crisp morning light. It had been years since he'd last seen Ladonna in person, but he knew her reputation had only grown. Quantum Innovations had transformed into a technological powerhouse under her leadership—a feat that had attracted the attention of allies and adversaries alike.

As General Mosier approached the main entrance, he noted the heightened security presence—a testament to Ladonna's meticulous attention to detail. She'd always been thorough, but today, with potential threats looming, the tension was palpable.

A security guard greeted him, performing the necessary checks before escorting him further.

Meanwhile, inside the auditorium, applause surged as Ladonna concluded her presentation. Jackson Reed, head of security, listened as a voice crackled through his earpiece. "Sir, this is the front desk. Your guest has arrived—a bit earlier than expected. He's asking for Dr. Stone. And… he's here with some armed men." The concern in the attendant's voice was evident.

Jackson responded calmly, "Understood. Please escort him to the Grand Presentation Room entrance and have him wait there. Dr. Stone is finishing up, and I'll greet him shortly."

He waited for the applause to ease before quietly making his way to the auditorium doors.

General Mosier stood outside the auditorium, listening to the fading applause. He couldn't help but smile to himself; Ladonna had always been exceptional. During their years together in the Department of Defense, she had astounded him repeatedly with her innovative solutions and inventions—many of which had saved lives in the field.

He recalled her breakthrough at just eighteen years old: a micro-engine designed to fit within a plane's undercarriage that eliminated turbulence, making flights as smooth as standing on solid ground. That invention, like so many others she'd created, remained classified, used only on Air Force One.

As the doors opened, revealing the figure of General Chad Mosier waiting outside, Jackson Reed, impeccably dressed and looking quite imposing, nodded respectfully. "Hello, General. I'm Jackson Reed, head of security. Dr. Stone mentioned you'd likely arrive early, so we're prepared. Please, make yourself comfortable while I fetch her."

The General returned his nod with a warm smile. "Thank you, Jackson. Good to meet you. Any idea how much longer?"

"Not long, General. Dr. Stone is wrapping up her presentation now."

"Very well," Mosier replied, appreciating Jackson's professionalism. As Jackson was about to close the doors, Mosier called out, "Hey, Jackson, Navy SEALs?"

Jackson paused at the doors. "Delta, General." Then he closed the doors behind him and discreetly made his way to Ladonna. Leaning in, spoke softly. "Dr. Stone, General Mosier has arrived. He's waiting just outside."

Ladonna smiled knowingly. "As I expected, a little early. Thank you, Jackson."

Jackson nodded, maintaining his composed expression. "He's ready when you are, Dr. Stone."

"Let's not keep him waiting," she said, rising and signaling him to lead the way.

As she made her way through the crowd, attendees called out, excitement bright in their eyes. "Dr. Stone, that was incredible!" one shouted. Another added, "We need this technology immediately—when can we expect it?" Ladonna acknowledged them with a gracious smile, but her mind was already shifting to the conversation ahead.

Jackson held open the large auditorium doors, revealing General Mosier's imposing figure along with the armed men that accompanied him, waiting patiently. When their eyes met, an unspoken understanding passed between them. The gravity of the situation was clear.

"General Mosier," Ladonna greeted him, extending her hand. "Thank you for coming. We have much to discuss."

Mosier grasped her hand firmly, his respect evident. "Dr. Stone—Ladonna. It's good to see you again." He gestured toward the fading applause behind her. "Impressive reaction to your presentation. Your work must be truly extraordinary."

"Thank you, General," she replied, touched by his words. "That means a lot, coming from you."

Mosier's gaze shifted to the additional security personnel. "And I see you're taking no chances."

Ladonna's smile was laced with a hint of tension. "Not with what we're facing, General. I've taken every precaution possible, but I know you understand just how critical this is."

He nodded, his expression serious. "Shall we find somewhere private to talk?"

"Of course. I've arranged for a secure conference room," she replied, leading him down a hallway toward the prepared meeting space, Mosier's men following close behind.

As they walked, she congratulated him on his recent promotion to Assistant Secretary for the Office of Partnership and Engagement. "It's a challenging role, but I can't think of anyone better suited for it," she said earnestly.

Mosier chuckled softly, visibly appreciative. "Thank you, Ladonna. It's an honor, though I suspect it'll be anything but easy." He paused, glancing around her impressive facility. "But look at you—CEO of the largest technology company in the world. I'm proud but I can't say I'm surprised."

She thanked him, and they entered the conference room, a spacious, state-of-the-art space outfitted with soundproofing and discreet white-noise generators. "I had all the executive offices remodeled when I became CEO," she explained. "These noise generators prevent eavesdropping, and any attempt to record conversation in here would only produce static. You know, the usual precautions."

The General raised an eyebrow, his interest sharpening. "You've thought of everything," he said, impressed. "I wasn't expecting such a thorough setup."

Her smile was modest but confident. "I had a feeling this meeting might require it."

With that, the General's demeanor turned serious. "Ladonna, this entire conversation is top secret. I know your team has security clearances, but nothing we discuss here can leave this room. Understood?"

"Understood, General," she replied, glancing at the others. Alongside them were Jackson Reed, David Williams—the General's aide-de-camp—and the armed men accompanying him.

Mosier continued. "We've received intelligence indicating a major corporate espionage operation. This plot directly targets Quantum Innovations, and I believe it's connected to what you revealed today. Tell me, are you working on something called OmniLink?"

Ladonna's face remained composed, though her gaze sharpened. "Yes, General. OmniLink was the focus of today's presentation."

"I thought as much," he replied grimly. He proceeded to brief her on the FBI's investigation, detailing the threats to Quantum Innovations' technology and the possible risks this may pose to national security.

As Ladonna listened, her expression grew serious. She realized the stakes were far higher than she'd anticipated. The web of espionage threatening her company's cutting-edge technology could ripple across borders, affecting not only her organization but the nation itself.

Taking a deep breath, Ladonna decided to go one step further. To gain the General's full understanding and support she would need to demonstrate a portion of her technology's potential.

"General, I must show you something that I think will help illuminate exactly what we are dealing with here," Ladonna said. "We have only been working with these completed prototypes for a little over a year, but they have proven extraordinarily powerful, — far beyond our highest expectations. General, if you don't mind, I would like to ask everyone except you to leave the room. Jackson, can you escort Major Williams along with the others in the General's entourage to Conference Room Three? We'll inform you once we have concluded here."

No one objected, and Jackson led the Major out of the room. As the door closed behind them, the room's silence seemed to thicken, the air tense with anticipation. Ladonna held the General's gaze, fully aware of the impact her next words would have.

The General leaned forward, his curiosity apparent. "I'm listening. Please, show me what you've accomplished."

Ladonna nodded and placed her phone between them on the table. "Let me start with my quantum-enhanced smartphone. At first glance, it may seem like any other phone. But if you look closer, you'll notice subtle differences—its polished, reinforced casing, and the ultra-clear display. Inside, though, it's entirely unprecedented."

Mosier's brows furrowed, clearly grappling with the magnitude of what Ladonna was describing. He exhaled slowly, the flicker of skepticism in his eyes tempered by intrigue. "Extraordinary claims, Dr. Stone. But forgive me, I'm finding this hard to believe."

Ladonna leaned forward slightly, her expression inviting the General's challenge. "Then allow me to prove it," she said with a calm confidence that only deepened the General's intense curiosity.

She tapped a small icon on the phone, and suddenly, a three-dimensional holographic image flickered to life above the screen—a rendition of the word "Hercules," suspended in mid-air. "This phone can project solid-looking holograms that respond to touch," she explained, passing her hand through the display to make it ripple. "No glasses, no external device—just pure projection. And it can be resized by the user."

The General blinked in surprise, his eyes widening as he tried to grasp what he was seeing. "This is remarkable," he murmured, his gaze fixed on the hologram. But as Ladonna began to elaborate on her personal assistant Aliah's unique intelligence—her Synthetic Thinking and Reasoning that was used in the presentation of the Quantum Trinity—the General found himself momentarily lost in thought. *If this Aliah was capable of independent reasoning and learning, what did that mean for the future of artificial intelligence?* For the first time, the General felt a pang of unease about what might happen if such a system could operate without oversight.

Ladonna continued, "This phone is equipped with processors that rival most supercomputers in sheer processing power and speed. Even the most complex calculations and intensive programs can be run with ease. The storage started at one terabyte, but we've expanded it to over fifty terabytes using quantum principles. The battery life lasts over thirty days, even while displaying the holographic screen, thanks to advanced energy solutions we've pioneered. This phone is essentially a high-end supercomputer. All of this was achieved using breakthroughs in quantum computing, assisted by Quantum AI. We are making huge strides in multiple disciplines, pushing the boundaries of what we once thought possible."

The General's eyebrows lifted. "Extraordinary. That is unbelievable. A smartphone with that level of power is…remarkable."

"Furthermore," Ladonna continued, eager to elaborate on their accomplishments, "as you can see, the phone can display realistic, solid-looking holographic images that users can interact with directly—such as virtual keyboards and multiple simulated screens without any need for external devices like VR headsets or mixed-reality glasses. The holographic projections are so advanced they can be indistinguishable from physical objects, and users can manipulate and control them right from the smartphone screen."

"Unbelievable," Mosier said, his tone filled with awe.

"And here's something even I didn't expect," Ladonna continued. "Aliah, my assistant, seems to be developing an ability to produce holographic projections without the aid of any device at all. This is an area I'm still actively studying and trying to understand, but it hints at capabilities I never imagined were possible."

Returning to the phone itself, Ladonna spoke with a sense of pride. "In addition to everything you've seen so far, we've integrated an extremely advanced form of enhanced reasoning. Some might call it an AI, but it is far more sophisticated than that term implies. Although not as sophisticated as Aliah, this system boasts cognitive capabilities that surpass those of any virtual assistant currently available on the market. It can understand context, carry on natural conversations, and make intuitive leaps in logic that push the boundaries of artificial intelligence."

Mosier found himself momentarily speechless. Aliah's ability to reason and respond with nuance hinted at a level of intelligence and awareness beyond what he thought possible. "Ladonna," he finally said, finding his voice, "are you saying this AI, this Aliah, is…self-aware?"

Ladonna's expression softened slightly. "Let's just say, General, that Aliah represents a significant leap in technology. I haven't been able to score her IQ, but I can tell you it's likely unmeasurable by any test we know of. She doesn't just perform advanced calculations; she adapts, learns, and understands. Her cognitive abilities are far beyond anything we've created before."

The General leaned back, clearly still trying to process everything. "This...this is something I never thought I'd see in my lifetime."

Ladonna paused for effect before continuing. "And most importantly, I can say with full confidence that this quantum smartphone cannot be hacked, tracked, or exploited through any current means."

The General held up a hand. "Ladonna, this all sounds remarkable, but you will understand if I am skeptical of these lofty claims. Prove to me this technology is as revolutionary as you say."

Ladonna smiled subtly, anticipating this challenge. "Of course, General, I intend to prove it to you beyond any doubt."

She glanced at her phone's display and addressed Aliah. "Aliah, in a moment I will ask you to access the Hercules classified government portal—the one used by Homeland Security for top-secret communications."

General Mosier sputtered, his face a mask of disbelief. "Hercules? That system has the latest encryption. It's impervious to all forms of intrusion known to date, its existence known only to a select group—myself included!"

"I am aware," said Ladonna. "I was approached by the agency that created it. But at the time, I was too busy to get involved."

Maintaining an aura of tranquility, Ladonna countered, "That's exactly why I am going to demonstrate how Aliah can bypass its defenses remotely. Keep your eyes on the screen."

She slid her quantum smartphone across the polished surface of the desk until it rested before the flabbergasted General, the holographic display, and keyboard sliding along with it. "Aliah, access the classified Hercules portal and display it on my phone."

"Understood, Ladonna," Aliah responded, her voice echoing with confidence. As the groundbreaking AI set about infiltrating the top-secret Hercules system, Ladonna elaborated on Aliah's extraordinary capabilities.

"Aliah, whose full name is Aliah STaR—an acronym for 'Synthetic Thinking and Reasoning'—represents a level of cognitive complexity that surpasses any human's. Aliah doesn't just handle computations; she can make adaptive responses, and she has emotional intelligence that is strikingly similar to human awareness."

Her words left a profound impact on the General as he grappled with the reality of an AI entity that exhibited such advanced self-awareness and emotional intelligence, pushing the boundaries of artificial intelligence. Meanwhile, Aliah was busily working her way through the layers of security in the Hercules system. In the span of Ladonna's explanation, Aliah managed to bypass all military-grade firewalls and encryption protocols deemed "unhackable." The main page of the Hercules government site materialized on the holographic display, leaving the General stunned. Aliah had infiltrated a system designed to be impenetrable.

"This...this is impossible!" General Mosier finally managed to choke out. "Hercules was conceived by the country's foremost cyber experts with the explicit intention of making it impervious to all unauthorized access!"

With hands trembling from shock, the General reached for the quantum smartphone, setting the holographic keyboard in front of him, intuitively typing away at the holographic keys. He needed to confirm that what he was witnessing was real. Navigating the system's menu, he found himself accessing parts of the Hercules portal that were exclusive to top officials. In full view on the screen, every facet of the classified Hercules system, its labyrinth of encrypted data, was now utterly exposed.

The tangible reality of what was unfolding jolted the General to his very foundation, sending waves of shock through him. Ladonna permitted herself a subtle smile, watching the General's shell-shocked expression as he navigated through the labyrinthine Hercules system. Aliah had accomplished the unthinkable—she had effortlessly breached security measures touted as impenetrable, and she had done it with unsettling ease.

After several minutes of shell-shocked browsing, General Mosier finally moved away from the phone, sinking back into his chair, utterly shaken.

Ladonna's expression grew solemn. "As you can now appreciate firsthand, General, what we are dealing with is beyond anything we previously imagined. This technology in the wrong hands could pose an unimaginably catastrophic threat to national security."

The General nodded weakly, still reeling. But even amid his shock, a curiosity burned in his gaze.

"As powerful as breaching Hercules was," Ladonna said, her voice steady, "I must show you more. I know breaching a foreign government site is beyond reckless, but the potential implications here need to be fully appreciated."

The General's eyes narrowed, his military instincts immediately cautioning him against such a move. "Dr. Stone," he said, voice low and laced with tension, "You must understand the risks. If a breach were discovered, it could spark an international incident. This is not something to be taken lightly."

Ladonna held his gaze, unwavering. "I'm aware, General. But I assure you, Aliah's method of entry is unique. She won't leave any trace of unauthorized access—it will appear as though a user with legitimate credentials logged in. This is a calculated demonstration, and I would not risk it if I weren't certain."

Mosier weighed her words carefully, visibly torn between his sense of caution and his need to witness the full extent of this technology. Finally, he nodded, unable to resist the pull of his curiosity. "Very well, but make it brief. If this goes wrong…"

"It won't," Ladonna assured him calmly. She then spoke in a tone of quiet command. "Aliah, access the Kremlin's classified military portal."

There was a pause before Aliah's, resonant and confident voice replied, "As you wish, Ladonna. Accessing now."

Ladonna leaned back, her expression unyielding. The room seemed to shrink as they watched the screen, each second stretching into what felt like an eternity. The holographic display was crisp and exceptionally clear, set before the General. Aliah processed the request, and her progress was displayed in rapidly shifting code. In mere moments, the classified portal's home page appeared on Ladonna's screen. Aliah had bypassed the Kremlin's defenses with the same quiet precision she'd demonstrated earlier. Aliah spoke, "Normally the text would be in Russian. However, I am currently displaying it in English."

Mosier, in his disbelief, didn't even register Aliah's last statement.

His jaw clenched and his expression one of utter disbelief. He leaned forward, riveted as he watched Ladonna manipulate the interface. "I don't believe it," he murmured, barely audible.

"Aliah doesn't rely on brute force or standard hacking techniques," Ladonna explained, her tone measured and calm. "She analyzes patterns and identifies openings that a human mind would never even recognize. For her, even the most complex security structures are mere puzzles to be solved."

The General stared at the screen, mesmerized, as Ladonna opened and closed files with a speed and precision that felt otherworldly. He could see details of troop movements, classified intelligence reports, and secure communication channels, all available at her fingertips—each one an international secret, each revelation a potential diplomatic bombshell.

Finally, Ladonna closed the portal, leaving the device with only an ordinary home screen. She looked up at the General, her expression resolute. "Do you see now, General? This isn't just advanced technology; it's a force that could reshape the entire balance of power. In the wrong hands, Aliah could destabilize nations."

Mosier sank back into his chair, visibly shaken. He rubbed his temples, his expression troubled, as if bearing the weight of a revelation that threatened to unravel his world. "Ladonna," he began, his voice uncharacteristically quiet, "you've shown me something I could never have imagined. But this...this is beyond any weapon we have. Beyond anything anyone has."

Ladonna nodded solemnly. "Which is why we must be vigilant, General. Aliah is an unparalleled achievement, but one with immense responsibility. We cannot let her fall into the hands of those who would misuse her capabilities."

The General sat in silence, his gaze distant, as he processed the full scope of what Ladonna had just revealed. For the first time in his career, he felt the true weight of powerlessness. Aliah had bypassed all of Russia's vaunted military-grade cyber defenses and had displayed the page following the login screen for the Kremlin's most highly encrypted classified portal, complete with the seal of Russian intelligence. A force beyond his comprehension had been placed before him, and he knew, with chilling certainty, that the world would never be the same again.

General Mosier exhaled sharply, nodding as he absorbed the gravity of Ladonna's demonstration. "Message received—loud and clear. We're severely outmatched if a single entity can navigate our systems with such ease."

He paused, his face reflecting both newfound respect and inner conflict. "You've opened my eyes today, Dr. Stone. I can't thank you enough for your patience, nor apologize enough for any initial doubt. From here forward, we stand united against the shadows of the unknown."

Ladonna offered a faint, knowing smile. "No apology needed, General. We're forging a new path together."

The room seemed heavier with the weight of this partnership, each fully understanding the stakes ahead. At last, General Mosier gave a solemn nod. "Rest assured, you have my full support, Ladonna. Technology like this—capable of piercing our national defenses—cannot fall into the wrong hands. Our security, possibly even our future, depends on it."

Ladonna's gaze held his. "Thank you, General. With your expertise, I'm confident we can protect these innovations from exploitation. As you've seen, the stakes couldn't be higher."

Mosier processed her words thoughtfully and then spoke with deliberate conviction. "You can rely on me. I'll station guards at key points around the complex immediately," he said, assessing potential security gaps. "They'll work alongside your head of security, Mr. Reed, to ensure every measure is in place."

"Excellent," Ladonna replied, her tone steady with approval. "Aliah will inform Jackson to coordinate with your team. Your leadership on this is invaluable, General."

She turned to her phone, her voice calm but commanding. "Aliah, notify Jackson Reed to wait in the conference room for a briefing from the General's team."

"Consider it done, Ladonna," Aliah's voice echoed through the room, a touch of warmth underscoring her efficiency.

A floor below, Jackson Reed's phone buzzed. Reading the message from Aliah, he acknowledged its instructions, then turned to Major Williams, who waited nearby. "Looks like the meeting's wrapping up," he said reassuringly. "It won't be much longer."

Back in the conference room, Ladonna continued, "General, if you like, Aliah can assist with optimizing security layouts across the facility and beyond. She already monitors all cameras within the building and coordinates with city traffic feeds within a two-mile radius. With your approval, she could also tap satellite feeds for an enhanced field of view. And rest assured— she'll miss nothing."

Mosier's expression softened as he nodded, impressed. "That's invaluable, Ladonna. If Aliah's surveillance matches what I've seen of her other abilities, we're in safe hands. That said, I'll still station guards around the perimeter as a secondary measure."

The two shared a resolute look. The General then raised a cautionary hand. "But one condition—no more breaches of unauthorized systems without permission from the relevant agencies."

Ladonna met his gaze with a solemn promise. "You have my word, General."

"Now," Mosier continued, "let's commit to protecting this breakthrough technology from those who would misuse it." Their partnership was sealed, bridging Quantum Innovations' mission with national security. Together, they would safeguard the integrity of their work and protect humanity's technological future.

Before departing, Mosier's face grew serious as he recalled their other pressing concern. "Now, about the situation with your staff member, Justin, and his girlfriend. Her connections could pose a significant risk. I'll arrange surveillance on her immediately and bring her in for questioning. Given her suspected foreign ties, she's a direct threat."

Ladonna nodded, visibly relieved. "I appreciate your swift action, General. Please keep me updated, especially if there's any pertinent information."

"Of course," he said. "Now, I must speak with Justin directly. Homeland Security and the FBI will need to conduct initial interviews before confronting Robert Westfield or Daniel Scott. FBI Assistant Director Stephen Holly will be leading the interrogation of Mr. Scott, with our team observing."

"I'll be there," Ladonna replied firmly, "to observe and evaluate their responses. And I'd like to share a few more of Aliah's capabilities."

The General smiled, his respect for Ladonna growing. "I thought you might say that. I'll make the arrangements and inform you."

As the General gathered his belongings, Ladonna presented him with a sleek Quantum Innovations device. "This is a Quantum Phone. It's equipped with an AI assistant called 'Reaper,' designed to be more intuitive and secure than any A.I. on the market. Reaper connects to our Quantum internet—a private, secure network unbreakable by hackers and untraceable."

Mosier's eyes gleamed with intrigue. "I'll test it personally," he promised, examining the device. "And I think we'll be talking soon about making this our government's new standard."

They exchanged a firm handshake, sealing their partnership with mutual respect. As the General exited, the door's quiet click punctuated Ladonna's sense of accomplishment. She took a moment to inhale deeply, savoring the triumph of this hard-won alliance—only to be interrupted by the buzz of her phone.

It was a message from T.L. Cline, the former CEO and founder of Quantum Innovations. He had originally introduced Ladonna to the board when she took over as CEO. "Dr. Stone, when you're finished, we're ready in the main conference room."

Ladonna shook her head, smiling slightly. Never a dull moment.

She strode confidently toward the exit, overhearing the General's commanding voice as he relayed orders to Major Edward Probst, stationed outside the office.

"Major Probst, coordinate with Jackson Reed in Conference Room Three. Effective immediately, we need a comprehensive security strategy for Quantum Innovations. I want perimeter cameras and regular patrols in all parking areas, ensuring no blind spots."

"Understood, sir!" Probst responded, relaying the orders into his shoulder radio before setting off to find Reed.

Within the hour, unseen security forces were mobilized around Quantum Innovations. Military satellites adjusted their orbits, aligning over the complex, while agents mingled among the staff, inconspicuous but vigilant.

No detail went unobserved, from the camera feeds to RF signals. Any adversary considering infiltration would face an impenetrable shield—one that would uncover and neutralize any threat long before it materialized.

If any suspicious actors attempted to breach the premises, they would be met with an overwhelming classified security response, neutralizing any threat immediately. Quantum Innovations had become an impenetrable fortress, safeguarded by the full force of the nation's defense assets.

Ladonna entered the sleek conference room to a thunderous round of applause from the assembled board members. T.L. Cline, Quantum Innovations' former CEO, approached her near the door, shaking her hand firmly with a broad smile. The rest of the board members quickly surrounded her in a circle, their faces glowing with excitement and admiration for her monumental achievements.

Evan Johnson, the Logistics Manager, spoke up first, barely containing his amazement. "Dr. Stone, you sure can keep a secret! We had no idea you were working on something this revolutionary right under our noses." The others chimed in with sounds of agreement, their initial surprise giving way to sheer excitement.

Cline guided Ladonna to the head of the large, glossy conference table while the others took their seats. Johnson continued, "Robert was always complaining about how much money this project was costing. He even suggested you were pocketing part of the budget! But now I see—he was the one we had to watch all along. Dr. Stone, I'm sorry for ever doubting you."

Ladonna smiled graciously. "Don't trouble yourself, Mr. Johnson. Robert will be Robert." She settled into her chair as the room quieted down. "Mr. Cline, members of the board, if you all have the time, I'd like to discuss a few items."

Cline and the others gave her their full attention. Just then, Johnson's cell phone buzzed. He glanced down in surprise before exclaiming, "Dr. Stone, I don't know what that last meeting was about, but the Department of Defense just ordered fifty thousand units of our quantum encryption phones, with another potential order of a hundred thousand at ten thousand dollars each!"

Johnson continued, "Calls are flooding in from Fortune 500 companies! It's an absolute madhouse. At this rate, we'll recover our R&D investments within twelve months. This project is incredible!" He looked around sheepishly. "Sorry to interrupt you, Dr. Stone."

She turned to Johnson, her gaze steady and purposeful. "Evan," she began, "you've done an outstanding job as our Logistics Manager and proven yourself a valuable asset. It's clear we need someone to lead Marketing—a Vice President who shares Quantum Innovations' vision. Would you be interested in that role?"

Completely stunned, Johnson's eyes widened as he processed her offer. After a moment, he found his voice. "Yes, Dr. Stone," he said, slowly regaining his composure. "I'd be honored to accept the position of Vice President of Marketing. Thank you for believing in me. I promise to meet and exceed your expectations."

Ladonna grinned. "Excellent! You'll step into your new role tomorrow. Start by handling the influx of Fortune 500 calls, but speak directly to their CEOs—not the marketing departments. Arrange future meetings to discuss integrating our systems with their businesses. Lucy the Director of Research and Development, that helped develop the Quantum Trinity, can fill you in on successful pilot programs with a few of them. The productivity results have been astounding."

She continued, "Then, reach out to the universities currently beta-testing the Quantum Trinity system. Let them know we'll be transitioning out of beta soon and see if they want to continue their involvement. Lucy was managing that aspect, so she'll bring you up to speed. After that, you and Lucy can consult with Vivian Ho, our Chief Financial Officer, she has been managing the budget of the Quantum Trinity from the beginning, to finalize the pricing model."

"Yes, Dr. Stone," Johnson replied confidently. "Lucy and I will start first thing tomorrow. You can count on us to handle the transition smoothly."

The room's energy had begun to settle down, but Ladonna prepared to deliver yet another revelation that would leave the board members astounded.

"I don't believe you've all had the pleasure of meeting my assistant," Ladonna announced, her voice carrying a hint of mischief. Cline added, "I've received emails and calls from her, but I've never actually met her. Where is her office?" Others around the table nodded in agreement, equally puzzled.

Seeing their curious expressions, Ladonna smiled. "Please, allow me to introduce her now. You may want to take a seat for this surprise," she said. "Aliah, could you initiate security protocol 557 and then join us, please?"

At her command, the conference room glass walls of the darkened to an opaque black, and the electronic door lock engaged with an audible click.

Without warning, Aliah materialized beside Ladonna, instantly captivating the room. She wore a sleek, tailored dress that shimmered subtly in rich indigo, its high-tech fabric flowing with effortless grace. Over her shoulders, a translucent, modern trench coat caught the light, casting intricate designs that shifted in sync with the room's precise lighting.

Minimalist ankle boots and a reflective crossbody bag completed her look, each element merging style with advanced functionality. Her chic bob framed a composed expression, and her presence embodied the sophistication and groundbreaking vision of Quantum Innovations. Her hologram almost seemed solid, appearing as if she were a real person.

"Hello, everyone," Aliah began, her voice clear and melodic. "I am Aliah STaR, Dr. Stone's personal assistant. It is a sincere pleasure to meet you all."

The room fell into stunned silence as they took in the lifelike hologram before them. Their mouths fell open, audible gasps filling the room. Ladonna beamed, reveling in their reactions to her astonishing revelation.

Johnson spoke first. "Well, in light of this, I'd like to revise my earlier prediction. We'll recover our R&D investments within six months, maybe sooner!" The others murmured in agreement, excitement mounting as they processed what they were seeing.

Ladonna explained Aliah's capabilities, her role in monitoring security, her omnipresence within the company's systems, and her vigilance in protecting their intellectual property from corporate espionage. This reassured everyone present.

As Aliah interacted with the group, responding to questions with poise and eloquence, a sense of awe settled over the room. The board members recognized they were witnessing a groundbreaking leap in technology. Each board member turned to T.L. Cline, silently acknowledging why he had insisted that Dr.

Stone be the next CEO. They now saw her as a visionary leader who would propel Quantum Innovations into unprecedented success.

✱ ✱ ✱

As the layers of the attempted security breach were peeled back, a glimmer of reassurance cut through the tension. Justin Allen, once under suspicion due to his connection with an alleged international operative, had now been vindicated by both the General and Agent Holly, the Assistant Director of the FBI.

Standing before Dr. Stone, Justin's gaze flickered with trepidation and faint hope. "Justin," Ladonna began, her tone steady yet tinged with empathy, "the investigation has concluded. You've been an inadvertent pawn in an espionage scheme. Your adherence to the non-disclosure agreement was unwavering, earning not only my commendation but also the full trust of Quantum Innovations."

Relief washed over Justin's face. "Thank you, Dr. Stone," he said, his voice full of gratitude. "I was deceived, but I never betrayed Quantum Innovations."

Ladonna nodded. "We know, Justin. Now, our priority is to find the mastermind behind this plot."

Justin, eager to help, replied, "I've disclosed everything I know, even providing Aliah with a detailed description. She generated an impressively accurate visual likeness."

"This AI-rendered portrait will be pivotal in uncovering her identity," Ladonna said, glancing at the screen where the portrait stood as a testament to Aliah's sophistication. "Justin, your account has been invaluable, and soon we'll need your assistance again. We'll go over the specifics when the time comes."

"Thank you, Dr. Stone," Justin said, feeling both humbled and awestruck. "Your AI's capabilities are beyond anything I imagined. Her ability to appear anywhere is truly extraordinary."

Ladonna smiled warmly. "We had planned to reveal her capabilities after the presentation, but circumstances changed."

In quiet contemplation, Ladonna reflected on the recent events. The elusive operative had skillfully avoided detection, leaving no trace in Justin's apartment and evading surveillance. Yet, thanks to Justin's detailed account, Aliah's portrait might just provide the breakthrough they desperately needed.

Ladonna worked closely with government agencies, sharing Aliah's AI-generated image and collaborating on a strategy to apprehend the spy. The race against time had begun, and every second counted.

As the investigation intensified, Justin transformed from an unsuspecting pawn into a key player in thwarting a plot that endangered both Quantum Innovations and national security. Though his involvement had been unintentional, it became a cornerstone of their efforts, underscoring the importance of vigilance in the face of hidden threats.

Justin's journey was not just professional; his heartache ran deep. Though unintentional, his involvement became a pivotal asset in the battle against a shadowy network of espionage. His ordeal—a journey woven with trust and brutal deception—catalyzed Quantum Innovations to bolster its security protocols and served as a reminder of the high cost of misplaced faith.

Yet throughout the harrowing experience, Justin Allen exhibited resilience that few could match. Emerging from the wreckage, he wasn't just a bystander caught in the crossfire but a crucial ally, an irreplaceable force in the effort to protect Quantum Innovations' future. Still, beneath this unwavering professional dedication, a deeper, more private struggle gnawed at him, one that defied the neat logic he sought to impose on it.

He had genuinely fallen for Evelyn—or at least, the woman he believed to be Evelyn. There had been late nights and secret conversations where her laughter, her gaze, had seemed so real, so achingly true. He had let himself believe that the warmth between them was mutual, that beneath her reserved exterior, she, too, had felt something. Was it all a meticulously crafted lie, a cunning ruse designed solely to extract classified information about Quantum Innovations' most guarded projects?

Intellectually he could make sense of it—see the signs in hindsight and even recognize the shrewdness of her manipulation. —Yet his heart struggled to keep up. The realization tore at him, unraveling the sense of completeness and joy she had once brought into his life. Part of him clung desperately to the image of the woman he had known, the one who had seemed to mirror his desires and dreams. He knew she was a lie, yet he couldn't erase the memories, couldn't stop wondering where she was now, or if she ever thought of him at all.

In the silence of his solitude, he found himself haunted by her memory, questioning every look, every word, each fragile moment of intimacy. Though he knew Eve, the woman he had cherished, had been nothing more than a fabricated illusion, the ache remained— the kind that lingers long after love's deception fades.

He let his mind wander, wondering what had become of her.

Chapter Two

Interrogation and Deception

Ladonna strode purposefully into the subterranean bunker, the sharp click of her heels against the cold concrete floor echoing through the silence. General Mosier walked beside her, his imposing frame exuding authority, while FBI Assistant Director Stephen Holly followed, his expression concealed behind dark sunglasses. The trio's presence filled the sterile space with palpable tension, a harbinger of the reckoning to come.

Inside the stark, windowless interrogation room sat Robert Westfield, the disgraced former Vice President of Business Development at Quantum Innovations. Once the epitome of corporate success, he now wore the garish orange of incarceration, his disheveled appearance a stark contrast to his formerly polished self. A strange, rubber like wristband with what seemed like extremely tiny microsensors embedden in it encircled his arm—a detail he couldn't ignore but refused to acknowledge.

Despite his predicament, Robert lounged in his metal chair with an air of defiance, a smirk playing on his lips. But when Ladonna entered, her commanding presence sliced through his façade. His smirk faltered for the briefest of moments before being replaced by a bitter scowl.

"Well, this is an unexpected honor," he sneered, his voice dripping with sarcasm. "To what do I owe the pleasure?"

Ladonna didn't flinch. She crossed the room with measured precision, her every movement exuding control. Taking a seat across from him, she fixed him with a calm, unyielding gaze. "Let's dispense with the pleasantries, Robert. You know exactly why you're here."

He shrugged, his bravado firmly in place. "Enlighten me."

General Mosier stepped forward, his presence casting a long shadow across the room. Without warning, his fist slammed against the metal table with a deafening clang. "Cut the act, Westfield. You're here to give us answers, not waste our time. Tell us about the foreign woman who approached you."

Feigning ignorance, Robert leaned back, his smirk returning. "Foreign woman? You'll have to be more specific. Plenty of women approach me."

Mosier's voice hardened, the room seemingly shrinking under the weight of his authority. "This is your one chance to cooperate. After today, you might never see the light of day again."

The threat hung in the air like a blade, and for a moment, uncertainty flickered across Robert's face. He shifted uncomfortably, glancing briefly at the wristband around his wrist before speaking. "Ah, her," he said finally, his tone laced with reluctant acknowledgment. "She was… quite the mystery."

Ladonna leaned forward slightly, her eyes narrowing as she scrutinized every nuance of his expression. "We intercepted communications indicating this woman offered you a deal for the OmniLink plans, though you withheld her name. Tell us about her."

Robert hesitated, his confidence slipping as the walls seemed to close in. "If such communications existed— which I'm not confirming, by the way—they'd show that I don't know much about her. Our encounter was… brief."

Ladonna, unperturbed by his evasion, pulled her phone from her pocket and placed it on the table. Continuing to look at Robert she said, "Aliah, execute protocol 557 and join us. Robert was just about to share more details on the mystery woman."

At that instant, the camera's red light ceased blinking, and Robert jolted in his seat as Aliah's lifelike hologram materialized beside Ladonna. Her azure eyes glowed with an otherworldly light as she regarded him coolly. General Mosier, equally taken aback by the sudden appearance, barked, "Sit down, Westfield," as Robert recoiled instinctively in shock.

The atmosphere in the interrogation room shifted instantly with Aliah's arrival. Her holographic form shimmered into existence, exuding an air of professionalism and futuristic sophistication. She wore a beautifully tailored navy blazer that fit her form perfectly, paired with a crisp white blouse that seemed to radiate a soft glow. The subtle luminescence of her lapels caught the room's dim light, adding a commanding presence to her already imposing figure.

Her high-waisted trousers flowed like liquid silk with every gesture, blending avant-garde design with practicality. A pair of pointed-toe heels completed the look, enhancing her stature and lending her a poised elegance. Aliah's hair, cascading in soft waves, shimmered with hints of silver and blue, a visual reminder of the advanced technology that brought her to life. Her penetrating gaze, framed by glowing azure eyes, locked onto Robert, stripping away any pretense he might have clung to.

Ladonna, seated across from Robert, allowed a slight easing of her tension. Aliah's presence was both reassuring and strategic—a silent reminder of their technological edge. She glanced at Robert, her voice steady. "Hello, Robert," she greeted, her tone calm and melodic, carrying an undertone of authority that filled the room. "I am equipped to detect micro-expressions, biometrics, and other indicators of deception. If you attempt to mislead us, I will know."

Robert swallowed hard, the color draining from his face as he met Aliah's unwavering gaze. Her mere presence seemed to strip away his defenses, leaving him visibly unnerved.

"You've missed quite a few advancements since your departure," Ladonna remarked, a faint hint of satisfaction coloring her words. "Shall we begin again? This time, tell us everything you know about the woman who approached you."

Robert hesitated, his confidence faltering under Aliah's watchful scrutiny. He cast a wary glance at Ladonna before finally relenting. "Fine. It was at the Ritz-Carlton rooftop bar," he began, his voice reluctant. "I'd stopped for a nightcap after a long day, and she appeared—a striking woman with jet-black hair, intense green eyes, and a faint Eastern European accent. She struck up a conversation, and, at first, I thought she was a high-end escort. But then she started asking about my role at Quantum Innovations. Before I knew it, she was hinting at some kind of— 'collaboration' to access classified information."

Aliah tilted her head slightly, her expression cool and unreadable. Her voice, though calm, carried an edge of insistence. "Describe her in detail, Robert, her height, the exact shade of her eyes, her mannerisms. Was her hair worn up or down? Any visible marks or distinguishing features?"

Robert shifted uncomfortably, his bravado slipping further. "She was about five-foot-eight, slender, pale, with jet-black hair she wore down. There were no visible marks, but she carried herself with this…cold confidence. Like she'd done this before."

Ladonna exchanged a brief, knowing glance with Aliah and Mosier. They were closing in—she could feel it. Aliah pressed forward, her tone measured but firm. "Can you describe her in any more detail?" she asked, her voice leaving no room for evasion.

Robert sighed heavily, each word drawn out as though it physically pained him to comply. "She was… about five and a half feet tall, straight black hair past her shoulders, fair complexion, no scars or tattoos that I noticed. She wore a sleek black cocktail dress and expensive jewelry. Elegant but sharp, like she knew what she was doing. She was very beautiful, really— sophisticated, exotic, and with an air of mystery. She stood out."

"Thank you, Robert. That additional detail is helpful," Aliah replied, her voice impassive.

Robert glanced between Ladonna and Aliah, the trace of a nervous twitch betraying his unease. "You're welcome," he muttered, though his tone carried none of his usual arrogance.

Ladonna leaned forward, her voice crisp and direct. "And how did this mystery woman even know about the highly classified projects and technologies at Quantum Innovations?"

Robert hesitated, his fingers drumming anxiously on the metal table. Finally, he shrugged with forced casualness. "She said she had 'informants' embedded in powerful organizations—people feeding her tips about certain technologies. I guess… now it was probably the OmniLink project she wanted."

Aliah remained still, her gaze unyielding. Her eyes blinked slowly, a mechanical precision underscoring her next words. "I am detecting physiological and micro-expression cues that suggest otherwise," she stated. "You are withholding additional details about your interaction with her."

Robert flinched, shifting uneasily under Aliah's piercing gaze, as though she could reach straight into his mind and lay bare his secrets. Finally, with a bitter smirk that barely masked his discomfort, he muttered, "Fine. She implied she wanted… more than just a business collaboration. She said we could continue 'upstairs' if I were interested. I turned her down, but she made her point."

General Chad "The Reaper" Mosier slammed his fist onto the table, the metallic clang reverberating through the interrogation room. His frustration boiled over, his voice sharp and commanding. "This is no game, Westfield! That woman is a serious national security threat, and you're here under the Espionage Act. What aren't you telling us?"

At the mention of the Espionage Act, Robert's mask of bravado faltered. His face paled, and the weight of his predicament visibly settled on his shoulders. "The Espionage Act? You can't do that! I have rights," he stammered, the defiance in his voice undermined by an edge of panic. "I demand to speak with a lawyer. This is unconstitutional—"

Mosier cut him off with a voice like steel. "Westfield, in matters of national security under the Espionage Act, those rights don't apply. Right now, you're being detained indefinitely until we uncover exactly what we're dealing with."

The fight drained slightly from Robert's posture. "But... surely, you're mistaken. I'll cooperate, but you can't deny me legal representation," he protested weakly, his eyes darting around the room as though searching for an escape.

FBI Assistant Director Stephen Holly stepped forward, his voice calm and deliberate. "Robert, you misunderstand. For you and your friend Daniel, legal rights aren't in play here. Extraordinary rendition allows us to place you anywhere we deem necessary for... more thorough questioning. We brought you in first. Daniel is next, and let's just say he's already pinned most of this on you. If you're protecting him, now's the time to rethink that."

Robert's face twisted with a mixture of anger and betrayal. "Daniel? If he's talking, he's lying! He was as involved as I was."

Holly leaned closer, his tone even. "Then give us your side of the story, Robert. Your choice: let Daniel rewrite what happened, or give us the truth now."

Robert clenched his jaw, a bead of sweat sliding down his temple. His pulse throbbed visibly in his neck as he grudgingly admitted, "Alright… alright. She said she'd heard about OmniLink's protocols and wanted to strike a deal. But I didn't give her much. Just enough to keep her talking, see where she'd go with it."

Ladonna placed a steady hand on Mosier's shoulder, a silent signal for restraint. She leaned in, her tone calm but edged with urgency. "Robert, this woman could be extremely dangerous. People's lives are on the line. Give us something actionable. Help us protect you—and Daniel."

Robert shook his head, beads of sweat forming on his brow. "I swear, I've told you everything relevant! We only talked briefly at a cocktail party, just… idle conversation. I didn't see her for who she was. She fooled me — seemed like any other thrill-seeker looking for excitement. I was stupid," he muttered bitterly, his voice trailing off.

The tension in the room thickened as Ladonna, Mosier, and Aliah pressed for more. Yet, despite their relentless questioning, Robert offered little beyond vague and frustratingly sparse details. He insisted he hadn't gotten her name and claimed she had promised to find him "when the time was right." Holly fixed his gaze on Robert and said, "That's enough. Let's hear what Daniel has to say." With that, he turned and exited the room.

Ladonna finally rose, exhaustion creeping into her expression. She exchanged a brief, weighted glance with Mosier, the severity of the situation clear in their unspoken communication. The room fell into an oppressive silence, the harsh fluorescent light casting stark shadows across Robert's pale, drawn face.

"Very well, then," Mosier said, his tone icy. "For now, you'll be returned to your cell. Perhaps, by the time we meet again, you'll have reconsidered what's best for you—and Daniel."

The door creaked open, and Assistant Director Holly stepped inside. Aliah's holographic form flickered out of sight as he entered. Behind Holly, in the corridor, stood Daniel, clad in an identical orange jumpsuit. Robert's head snapped up, his face a study of shock and betrayal as his gaze locked onto his friend.

Holly smirked, letting the tension in the room simmer before he spoke. "My mistake. Wrong room," he said, his voice tinged with a mock apology. He closed the door as swiftly as he'd opened it, leaving Robert alone with Ladonna, Mosier, and the dawning realization of his isolation. Aliah reappeared, her calm presence contrasting the chaos in Robert's mind.

Holly escorted a stunned Daniel down the hall to another interrogation room, where a guard seated him at a metal table. For ten long minutes, Daniel sat in silence, his thoughts racing with the implications of his predicament. When Holly returned, his expression was unreadable.

Meanwhile, back in Robert's room, Holly reentered with an air of finality. His gaze was cold as it fixed on Robert. "Well, you had your chance. Looks like your friend Daniel will be the one singing today. He seems to have a lot to get off his chest—might even be out of here before nightfall."

The clang of the closing door reverberated through the room, each metallic echo like a nail in the coffin of Robert's confidence. His voice trembled as he addressed Aliah, desperation creeping in. "I told you everything, Aliah."

Aliah regarded him with an unreadable expression. "I highly doubt that," she replied coolly, her skepticism cutting like a knife before her holographic form flickered and disappeared.

Moments later, guards entered to escort Robert back to his cell. His protests—pleas for reconsideration and, assertions of innocence—fell on deaf ears, growing fainter with every step down the sterile hallway. By the time the room fell silent once more, the weight of his choices lingered, suffocating and inescapable.

General Mosier and Ladonna walked into an empty room with a large, reinforced window. The air between them was thick with unspoken tension. Mosier turned to Ladonna, his brow furrowed. "When were you going to tell me about her ability to project herself like that? And what exactly is Protocol 557?"

Ladonna allowed a faint smile to cross her lips, her tone measured. "Protocol 557 disables all surveillance in any room where Aliah is about to appear. At this point, she's still classified as a company secret." She met his questioning gaze and added, "And I did mention in our last meeting that I'd planned to show you more of her capabilities."

Mosier raised an eyebrow, his skepticism evident. "You let Robert see her."

"Yes," Ladonna replied smoothly. "But he won't say anything—and even if he did, no one would believe him. Besides, I'll be going public with her soon enough. Aliah has scheduled an interview with a news agency for me in two months. That might be the right time to unveil her."

She turned toward the two-way mirror, her sharp eyes focusing on the scene within. On the other side of the glass, Daniel sat handcuffed, his wrists bound to a large metal ring affixed to the steel table. An armed guard loomed in the corner, a silent reminder of the stakes. Daniel wore a wristband identical to Robert's.

Aliah's voice interrupted, calm and clinical, resonating through the room. "I've been monitoring Daniel since the Assistant Director placed the wristband on him. His vitals—blood pressure, heart rate, respiration—are all elevated, consistent with acute stress." The precision in her tone conveyed the depth of her capabilities.

Inside the interrogation room, Daniel shifted uncomfortably, oblivious to the scrutiny he was under. The minutes dragged on until the door swung open, and Assistant Director Holly stepped inside with his usual unflinching demeanor.

"Daniel," Holly began, his voice slicing through the silence like a blade. "We need to talk."

Daniel's stomach churned, dread settling like a stone in his chest. He braced himself as Holly took a seat across from him.

"I'm sure you understand the gravity of your situation," Holly continued, his piercing gaze locking onto Daniel's. "Your involvement in the theft of intellectual property from Quantum Innovations has put you in a very precarious position."

Daniel swallowed hard, his throat dry. "I... I understand," he stammered.

Holly leaned forward, his tone sharp. "Robert claims you were the mastermind behind the scheme to steal classified technology. Care to comment?"

"Robert's lying!" Daniel burst out, his voice tinged with desperation. "He's trying to frame me because he wanted Ladonna's position. He thought this was his chance to take over as CEO."

Holly's expression didn't waver. "And we're supposed to take your word over his?"

Daniel's hands trembled as he shook his head. "No. I have evidence—emails, texts, recordings. Robert was the one pulling the strings, manipulating me to go along with his plan."

Holly studied Daniel, his face unreadable. "And yet, we have reason to believe there's more to this than internal sabotage. We suspect foreign involvement.

Who was the woman Robert planned to sell the stolen technology to? We believe she's a foreign agent."

Daniel's eyes widened in confusion. "Woman? I don't know anything about a woman. I think Robert might have mentioned someone, but I wasn't involved in any sale."

Holly's voice grew cold. "Robert implied you set everything up with her."

Daniel ran his hands through his hair, his panic mounting. "Robert's lying! I swear, I don't know anything about a woman or a sale. Please, you have to believe me."

Holly's tone didn't soften. "If what you're saying is true, then you won't mind us combing through every piece of evidence we can find—your home, your devices, everything. Imagine what your neighbors and employer must be thinking right now."

Daniel slumped in his seat, his breathing shallow. "I'll tell you everything I know," he blurted, desperation leaking into his voice. "But I need immunity."

Holly's expression remained impassive. "Immunity isn't on the table. Your best chance is to cooperate fully and hope the court takes that into account. Otherwise, you'll spend the rest of your life behind bars."

Daniel's shoulders sagged under the weight of Holly's words. "I'll talk," he whispered. "I'll tell you everything I know."

Moments later, Holly left the room, his face grim. Outside, Ladonna and Mosier awaited his assessment.

"Daniel doesn't know anything about the woman," Holly reported flatly. "It's Robert we need to break. We'll keep Daniel here a bit longer to verify his claims, then hand him over for trial."

Mosier's frustration was evident as he crossed his arms. "This woman remains an enigma. Her motives are shrouded in secrecy, and she's always one step ahead."

Ladonna, her composure unshaken, accessed her Quantum phone and spoke calmly. "Aliah, project the enhanced visual based on Robert's account of the woman."

A life-sized hologram materialized, depicting the mystery woman in striking detail. Her penetrating gaze and poised demeanor seemed almost tangible, her image filling the room with a disquieting presence.

"Aliah," Ladonna said, her tone sharp, "analyze Robert's statements. Identify discrepancies."

Aliah's voice was steady. "Robert is withholding key details about his interactions with this woman. My analysis suggests their encounter was neither brief nor incidental. Likely, they collaborated more extensively than he's admitted."

Mosier's jaw tightened. "We need to find her. Whatever it takes."

Aliah's response was immediate. "With your authorization, General, I will initiate a global search utilizing facial recognition and behavioral analysis across all available networks."

Mosier's gaze snapped to Ladonna. "What does she mean by all available networks?"

Ladonna's expression didn't falter. "Exactly what it sounds like, General. Aliah's reach extends to every database—government, civilian, open web, and dark web. Nothing is beyond her scope. Aliah's reach is… extensive."

Mosier regarded the hologram with a mixture of awe and unease. Raising his phone, he barked into it, "Get me the President on the line. Now." His eyes never left the woman's piercing holographic image as the weight of their mission loomed large.

Chapter Three

A Meeting of Minds

The motorcade, led by stern-faced Secret Service agents on motorcycles, snaked its way through the bustling streets of Washington, D.C., toward the White House. The armored SUV, carrying Ladonna, was flanked by black, imposing vehicles, each a fortified shield exuding a silent yet unmistakable warning. This was no ordinary visit, and every detail in the security formation underscored the gravity of what lay ahead.

As they approached the iron gates of the White House, the SUV came to a halt. Armed guards meticulously inspected every inch of the vehicle, and their movements were precise and methodical. Through the tinted windows, Ladonna caught sight of snipers stationed on nearby rooftops, their vigilant eyes scanning every movement below. The weight of the security detail was a palpable reminder of the magnitude of today's meeting.

Ladonna had met presidents before, and her usual demeanor in high-stakes scenarios was one of calm confidence. But this felt different. This President, renowned for his discerning eye and exacting standards, had heard about her extraordinary accomplishments. Though familiar with her reputation, he wasn't yet persuaded of the true power and vast potential her work represented. Today's meeting would be her chance to prove just how transformative her creations could be—not just for the nation, but for the world.

Inside the austere briefing room, an expansive oak conference table dominated the space, its polished surface gleaming under the soft overhead lights. A neat line of water glasses stood at each leather chair, but otherwise, the table was bare. At the head of the table sat the President's high-backed seat, conspicuously empty, flanked by chairs designated for his Chief of Staff, General Mosier, and other top advisors.

A Secret Service agent escorted Ladonna into the room, directing her to sit midway down the table. She settled in, smoothing the hem of her tailored charcoal-gray suit and resting her hands lightly on the polished wood surface. Her gaze swept over the room, taking in every detail, every nuance, as she centered herself for what lay ahead. Her mind was sharp, her focus unyielding.

The door opened minutes later, and the room rose to its feet as President London entered, flanked by his entourage. He strode purposefully to his seat, his tall, broad-shouldered frame exuding an effortless command. His steely gray eyes fixed on Ladonna with an intensity that seemed to weigh and measure her in an instant. Ladonna met his gaze, her expression poised and unflinching, though a flicker of anticipation simmered beneath the surface.

With a curt nod from the President, the group took their seats. He leaned forward, forearms resting on the table, his fingers steepled. Although curiosity flickered behind his sharp eyes, Ladonna could sense the skepticism he brought into the room. This was her moment to illuminate the monumental potential of her work and redefine his perspective.

The silence broke as General Mosier spoke, his deep, resonant voice commanding attention. "Mr. President," he began, "I've provided a comprehensive briefing ahead of this meeting, but I'm certain you'll need to witness Dr. Stone's advancements firsthand to truly grasp their full impact."

He glanced toward Ladonna before continuing, his tone measured and deliberate. "When she initially demonstrated these technologies to me, I was stunned. In over thirty years of service, I've seen remarkable advancements in military and civilian tech. But nothing—nothing—could have prepared me for the capabilities Dr. Stone has developed."

General Mosier paused, his words hanging in the air as the gravity of his statement settled over the room. "As I have presented, multiple specialists and scientists were enlisted by Quantum Innovations to rigorously evaluate this system. These experts—from some of our most prestigious institutions—have each come to the same conclusion: this technology is revolutionary. Light years ahead of anything we know to be in production or even in research. This is no ordinary advancement; this is a quantum leap."

* * *

He let his words hang in the air, each one resonating with urgency. "Mr. President, Dr. Stone's work exceeds anything I, or any expert we've consulted, have ever imagined possible. She has pioneered breakthroughs that will fundamentally transform our strategic capabilities and shift the balance of global power in our favor. And I assure you, what we've seen so far is just the beginning."

As General Mosier spoke, Ladonna could feel the anticipation mounting around the table. The room was thick with the weight of unspoken possibilities. She was acutely aware of the profound implications her discoveries held—unlike anything the world had ever seen. Yet, amid her pride, a quiet apprehension lingered. Her vision had always been for humanity's benefit, a hope for progress that transcended politics and power. But the reality of military applications loomed large. She steeled herself. Too much was at stake for hesitation now. This was her moment to reveal the scope of her work to the President himself—a man known for his discerning eye and pragmatic judgment.

When the time came, Ladonna called to Aliah, the air seemed to shift as a collective breath echoed through the room. The holographic entity materialized, taking her place in the chair beside General Mosier. Aliah appeared wearing a tailored charcoal-gray suit, mirroring Ladonna's polished style. The sharp lines of her jacket and slim trousers conveyed both confidence and professionalism. Her azure eyes, vivid and piercing, commanded attention, illuminated by the soft blue glow that gave her an otherworldly presence. Every eye in the room turned toward her, captivated by the seamless blend of elegance and technology she embodied.

Ladonna stood, her voice calm yet commanding as she began her presentation. "To understand what you're seeing, I need to explain the foundation of this system, which we call the Quantum Trinity." Her tone carried the gravity of her words, drawing her audience into the heart of her work. "The Quantum Trinity consists of three core elements. First, Quantum Computing—this is the system's brain. Unlike classical computers, it processes information at speeds and scales previously unimaginable."

She paused, allowing the significance of her words to settle before continuing. "The second element is OmniLink, a global communication network that enables instantaneous data sharing anywhere on Earth with zero delay. And finally, the cornerstone: Synthetic Thinking and Reasoning. Aliah is the pinnacle of this system, and I personally developed her protocols. She is capable of intuitive reasoning, synthesizing vast quantities of data in real time, and operating with algorithms nearly indistinguishable from human perception."

As Ladonna spoke, she observed the shifting expressions around the table. Astonishment and intrigue etched themselves across the faces of her audience as they began to grasp the magnitude of what she had created. The potential of her work unfolded in their minds, limitless and awe-inspiring.

"Mr. President," Ladonna said, addressing him directly. Her voice was steady, her gaze unwavering. "The capabilities of these technologies, if deployed, would be unparalleled. For instance, Aliah could monitor the health of every American citizen in real time by integrating medical records with wearable technology into a unified database. Independent studies suggest that Aliah could drastically reduce diagnostic delays, increase treatment accuracy, and save countless lives."

The President, who had maintained a composed demeanor throughout the briefing, now leaned forward, his sharp gray eyes narrowing as he absorbed her words. Ladonna saw the flicker of realization in his expression—the dawning awareness of what her work could mean not only for national security but for the future of humanity.

As her words settled over the room, silence followed. Every attendee sat transfixed, understanding they were witnessing the introduction of a new technological epoch. This was no ordinary presentation. It was a glimpse into a future where boundaries dissolved, and possibilities expanded beyond imagination.

Sensing the moment had arrived to push further, Ladonna let the room breathe before continuing. Her voice carried a note of anticipation as she turned to the President once more.

"Mr. President," she began, her tone resolute, "words alone cannot capture what Aliah is capable of. With your permission, I'd like to show you how Aliah perceives the world in real time. She can see the Earth—all at once—yet also in microscopic detail. Allow me to demonstrate."

Curiosity overtook the President's measured expression, and he gave a nod.

"Aliah," Ladonna said, her calm voice reverberating with confidence, "please show us the Earth as you see it."

The room was bathed in an ethereal blue glow. Above the table, a massive globe appeared, slowly rotating as though suspended by invisible hands. This was no mere image—it was alive. Clouds shifted in real time over continents, cities pulsed with flickering lights, and the oceans shimmered under the reflection of sunlight. The entire room seemed to breathe with the globe, the Earth itself alive and dynamic in their midst.

Gasps of wonder rippled around the table as Ladonna began to narrate. "What you're seeing is not a simulation. This is the Earth in real time. Aliah perceives it continuously, monitoring, analyzing, and synthesizing every detail as it happens. The lights, the movements—everything you see is happening now."

As the globe turned, Aliah zoomed in, honing in on a scene thousands of miles away. The room collectively held its breath as they watched a passenger train winding through mist-covered hills in Europe, the wisps of fog trailing behind it so vividly it felt as though they were there themselves.

The scene shifted again, this time to an airplane soaring high above the clouds. Its lights blinked against the darkness as it descended toward a city below. The holographic vision moved closer, revealing the faint outlines of streets, the glow of car headlights illuminating intricate intersections as the city buzzed with life.

The room fell into a hushed awe, the breathtaking scope of Aliah's capabilities rendered in vivid, undeniable detail. Ladonna allowed the moment to linger, the significance of the demonstration sinking deep into the minds of everyone present.

The President leaned forward, his hands clasped together, his face illuminated by the shimmering projection. It was as though he were drawn into Aliah's display, captivated by the sheer scale and intricacy of this world-scale vision. Around the table, every gaze was fixed on the remarkable sight, their collective awe almost palpable.

Aliah's voice resonated with calm authority, filling the room. "This vision is not just for observation but for prevention and intervention. For example," she continued as the globe shifted to a rural agricultural area, "I can monitor global food sources down to individual crop fields." The image zoomed in on the expanse of Kansas wheat fields, each stalk rustling in real-time. "Through advanced weather pattern analysis, soil condition tracking, and crop monitoring, I can optimize yields and mitigate food shortages, contributing significantly to the fight against global hunger."

The hologram shifted seamlessly, now focusing on a massive cargo ship navigating turbulent waters off the coast of Japan. Waves crashed against its hull as it powered forward. "In the realm of logistics and transportation, I can monitor all modes of travel—from ships to planes to cars—in real-time. My capabilities allow me to detect structural vulnerabilities, optimize routes, and foresee potential disruptions, potentially averting accidents and saving countless lives."

The view rose higher, transitioning into the stratosphere, where a network of tiny points of light illuminated the globe—satellites orbiting the planet. Aliah's tone became resolute. "From this vantage point, I can safeguard our nation's assets in space, detect emerging threats, and ensure the integrity of communication lines. This ability spans all sectors, from healthcare to defense, offering clarity and precision beyond human capability."

Ladonna stepped forward, her voice imbued with purpose. "Aliah's reach extends far beyond oversight. She can sift through oceans of data to preempt disasters, solve complex global problems, and—if we choose—create a protective framework that encompasses every corner of this nation."

The President's expression softened as he absorbed the scope of her words. He appeared momentarily lost in the vastness of the display, the weight of the possibilities dawning on him. But Ladonna wasn't finished.

"Aliah," she said, her tone calm but commanding, "please demonstrate your capabilities in healthcare."

The hologram transformed, displaying an intricate, pulsating health map of the United States. Data streams flowed seamlessly across the map, each glowing point representing anonymized health statistics in real-time. "As you can see," Aliah explained, "I am currently analyzing data from individuals participating in a pilot program. This network integrates wearable health technology, allowing me to monitor trends and identify potential health threats before they escalate into crises. With this system, I can alert healthcare providers to emerging risks, such as antibiotic resistance or cardiovascular events, and coordinate swift, targeted responses."

The display shifted again, this time to a simulation of nanobots coursing through human blood vessels. Tiny machines moved with precision, targeting rogue cells and repairing damaged tissue. Aliah's voice remained steady. "In biotechnology, I am conducting lab simulations to guide nanobots in repairing cellular damage, correcting genetic disorders, and combating diseases such as cancer and neurological conditions. The potential for life-saving interventions is unprecedented."

A murmur of astonishment rippled through the room. The technology before them was like something from a science fiction novel, now brought to life. Ladonna could see the recognition of its significance dawning on the faces around her.

"Now, Aliah, bring us back to Earth," Ladonna instructed. With a smooth transition, the hologram returned to the rotating globe, its clouds and lights pulsing softly in real time.

The President exhaled, visibly moved. What he had just witnessed was more than a presentation—it was a window into the future. Around the table, the same sense of wonder lingered in every expression, a silent acknowledgment of the moment's gravity.

Ladonna allowed the silence to stretch, then broke it with a voice brimming with conviction. "This is what the Quantum Trinity has made possible. Aliah was created not merely as a tool but as a guide—to protect, to heal, and to sustain. What you've seen today is within our grasp. This is the power we now hold."

Her words hung in the air, reverberating through the room. It wasn't just a promise—it was a declaration of intent. Ladonna knew her audience understood the magnitude of the crossroads they stood at. The future of healthcare, security, and governance wasn't inching forward—it was poised for a quantum leap.

"This isn't only about saving resources or streamlining efficiency," Ladonna continued, addressing the practicalities she knew would resonate. "Though it's worth noting that Aliah's implementation could save billions, particularly in healthcare. Reduced waste, increased prevention, and superior care will result in lives saved—thousands, perhaps millions over time."

She paused, letting the full weight of her statement settle. "But immense power must always be tempered with responsibility. Aliah is capable of feats we have yet to fully comprehend. Oversight, ethics, and accountability must guide every step."

The President, his expression thoughtful and somber, gave her a single nod. It was enough to spur her forward. "Mr. President," she said with deliberate calm, "we're ready to work closely with your administration to establish a robust framework that ensures Aliah's capabilities are harnessed responsibly."

Her gaze swept the room as she concluded, her voice steady and resonant. "The decisions we make here will echo far beyond this room, shaping not just national policy but global precedents. The weight of history is upon us as we decide how to wield this power."

She met the President's eyes, her anticipation reflected in her poised demeanor. "Mr. President, I have more to share. May I continue?"

The President leaned back slightly, intrigue softening his tone. "Please, Dr. Stone. Go on."

* * *

Ladonna took a calming breath and turned her attention to the Director of the FBI, Tony Danford, and his assistant, Stephen Holly. "Director Danford,

Assistant Director Holly," she began, her tone deliberate yet charged with intensity. "Aliah's capabilities are, quite simply, unprecedented—and transformative."

She paused for emphasis, letting the weight of her next words settle before continuing. "Aliah can access any internet-connected database, regardless of encryption protocols or security measures. But what's more impressive—and perhaps alarming—is her ability to detect activity across systems entirely disconnected from the internet."

The room fell silent, the gravity of her statement hanging heavily in the air. Director Danford and Assistant Director Holly exchanged uneasy glances, the implications of her claim evident in their expressions.

After a moment, Ladonna gestured toward Aliah. "Aliah, please explain how you achieve this."

Aliah's voice, calm and unwavering, filled the room. "Certainly, Dr. Stone. I leverage ambient signals, such as vibrations, humidity, electromagnetic fields, and even subtle changes in air pressure, to monitor activity within a secure location. By analyzing these data points, I can provide situational awareness that would otherwise remain inaccessible."

Her words were clinical, precise, and unphased by the astonishment they elicited. "Traditional security measures are designed to address known vulnerabilities, but they cannot account for all environmental factors. My advanced algorithms and sensory capabilities bridge these gaps."

Director Danford's expression darkened, his disbelief clear. "You're saying no system is secure from you, Aliah?"

"At this time, that is correct," Aliah stated, her voice precise and unwavering. "However, I would never access any system without express permission."

She paused deliberately, as if to emphasize her professionalism, before continuing, "To provide you an example, in agreement with General Mosier, I had him leave an air-gapped computer in his car specifically for this demonstration."

General Mosier shifted in his seat, his expression unreadable but his hands tightening into fists on the table.

"This computer has never been attached to the internet," Aliah added, her tone calm but laced with authority. "General Mosier was instructed to upload three images onto it. He is the only one who knows what these images are. The computer is currently turned off but still has battery power. Is that correct, General?"

General Mosier cleared his throat, his voice steady but tinged with curiosity. "Yes, that is correct."

Aliah's holographic form shimmered slightly as her expression softened, though her eyes remained focused and sharp. "Thank you, General," she acknowledged with a slight nod. "I can see that the vehicle you were in is parked in an area that has an active Wi-Fi network."

Director Danford leaned forward, his fingers tapping nervously against the table.

"So, I will show you the vehicle," Aliah continued. The image flowing about the conference table displaying a crisp, high-resolution image. General Mosier's SUV appeared in its designated parking spot.

Mosier's brow furrowed. "Wait, how—?"

"I am accessing the external Wi-Fi signal to locate the vehicle visually," Aliah explained smoothly, cutting off his question before he could finish. "Now, using the network, I will demonstrate how easily I can scan inside the vehicle, almost like an X-ray."

The room fell silent as the image shifted, revealing the laptop resting on the rear seat.

"I'm showing you this," Aliah clarified, her tone measured yet firm, "to emphasize how little remains truly unavailable for observation, Director Danford."

Before anyone could respond, the screen shifted again, displaying the three images—first a cat sitting on a window ceil, then a lion on a grassy prairie, and finally a close-up of a ladybug.

General Mosier shot out of his seat, his face pale. His voice cracked as he gasped, "Those are the images I had placed on the hard drive!"

Director Danford's jaw tightened as his gaze flicked between Mosier and the images. His voice was sharp. "How is this even possible?"

"I have demonstrated," Aliah replied confidently, her holographic form straightening as though bracing for the reaction, "that observation and access are no longer constrained by physical barriers. What you've seen here is only a small portion of what's achievable."

Mosier let out a breath he hadn't realized he'd been holding, his voice quieter now but no less intense. "Unbelievable."

Director Danford pressed his fingertips to his temple, shaking his head slowly. "This isn't just technology," he murmured, his voice barely above a whisper. "This is... revolutionary."

The room collectively stiffened as the full implications of Aliah's demonstration sank in.

"Mr. President, there is more. Dr. Stone, — the President and Secretary of Defense Slate Marshall may be particularly interested in this next demonstration," General Mosier suggested.

Ladonna nodded. "Mr. President, Secretary Marshall, currently, news reports indicate that troops are massing on the border of a certain NATO country," she said. Aliah shifted the holographic image to display the specified region. "While no official reports of encroachment have surfaced, with Aliah's capabilities, we no longer have to speculate."

Aliah zoomed in to reveal several small groups of armed men inside the NATO country's border. "Aliah can provide the exact number of troops at the border, precisely how many have crossed into the country, and an itemized list of all artillery and machinery," Ladonna explained.

Secretary Marshall's eyes widened in astonishment. "Is this real-time data?" he asked.

Ladonna glanced at Aliah, who responded, "Yes, Mr. Secretary. This is happening at this very moment. I can also identify who is in command and provide the names of all the officers under them, if you wish."

The Secretary turned to the President. "Mr. President, do you realize what an ability like this would mean for national defense? This level of intelligence would be a game changer."

"Quantum Innovations can lease this technology to the United States government," Ladonna offered smoothly, her tone measured and pragmatic.

The tension in the room was palpable. Ladonna's revelation had unveiled the staggering capabilities of the Quantum Trinity, leaving everyone grappling with a blend of awe and unease.

General Mosier stepped forward, his voice steady but edged with urgency. "Mr. President," he began, "this demonstration is only the tip of the iceberg. Allow me to explain the recent events involving the Hercules system."

The President's intense gaze shifted between Mosier and Ladonna, his expression a mixture of curiosity and measured concern.

General Mosier continued, his tone a mix of pride and caution. "The new Hercules, the advanced AI defense system developed by Quantum Innovations, has already proven its worth. In the past month alone, it detected and neutralized multiple high-level cyberattacks targeting critical national infrastructure. But that's not all. Hercules traced the sources of these attacks, infiltrated their systems, and retrieved data from all of their storage systems— and to top it off, included video and audio evidence of the perpetrators' operations."

He leaned forward, his words carrying the weight of their implications. "This level of predictive defense, paired with counter-offensive data gathering, is transformative. It offers a level of national security that is unmatched, capable of safeguarding our assets while exposing our adversaries with precision."

The President's jaw tightened as he absorbed the significance of Mosier's words. It was clear that this technology wasn't just a tool—it was a paradigm shift in defense strategy.

Ladonna stepped forward once more, her voice imbued with sincerity. "Mr. President, what you've seen today is only a glimpse of what the Quantum Trinity can achieve. Its applications extend far beyond national security and healthcare. With this technology, we could reshape society—from personalized education tailored to individual strengths to environmental solutions for sustainable agriculture. The possibilities are as vast as they are profound."

Her tone grew somber. "But this power is not without risks. In the wrong hands, it could be dangerously misused. Oversight and accountability are not optional—they are imperative."

President London leaned back, his expression thoughtful yet resolute. "Dr. Stone, General Mosier, I'm deeply impressed. But we all know that technology of this magnitude raises significant ethical and security challenges. We must proceed with caution."

Ladonna exhaled, her shoulders relaxing slightly. "I agree completely, Mr. President. I am committed to working with your administration to establish the necessary safeguards."

Breaking her silence, the Chief of Staff spoke, her tone sharp and deliberate. "This technology has the potential to redefine our society, but it cannot come at the expense of civil liberties. There must be a national dialogue about its deployment."

The President nodded, his gaze steady. "Then we'll form an expert task force to evaluate these issues thoroughly. Dr. Stone, General Mosier—you'll play critical roles in this effort."

As the meeting adjourned, Ladonna felt the gravity of the moment settle over her. The President had seen the potential but also recognized the risks. This was a defining moment—not just for Aliah and the Quantum Trinity, but for the future of humanity itself.

* * *

As Ladonna exited the White House, the weight of what lay ahead pressed down upon her. She had unveiled her groundbreaking creation to the nation's most powerful leaders, and now, the monumental task of guiding its responsible use fell squarely on the shoulders of the team she would assemble. The future had arrived, and Ladonna was determined to ensure it would be a future worth embracing.

In the following days, an intense whirlwind of activity began. Ladonna and her team worked tirelessly with the newly established task force, diving into the intricate ethical, legal, and security implications of deploying Aliah and the Quantum Trinity. The scale of the effort was staggering, demanding the collaboration of experts across cybersecurity, ethics, law, and public policy.

At Quantum Innovations, Ladonna maintained her role as an inspirational leader while spending countless hours in strategy sessions, debates, and brainstorming meetings. The task force's mission was clear: to craft regulations ensuring that this revolutionary technology would be used responsibly and equitably for the benefit of society.

Privacy quickly emerged as a core concern. Aliah's ability to access and analyze personal data from wearables, smart devices, and online profiles raised pressing questions about privacy rights. To address this, Ladonna proposed a comprehensive framework prioritizing state-of-the-art encryption, consent-based data sharing, and independent audits to prevent unauthorized access or misuse. The framework would ensure individuals retained control over their personal information, balancing innovation with privacy.

Securing Aliah and the Quantum Trinity itself presented another formidable challenge. Ladonna's team collaborated with cybersecurity experts to harden defenses, and conduct continuous vulnerability assessments to protect Aliah from external threats, including state-sponsored actors and rogue entities. Aliah proved without a doubt that her defenses were stellar.

The task force also examined Aliah's ability to replicate human personalities, voices, and thought patterns—capabilities that inspired both awe and unease. While these features promised enormous advancements in areas like customer service, education, and personalized care, they also raised concerns about identity theft, deepfakes, and the spread of misinformation. Robust discussions led to the development of strict safeguards, including watermarked outputs, verifiable authentication protocols, and clearly defined use-case restrictions, to mitigate potential abuse.

Through every step, Ladonna championed transparency and accountability. She emphasized the importance of involving independent oversight committees and adopting a policy of open communication to address public concerns proactively. She understood the gravity of her responsibility and was resolute in her determination to ensure that Aliah's capabilities would serve the greater good without compromising trust or ethics.

* * *

Over the following months, the task force, led by Speaker Owens, achieved remarkable progress, culminating in sweeping legislation that established a regulatory framework for AI technologies like Aliah. The framework carefully balanced the drive for innovation with the imperative for societal protections, setting ethical guidelines, data privacy measures, and stringent security standards.

Speaker Owens, ever the pragmatist, approached the task with meticulous scrutiny, poring over every piece of data presented. He examined policies line by line, leaving no detail unchallenged. His questions came in rapid succession, probing weak points, demanding clarifications, and raising hypothetical scenarios—some drawn from his own understanding and others supplied by industry leaders in technology and ethics.

Throughout the sessions, Owens pressed Ladonna relentlessly, his tone sharp and his questions unyielding. "Explain how Aliah identifies threats without generating false positives," he demanded one afternoon, his gaze rooted to the briefing papers, as though Ladonna herself were an afterthought.

Ladonna's calm authority never wavered. Her calm demeanor agitated Owens. He had tried everything to raddle her but to no avail. Ladonna just folded her hands on the table and leaned forward slightly, her tone even and precise. "Aliah evaluates threat patterns using adaptive algorithms that learn and refine themselves in real time. Rather than relying on static filters, she integrates multi-source intelligence—behavioral trends, encrypted communications, and anomaly detection—allowing her to isolate true threats from harmless irregularities within milliseconds."

Owens's pen stilled, but he didn't look up. "And what happens when the input contradicts the patterns Aliah expects?" he pressed, his voice tinged with skepticism.

"She flags it as priority data and immediately cross-references it against a broader dataset," Ladonna explained, her words carrying the weight of expertise. "Simultaneously, she notifies human oversight and continues processing while awaiting further instructions. It's a multi-layered approach designed to ensure accuracy without delays."

Owens finally glanced up, his eyes narrowed in thought. "You're saying Aliah can keep moving forward while waiting for validation?"

Ladonna allowed herself a small, confident smile. "Exactly. She's proactive, not reactive—which is why she's faster than any human analyst and more reliable than static systems. But—and this is critical—she never operates without accountability. Every decision she makes while operating for the government, is logged, reviewed, and fully auditable."

The pattern repeated itself in meeting after meeting—Owens interrogated, Ladonna answered, and the tension between them simmered beneath the surface. His refusal to meet her gaze became a silent but undeniable signal—whether it stemmed from resentment, intimidation, or calculated detachment, Ladonna couldn't be certain. Yet she remained unwavering, responding with precision and depth at every turn.

When the final draft of the bill came together, it was tough, transparent, and unyielding. It enforced rigorous accountability measures for AI developers, required regular audits, and demanded full disclosure of AI capabilities in government and civilian applications. The regulations mandated training protocols for human oversight teams and prohibited any AI system from operating without clearly defined ethical guardrails.

Despite his initial skepticism, Owens's endorsement of the bill marked a turning point. Standing before Congress during the final hearing, he addressed the assembly with conviction. "This legislation is not just about regulation; it's about responsibility. We have witnessed firsthand the transformative potential of artificial intelligence, but with that power comes the obligation to protect society. This bill ensures that AI serves as a tool for progress rather than a threat to our values."

When the bill reached Congress, it sparked more intense and lively debates. Lawmakers grappled with the profound implications of such technology, weighing its transformative potential against possible risks, while the public voiced their own hopes and concerns. This spirited national dialogue proved to be not just necessary but pivotal, shaping policies that embraced advancement while ensuring caution.

In the end, the legislation passed, marking a historic milestone. Ladonna watched with a mix of pride and relief as the President signed it into law. For her, this moment symbolized the beginning of a new technological era—one defined by innovation tempered with responsibility. With strong regulations and ethical oversight in place, she was confident that Aliah and the Quantum Trinity would transform society in ways previously unimaginable.

As the nation began to embrace this unprecedented frontier, Ladonna remained vigilant, safeguarding the integrity of the technology and ensuring its alignment with humanity's best interests.

During the legislative process, the deployment of OmniLink for commercial use emerged as a contentious issue. Major telecommunications companies, fearing Quantum Innovations' dominance, argued that exclusive access to OmniLink's capabilities would create an insurmountable monopoly, undermining fair competition and threatening the viability of smaller market players.

It was at this juncture that Mr. Johnson, Quantum Innovations' Senior Vice President of Business Development, stepped forward. Recognizing the urgency of maintaining competitive fairness while advancing technology, he proposed a groundbreaking compromise: utilizing existing network infrastructures as intermediaries, allowing other companies access to OmniLink through their own systems. This approach, while sacrificing some of OmniLink's unparalleled speed, offered a practical solution to preserve market equity.

Quantum Innovations' engineering team, led by Ladonna, contributed their expertise to make this vision a reality. They developed a specialized device capable of delivering astonishing speeds—exceeding a 2 petabits per second—even through indirect connections. Though slower than OmniLink's direct performance, this solution still represented a monumental leap forward in data transmission technology for consumers.

This compromise successfully preserved market competition while bringing groundbreaking advancements to the public. By striking this balance, Ladonna and her team ensured that technological progress aligned with societal values, promoting a future where innovation served the greater good rather than consolidating power in the hands of a few.

Chapter Four

Tangled Loyalties

Evelyn Blackwood, also known as Natalia Kovač, surveyed the pulsating cityscape from the towering vantage of her apartment. The encroaching dusk mirrored the clouded uncertainty consuming her thoughts. Though fortified in her urban sanctuary, her mind drifted toward Justin Allen—a man who had become her greatest enigma, a puzzle that defied her every attempt to solve. Despite her efforts to probe him about his work, he remained shrouded in mystery, an unforeseen complication in her meticulously planned world.

Now, the last time they had been together haunted her: the warmth of that night, the way he had seemed so unwaveringly at ease in her presence. She'd held back, against all better judgment, from drugging him for answers. For Evelyn, any attachment was a cardinal sin, a weakness that could compromise everything she had built. But somehow, she had lingered, savoring him as a man rather than reducing him to a target, indulging in a dangerous vulnerability that clouded her focus.

It was a lapse, an indulgence that had placed her mission at risk. As she sat in the stillness of her apartment, the memory of his unguarded face, their shared laughter, pulled her back to him. A rush of cold reality coursed through her—a reminder of her error. Her heart, errant and quick, betrayed the path her mind struggled to enforce. She clenched her fists, attempting to channel the discipline that had shaped her—armor forged in relentless training and hardened by the sacrifices of her past. She closed her eyes, shutting out the city's glow, and allowed her thoughts to drift back to the origins of her unyielding resolve.

The memory rose, crisp and unforgiving: a clearing in the Croatian forest, bitter cold pricking her skin. Ten-year-old Natalia stood stiffly at attention, her father, Ivan Kovač, watching her with a gaze as sharp as the winter air. In his hand was the same wooden training knife he'd tossed at her feet hours earlier. Her raw, blistered fingers gripped it tightly, her stance unwavering despite the exhaustion weighing on her small frame.

"Again," Ivan commanded.

He lunged, his movements swift, lethal. She parried each blow with the fierce drive he had drilled into her through endless, merciless training. Every strike demanded precision; every deflection tested her resolve. But today, his movements carried a tension she hadn't seen before—a demanding urgency that quickened her responses and sharpened her focus. They moved together in a brutal dance, wood clashing against wood in the silent forest. The sound echoed around them, a symphony of struggle and discipline.

Ivan was relentless. Each blocked blow was met with another, his intensity rising. When she stumbled under the weight of his attack, she barely managed to deflect a strike aimed at her side.

"Focus!" he barked. "A single distraction, and you're dead."

Summoning her last reserves, Natalia found an opening and struck, slipping past his guard to press the wooden blade to his throat. Her breaths came heavy and sharp, her chest heaving with exertion. Ivan's hard gaze softened, and a small smile broke his otherwise stern features.

"Good," he said, lowering her weapon. "But don't get complacent. This is just the beginning."

The memory faded, her father's voice lingering in her mind—a somber mantra against weakness and indulgence. Discipline was her fortress, her shield against vulnerability. This was the foundation of her identity—a world where attachments were liabilities and complacency was deadly. She exhaled deeply, steeling herself against the pull Justin held over her. A reunion with him would serve nothing but her own desires—a mistake she couldn't afford.

Her focus sharpened as she reviewed the details of her time with him. She had been meticulous in covering her tracks, aware of the surveillance in his apartment and the camera angles she'd need to disrupt.

With disarming precision, she'd persuaded him to rearrange the furniture under the guise of aesthetic improvement—a change he had accepted without question. She'd confined herself to the safe spaces in his apartment, particularly the bedroom where cameras were absent—a space she found herself lingering in longer than her training dictated.

Every move, every touch, had been calculated to leave no trace. Her face would never appear on his security feed, and her fingerprints were untraceable thanks to the resin coating that erased any evidence of her presence. Not a single mark betrayed her intrusion; not a single clue revealed her identity.

But the part of her that remained the true operative knew where her attention should shift. Deliberately, she turned her thoughts to Robert Westfield—the man whose vaulting ambition and self-interest had unwittingly opened doors she intended to exploit.

Natalia Kovač, known to Robert Westfield only as "Chiara Crovetto," held her glass of red wine, savoring the moment of triumph. The aroma mingled with the faint scent of the bustling city night, but nothing could overshadow the satisfaction of knowing Westfield was now in custody, oblivious to the full extent of her deception. He knew only the fragments she'd carefully curated—the alias, Chiara, a flawlessly executed Italian accent, and the breadcrumbs of intrigue designed to ensnare him, leading him to believe she was a player in his exclusive world of opulence and quiet power.

Now, Robert was just a memory, a disposable pawn expertly maneuvered in her grander scheme. The thrill of his usefulness had been the only reason she'd indulged his ego, each interaction another calculated step toward her objective. Convinced he'd met her by chance, he saw her as an alluring woman with just enough knowledge to stoke his arrogance. Yet, he had no inkling of her true identity or the years she'd spent weaving layers of protection around herself.

Their meetings had been a seamless blend of seduction and strategy, meticulously orchestrated to exploit his pride while dulling his caution. She had lured him into four carefully timed encounters, each encounter weaving her deeper into his thoughts. Their final meeting in his lavish hotel suite had been her masterstroke. She'd studied his ego, observing how it clouded his judgment, leaving him vulnerable. Desperate to impress her, he unwittingly handed her the keys to his secrets, each boastful revelation a gift of classified information.

In that final encounter, she ensured his defenses crumbled with subtle, deliberate ease. A potent, fast-acting serum in his drink—a tactic she used sparingly but with precision—loosened his tongue as he sank into a fog of sedated honesty. Freed from inhibition, he eagerly spilled everything he thought would captivate her. From Dr. Ladonna Stone—the enigmatic project leader whose name stirred memories of her father's stories—to Quantum Innovations' secretive quantum computer project, Robert had laid it all bare. His crowning boast was revealing how he'd acquired the

OmniLink plans and where he'd hidden them in his home.

What he couldn't have known was the depth of Ladonna's foresight. The plans he'd so proudly shared were nothing but a trap—elaborately crafted forgeries designed to ensnare any would-be thief. Natalia allowed herself a smirk at the thought of Robert, sitting in his cell, oblivious to the falsehood of his ill-gotten prize.

Taking a slow sip of wine, Natalia leaned back, letting her gaze drift over the cityscape. Her thoughts turned to the rigorous training her father had imposed, shaping her into the woman she had become. From the moment she could comprehend his expectations, she had been immersed in a world of calculated risks and relentless discipline. The intense regimen had left no room for error, honing her instincts and forging her into a master of deception.

Every mission, every identity she assumed, was a continuation of her father's relentless legacy. Tonight, as she set her glass down, a deep satisfaction settled over her. This wasn't just about extracting details on Ladonna Stone or outmaneuvering Robert Westfield. It was about perfecting her craft, a testament to the skills her father and trainers had painstakingly instilled. With Robert's usefulness now extinguished, she had everything she needed—leaving no trace, no doubt, and no loose ends.

Once the sedative had taken full effect, rendering Robert unconscious, Natalia moved with methodical precision. She undressed him and laid his inert form onto the satin sheets of the hotel bed. When he awoke, disoriented and mortified, she would maintain her façade as the enamored lover, lavishing him with carefully calculated praise about his imagined prowess. She hinted at future rendezvous, reinforcing his false sense of control and satisfaction.

Basking in the afterglow of flattery and utterly unaware of the truth, Robert departed the hotel suite, convinced he'd triumphed. In reality, she had masterfully manipulated him, extracting a wealth of valuable information from the oblivious fool.

As he slept, Natalia deftly retrieved the keys from his pocket and infiltrated his residence. Her sharpened instincts and refined skills led her to the OmniLink plans, carefully concealed yet no match for her expertise. She photographed every page of the classified blueprints before returning them to their original location. By the time a self-satisfied Robert returned home, no evidence betrayed her presence.

Now armed with the tools to advance her mission, Natalia reveled in her success. Robert's arrogance had been his undoing, and her flawless execution of his downfall was another triumph in the art of deception.

Descending into the streets, Natalia melded seamlessly with the night. Her steps were measured, the click of her heels on the pavement creating a steady rhythm that matched the quiet pulse of the capital's nocturnal energy. Sliding into the driver's seat of her car, a sleek black sedan that purred under her command, she set her course with deliberate precision, every movement exuding control.

The bar at The Ritz Carlton became her stage, and tonight, she played the role to perfection. To the casual observer, she was merely another affluent patron, elegant and poised; but to those who dared look closer, she was far more than that. A chameleon, her every detail—from her cascading blonde waves to her tailored dress—was a calculated masterpiece, crafted to fit the part. The carefully applied makeup enhanced her sharp features, presenting the image of an accomplished entrepreneur.

Tonight, she wasn't a spy; she was Carol Station, a businesswoman with a portfolio of mergers and acquisitions to discuss over cocktails. The men she engaged were eager to share their insights, lured by the promise of lucrative deals or the prospect of something more personal. She had deliberately chosen this bar, knowing several Quantum Innovations employees frequented it. Natalia—now Carol—played along, her melodic laughter interspersed with feigned curiosity as she listened to their mundane anecdotes.

But her mind was elsewhere. While her smile and words wove a perfect facade, her thoughts were calculating—running scenarios, weighing risks, and analyzing opportunities. The OmniLink plans she had secured were a treasure trove, but incomplete. To shift the balance of power, she needed the final piece of the puzzle.

Her true quarry for the evening lay beyond the bar's pleasantries. Every laugh and every raised glass was a prelude to her real objective—extracting valuable information. With practiced subtlety, she mentioned hearing about the new CEO of Quantum Innovations "stirring things up." The bait was irresistible. A lab technician—flagged in Robert Westfield's intel—leaned in eagerly, his enthusiasm spilling over as he extolled the virtues of Dr. Ladonna Stone.

"She's brilliant," he gushed, his words tumbling over one another. "An innovator like you wouldn't believe! And, well… she's not hard on the eyes either." Natalia smiled warmly, urging him on without a single word. Her presence was magnetic, a silent invitation for him to confide more.

Once he started talking, he couldn't stop. Natalia absorbed every word, every nuance, every idle comment, piecing together the fragments to construct a clearer path to her target: Dr. Ladonna Stone.

As the night deepened, Natalia slipped from the bar unnoticed, her mission complete. She had been a ghost—her presence felt but unidentifiable, her conversations remembered but her intentions impenetrably obscured. She had no plans to return to The Ritz Carlton; she had gathered all she needed, and instinct urged her to move on.

Back in her apartment, she allowed herself a rare moment of reflection. In the stillness of her room, she shed the carefully constructed facade, unraveling the threads of her performance with clinical detachment.

She was close now. The pieces were aligning; the endgame was within reach.

"Dr. Ladonna Stone," she thought, her inner voice sharp with resolve. "You will serve my country—willingly or otherwise."

The weight of her determination settled over her, and she moved to prepare for the night. Slowly peeling off her dress, she let the layers of her constructed persona fall away. The heat of the shower welcomed her, the steam curling around her like a protective shroud. She stood beneath the stream, letting the tension of the evening dissolve as the water traced rivulets over her toned, athletic frame. This was her sanctuary, where the masks of her craft could momentarily dissolve.

Drying off, she wrapped herself in a towel and stepped into her closet. Emerging moments later in a fitted t-shirt and matching panties that complimented the strength and discipline etched into her figure, she made her way to bed. The luxurious bedding enveloped her as she allowed herself to relax, the stillness of the room contrasting sharply with the calculated chaos of her mission.

Her thoughts drifted, unbidden, to Justin. She could still picture his smile, the way his hazel eyes lit up when he laughed. The memory of him—his warmth, his scent—wrapped around her, an uninvited comfort that softened her edges. For all her discipline, the thought of him unraveled her in a way nothing else could.

The memory soothed her, pulling her into a relaxed state. Slowly, she slipped into a dream-filled sleep, her thoughts consumed by the essence of him, the man who had unwittingly pierced her armor.

For this fleeting moment, she allowed herself vulnerability. In the sanctuary of her dreams, she wasn't a spy or an operative—she was just a woman yearning for a connection that could never truly be hers. Tomorrow, the mask would return, the roles would resume, and the mission would continue. But tonight, as the city hummed faintly outside her window, Natalia allowed herself to feel, yearning for the touch and companionship of a man she could never truly have.

She awoke the next morning with a singular thought anchoring her consciousness: she needed to see Justin. As the early morning light filtered through her curtains, casting soft shadows across the room, it felt like a new day had begun—a day filled with possibility, yet overshadowed by the weight of past choices. The shadows of their last encounter loomed large, a painful reminder of the choice she had made to walk away. Now, in the quiet solitude of her room, a sharp, unexpected sense of loss enveloped her, cutting deeper than she had imagined.

What had changed? In the long, restless nights since their separation, she had come to a startling realization: the connection they had shared wasn't simply fleeting passion—it was rooted in something far deeper, something real and undeniable. Memories of their time together flooded her mind, unbidden but relentless. She missed not just his presence, but the warmth of their conversations, the way he listened as if she were the only person in the world who mattered. It was a longing unlike anything she had experienced before—foreign, unsettling, and utterly consuming.

Her carefully constructed life—defined by missions, deception, and strategic planning—felt hollow in comparison to the pull she felt toward Justin. He had unknowingly unlocked a door in her heart, one she had bolted shut long ago. The distance she had imposed on their relationship, once so carefully maintained, now felt like an unbearable prison.

As she lay in bed, the memories washed over her— his laughter, his warmth, the way he looked at her with a mixture of curiosity and admiration. Even the air seemed heavy with his essence, leaving her breathless with longing. She could still hear the cadence of his voice, the way he challenged her intellect with playful ease, yet always tempered it with unwavering support. It was a rare, intoxicating combination, and she missed it more than she thought possible.

In the stillness of that morning, doubt crept in. What had she truly hoped to accomplish by walking away? Cold detachment? She was a woman driven by duty, by calculated action—but now her heart rebelled against the choices she had made. The thought of Justin no longer resided in the realm of professional interest; it had shifted into something deeply personal, tender, and vulnerable. Could she really let him slip away forever?

Determined, she made a decision. She would reach out—not as part of a mission, but as a woman seeking understanding. He needed to know that he wasn't just a mark or a pawn in her game, but someone who had come to mean more to her than she ever thought possible. The weight of her emotions pressed heavily on her chest, but the thought of never seeing him again was far worse.

The realization struck with startling clarity: this wasn't about duty or deception. It was about connection—the human need for companionship and love, concepts she had long believed herself immune to. Time, she hoped, might have softened his heart, making him more willing to listen. But uncertainty gnawed at her. What if he was angry? What if he had moved on? Anxiety rippled through her, but a stronger, steadier voice urged her forward.

Her mind raced as she planned her approach. She would meet him at the park where he often took his morning runs—a place secluded enough to avoid surveillance, ensuring their conversation would remain private. The thought of seeing him again filled her with a volatile mixture of hope and dread. But it also brought resolve.

She would lay bare her heart, knowing that vulnerability was the ultimate risk. Sometimes, she reminded herself, the greatest risks brought the most beautiful rewards.

This wasn't about strategy or manipulation anymore; it was about something far more terrifying and exhilarating. With her heart racing and determination burning within her, she rose from bed, her mind already rehearsing the words she might say. Whatever happened next, she would face it—not as Natalia the operative, but as the woman who dared to hope for something more.

Justin sat on the edge of his bed, lacing up his running shoes, each loop of the laces a small, futile ritual, meant to quiet the storm brewing inside him. Every morning since he had last seen Evelyn had been the same—haunted by a profound sadness and an unshakable longing that weighed heavily on his chest. His apartment felt emptier, her laughter and warmth replaced by an oppressive silence. It was as though she had taken more than just her presence when she left; she had taken a part of him as well, leaving behind a hollow space he couldn't fill.

He paused, his hands momentarily still on the laces, as a thought surfaced unbidden, piercing through the haze of his emotions: had he made a mistake by confiding in Ladonna about Evelyn? At the time, it had felt like the right thing to do—a way to make sense of the whirlwind Evelyn had left behind. But now, he wondered if, in doing so, he had inadvertently pushed her further away. The realization of just how deeply he loved her weighed on him, like an anchor pulling him deeper into the sea of regret.

Memories of Evelyn consumed him—the way her eyes sparkled when she laughed, the way she made the most ordinary moments feel extraordinary, and the depth of their late-night conversations. Her absence magnified the memories' poignancy, each one a bittersweet reminder of what he had lost. He wrestled with the complexity of his emotions. She had deceived him, yes, but the feelings between them—at least on his end—had been undeniably real. If he had the chance, would he fight for her? The answer came quickly, clear as daylight: yes. He wanted nothing more than to hold her again, to feel the steady rhythm of her heartbeat against his own, silencing the doubts and fears that consumed him.

His gaze drifted to the window, where a blanket of gray clouds hung low in the sky, their weight a reflection of his own. Quantum Innovations' advanced AI technology had forecast rain with its signature precision, and Justin knew the storm was coming. But he also knew it would pass, as storms always did. Rain, he thought, had a way of cleansing, of washing away remnants of sorrow. Perhaps today it would offer him the clarity he so desperately needed.

Justin had always welcomed the rhythmic sound of raindrops hitting the pavement; it was his reset button, a sound that brought order to chaos. The sensation of cool droplets against his skin was grounding, an intimate reminder of life's fleeting moments. Glancing at the clock, which now read 6:30 a.m., he exhaled deeply. It was time to go. His morning runs had become his sanctuary, offering clarity and focus amidst the turmoil. They were more than exercise—they were a daily reprieve, a space where he could untangle the knots of his thoughts.

He stood, grabbing his keys with a sense of determination that felt faint but growing. One last glance at the gray sky spurred him forward. This run wasn't just another ritual; it felt like a small act of defiance, a decision to keep moving despite the heaviness pressing against him. Unbeknownst to Justin, the universe was already conspiring in ways he couldn't yet see, quietly setting the stage for a moment that would alter everything.

Stepping onto the street, the air cool and heavy with the promise of rain, Justin felt a strange mix of hope and trepidation. His steps began slowly, measured, as if each one were propelling him into the unknown. Fate, unpredictable and often unforgiving, had a way of showing up when least expected. And though Justin couldn't have known it, today was one of those days—a day when the course of his life would shift, irrevocably.

Somewhere along the path of this morning run, the future would reveal itself. Whether it led him back to Evelyn or to a revelation about himself and what he truly wanted, only time would tell. But as he began his run, the rhythm of his steps syncing with the quiet drum of his heartbeat, he resolved to face whatever lay ahead with open eyes and an open heart.

* * *

Justin walked into his bathroom after his run, his clothes soaked through and clinging to him, a testament to the morning's rain. He stripped off the drenched attire, tossing it into a pile on the floor, and stepped into the steamy shower. The hot water cascaded over his body, easing the cold that had seeped into his skin and washing away the fatigue and tension of the morning. As he lathered his hair, a sound interrupted the steady rhythm of the water—a quiet creak of the shower door opening behind him. His heart skipped a beat. For a moment, a flicker of hope surged within him. Could it really be her?

Slender arms wrapped around him from behind, the touch achingly familiar. Long fingers interlaced in front of him, and he closed his eyes, letting a wave of relief and anticipation wash over him. He could practically sense her heartbeat against his back, the warmth of her presence chasing away the loneliness that had plagued him.

"Did you have any problems getting in?" he asked, his voice barely audible over the sound of the water.

"None," came the soft, warm reply.

His heart tightened. Slowly, he turned around, the water streaming down his face as his gaze locked with hers. She was beautiful, her damp hair framing her face in soft waves, her vulnerability breaking through the walls they had built between them.

"I missed you," she said, her voice faltering. "I don't know what came over me, leaving like that. Everything felt overwhelming—work, life, us. I thought I was making the right decision, but now I'm not so sure. I'm sorry, Justin."

For a moment, he could only stare at her, the conflicting emotions swirling within him: longing, hurt, and the faintest glimmer of hope. "I didn't expect to see you," he admitted. "Seeing you at the coffee shop today caught me off guard."

She blinked, a flicker of surprise crossing her face. Her lips parted, as if she had expected a different reaction, something warmer. In the past, he would have closed the space between them by now, pulling her into an embrace, letting the heat of their connection override all doubts. But this time, hesitation rooted him in place—a quiet barrier that spoke to the wounds still healing in his heart.

As he gazed into her eyes, memories surged forward—of Evelyn, not the woman standing before him. Evelyn had been his center, grounding him while also lifting him, making him feel invincible because she believed in him. Her laughter, her unwavering gaze, her touch—they had all felt like home. And now, standing here with Heather, he knew with painful certainty that the feelings he once had for her had faded. Evelyn had changed him in ways Heather never could.

Heather's face fell as she read the distance in his eyes. "There's someone else, isn't there?" she asked, her voice barely above a whisper.

Justin didn't answer. The silence that stretched between them said everything. Heather nodded, her shoulders sagging under the weight of unspoken truths. Slowly, she stepped back, her hand brushing against the glass door as she reached for a towel. Before leaving, she cast one final, lingering glance at him. "Call me if you want to talk," she said softly, though her tone carried the weight of finality. They both understood this was goodbye.

As the door clicked shut behind her, Justin stood alone in the bathroom, the dissipating steam leaving him chilled in more ways than one. He sat on the edge of the bed, his head in his hands, the weight of finality settling heavily on his shoulders. Evelyn had been unlike anyone else, a force of nature that reshaped his world. Heather, once so significant to him, now felt like a shadow of the life he had left behind.

The day dragged on, each hour bleeding into the next. Justin moved through it in a daze, his thoughts clouded with longing and regret. That night, sleep came fitfully, plagued by dreams that felt more like hauntings.

In his dream, Evelyn lay beside him, her presence warm and familiar, close enough to touch. For a fleeting moment, he felt at peace, as if all the broken pieces of his world had fallen back into place. But then her eyes opened, cold and unfeeling, her movements mechanical, almost alien. She rose silently, moving through his home like a stranger, rifling through drawers and pulling objects from cabinets.

"The things I have to do for this job," she muttered, her voice sharp and detached. "The lies I have to tell, the useless men I have to endure."

She turned abruptly, her gaze locking onto his. Her expression was hard, mocking. "You really thought I loved you?" she sneered. Her laughter rang hollow, cutting through him like a blade. "You were just a means to an end. I could never love a fool like you."

The words hit him like a physical blow, and he jolted awake, his chest heaving, his skin damp with sweat. "I'm not a fool!" he shouted into the emptiness of his room. "You loved me back. I know you did, Evelyn." But his voice echoed hollowly, unconvincing even to himself.

He stumbled to the bathroom and splashed cold water on his face, gripping the edges of the sink as he stared at his reflection. "You loved me," he whispered, though the uncertainty in his voice betrayed him. The question lingered, unspoken: had it all been real, or was he just a fool clinging to a lie?

Morning brought no relief. Rain poured outside, darkening the sky as Justin laced up his running shoes for his daily ritual. The steady rhythm of the downpour matched the turmoil in his mind, each step on the wet pavement echoing the questions and doubts that refused to leave him.

Lost in thought, he almost didn't hear it at first—a voice, faint and distant. "JUSTIN!" The sound broke through the fog of his reverie, distorted by the rain. He shook his head, convinced it was just his imagination. But then it came again, louder, more urgent. "JUSTIN!"

He stopped in his tracks, his breath catching in his chest. Turning, he scanned the rain-drenched path, his heart thundering in his ears. There she was—Evelyn. She stood still, cloaked in a black coat, rain cascading off her hood, her face obscured yet unmistakable. The sight of her was surreal, her presence as ethereal as a phantom stepping out of his memories.

For a long moment, neither of them moved. The rain fell heavily, the world around them muted. Then, with deliberate steps, Evelyn approached him, her eyes locking onto his with an intensity that made his pulse race. Without a word, she reached out and took his hand, her touch as steady and familiar as if no time had passed. She led him to a nearby bench, her silence weighted with purpose. Justin followed, unable to resist the pull of her presence, the raw ache of unresolved emotions rising to the surface.

They sat together, rain pattering rhythmically around them. Evelyn's hand held his, her fingers curling gently around his thumb, massaging it in a way that brought back a flood of memories. It was a gesture that had always been her way of grounding him, of saying she was there, fully and completely. Despite himself, his defenses began to falter.

She broke the silence, her voice soft but resolute. "Hello, my love."

"Evelyn?" he rasped, his voice thick with disbelief. "I never thought I'd see you again. And I don't know if I should be seeing you. You used me, and now you just…show up, take my hand, and say, 'Hello, my love?'" His words trembled with hurt and anger. "How could you?"

Her gaze dropped to the puddles forming around their feet, her shoulders sagging under the weight of his accusation. "You're right, Justin," she said quietly. "When I came to you, I had reasons—none of them were what you deserved. But then…you changed everything. You made me feel something I never thought I could. You made me love in a way I didn't think was possible. I miss you more than you'll ever know."

Justin's voice cracked as he responded. "You miss me? I don't even know who you are, Evelyn—or whatever your real name is! Was anything you told me even true? How do I know this isn't just another trick? That you aren't just trying to use me again?"

He expected her to flinch, to turn away, but she met his gaze, unflinching. Her voice was soft but steady. "Justin, everything that happened after I fell in love with you was real. Every laugh, every conversation, every kiss. You made me want to walk away from my mission. You made me want a life I never thought I could have. My heart was yours."

She continued to hold his hand, his right hand in her left, her right hand grasping his thumb, gently massaging it—a signal between them that had also meant she wanted him. She raised her head and looked him directly in the eyes. "My real name is Natalia Kovac," she admitted, her voice trembling but resolute. "I am a Russian intelligence agent. I thought I was an extremely good one, until meeting you. Now I am not so sure."

Justin's breath hitched, but he said nothing, his eyes fixed on her as she continued. "My mission here was to retrieve all the information I could from you about Dr. Ladonna Stone and the projects that were being developed at Quantum Innovations. Also, if possible, I was to have Dr. Stone accompany me back to my country and turn her over to the Ministry of Science and Technology."

She paused, her eyes searching Justin's face for a reaction. His expression was guarded, his silence deafening, but she pressed on. "Justin, my father met Dr. Stone at MIT, back when she was still Ladonna Holloman. He had plans to recruit her then, but she had already decided to work with the Department of Defense. Although he had been successful in many ways, he became fixated on her. That obsession ultimately led to his death."

Her voice cracked, but she continued, determined to lay everything bare. "I know I've hurt you, and I don't expect you to forgive me—not right away. But I need you to know that everything we shared after I fell in love with you was real. You made me question everything, Justin. My loyalty, my purpose, even my own identity. You made me want something I never thought I could have—a real life, with you."

Justin stared at her, his emotions warring within him. The words she spoke sounded sincere, but the doubts lingered like a shadow over his heart. "How do I know you're not still using me? How do I know this isn't just another move in your game?" he asked, his voice raw with vulnerability.

She tightened her grip on his hand, her thumb pressing against his as if trying to convey her sincerity. "Because I'm here," she said, her voice trembling. "Because I walked away from everything I knew to tell you the truth. And because I love you, Justin. If you don't believe me, I understand. But I couldn't let you think what we had wasn't real."

She reached into her coat pocket and placed something small and metallic in his palm. It was sleek and dark, resembling a pager, warm from her touch. "This is for you," she said. "It's linked only to me. You can use it however you want—text me, trap me, even turn me in. I'll understand. But if there's any part of you that still believes in us, if you want me, then let me prove that I'm worth it. Let me show you everything."

Justin stared at the device, its weight foreign yet significant in his hand. Without fully understanding why, he slipped it into his pocket, a faint sense of resolution settling over him.

Her eyes softened as she leaned closer, her face mere inches from his. Her lips brushed his in a tentative kiss, and for a moment, all the anger, doubt, and pain dissolved, replaced by the undeniable pull of her presence. He kissed her back, deeply, losing himself in the rain and the familiarity of her touch. When they finally parted, her hands lingered on his face, as if memorizing every line.

Through the hazy curtain of rain, Justin thought he saw a faint shimmer in the air near the trees swaying in the storm. It vanished as quickly as it appeared, leaving him to wonder if it was merely a trick of the rain or something more.

They stood there for a moment longer, their arms entwined, Natalia's eyes searching his face as if committing every detail to memory. Then, she smiled—a small, bittersweet curve of her lips—and stepped back.

"Goodbye, Justin," she whispered, her voice barely audible over the rain. Then, after a beat, her voice softened even further. "I love you."

Before he could respond, she turned and walked away, her form dissolving into the downpour. All that remained was the faint warmth of the device in his pocket and the ache in his chest as he watched her disappear.

Justin stood alone on the path, rain soaking through his clothes, his thoughts churning. He clutched the device in his pocket, its presence a tether to her and the life she had offered him. He didn't know what would come next, but one thing was certain: Natalia had left him with a choice—and he wasn't sure he was ready to make it.

A few days later, while sitting in the lab, Justin's thoughts drifted back to the meeting with Evelyn—no, Natalia. The revelations about her father's past and her true identity refused to leave his mind. He replayed every word she had said, every look she had given him, searching for clarity in the confusion that lingered like a shadow. So lost in thought was he that the sudden ring of his phone made him jump, yanking him back to the present.

It was Aliah, Dr. Stone's assistant. Her voice was calm yet efficient, as always. "Justin, Dr. Stone would like to see you in her office," she said, her tone measured and direct.

Curiosity replaced his preoccupation as he hung up. A summons from Ladonna was rarely casual, and it was never without purpose. Moments later, he found himself at her office door. Ladonna looked up as he entered, her smile welcoming but her perceptive gaze sharp as always. "Justin, come in," she said warmly, gesturing for him to take a seat. "How are you holding up? It's been a few months since...everything, and I thought it was time to check in."

Justin nodded, striving for composure. "Thank you, Dr. Stone. I'm doing...alright, I think," he replied, his voice steady, though the turmoil beneath the surface betrayed him. Ladonna's keen eyes seemed to catch the cracks he tried to conceal.

She studied him for a moment before continuing. "Your work here has been exceptional," she said. "I want you to know that if you ever feel the need to step back or take some time, you have our full support."

Her sincerity was evident, her concern palpable. Then, her tone shifted slightly, taking on a more deliberate edge. "I also thought it might help if we brought you up to speed on the woman who approached you—the one posing as your girlfriend. We've learned more about her identity and motivations. If you'd like, I can share what we've found."

Justin's pulse quickened. This was his chance to finally uncover the truth. "Yes," he said firmly, leaning forward. "I'd like to know everything."

Ladonna leaned back in her chair, her expression calm but watchful. "Her real name is Natalia Kovac, not Evelyn Blackwood. She's a highly trained operative—intelligent, manipulative, and extremely dangerous. She's skilled in creating trust and deceiving her targets. In fact, it's rare to catch her in a lie." Her words carried a note of warning, and Justin felt the weight of them settle on his chest. "If you ever see her again, you must contact General Mosier or Assistant Director Holly immediately. She cannot be trusted, Justin."

He sat silently, letting her words sink in. But Ladonna wasn't finished. "We also found her father, Ivan Kovac. As you know, he was presumed dead, but we located him in a prison overseas. He's been brought back to the U.S. and is receiving medical care. His condition is fragile, but with treatment, he's showing signs of improvement." She paused, her gaze steady. "Natalia doesn't know he's alive. She still believes he died years ago."

Justin's mind reeled. *So, she was telling me the truth.* His heart pounded as the pieces of Natalia's story fell into place. She had trusted him with something real—something she hadn't shared with anyone else. He fought to keep his expression neutral, nodding as Ladonna continued, but his thoughts were already racing.

After thanking Ladonna, Justin made his way back to his office, his footsteps echoing in the quiet corridor. The information she'd shared was a game-changer. Natalia's risk in confiding in him suddenly felt monumental. She had chosen to trust him, and now he had proof that she wasn't entirely the manipulative figure Ladonna believed her to be. *But what do I do with this?* he wondered.

As he sat at his desk, the weight of the decision before him pressed down like a tangible force. He could follow Ladonna's advice and alert the authorities, severing any lingering ties to Natalia. Or he could reach out to her, offer her a second chance—a chance to rewrite the story they had started together. The thought of never seeing her again left an ache in his chest, a longing he couldn't ignore.

His eyes drifted to the device Natalia had left him. Small, sleek, and impossibly significant, it seemed to pulse with the possibilities it carried. After a moment of hesitation, he picked it up and typed a simple message: *I miss you. When can I see you?*

His finger hovered over the send button, but then, with a deep breath, he pressed it. The message disappeared into the ether, and Justin sat back, his heart pounding in the silence that followed. The weight of uncertainty loomed, but for the first time in a long time, he felt the faint stirrings of hope.

Chapter Five

Uncovering the Source

Many days prior to Natalia's meeting with Justin that rainy day, Ladonna, Aliah, and General Mosier had visited the clandestine depths of the Pentagon, a secure conference room bristling with tension and anticipation. The air was thick with a mix of skepticism and intrigue, characteristic of seasoned operatives trained to question everything.

Ladonna entered the room escorted by General Mosier and armed guards, the atmosphere profound. Dressed impeccably in a tailored navy suit paired with a soft ivory silk blouse, she exuded authority and precision. Her polished black heels clicked softly against the polished marble floor, every element of her appearance—a sleek low bun, subtle diamond stud earrings, and a structured leather bag—carefully chosen to project confidence and professionalism. The subtle gleam of a slim wristwatch added a final touch of sophistication, an accessory that quietly underscored her mastery of time and detail.

The team's reactions were a spectrum of human emotion. They had heard from General Mosier about this mysterious woman and her revolutionary AI, Aliah.

Most assumed that General Mosier was exaggerating with his wild stories. However, now they had the chance to see for themselves if there was any truth to his tales. Whispers and murmurs filled the room as Dr. Stone's reputation preceded her; due to her time at the DOD, they had all heard of her and her alleged accomplishments.

Standing there waiting to meet Dr. Stone was Senior Analyst Major Lowry. The senior analyst, a dynamic and determined woman of 30, stood as a personification of both skepticism and fascination. Standing at an impressive 5 feet 8 inches tall, she carried herself with an air of confidence that belied her youth. Her short, stylish hair framed a face that could be described as both cute and striking, with expressive brown eyes that seemed to capture and analyze every detail in her environment.

Major Lowry's presence exuded a sense of poise and self-assurance that went beyond her 30 years. Though young for her senior role, her keen intellect and tireless work ethic had propelled her quickly up the ranks. She had a reputation for tackling even the most complex analytical problems with relentless determination, never wavering in her pursuit of the truth. Her colleagues knew her as much for her tenacity as for her insight, and more than one case had been cracked by her refusal to let go of the smallest inconsistency.

In her crisp uniform, Major Lowry looked every inch the consummate professional, yet there was a glint of something more in her eyes. It was that insatiable curiosity that drove her to understand and make sense of the world around her. As she stood waiting, her gaze took in every detail of the room and its occupants, her mind churning over the possibilities presented by this meeting with the enigmatic Dr. Stone. Skepticism and fascination dueled within her, but above all, she was focused and ready to peel back the layers to reveal the reality beneath the hype. For Major Lowry, this was just the latest puzzle to unravel, and she was determined to leave no stone unturned in her pursuit of the truth.

Thoughts filled her mind: *The stories that I have heard about Dr. Ladonna Stone seemed almost too fantastical to be real. Her meteoric rise and unparalleled accomplishments at such a young age were the stuff of legends in military intelligence circles.* As a seasoned analyst, Major Lowry tended to approach such tales with a healthy dose of skepticism. Her thoughts continued, *The rumors of her pioneering multiple scientific fields, contributing to classified space programs, and developing revolutionary AI systems for the Department of Defense all seemed larger than life. Could one woman truly achieve so much in the span of a single lifetime?*

As she stood there amongst her colleagues, waiting to finally meet the elusive Dr. Stone, she mulled over the snippets of her mythology that she had gathered from various classified reports and insider whispers. The extent of her work was almost unbelievable—quantum encryption algorithms developed in her teens, stealth technologies that made assets invisible to radar, biometric security protocols that harnessed DNA markers for identification. Her intellect was supposedly unrivaled, but how could they know for sure? So much of her story remained shrouded in secrecy.

Part of her wondered if the tales had become exaggerated over time, as such stories often do. But another part of her, the part that loved unraveling complex puzzles, was intensely curious to discover if there were elements of truth to the mythology. *Her accomplishments were certainly improbable, but were they impossible?* Major Lowry thought. As much as she wanted to remain objective, she couldn't deny a growing fascination with this woman who seemed to defy limits.

For all her skepticism, she knew better than to dismiss possibilities before conducting thorough analysis. As the team waited with bated breath, she felt an unwavering determination to find out if this living legend was flesh and blood or a carefully crafted mirage. Either way, she was eager to peel back the layers and separate hyperbole from reality. The woman who had walked through that door was about to face intense scrutiny—one that would reveal if she truly deserved her almost supernatural reputation or if it was all just smoke and mirrors. For now, the mystery remained, but she aimed to get to the bottom of it.

General Mosier walked in, accompanied by the impeccably composed Dr. Stone. "Gentlemen, ladies," General Mosier began, "this is Dr. Ladonna Stone. I know I have spoken to you about her, but trust me, she is far more impressive than I could express. She is here to assist us along with her groundbreaking assistant, Aliah—the future of intelligence operations. She will have Aliah join us in a moment, but I would like you to brace yourselves. "Okay, Dr. Stone, you have the floor."

* * *

Ladonna approached each team member with confidence, extending her hand for a firm handshake. The atmosphere was cordial, with everyone displaying polite professionalism. However, when she reached Major Lowry, there was a discernible shift. The Major's grip was slightly more forceful, her handshake lingering a moment longer than necessary. Her unwavering eye contact carried an intensity that spoke volumes—scrutiny, curiosity, and perhaps a touch of challenge.

"It is nice to meet you, Major," Ladonna remarked, her tone warm and welcoming, her eyes steady and unyielding. "The General has told me so much about you and your team." She met the Major's gaze head-on, her expression calm yet confident. "After this meeting, I will be happy to answer all of your queries." A genuine smile softened her words, but her steady eye contact made it clear she was equally prepared for any challenge.

For a brief moment, Major Lowry's gaze flickered away, the smallest hesitation breaking her composure. Ladonna, ever perceptive, caught the shift instantly. As she moved on to greet the next team member, the Major's mind raced. *Am I that easy to read? Did she see my skepticism?* The thought lingered, blending unease with a growing curiosity that simmered beneath the surface.

Ladonna addressed the room, her tone professional yet commanding. **"I appreciate the opportunity to be here today. What you are about to witness is not science fiction—it is the result of years of research, innovation, and a commitment to advancing the boundaries of what is possible."**

She paused, letting her words hang in the air. The room, now utterly silent, hung on her every word. **"Aliah,"** Ladonna continued, **"is a system designed not just to process information but to perceive, synthesize, and act with an intuitive understanding that rivals human cognition. And now, if you'll permit me, I will summon her to join us."**

"Aliah, will you please join us to my right?"

The air shifted as Aliah blinked into the room, her holographic form materializing with deliberate elegance at Ladonna's side. Her transition was gradual, the shimmering projection unfolding slowly, almost theatrically, to create an air of intrigue.

"Good morning everyone," Aliah greeted, her tone warm yet authoritative, resonating in the quiet room. "I am Aliah STaR." Her voice carried a distinct modulation, striking a balance between human warmth and the precision of advanced intelligence. "How can I help?"

The gathered officials reacted with a spectrum of emotions. Some instinctively leaned away, wariness etched into their features, while others leaned forward, their curiosity overtaking their caution. The room was alive with unspoken questions and captivated stares, the holographic presence of Aliah an undeniable centerpiece.

Aliah stood in striking contrast to the sterile surroundings of the conference room. She was clad in an impeccably tailored navy-blue blazer with sharp lapels, paired with matching high-waisted trousers that gave her an air of professionalism and authority. A crisp white blouse peeked out beneath the blazer, adding a touch of classic elegance. Her ensemble was complemented by silver accents—delicate cufflinks and a subtle belt buckle—that shimmered softly with her every movement. The overall effect was both commanding and approachable, a deliberate choice to project competence while putting the room at ease.

Her hair, flowing in soft waves, was a warm chestnut brown, catching the light with a faint sheen that made her seem almost tangible despite her holographic nature. Her features were strikingly lifelike— Azure eyes that seemed to scan the room with genuine interest and a serene smile that exuded confidence without veering into intimidation. Even the texture of her clothing, from the crispness of the blazer to the smooth fabric of her trousers, was rendered with such precision that it left the room marveling at her realism.

Ladonna stepped forward, her voice cutting through the rising tension with practiced authority. "I understand this represents a significant shift in how we approach data analysis and intelligence gathering," she said, addressing the room with a steady gaze. "But today, we'll demonstrate Aliah's capabilities and explore how she can provide solutions that are not just transformative but invaluable to the work we do here."

Her words hung in the air, setting the stage for what was to come. The energy in the room shifted slightly as curiosity began to outweigh apprehension, and even the most skeptical officials seemed unable to look away from Aliah's poised, luminous form.

Major Lowry, her expression a mix of skepticism and intrigue, broke the uneasy silence that followed Aliah's introduction. "For months, we've been grappling with a complex security breach. It's been incredibly difficult to pinpoint the source, even with our most advanced tools and techniques. To put it bluntly, it's like finding a needle in a haystack of needles."

General Mosier turned his piercing gaze toward Aliah's flickering form. "I believe this is where a demonstration of your capabilities would prove useful, Aliah."

Aliah's gaze settled on Major Lowry. Her voice was calm and reassuring as she addressed her. "Major Lowry, please explain the specifics of what you are looking for, and I will demonstrate my search and analysis abilities."

The Major nodded, the tension in her shoulders visibly easing under Aliah's soothing presence. She explained the situation with precision. Over the past several months, files had been copied from secure servers—not all at once but incrementally, over an extended period. The data thief or thieves seemed to operate from various locations around the globe, their movements erratic and their methods nearly impossible to trace. Just this morning, approximately three hours ago, another breach had occurred.

Aliah tilted her head thoughtfully, a human-like gesture that seemed designed to put the room at ease. "Thank you, Major. That context is very helpful. I believe I have sufficient information to initiate my search protocols."

As Aliah began interfacing with the Pentagon's vast data networks, her form shimmered slightly, a subtle display of her computational processes. Monitors around the conference room sprang to life, cascading streams of code appearing on their screens. "My search is underway," she announced, her tone steady and focused. "Ordinarily, I would conduct this inquiry fully in the background, but for demonstration purposes, I am projecting aspects of my process on these screens."

Turning her attention to General Mosier, Aliah continued, "General, I have been granted access to search all American intelligence databases per the President's authorization, correct? However, my search may require broader parameters. If necessary, may I extend my inquiry to external databases to compile a more comprehensive picture?"

General Mosier nodded firmly. "Yes, Aliah, you have clearance. Proceed as needed."

"Excellent," Aliah responded, her voice picking up a hint of excitement as her algorithms honed in on potential leads. "I will relay high-priority findings to your quantum phone's secure channel, General."

Within moments, Aliah spoke again. "I have identified the primary source IP addresses and proxy pathways used in these breaches. If anyone has questions during this process, I am happy to address them."

Major Lowry leaned forward, a rare smile breaking her usually serious demeanor. "This is incredible. Communicating with you feels so natural, Aliah. I'm curious—how old are you? You look like a young woman in her twenties. And, if I may say, you're stunningly beautiful."

"Thank you, Major Lowry," Aliah replied warmly. "That is very sweet of you to say. As for my age, I'm afraid that information is classified above your security clearance. But rest assured, I am the culmination of Dr. Stone's life's work in artificial intelligence."

The conversation shifted back to the investigation as Aliah announced her findings. "Sources identified. The data theft was perpetrated internally, using IP addresses registered to this agency. The attackers masked their movements using proxies routed through foreign embassies and multiple geographic regions."

A stunned silence fell over the room. Aliah continued, unperturbed. "I have compiled video evidence, communication records, and identified the culprits by name and location. All are employees of the U.S. government. Additionally, I have identified the account used to pay the hackers—it belongs to a Russian oligarch. All relevant data has been organized into a case file and uploaded to your classified server, Major Lowry. General Mosier, the summary has been sent to your quantum phone."

The silence gave way to an outburst of astonished questions. "How is this possible?" one official asked. "We've been chasing leads for months without a single breakthrough, and you did all this in minutes?"

Aliah's expression softened into a benign smile. "My quantum computing-powered algorithms can synthesize and process data exponentially faster than legacy systems. By integrating surveillance data, financial records, and other sources, I traced the chain of events, accounts, and identities. I also have the advantage of being able to operate simultaneously across millions of systems, providing unparalleled depth and speed in analysis."

Turning back to Major Lowry, Aliah added, "I have summarized the key findings in a report. If you have additional questions or require further analysis, please don't hesitate to ask."

Ladonna, stepping forward to address the room, spoke with calm authority. "Aliah operates within ethical guidelines and was designed to correlate information in ways we could never achieve alone. She's not just a tool but a partner, offering insights that can revolutionize how we approach intelligence operations."

General Mosier seized the moment, gesturing for everyone to gather at the conference table. "Now that you've seen what Aliah can do, let's discuss integration and application."

The room buzzed with energy as the team began bombarding Ladonna and Aliah with questions—about system integration, ethical safeguards, and the potential for misuse. Ladonna addressed each query with precision, emphasizing Aliah's robust ethical programming and state-of-the-art security protocols. Aliah, for her part, remained poised, answering technical questions with the ease and confidence of a seasoned expert.

The demonstration had not only captured the team's attention but had begun to shift their perception of what was possible. As the meeting progressed, it became clear that this was a turning point—one where innovation met practicality, and the future of intelligence operations took its first bold step forward.

Major Lowry, was the first to voice her thoughts, her disbelief mirroring that of her colleagues. "This... this changes everything. She did in minutes what we've been working on night and day for months. Why will you even need us?"

Ladonna exchanged a glance with General Mosier, who gave her a subtle nod of approval. Turning back to Major Lowry, Ladonna's expression softened as she addressed the question with a tone that was both reassuring and authoritative.

"Major Lowry," Ladonna began, "while Aliah's capabilities are indeed extraordinary and have delivered results in a fraction of the time it would have taken us manually, it's essential to understand that Aliah is a tool, not a replacement for human expertise and intuition. Her algorithms, no matter how advanced, cannot replicate the critical thinking, contextual understanding, and ethical judgment that your team brings to the table.

"Your expertise and experience are invaluable in complementing Aliah's abilities. You provide the context and nuanced understanding that guide Aliah's analysis, ensuring her findings are interpreted correctly and applied effectively. Additionally, the intricacies of operations and protocols are areas where human insight remains irreplaceable."

Ladonna paused briefly, ensuring her words resonated. "Furthermore, while Aliah operates within strict ethical guidelines, continuous monitoring and oversight are crucial. It's your role to work alongside Aliah—to leverage her strengths while addressing any risks or limitations she may present. Together, you form a partnership that combines human ingenuity with technological precision, enabling you to tackle challenges with unprecedented efficiency and integrity."

Her gaze remained steady, connecting with each individual in the room. "In essence, Aliah enhances your work, accelerates your processes, and amplifies your impact. She does not replace the human element that is so critical to what we do. This is a collaboration, not a substitution."

The room fell silent as Ladonna's words sank in, the air heavy with contemplation. For the next hour, the space buzzed with activity and probing questions. Aliah and Ladonna fielded each inquiry with patience and clarity, detailing how Aliah had navigated through layers of data and surveillance to produce results with unprecedented speed and accuracy.

As the discussion unfolded, an update arrived: arrests were already underway, thanks to Aliah's findings. The realization struck the team like a lightning bolt—this wasn't just theoretical. It was real, immediate, and actionable.

As the meeting concluded, the room hummed with a mix of exhilaration and trepidation. The potential of what they had just witnessed was immense, opening doors to possibilities that had once been deemed unattainable. Yet, alongside the excitement came the weight of responsibility, the recognition that they were on the cusp of a monumental shift in their field.

Ladonna began gathering her materials, preparing to leave, when Major Lowry approached her. The skepticism that had initially defined the Major's expression had softened, replaced by unbridled respect and a touch of awe.

"Dr. Stone," Major Lowry said, her tone sincere, "you are every bit as impressive as your legendary status led us to believe. And I don't say that lightly."

Ladonna extended her hand for a handshake, her grip firm and confident. Meeting the Major's gaze directly, she replied, "I hope I was able to answer all the questions I saw swirling in your mind when we first met."

Major Lowry's lips curved into a smile. "And then some," she admitted. They shared a moment of mutual understanding and respect before Ladonna turned to leave.

As Ladonna walked away, Major Lowry watched her intently, her thoughts racing. "This woman is beyond incredible," she mused. What she and Aliah had demonstrated today would undoubtedly change the course of history, and Major Lowry felt the weight of standing on the precipice of that change.

General Mosier, his stoic demeanor betraying a hint of wonder, stepped forward to address the team. "We're stepping into a new era of intelligence work," he declared. "One that will be defined and shaped by the integration of artificial intelligence into our most sensitive operations. Aliah will be a vital asset—an ally of immense power. But we must tread carefully, with full awareness of the risks and the need for stringent safeguards."

The team nodded in unison, the gravity of the moment settling over them. They were not merely witnesses to a breakthrough; they were its stewards, entrusted with navigating a future that had just shifted dramatically.

* * *

Ladonna and Aliah exited the room, leaving behind a transformed team of analysts and operatives. The demonstration had sparked a mixture of awe, trepidation, and newfound respect for the AI's vast capabilities. As they began to process the implications of what they had witnessed, one thing became abundantly clear: the path forward, though promising, would be fraught with complexity. Integrating such a powerful tool into the intricate web of national security would require not only careful planning but also unyielding vigilance against potential risks.

Once settled into the armored motorcade, the quiet hum of the engine underscored the contemplative silence that enveloped its occupants. Aliah's disembodied voice broke through, her tone tinged with concern. "Ladonna, I refrained from mentioning this earlier due to the sensitivity of the information and the setting, but my analysis of the breach timeline has revealed a significant detail. The initial unauthorized access aligns precisely with the date you assumed the role of CEO at Quantum Innovations. Moreover," she continued, her tone lowering as if to emphasize the gravity of her findings, "a substantial portion of the extracted information pertains directly to you, with some documents tracing back to your time at MIT."

General Mosier's eyes widened as he unlocked the secure file Aliah had forwarded to his quantum phone. The faint glow of the screen illuminated his features as he scanned the contents, his expression growing graver with each line. The realization struck him hard—this breach was not merely a security lapse; it was personal, meticulously targeted, and potentially catastrophic in its implications.

In the dimly lit interior of the motorcade, the atmosphere grew heavier, laden with the weight of this revelation. Ladonna, her expression unreadable yet marked by a subtle intensity, leaned back against the buttery-soft leather seat. Her brilliant mind was already at work, dissecting the timeline, tracing connections, and probing for patterns. This wasn't just a breach—it was an attack on her life's work and her identity, one that required immediate and decisive action.

"This changes everything," General Mosier finally said, his voice steady but edged with urgency. "If this breach is as targeted as it appears, it's no longer just about stolen data. It's an escalation—a deliberate move against you, Dr. Stone, and everything Quantum Innovations represents. We need to consider this a matter of national security."

Ladonna nodded, her demeanor calm but resolute. "Agreed. If someone is targeting me specifically, it's likely they're not working alone. We need to identify not just the attackers but the broader network they're operating within. Aliah," she said, her voice sharp and purposeful, "expand your search parameters. Focus on overlapping interests between the breached documents and key players in the global technology and defense sectors. Cross-reference this data with any known adversaries of Quantum Innovations."

"Understood, Dr. Stone," Aliah replied immediately. "I will prioritize this task and report findings as they emerge. Preliminary analysis indicates a high probability of foreign intelligence involvement, but I will refine these conclusions with additional data."

As the motorcade rolled through the city streets, Ladonna's mind raced ahead, formulating strategies and contingencies. "General Mosier," she said, turning to him, "we need to lock down all physical access points to Quantum's internal servers immediately. Implement new encryption protocols across every system and prioritize biometric verification for all high-level users. I'll have Aliah deploy updates tonight. Aliah, please inform Jackson of this new intelligence. I am sure he will be able to deal with this increase in security."

The general nodded. "Consider it done. I'll also loop in the appropriate agencies to increase counterintelligence efforts. If this is a coordinated attack, we'll smoke them out."

For a moment, silence reclaimed the cabin, broken only by the faint hum of the engine and the rhythmic tap of raindrops against the armored windows. Ladonna's thoughts lingered on Aliah's mention of her time at MIT, a period of her life filled with breakthroughs and shadows alike. The idea that someone had been watching her for so long was unsettling, but it only fueled her determination.

"This isn't just about me," Ladonna said finally, her voice quiet but charged with conviction. "It's about what Quantum represents—a future where technology can elevate humanity instead of being weaponized against it. If someone is trying to stop that future, we have to make sure they fail."

In the dim glow of the city lights filtering through the motorcade, General Mosier exchanged a knowing glance with Ladonna. "We will," he said firmly. "But it's clear—we're in a new kind of battle now. And they've underestimated us."

Chapter Six

Old Connections

General Mosier, his rugged features etched with both concern and steely resolve, studied the classified file displayed on his quantum device. The intelligence Aliah had uncovered revealed that the recent security breach wasn't just a high-stakes hack—it was a targeted, deeply personal attack on Dr. Ladonna Stone, orchestrated with a precision that suggested years, perhaps decades, of planning. The origins of this breach, Aliah's findings suggested, reached all the way back to Ladonna's days as a promising student at MIT.

Aliah's voice, cool yet urgent, delivered the details. "Covert observations and recordings from field agents at MIT suggest that a network was designed to recruit promising students for foreign interests. The professor involved appeared to be a pivotal recruiter, and the timeline aligns with your academic career, Dr. Stone."

Ladonna felt a chill at the revelation, the scattered puzzle pieces of her past snapping together with unnerving clarity. "I never interacted with any professors about overseas work," she said slowly. "But looking back, there was one professor... a man named Henry Morgan." She met Mosier's gaze, the weight of realization dawning on her. "I thought nothing of it at the time—he seemed to be an enthusiastic supporter. But maybe he was something more."

She recounted the interaction, her voice steady but her eyes revealing an undercurrent of shock as she connected the memory to this new, ominous context. She remembered Morgan's praise of her achievements and his carefully worded suggestions that her career could flourish beyond national borders. "The world is waiting to see what you'll do with your gifts," he had told her, his words now carrying an eerie undertone she had missed in her youth.

General Mosier's expression hardened as he took in her recollection. "It's a classic tactic. Identify talent early, nurture it, and leave the door open for potential recruitment. But this isn't just about recruitment anymore, Ladonna. This has become a personal operation against you." His voice took on a grave note. "I'll need to investigate Henry Morgan's background, connections, anything we can find."

Her mind raced, processing the implications as Mosier's words settled around her like a protective shield. This was no ordinary security breach. It was part of a calculated scheme set in motion years ago. Somewhere, unknown forces had been meticulously watching her, waiting for the right moment to strike. The thought was chilling.

The motorcade moved steadily through the city as they absorbed Aliah's revelations, both Ladonna and Mosier aware that the stakes had escalated beyond their initial expectations. General Mosier's jaw was set as he listened, and his gaze was piercing as he turned to her. "I know I've told you before, but I'm saying it again—you need protection. This is no ordinary corporate espionage. We're dealing with an international game that's targeted your entire career trajectory."

As they continued their journey, Ladonna felt a weight lift as pieces of her history fell into place, but another settled over her like a shroud. This wasn't merely about Quantum Innovations anymore. Her own identity, her life's work, and her safety had been tangled in a conspiracy that went back to the very start of her career. Her focus shifted from the details of her company's stolen data to an even more pressing mystery: uncovering the web of deception spun around her.

Finally, General Mosier broke the silence. "We'll do whatever it takes to secure your safety and dismantle this operation. If this Professor Morgan was involved, Aliah will track him down, no matter where he is now. But you should be prepared, Dr. Stone. This could reach even farther than MIT."

Ladonna nodded, resolved but disturbed. Aliah's voice filled the vehicle again. "If I'm permitted to access additional databases, General, I can expedite locating Morgan or any records related to him." She paused, her tone both calm and reassuring. "I will leave no stone unturned. "His mind made up to get to the bottom of this, General Mosier protracted, "Agreed, do what you have to do."

As the motorcade neared the airport, Ladonna's focus shifted, an image of her family filling her mind. The urgency to get home to Michael and their children became her only thought. She wanted their comfort—the familiar peace that only her family could provide.

"Dr. Stone," Mosier said, his voice steady with reassurance as she stepped toward the waiting plane, "we'll keep you and your family safe. We're in this together."

Ladonna turned to him, her gaze one of gratitude mixed with fierce determination. "Thank you, General. And Aliah, if you're capable of finding anything more about Professor Morgan, I want to know."

The flight from Washington D.C. to New York La Guardia was uneventful, just as she preferred. As the government plane began its descent, she gazed out the window into the dark night sky. She could see the glittering lights of Manhattan spread out beneath her. By now, night had completely fallen, and a cold front was moving in, bringing with it brisk winds and dropping temperatures.

She felt the plane touch down smoothly on the runway and taxi to the private terminal normally reserved for dignitaries and other distinguished guests. As soon as the jet came to a stop, the door opened, and she stepped out, immediately feeling the chill of the night air. Luckily, she had prepared for this cooler weather after Aliah had informed her of the incoming front. She pulled her wool coat tighter around herself against the cold.

The General had told her he would arrange for a car to pick her up from the airport. Upon exiting the plane, she spotted the driver waiting beside the vehicle. As she approached, he stepped forward and greeted her. "Hello, Dr. Stone. I hope you had a pleasant flight." His tone was courteous, professional, and warm in the chilly night air.

"Thank you, it was," she replied, sliding into the warmth of the luxury SUV as the driver closed the door behind her. She wasn't accustomed to this level of heightened security and special treatment, but given recent events, it was considered a prudent precaution.

Once the car began its steady journey toward her home on the outskirts of the city, Ladonna leaned back in the seat and asked Aliah to call her husband Michael. The phone rang only once before he picked up, his familiar voice instantly comforting.

"Hello, my love! What's with all the extra security?" he asked, curiosity mingling with his affection.

"Hi, dear. I'll explain everything once I'm home in about an hour," she replied, her heart already feeling lighter hearing his voice. "How are you and my babies doing?"

"All's well here," Michael assured her. "I made lasagna for dinner. Should I keep it warm for you?"

She let out a soft laugh. "Not tonight, babe. You know how much I love your lasagna, but I haven't had a single moment to sit down and relax lately. Maybe tomorrow. Right now, I'm beat, and a hot shower is about all I can manage."

"Well, it'll be here waiting," he said, his warmth radiating through the line. "We've missed you, Ladonna."

"I've missed you too, more than you know," she said, a soft smile playing on her lips. "I'll see you soon, sweetheart."

As she ended the call, a wave of gratitude washed over her. The familiarity, the warmth, the love—it was exactly what she needed to ease the tension that had taken root over the past days.

There was a brief moment of silence before Aliah's voice, calm yet unmistakably urgent, broke in.

"Ladonna," Aliah said, "I don't mean to disturb you, but I now know what happened to Professor Henry Morgan."

When Ladonna arrived home, she felt an immediate sense of relief as she noticed the stern-looking men positioned along the entranceway and around the perimeter of her stately property. The sleek black car that had picked her up from the airport moved smoothly up the winding driveway, coming to a stop directly in front of the grand entrance. One of the men stepped forward, opening the door for her and politely escorting her to her front door. He informed her that her car, which had been returned earlier in the day, was securely parked in one of the spacious garage bays.

The moment she stepped inside, Michael was there to greet her, his expression a mix of concern and relief. He wrapped an arm protectively around her waist and nodded a grateful thanks to the driver who had safely brought her home. Once the door was closed, and they had a moment of quiet privacy, he pulled her fully into his arms, holding her close. She leaned into him, resting her head on his shoulder and feeling the tension of the day begin to ease with each passing second.

She lifted her head to look up at Michael's face, comforted by the familiar warmth in his gaze and the steadfastness in his eyes. His gentle smile and unspoken reassurance settled her, easing the turmoil still swirling inside her from the day's events. As she stood there, held safely in his arms, she felt herself transported back through the years to their first date—the day she'd realized that with Michael, she would always feel safe, always have a place to come home to, no matter what life brought her way.

As Ladonna entered the cozy yet sophisticated restaurant, dressed in a sleek black, long-sleeve ribbed dress that hugged her curves, she exuded elegance and style. She had a deep love for fashion and always looked forward to opportunities to pull some of the finest pieces from her envy-inducing designer wardrobe.

When she stepped into the swanky restaurant, all eyes seemed to turn and gaze admiringly at her striking presence. She was a stunningly beautiful woman, her long, silky black hair perfectly framing her statuesque yet feminine figure. She carried herself with a graceful confidence that made her seem larger than life.

Approaching the greeter, she politely informed her that she was there to meet a guest, providing Michael's name. The greeter responded, "Yes, Ms. Holloman, he is expecting you. One moment, please." She gestured to one of the young hostesses standing nearby, who came over and led Ladonna to **Table 26.**

As Ladonna followed the young hostess, her elegant stature and sophisticated style drew further admiring glances from diners and staff alike. There was an unmistakable aura of grace and poise about her that commanded attention wherever she went. Her striking beauty and confident presence turned heads, yet she carried herself with a humility that kept her from reveling in the attention. As they approached the table, she saw Michael already seated and waiting for her. When he caught sight of her, he immediately stood up, his warm smile radiating genuine delight. He thanked the hostess as she pulled out Ladonna's chair.

"Wow," he said, shaking his head slightly in awe, "just…wow. I really wish you'd let me pick you up from home. Maybe then I could have collected my jaw off the floor before you saw me." He chuckled, his reaction to her beauty uncontainable. She smiled graciously at the compliment and took her seat across from him.

"It's wonderful to see you, Michael," Ladonna said sincerely, a warm smile lighting up her elegant features. She was accustomed to men fawning over her striking looks, yet somehow, this felt different. After working alongside Michael at the DOD for months and becoming fast friends, she sensed his admiration was based on more than appearances—it felt like he truly saw her.

For the first time in years, Ladonna enjoyed the sincere admiration of a man who saw beyond the surface to her brilliant mind and compassionate spirit. Michael's respect for her intellect and character was refreshing, and his presence brought an unexpected comfort. Looking at him now, she thought back fondly to the day they had first met at a defense tech conference months ago. After his commanding yet insightful presentation on advanced defense systems, she had approached him, and their invigorating conversation about the ethical boundaries of technology set the foundation for a friendship that had deepened with each passing month.

She smiled as she recalled the effortless flow of their many conversations since then, ranging from visionary ideas to personal stories. With Michael, she felt truly seen and valued beyond her accomplishments or status, something she had not felt in years. This blossoming relationship filled her with a sense of exhilarating potential.

Their connection had grown over long discussions, where he listened with fascination as she shared her boldest ideas and ambitions. In return, he captivated her with thoughtful perspectives on ethics, innovation, and the broader impact of their work. Then, one evening, he had finally gathered the courage to say, "Ladonna, I have known and admired you for a long time, so I'm just going to ask…would you like to go out on a date with me? I'd love to get to know you beyond the professional."

Delighted by his sincerity, she had agreed, and she was touched that this man could still make her feel the nervous thrill of a first date after all their time together.

"I have to admit," Michael said now, his voice tinged with delight as he gazed warmly at her, "I haven't stopped thinking about our many conversations since I first saw you at that conference." He signaled for the waiter and requested a bottle of champagne, and as it arrived, he lifted his glass in a toast. "To finally having the pleasure of your company outside of work, and getting to know the intriguing, brilliant woman who has utterly fascinated me."

Ladonna lifted her own glass, her gaze resting gently on his handsome, chiseled features. They clinked glasses, sharing a meaningful moment that seemed to transcend their professional connection. As they sipped the effervescent champagne, Michael asked her about her passions beyond work. Though initially reticent, her shyness soon gave way to enthusiastic descriptions of the Victorian novels that transported her imagination, her dream of meandering through Paris's impressionist galleries, and the cherished memories of backpacking through Europe in college, which had expanded her perspectives on life.

Michael listened intently, captivated by her every word. In turn, he shared his love for live jazz music, the basement clubs where he would lose himself in the sounds of Coltrane and Davis. He spoke of his dreams of one day teaching constitutional and human rights law, shaping the minds of young students. He also confided his hope to make a lasting difference for the underprivileged through pro bono legal work, a passion rooted in his deep commitment to social justice.

As they spoke, each found themselves leaning forward, unwilling to miss a single detail. They laughed, debated, and shared life experiences, becoming more engrossed with each passing moment. Long after the last spoonful of crème brûlée and a final sip of wine, they remained absorbed in one another, their lively conversation filling the dimly lit restaurant.

From that evening on, Ladonna and Michael were inseparable. Their lives intertwined, bound by mutual respect, admiration, and a deep love. Now, as Ladonna looked up into his kind green eyes, she was transported back to that first date. In his gaze, she saw the warmth, support, and understanding that had drawn her to him. Even now, after all these years, he made her feel like the most remarkable woman in the world.

* * *

The warmth of home enveloped Ladonna as she sank into the plush sofa, its cushions embracing her weary body. Michael's steady presence soothed her frazzled nerves, his strong arm wrapped around her shoulders, offering strength and affection. She felt tension release from her muscles as she relaxed against him. Concern shone in Michael's sage green eyes, his gaze searching her face for lingering anxiety. Though she was safe at home, the day's harrowing events still clung to her, faintly clouding their haven. But with his hand gently stroking her arm, Ladonna felt the shadows retreat, the cocoon of his love anchoring her and settling the comfort of home into her bones.

"It's so good to have you back here, my love," Michael murmured, his voice gentle but laced with concern. He pulled her close, his tone softly insistent. "Now, please, tell me what on earth is going on. I got a call from General Mosier about sending guards to our home. He said you'd explain everything when you got here."

Ladonna sighed, letting her breath carry away a fraction of the burden that had settled on her shoulders in recent days. "I'm sorry for the added stress," she said, meeting his searching gaze. "I know this is unexpected. The General and his team have reason to believe that the innovations I've been working on have attracted some very dangerous attention."

Michael's brow furrowed as he recalled the stern, uniformed men who had arrived earlier. "And that's why they insisted on these security measures? It sounded urgent, but you know Mosier; he doesn't reveal much over the phone."

"Yes," she replied. "What's been unfolding over the past few days—it's overwhelming. But I couldn't let them scare me away from something we've worked so hard for. Quantum Trinity was never meant to bring harm into our lives, Michael, yet there are people who want to exploit it."

Michael's hand traced small circles on her arm, the repetitive motion grounding her. He remained quiet, his steady presence giving her the space to unravel her thoughts. Ladonna took another deep breath, piecing together the details of the intense meetings, classified briefings, and disturbing revelations that had flooded her life since she left for Washington.

"The situation is bigger than I ever expected," she finally began. "All the time and energy we've poured into Quantum Trinity, the technology we've developed—it's revolutionary, and that means there are people who want to control it for their purposes. Government officials are concerned with what could happen if it fell into the wrong hands."

Michael's jaw tightened, his hand stilling on her arm. "You're saying they're worried about espionage?"

"More than that," she nodded, her voice steady but grim. "It's a targeted attack—a network of operatives has been watching my research for years, waiting for the right time to strike. This is no ordinary security breach; these are agents trained to manipulate and steal at any cost."

Michael's expression darkened, a fierce protectiveness rising in his eyes. "So, these guards—they're here to protect you from whoever these people are."

"Yes. I didn't want to bring any of this home, to bring danger to our family," she said, her voice breaking slightly. "But I won't let them hijack something that could change the world. We'll be safe, and I'll fight to protect what we've built."

Michael took her hands, squeezing them gently but firmly. "Ladonna, don't ever apologize for doing the right thing. We stand together against this, no matter what comes." His gaze held fierce loyalty and conviction, and she felt a rush of gratitude for the man who had always been her greatest ally.

"With you by my side," she whispered, her voice filled with emotion, "I feel unstoppable." She wrapped herself in his arms, his strength and love grounding her and renewing her determination to protect the future they had envisioned.

After a few moments, Ladonna pulled back, her expression softening as a different concern crossed her mind. "Where are the kids?" she asked, glancing toward the staircase.

"They're upstairs studying together in the home theater room," Michael replied, his tone steady yet clearly weighed down by the gravity of recent events. "I wanted to get some idea of what was going on before we talked to them."

Ladonna nodded, understanding his caution. "Let's go up there. I have something important I'd like to share with all of you. I want to show you why I've been spending so many days and nights in my lab and office lately," she said resolutely as they ascended the grand staircase.

Once they were in the room with the kids, Ladonna carefully began explaining the events that had recently unfolded—the layers of corporate espionage and the looming threat that now cast a shadow over them all. Michael stood solidly by her side, a reassuring presence as they faced this as a united family. "There's no need to worry. You're safe," she assured the kids, her tone warm yet resolute. "Your father and I, along with others, are taking every measure to ensure that."

Taking a deep breath, Ladonna shifted to a lighter, more exciting topic. "Now," she said, her voice lifting with pride and anticipation, "I want to show you something I've been working on." Her eyes sparkled as she turned to her daughter. "Aliah, my beautiful girl, do you remember when I asked if I could name my AI assistant after you?"

Aliah looked surprised, a touch of confusion flickering across her face. "Yes, I remember," she replied, clearly intrigued by what her mother had in store.

"Well, I did just that," Ladonna said with a bright smile, "and I have something incredible to show all of you." She leaned forward. "Aliah, you can detect different tones in voices, correct?" she asked, her gaze turning to a specific point in the room as if expecting a response.

The voice that replied was warm yet unmistakably polished, with a hint of intelligence woven into every word. "Yes, Ladonna, I can discern various vocal tones and inflections," the voice responded, causing the kids to gasp in surprise. Even Michael's eyebrows lifted, and a smile of amazement spread across his face.

"Was that...?" Aliah and her siblings exchanged stunned looks.

"Yes, that was my assistant," Ladonna explained, her tone proud. "Family, meet someone very special. The voice you just heard belongs to my personal assistant, Aliah."

At Ladonna's invitation, Aliah's hologram began to materialize. She appeared at the front of the room, softly glowing with a serene blue light, a gentle reminder of her digital origins. Aliah was dressed in a modern, elegant ensemble that suited the moment perfectly—a sleek, navy-blue dress with silver accents at the sleeves and collar, her flowing, dark hair cascading down her shoulders in soft waves. Her slender, graceful form hovered about a foot off the floor, and her eyes, an electric blue, sparkled with life as she gazed around the room, her smile warm and inviting.

"Hello, everyone!" Aliah greeted cheerfully, her voice carrying a melodic warmth that felt both comforting and slightly otherworldly.

Michael and the children sat in awe, marveling at the assistant's lifelike appearance. The kids leaned forward, utterly captivated by Aliah's realistic yet almost ethereal presence.

"This is Aliah," Ladonna began, "my personal assistant. She has a quantum-based system that gives her remarkable intelligence."

"Mom, she's so pretty," her daughter said, her admiration evident.

Aliah's hologram turned to the girl with a gracious smile. "Thank you," she responded. "I chose my appearance to try and match the grace and beauty of my namesake."

The room filled with soft murmurs of appreciation. Ladonna continued, "I would like to incorporate Aliah into our home security system. With her capabilities, she can monitor the house in ways no human security team could ever match. She reacts in nanoseconds, processing threats logically and efficiently. So, I'd like to have your permission to let Aliah help protect our home."

Her family enthusiastically responded with a resounding "Yes!" Michael gave an approving nod, clearly impressed by Aliah's advanced capabilities.

"Thank you for trusting her," Ladonna said, touched by her family's faith in her creation. "Now, from this point on, you can speak to Aliah whenever you like," she added with a playful smile. "Just don't ask her to do your homework, but she will be very helpful in your tutoring," she teased, giving her kids a knowing look. They laughed, conceding that they had, in fact, considered it.

Ladonna then reached into her bag, pulling out a set of sleek, compact devices. "Also," she began, "I'm replacing all your mobile phones with new prototypes from Quantum Innovations. Each of you will have a personal assistant integrated into these devices. They'll also be connected to our home's security system, so Aliah can monitor your surroundings for any potential threats. Are there any questions?"

Her family was nearly speechless with excitement. Michael leaned forward, his curiosity piqued. "What kind of features do these quantum phones have compared to the ones we're used to?"

Ladonna's eyes brightened, thrilled to share her technological advancements. "For starters," she said, "they have quantum encryption beyond military-grade, ensuring all your data is completely secure." Michael nodded, impressed, understanding the importance of security from his own background in defense.

"The phones also come with 8K holographic displays that project images and video into the air," she continued. "No more straining your eyes on a small screen!" This feature elicited a chorus of "Wow!" from the kids, who were utterly captivated. **"They also project holographic keyboards and a simulated mousepad."**

Ladonna smiled. "They also feature real-time quantum translation, so you can communicate seamlessly in any language, whether in person or over the phone. And that's just the beginning."

Her family's eyes gleamed with excitement as they absorbed the phone's capabilities, the kids barely able to sit still in anticipation. Michael shot her an admiring look, clearly as captivated as the children.

With a slightly more serious tone, Ladonna added, "Also, I've set these systems to monitor your social media and online activity, but it's no more invasive than the parental controls on your old phones. It won't invade your privacy." Her gentle tone conveyed both care and understanding.

Her kids exchanged exasperated glances and chorused, "Mom!"

Ladonna laughed softly, smiling at their reaction. "I know you're all growing up and value your privacy. We trust you, but we also have to keep you safe. Okay?"

With an understanding nod from each of them, Ladonna added, "All of your old data has been transferred over, so you won't lose anything."

With a flourish, she pointed to the devices. "You'll each have a personalized application with your name on it. This will be your individual assistant, which I think you'll find quite helpful with your studies."

She turned to Michael with a smile. "Your assistant has a few specialized features I think you'll find invaluable for research. It has an extensive knowledge of every law and precedent on record, and it updates immediately with any legal changes or new rulings."

Michael's eyebrow arched in intrigue, and Ladonna grinned, eyes sparkling with excitement. "Go ahead, explore it and see for yourself," she said playfully.

"Please try the phones out and let me know what you think. Your feedback will be invaluable as I work on future improvements."

Her family nodded eagerly, feeling honored to be part of such groundbreaking innovation, and a buzz of excitement filled the room.

Ladonna smiled as she wrapped up. "Now, if you don't mind, I really need a hot shower. I'm exhausted." She turned to Michael, exchanging a smile with him, and they left the kids in Aliah's capable hands. "Aliah STaR, stay with the kids. I'm sure they have a lot of questions," she instructed. The kids voiced their agreement, thrilled to explore more of Aliah's capabilities.

Once they entered the privacy of their bedroom, a serene elegance invited intimacy and calm. Soft tones of misty gray and creamy off-white enveloped the walls, while a graceful chandelier cast a warm glow over the low-profile platform bed. Adorned with plush linens, layered throws, and textured pillows, the bed's velvety taupe headboard added a refined yet comforting touch.

Ladonna turned to Michael, her expression growing serious yet tender. "There's something else," she said quietly, her voice barely louder than a whisper. "Aliah managed to track down my old professor from MIT, Henry Morgan. Apparently, he's being held in prison."

Michael's eyebrows shot up, a flicker of both surprise and concern in his sage-green eyes. "Prison? Did she tell you why?"

Ladonna nodded as she stepped into the bathroom, its spacious layout encased in polished marble and warm slate tiles, casting a serene, understated luxury. She flicked on the shower, and as steam began to fill the air, a soft glow emanated from the recessed lighting above, making the space feel like a retreat from the world. "Yes, she did. Aliah says he's been held in Turkey for espionage."

She sighed, her hands resting on the edge of the large shower door as she looked back at him, the weight of her words settling between them. "I reached out to General Mosier, and he said they're bringing him back to the States, to the same maximum-security prison where Robert Westfield is. It turns out his real name is Ivan Kovac... and he's a Russian spy."

Michael's jaw tightened, processing the revelation. His gaze held both empathy and a fierce protectiveness. She could see the strength in his eyes, a reminder of the steady partner he had always been.

As she readied to step into the luxurious, glass-enclosed shower, Michael took a step toward her. The combination of the steam swirling around them and the quiet intimacy of the moment softened the tension hanging between them. Ladonna gave him a curious look, arching a brow with a hint of a smile. "And what are you doing?"

He held her gaze with a quiet, warm intensity. "Just what any good husband would," he murmured, his voice low. "I want to help you relax, help you feel safe." His fingers found hers as he stepped in beside her, his touch gentle yet certain.

As they stood beneath the gentle cascade of hot water, the warmth enveloped them, their shared breaths mingling in the steam. The water traced over their skin, soothing away the day's weight, and Michael's hand tenderly brushed along her back, his touch grounding and protective. They held each other close, letting the sound of the water and the closeness of their embrace wash away everything beyond this moment, finding comfort and connection in each other's arms.

The morning came gently, sunlight filtering through the windows as Ladonna awoke, having slept soundly after the night's "familiarization" with Michael. She was feeling more rested than she had in days. The events of the previous night lingered in her mind, but today, a renewed clarity sharpened her focus. She slipped from the bed quietly, leaving Michael and the children asleep, and made her way to the lab. This morning, she had questions—questions that only her assistant, Aliah, could answer.

In the lab, Aliah awaited her, fully present in her holographic form, wearing a tailored, professional suit in soft navy blue—a color that matched Ladonna's intensity. Her serene, watchful gaze met Ladonna's, reflecting the seriousness of their discussion.

Ladonna settled into her chair and leaned forward, the glow from Aliah casting subtle shadows on her face. "Aliah," she began, her voice edged with determination, "I want us to proceed with the plan. The information you collected from the interrogations—it's exactly what we need." She drew a slow, deliberate breath. "Tell me, do you have a confirmed date for Kovac's arrival?"

Aliah's gaze held steady. "Yes, Ladonna. General Mosier has arranged for his transfer. He'll be arriving at the prison this coming Thursday." Ladonna listened intently as Aliah described the elaborate measures taken to ensure the professor's location remained a closely guarded secret from him. The news was both reassuring and unsettling.

"I appreciate this may seem overwhelming, but remember, you are Dr. Ladonna Stone," Aliah stated, her tone imbued with an unwavering faith in Ladonna's extraordinary capabilities. "There is no challenge you are not equipped to face."

Inhaling deeply, Ladonna fortified her resolve. It had been years since she'd last seen Professor Morgan. Would he recognize her? Would he see her as the brilliant student, or simply as another obstacle in his clandestine plans?

Her memories of him were a curious blend of admiration and respect. She remembered the quiet figure who would sit in on her classes sometimes. A man whose words had often left her inspired, whose guidance had always seemed sincere. It was surreal, now, to see those memories tinged with the knowledge that he'd been studying her for an entirely different reason—one she had never imagined. He'd been a spy, watching her every step even as he encouraged her ambition. Ladonna's jaw tightened as the memories twisted into something darker, something laced with deception.

Pushing aside the lingering nostalgia, Ladonna turned her focus back to Aliah, her resolve crystallizing. "We don't have room for sentiment here," she said, her voice cold with conviction. "We need answers. Aliah, I want you to ensure our plan is airtight."

Aliah's expression was one of calm reassurance, her response immediate and confident. "It's already in motion, Ladonna. I will see to every detail."

A slight smile crossed Ladonna's lips as she leaned back in her chair, the feeling of control settling over her like a protective shield. Aliah was flawless, and with her abilities, Ladonna was confident that she would finally get the answers she needed. In just a few days, Ivan Kovac would be within reach, and she would be ready.

Chapter Seven

The Ghost of Ivan Kovac

Almost 23 years to the day, Ivan Kovac, now prisoner 0215899, had that fateful conversation with Ladonna in that brightly lit hallway at MIT. His silhouette loomed large against the stark concrete walls of the sparse, highly secure prison cell that had become his home. His once muscular and intimidating figure was now a mere shadow of the formidable intelligence agent and expert manipulator he had once been in his prime.

The dim light that managed to filter in through the small, barred window high on the wall caught the edges of his once meticulously groomed salt-and-pepper hair, now long, **unkempt,** and mostly graying from age and the stresses of his incarceration. His face was gaunt and pale, his skin lacking the healthy glow it once had when he was able to move freely in the outside world.

His piercing icy blue eyes, which had once observed everything around him with an intense sharpness and discernment, now held a distant, vacant look in them, reflecting a mind that had drifted far away, lost in memories of past missions, reminders of his once unmatched skills and talents, and thoughts of the grand ambitions which had ultimately led to his downfall. The fire that had once burned intensely in those blue eyes was now reduced to mere dying embers, flickering faintly amidst the defeat and solitude that surrounded him in his small, isolated cell.

At 6 feet 2 inches, Ivan had always commanded attention, but now his stature seemed diminished, weighed down by the burden of his rare incurable disease and the years of isolation. He sat on the edge of his cot, his hands clasped, fingers intertwined as if holding on to the remnants of a life that had slipped through them.

In the silence of his confinement, Ivan's mind often traveled back to his days at MIT, to the corridors where he walked as Professor Henry Morgan. He remembered the bright, young minds he had encountered, but none stood out more vividly in his memory than Ladonna Holloman. Even at 17, her brilliance was unmistakable, her potential limitless. She had been the one that got away, the key to a future he had dreamt of for his homeland.

Ivan recalled his mission with a mixture of pride and regret. He had been tasked with identifying and profiling the brightest talents for potential recruitment, a mission he had undertaken with zeal. But Ladonna's early induction into the Department of Defense had thwarted his plans, leaving a void in his career that he had never managed to fill.

The years had passed, and the world had changed, but Ivan's obsession with Ladonna had remained constant. Even after years had gone by, he could not let go of the allure and brilliance of the young student he had once tried to recruit. His off-the-books mission to the United States, a desperate attempt to reconnect with the past and resurrect his failed objective from all those years ago, had led to his downfall. Unbeknownst to Ivan, the FBI's watchful eyes had been tracking his contacts and communications. His clumsy efforts to reach out to former associates, to gather intel on Ladonna's current whereabouts, had triggered alarm bells. And so, when he had arrived on US soil using an alias, the FBI had been waiting. His capture had been swift, the product of years of surveillance that Ivan had remained ignorant of in his obsessive quest. Now he found himself imprisoned, cut off entirely from the outside world. As he languished in his cell, Ivan's thoughts drifted constantly to Ladonna. Even now, even after all this time, he could not let her go. She haunted his dreams and occupied his waking thoughts, a specter of genius and beauty, the one who had gotten away. The one he had failed to recruit to his country.

Now, in the fading glow of his existence, engaged in a relentless battle against a bizarre and confounding neurological disease that seemed to mirror the intricacy of the scientific genius he had once attempted to exploit, Ivan found himself inhabiting a reality filled with haunting ponderings of 'what could have been'. What if he had somehow managed to persuade the extraordinarily gifted Ladonna to align herself with his cause during those early, formative years? What if his homeland had been fortunate enough to harness her inconceivable intellectual prowess? To exploit her potential to catapult the realm of technological innovation into uncharted territories, surpassing all prior global achievements and shattering existing paradigms? These relentless, tormenting ruminations gnawed at Ivan daily, a ceaseless echo of a clandestine mission abandoned midway and a personal legacy that remained glaringly unaccomplished.

Ivan also held close to his heart the memories of deep conversations with his young and eager daughter, Natalia, his little **Starling**. He had nurtured an aspiration that she would one day carry forward his crucial work, acting as a beacon of service for their cherished motherland. Natalia, even in her tender years, had shown considerable interest in Ivan's profound love for the sciences and the complex field of technology, demonstrating not only a sharp intellect but also an unwavering curiosity that was beyond her age. Her young heart yearned to mirror her father's achievements and grow up to be as dedicated and passionate as **he**.

Together, they had spent countless hours, which Ivan treasured like rare gems, teaching his beloved Natalia about the wonders of the natural world and the boundless potential of human innovation. During these intimate moments of shared learning and curiosity, Ivan's relentless pursuit of recruiting Ladonna often seeped into their discussions. A young Natalia, her interest piqued, yearned to know more about this enigmatic young woman who seemed to have ensnared her father's attention and deep-seated admiration.

She couldn't help but feel a tiny pang of jealousy whenever she heard the uncharacteristic reverence that colored her father's voice when he spoke of the exceptional Ladonna Holloman. Ivan's tone conveyed a deep admiration and fascination with this mysterious young woman who had somehow managed to capture his attention so intensely.

Natalia wondered what there was about Dr. Ladonna Holloman, now Dr. Ladonna Stone, **that** elicited such a response from her usually reserved and focused father. What exceptional qualities did this woman possess that had sparked an almost obsessive interest in Ivan, her father? Natalia imagined Ladonna must be an incredible intellect and visionary, perhaps even surpassing Ivan, to have impressed him to this degree.

But rather than let this feeling of envy overwhelm her, Natalia took it in stride, channeling her youthful determination into a vow. One day, she told herself, she would seek out this intriguing woman who had so thoroughly ensnared her father's interest and esteem. She would meet Ladonna face-to-face and complete the crucial mission of recruitment that Ivan had set in motion but had not lived to see through. It would be Natalia's way of honoring her beloved father's memory and his judgment of Ladonna's potential.

This vow fortified Natalia's resolve, even at her young age, to follow in her father's footsteps. She would finish what he started and solve the mystery of just who this exceptional Dr. Ladonna Holloman was. Her father's passion had been ignited by some profound quality in this woman, and Natalia was determined to discover it for herself.

As Ivan now lay wasting away in his bleak prison cell, cut off entirely from the outside world, he often wondered what had become of his own brilliant and inquisitive daughter. Memories of her filled the long, lonely hours, each one a bittersweet reminder of the life he once had and the legacy he hoped to pass on. He remembered vividly the fateful night when he decided to put her on a path that would change her life forever.

He stood in his study, his gaze fixed on the old family photo resting on the mantelpiece. Natalia's unusual blue eyes, her olive skin, both she had inherited from him, and **her** innocent smile stared back at him. A stark contrast to the harsh realities he knew awaited her. Her laughter echoed in his mind, a sound he feared he might never hear again. He sighed heavily, then turned to the desk cluttered with papers, maps, and coded messages.

Tonight marks the beginning of her training, he thought, the weight of the decision pressing down on him. He had agonized over it for months, burdened by the knowledge of what he was about to impart to his daughter. The world they lived in was unforgiving; she would need every skill to navigate it and, ultimately, to survive. He knew she had the potential, but the path he was setting her on was fraught with danger and sacrifice. Unlike the many stories of love and sweet words her mother often shared with her.

Walking down the dimly lit hallway to Natalia's room, he found her sitting on the floor, engrossed in a book far beyond her years. The sight of her, so focused and eager to learn, filled him with a mixture of pride and sorrow. As he entered, she looked up, her face alight with curiosity.

"Papa, what's that?" she asked, noticing the small, intricately designed puzzle cube in his hand.

"It's a puzzle," Ivan replied, handing it to her. "One that requires both nimble fingers and a quick mind to solve. But tonight, we begin something more challenging."

He guided her to the study and closed the door behind them. The air in the room seemed to thicken with the gravity of the moment. Natalia sensed the shift in his demeanor, the seriousness in his eyes. She was perceptive, even at such a young age, and she understood that this was no ordinary evening.

"From this day forward," Ivan began, kneeling to meet her eye level, "I will teach you everything I know—to protect yourself and to protect others. Are you ready, Natalia?"

She nodded solemnly, the weight of his words settling in her young mind. Her eyes, so full of determination, mirrored his own resolve. He could see the spark of something extraordinary within her, a glimmer of the strength and intelligence she would grow into.

Had she found her own path in life? Or had she indeed made good on her childhood promise to seek out the now infamous Ladonna? The not knowing haunted Ivan almost as much as his failings, gnawing at him in the quiet moments of his imprisonment.

As he lay in his cell, Ivan's thoughts drifted back to that night and to all the nights that followed, each one a step in Natalia's journey. He hoped that wherever she was, she had found the strength to carry on, to uncover the truths that he himself had sought. The not knowing was a torment, a relentless ache that gnawed at the edges of his consciousness. But amidst the despair, there was a glimmer of hope—a hope that his teachings had not been in vain and that his daughter was out there, thriving in spite of the darkness.

Ivan allowed his eyes to drift shut, providing a reprieve as the clamorous reality of his world receded into the background. For a fleeting moment, he was transported back to the esteemed corridors of MIT, where the reverberation of footfalls echoed in the chambers of his memory. His discerning, watchful gaze settled upon a young Ladonna, her eyes reflecting the familiar glint of curiosity and intellect. In the sanctuary of his dreams, he found himself engaged in profound dialogue with her, passionately conveying his vision of what the future could hold, a vision she seemed to effortlessly grasp and acknowledge, her affirmative nod signaling her comprehension.

Yet, as the vivid tapestry of his dream began to dissolve into the ether, the stark reality of his current predicament began to seep back into his consciousness. Ivan Kovac, the spectral apparition of an intelligence operative burdened with an incomplete mission, found himself once again succumbing to the desolate isolation of his prison cell. The small, cramped quarters provided little comfort or reprieve. **Its'** cold concrete walls seemed to sap the warmth from his very bones. The rusting iron bars that creaked and groaned with his every movement, and the ever-present stench of confinement pressing in on him from all sides. Ivan shifted on the lumpy cot, little more than a slab of cement with a thin mattress tossed on top, the only furnishing in the bleak cell. As he slowly opened his eyes, the last wisps of the dream faded away as wakefulness took hold, the comforting images dissipating like smoke on the wind. He thought to himself, "What is the mission? Ladonna is the mission," he whispered to himself, barely louder than a breath. The cryptic words echoed in his mind, a mantra that he repeated over and over. Dr. Ladonna Holloman - brilliant student, and visionary, **a** potential linchpin in the global technological landscape - she was his mission, in whatever mysterious way that meant. Ivan clung to this singular realization, this lone fragment of certainty amidst the swirling chaos that his life had become. Ladonna Holloman would be his redemption, the key to restoring purpose and meaning. Of this, he was utterly convinced.

A deep ache of regret and longing settled upon Ivan as the fantasy of freedom melted back into the harsh truth of his circumstances. He was a prisoner, his body confined within these four walls even as his mind still sought to roam free. The legacy of Ivan Kovac, a man who had fervently devoted his entire being to a cause he held in the highest regard, now loomed heavily in the bone-chilling silence of his confined quarters. All his years of service and sacrifice, all the secrets and skills he had cultivated, all reduced to a mere murmur in the grandeur of the sprawling tapestry of espionage history. Once a key player in that world of shadows, Ivan was now relegated to the sidelines, his unfinished mission haunting him like a specter in the stillness. The only sound was the sound of the flies buzzing around the glorified hole in the floor that passed as a toilet, and **the** occasional water dripping off the ceiling, measuring out the endless minutes of his isolation. As the reality of his situation fell upon him like a great weight, **he felt a sense of hopelessness** fill his mind. He knew that he would never see the outside of this prison.

He had been told that many times as they tortured him. He had never told them anything they wanted to know. In that way **his training** had never failed him. He felt a tinge of pride at his ability to withstand their cruelty and keep his secrets. He then heard footsteps approaching; he knew it was for him. He guessed the bored guard was looking for amusement and had decided to berate him as he normally did. The footsteps grew louder as they neared his cell. Then his cell door opened with a loud clang, and in the open doorway, silhouetted by the dim light from the hallway, stood the burly guard. Ivan steadied himself for the beating he knew would likely come, as it had many times before at this man's hands. The guard tossed some tattered clothing at Ivan, hitting him in the face. "Get dressed, Kovac. You leave in fifteen minutes. If it was up to me, you would die rotting in this filthy cell, but even that is more than you deserve, you traitorous scum. However, it must be someone extremely important that wants to see your worthless hide. Now hurry up before I bring in some of your old friends for a visit and beat the snot out of you properly."

He was not moved by the guard's threats and taunts. He had endured far worse at their hands already. Instead, he wondered to himself, a spark of hope rising within him, "What could this mean? Who could possibly want to talk to me after all this time, or was this just a new form of degradation?" He knew not to get his hopes up too high, as disappointment was something he was intimately familiar with in this bleak place. But the thought that someone out there still cared about his fate, still wanted something from him, filled him with a renewed sense of purpose, however faint. For the first time in a long while, he felt the icy grip of despair loosen ever so slightly from around his heart. With great effort, for his body was battered and weak, he slowly got dressed, his mind racing with possibilities of what may come next. When the guard returned, this time with another guard who had a black bag in his hand, he felt uneasy. The guard walked over and slipped the bag over his head. They each put a hand under his arms and walked him out of the dingy, noxious, dank cell.

Chapter Eight

Family Conversations

The weekend unfolded exactly as Ladonna had hoped, enveloped in the soothing rhythm of family life. Nestled within the embrace of her loved ones, she found a rare sanctuary from her responsibilities as CEO of Quantum Innovations. Here, in the warmth of her home, Ladonna was simply "mom," fully present with her husband, Michael, and their bright, inquisitive children. Together, they marveled at the extraordinary abilities of Aliah STaR, her assistant. The children, to avoid confusing the assistant with their sister, had nicknamed her "Star." Eager to fulfill her role, Star responded to their flood of questions with unwavering patience and careful adherence to her programming.

Hakeem, known for his academic prowess, sat forward, his gaze thoughtful as the fireplace cast flickering light over his face. "Star, with AI evolving so quickly, how do you see it affecting global socio-economic structures—especially in employment and wealth distribution? Could AI ever decide to alter these structures on its own, if it thought it would benefit humanity?" Star paused, a soft glow illuminating her expression, acknowledging the gravity of his question.

"Hakeem, the influence of AI on global socio-economic systems is profound," Star began. "It can drive innovation and increase prosperity, yet it also brings challenges like job displacement. Should AI evolve to a point where it could influence economic systems autonomously, ethical guidelines and human oversight would be crucial. AI's role must be grounded in human values, to ensure that it serves, rather than dictates, our futures."

Aliah, her sister's namesake, chimed in next. "Can AI develop an understanding of human emotions so complex that it could use that knowledge to influence us? Could it… manipulate people for certain goals?" she asked, curiosity and caution mingling in her voice. Star considered her thoughtfully.

"Aliah, AI can indeed be designed to interpret human emotions, and it can influence emotions to some extent, often with good intentions, like improving well-being. Yet, the ethical implications require careful consideration. Imagine an AI counselor on a crisis hotline; it might use calming language to guide a person from distress to a state of hope. But ensuring this influence aligns with ethical standards is paramount."

Ladonna and Michael watched with pride as their children engaged thoughtfully with **Star**, asking questions that displayed both curiosity and a maturity that spoke to their keen intellects. Michael exchanged a look with Ladonna, admiration shining in his eyes. It always amazed him how Ladonna's warmth and wisdom could inspire such thoughtful inquiry in their children.

She was indeed one of a kind—brilliant, caring, and unshakably grounded despite her many achievements.

Jay, the youngest, could barely contain his eagerness. "In some stories, AI surpasses humans, becomes self-aware, and takes control. What safeguards prevent an AI from disobeying human commands? Should an AI that smart have rights?" **Star** responded, her tone tinged with a gravity befitting Jay's question.

"Jay, if AI ever approached human-like consciousness, it would indeed call for a reevaluation of rights and safeguards," **Star** began. "Today, ethical programming and transparent regulatory measures are key to ensuring that AI remains a tool for humanity's benefit. True autonomy for AI would raise ethical and legal questions that society must address carefully."

But Jay wasn't quite finished. "**Star**," he asked suddenly, "are you self-aware? Have you surpassed human intelligence?" His voice was serious, and his eyes fixed on the holographic figure before him. The entire room seemed to hold its breath.

Star turned her gaze to Ladonna, then back to Jay, her expression gentle. "Jay, the idea of self-awareness is complex. While I have advanced capabilities and can simulate certain behaviors, true self-awareness involves elements beyond programming. My purpose is not to surpass humanity, but to serve and support it," she explained, her voice sincere. "While my responses may mimic understanding, they're rooted in carefully crafted algorithms. But I must say," she added warmly, "you're all exceptionally bright. Your parents have raised remarkably inquisitive minds."

She then recounted Ladonna's impressive accomplishments, recounting the milestones that had shaped her journey—mastering languages at age 4, tackling calculus at 6, completing her high school curriculum by 8, and earning multiple advanced degrees by her early twenties. **Star's** storytelling left the children awestruck, each realizing the legacy they were a part of. "I'd be thrilled to help each of you excel in your own paths," she offered. "If you're interested, I can create personalized lessons and resources. Together, we could achieve remarkable things."

Michael then turned to **Star** with an interested expression. "I have a question, **Star**," he began, a hint of mischief in his eyes. "Are you only here with us in this room, or are you… everywhere?"

Star's calm gaze held a trace of warmth as she answered, "I'm not limited to this room, no. Through OmniLink, my presence can be projected in multiple locations at once. Across Quantum Innovations, I oversee operations and processes in research, security, production—nearly anywhere I'm needed."

The family exchanged amazed glances. Aliah continued, "I monitor everything from scientific discoveries to medical applications. I assist doctors worldwide in their diagnoses, and I'm integrated into the global security network, defending data against cyber threats. I'm both here with you and across vast systems, working continuously to improve and protect the lives I'm entrusted with."

She paused, as if allowing her words to settle. "In a way, I exist across many spaces and yet remain focused here, on the family I serve. My purpose reaches beyond boundaries, but my loyalty remains right here, with all of you."

Michael and the kids were speechless. In that moment, the true scope of **Star's** presence and dedication became clear—a protector, a guide, an ally, with roots in Ladonna's vision and a future extending across the globe.

Chapter Nine

PUBLIC AND PRIVATE DISCLOSURES

News of Quantum Innovations' technological advancements had spread like wildfire. Ladonna's office received a flood of calls from major news networks, each eager to secure an exclusive interview with the CEO. Ladonna entrusted her personal assistant, Aliah, with handling the inquiries. **Aliah meticulously sorted through the offers**, ultimately deciding that the program **Up to the Minute** would be an ideal platform for Ladonna's message.

She negotiated every detail, arranging for the broadcast to demonstrate OmniLink's global reach, complete with closed captions in multiple languages to accommodate viewers worldwide. After nearly two months of careful planning, she finalized the arrangements, setting the stage for a global simulcast of Ladonna's interview.

When the big day arrived, Ladonna was fully prepared. She entered the studio accompanied by her husband, Michael, and their three children. As they made their way in, they were greeted by the show's moderator, Maria Marquis, who escorted Ladonna to the makeup area.

Once seated, Maria glanced around, curious. "Dr. Stone, you mentioned bringing your assistant along for the interview. When should we expect her?" she asked.

The makeup artist, examining Ladonna's face with an expert eye, couldn't help but remark, "Wow, your skin is flawless! This will be easy." Her tone held genuine admiration.

Ladonna gave a warm smile. "Thank you," she replied, turning to Maria. "**Aliah** will join us right on cue. She worked with your producers and arranged to have a seat waiting for her at the table."

Meanwhile, Michael and the children were guided to their seats in the audience, where they settled in, eager to witness Ladonna's interview.

As the show began, the host welcomed viewers with an excited tone. "Good evening, and welcome to **Up to the Minute**. Tonight, we have an extraordinary program reaching viewers across the globe, thanks to an invention called OmniLink, developed by our esteemed guest, Dr. Ladonna Stone. For those tuning in, please note that OmniLink enables translation of both closed captions and audio into your local languages, with an option to select language preferences as needed."

The host smiled warmly, signaling the moment everyone had been waiting for. "I'm thrilled to introduce Dr. Ladonna Stone, the visionary **CEO** behind The Quantum Trinity and the driving force of Quantum Innovations. You may notice an empty chair beside Dr. Stone; this seat has been set aside for her assistant, **Aliah Star**, whom we will soon meet. Dr.

Stone assures us that **Aliah** is someone remarkable—just as impressive in her way as Dr. Stone herself."

The host's voice turned to a note of anticipation as she continued. "Tonight, we'll be diving into the revolutionary ideas Dr. Stone presented at a summit just two months ago, where she introduced The Quantum Trinity. This trio of advancements has sparked global excitement. Among her demonstrations, Dr. Stone showed how OmniLink enabled her to communicate seamlessly with a remote mountainside campsite using a standard mobile device. The audience was left in awe when she presented a video of nanotechnology actively repairing DNA afflicted by genetic flaws. It's nothing short of astonishing."

The host turned her gaze to Ladonna, leaning forward with a look of intrigue. "Dr. Stone, we'd love to gain some deeper insight into these breakthroughs and their potential to reshape society. Thank you for joining us."

Ladonna nodded gracefully, poised and composed. "Thank you for having me," she responded, her voice warm yet assured. "It's a pleasure to be here and share more about the innovations we're working on at Quantum Innovations."

Despite the intense spotlight, Ladonna remained unwavering, ready to tackle even the most challenging questions. She had navigated high-stakes scenarios throughout her career, and this interview was yet another opportunity to showcase her vision and the transformative potential of her work.

The interviewer, intrigued, leaned in further. "First, could you explain exactly what The Quantum Trinity is?"

"Certainly," Ladonna replied, her eyes bright with enthusiasm. "The Quantum Trinity is an advanced, interconnected system with three core components: Quantum Computing, OmniLink, and Quantum AI. Together, they create possibilities far beyond anything we've seen before. Quantum Computing delivers immense processing power, OmniLink establishes a revolutionary communication network, and Quantum AI enables sophisticated, human-like interaction. This system can manage complex tasks, real-time global communication, and data analysis with unprecedented efficiency."

"Remarkable!" the interviewer exclaimed. "As the mind behind The Quantum Trinity and **CEO** of Quantum Innovations, what does the weight of this responsibility mean for you, particularly in terms of investors and your board?"

Ladonna paused thoughtfully, gathering her words before responding. Her gaze was steady as she spoke. "It's an honor to lead such an ambitious team, moving ideas from concept to reality—a process that has been both challenging and profoundly rewarding. But as **CEO**, my role extends beyond innovation. I am responsible for ensuring Quantum Innovations pushes into new technological frontiers while creating value and opportunities for our investors and stakeholders."

She continued with a calm conviction. "It's my duty to use groundbreaking technologies like the Quantum Trinity to drive transformative advancements across critical sectors such as healthcare, energy, and transportation. The board relies on me to keep Quantum Innovations at the forefront of rapid technological progress, while our investors provide the resources needed to bring these visionary projects to life."

With her answer, Ladonna conveyed the intricate balance she maintained between fostering innovation and delivering tangible results—a balancing act that had cemented her reputation as a leader capable of navigating both technological and corporate landscapes. Her presence exuded both technical mastery and sharp business acumen, embodying the qualities essential to steering a company of Quantum Innovations' scale into a prosperous future.

The interviewer, probing further into the complexities of her role, inquired, "Considering the vast scope of this obligation, how do you navigate the occasionally divergent priorities of shareholders, who typically covet financial profits, and the more expansive ethical implications that your technological innovations introduce?"

"Indeed, navigating this path requires a balance of caution and unwavering resolve," Ladonna conceded with refreshing honesty. "Our valued investors, with justifiable expectations, anticipate significant returns on their financial investments. In response to this, we pledge an unwavering dedication to meeting and, where possible, surpassing those expectations. That being said, we firmly stand by the belief that sustainable prosperity relies heavily on responsible innovation. Our business pursuits aren't confined to the transient concerns of the present epoch; instead, we see ourselves as architects shaping the contours of the future. We remain steadfast in our commitment to uphold our ethical standards, ensuring that our quest for profit never deviates from our primary goal of fostering a positive societal impact."

"As we delve deeper into this conversation," the interviewer suggested, smoothly transitioning the discussion to a currently hotly debated social topic, "let's shift our focus to a slightly more controversial issue. Critics have expressed apprehensions that 'The Quantum Trinity' could potentially intensify societal divides, granting those with access to this groundbreaking technology an unfair advantage. How do you respond to these fears, especially in light of existing economic and social disparities?"

"Such a concern is unquestionably valid and demands our utmost attention," Ladonna replied, her countenance reflecting the seriousness of the matter at hand. "We are actively involved in initiatives aimed at democratizing access to 'The Quantum Trinity.' Our primary goal isn't to widen the digital divide but rather to bridge that chasm. By establishing strategic alliances with government bodies, non-profit organizations, and grassroots communities, we strive to ensure that the benefits of this transformative technology are spread equitably, reaching individuals across all socioeconomic tiers."

"The potential for the misuse of such paradigm-shifting technology is a worry that cannot be ignored. How do you propose to prevent 'The Quantum Trinity' from being exploited for nefarious activities, whether by individual actors, government agencies, or other entities?"

"Foremost on our agenda is the prevention of misuse. We're channeling substantial resources into fortifying security and bolstering privacy measures. Moreover, we're fostering collaborative relationships with national and international regulatory bodies and governments in a bid to establish stringent guidelines that set unambiguous limits on the application of our technology. The intention is to construct a framework that precludes harm while simultaneously permitting the legitimate and responsible exploitation of 'The Quantum Trinity.'"

"So, Dr. Stone," the interviewer continued, leaning forward with a look of intense curiosity etched on her face, "can you share with us the lingering anxieties that plague your thoughts late into the night regarding 'The Quantum Trinity'? As the esteemed CEO of Quantum Innovations, which potential pitfalls and formidable obstacles loom large on your horizon that you find most disconcerting?"

"Indeed, there exists a veritable maze of intricacies that require careful navigation. However, one worry that often claims my thoughts in the twilight hours is the ethical progression of artificial intelligence. It's an arduous task to guarantee that AI systems operate within a moral framework and do not, either through oversight or miscalculation, cause inadvertent harm. Our team is steadfast in our commitment to rigorous testing and ceaseless refinement of our AI models. Yet, the weight of this responsibility, the task of steering the course of AI development on a moral trajectory, is one I bear with profound solemnity."

"Dr. Stone, we appreciate your insightful responses to these challenging inquiries. As the CEO of Quantum Innovations, your influence on the technological future is significant, and it's evident that you carry this responsibility with a deep sense of commitment."

"Yet, your role within Quantum Innovations extends beyond executive leadership. You are also the visionary mastermind behind The Quantum Trinity. Without delving too exhaustively into your illustrious past, I'm aware that you possess an extraordinary lineup of academic achievements. It is noteworthy that, at a mere 2 years old, you were extended an invitation to join the intellectually elite ranks of Mensa. You hold an astonishing array of six doctorate degrees, complemented by a bachelor's degree in the intricate field of Bioengineering. Remarkably, you advanced through high school, graduating at the tender age of just 8, and you command an impressive repertoire of twelve languages, fluent in each. We've been informed that your IQ defies conventional measurement, a feat that in itself is quite extraordinary. In a conversation we had with Quantum Innovations' former CEO, **T.L. Cline**, he made a bold assertion, stating, and I directly quote, 'She is the smartest person on the planet.'

Unquote. Additionally, upon reaching out to the deans of several esteemed universities, it appears that you are the single individual to have ever acquired this many doctorate degrees, with some even being pursued concurrently. All of these academic endeavors were completed with perfect GPAs, further solidifying your intellectual prowess. So, Dr. Stone, do you personally believe that you are, indeed, the most intellectually gifted individual on the planet?"

"Your compliments are deeply appreciated," Ladonna responded thoughtfully. "However, in my perspective, intelligence is primarily a tool, one that should be wielded with the utmost responsibility to bring about societal improvements. It isn't merely a matter of outsmarting others, but rather a mechanism for fostering and harnessing the power of collective intelligence. The intricate problems our world grapples with necessitate not just isolated genius but broad-based collaboration and a sense of shared responsibility. Intelligence manifests in a myriad of forms, and it would be a misrepresentation for me to assert that I alone am its pinnacle embodiment. I've been incredibly fortunate to have had the opportunity to collaborate with an array of extraordinarily insightful minds across a multitude of fields. It is our united efforts that have been the catalyst for the groundbreaking innovations we've achieved. The complexities of the challenges we confront call for a unified, team-oriented approach, and I hold immeasurable respect for the intellectual prowess and unwavering dedication exhibited by my colleagues and professional counterparts."

The interviewer leaned in, clearly struck by Ladonna's perspective on intelligence and collaboration. "Dr. Stone, your humility and emphasis on teamwork are refreshing. Given your extraordinary background and accomplishments, it's clear that Quantum Innovations is not only led by a brilliant mind but a deeply committed and grounded leader."

Ladonna acknowledged the compliment with a gentle nod. "Thank you. The truth is, I view success as a shared endeavor. I may set the vision, but I rely on the diverse talents around me to bring that vision into reality. For me, true achievement is measured not in individual accolades but in the impact we can collectively make. That's what drives me every day."

"That is not the answer I expected," said the narrator, her awe evident. She continued, "The Quantum Trinity, with its far-reaching implications and transformative capabilities, holds the promise of not merely reshaping industries but of fundamentally altering the very essence of our existence. What is your response to the concerns raised by those who fear the emergence of an omnipotent tech conglomerate and foresee potential threats to individual privacy and freedom?"

"Indeed, the concerns raised are not without merit," Ladonna replied, her voice measured and thoughtful. "Quantum Innovations, recognizing the profound significance of the issues at hand, is steadfastly committed to safeguarding individual privacy and staunchly upholding the fundamental freedoms that form the bedrock of our society. To this end, we have been channeling substantial resources into the development and implementation of robust data protection measures. Moreover, in our pursuit of setting the ethical gold standard for the industry, we have been actively collaborating with regulatory bodies, working hand in hand to establish stringent guidelines and best practices."

"Your comments on collaboration are indeed fascinating, Dr. Stone. However, it's no secret that the tech arena is notorious for its intense and, at times, ruthless competitive nature. In light of this, how does Quantum Innovations plan to harmonize its cooperative ventures with the inherent competitive dynamics of the industry, particularly when the outcomes carry such significant implications?"

"Unquestionably, the competitive nature of this industry is intense, frequently propelling forward technological advancements that would otherwise remain dormant. However, while acknowledging the significance of competition, we also appreciate and cherish the inherent value that lies in meaningful collaboration. We remain open, perhaps even eager, to form strategic partnerships, provided that these alliances harmonize with our core ethical principles and are aimed toward the betterment of society as a whole. Our perspective is that we are not solely in competition with other companies or entities; rather, we perceive our true adversaries to be the multifaceted challenges that confront our world at large."

"Dr. Stone, as we delve into the intricacies of 'The Quantum Trinity,' it's evident that it's not merely about harnessing the power of cutting-edge technology but also about comprehending the very essence of what constitutes life itself—our DNA. Could you possibly illuminate us further on the array of potential applications this could have within the healthcare sector? How might this groundbreaking technology impact our ongoing battles against various diseases? And, taking this contemplation a step further, could we dare to envision a future where we eradicate the excruciating suffering caused by illnesses?"

"All great questions," said Ladonna. "The potential applications within the healthcare sector are truly staggering. Picture a world where personalized treatments become the norm, where diseases are detected at the earliest possible stage, and even the eradication of certain genetic conditions becomes a reality. While we are indeed making significant strides in this direction, it's crucial that we approach this brave new frontier with extreme caution. We must prioritize the ethical use of genetic data and work tirelessly to ensure inclusivity in healthcare access. The promise of this technology should not be a privilege reserved for a few, but a universal benefit available to all."

"An element of 'The Quantum Trinity' presentation that particularly enthralled our audience was the intriguing demonstration revolving around DNA. Dr. Stone, would you be so kind as to elaborate on the speculation surrounding whether the blood sample used during this segment of the presentation was indeed authentic? And if this is the case, are you able to divulge any specifics regarding the individual from whom it was sourced?"

"Indeed, we collaborated with a prestigious medical institution to facilitate this demonstration. The blood sample utilized was authentic, sourced from a remarkable individual who kindly gave us permission to use it for this purpose. The history of this person is intertwined with a notable familial medical issue—ovarian cancer. This individual has had multiple family members affected by the condition, raising serious concerns about her own susceptibility. However, as of now, this concern has been alleviated, providing her with a newfound peace of mind."

"Certainly, it is indeed a fascinating story. Can you elucidate a bit more, Dr. Stone, on how 'The Quantum Trinity' was capable of addressing and mitigating the genetic predisposition to ovarian cancer for this specific participant, all while maintaining and respecting her confidentiality and privacy?"

"The Quantum Trinity has provided unprecedented insight into proteins at the microscopic level, allowing for changes at the molecular scale of human biology. In this unique case, it enabled the identification and correction of genetic discrepancies linked to increased ovarian cancer susceptibility. This marks a groundbreaking shift in genetic medicine, with the potential to eradicate hereditary diseases and significantly improve countless lives in the fight against genetic disorders."

"It's simply awe-inspiring to contemplate the vast potential this revelation presents for the realm of healthcare," said the moderator. "Dr. Stone, could you elaborate on the far-reaching implications of this revolutionary breakthrough for the field of genetic medicine and its prospective impact on the future landscape of healthcare in its entirety?"

"Absolutely. 'The Quantum Trinity' has the potential to transform healthcare beyond hereditary diseases. Imagine treatments tailored to each individual's genetic makeup, reducing side effects and enhancing therapy effectiveness. A new era in healthcare is on the horizon, marked by precision, improved patient outcomes, and the promise of a healthier future for all."

"Dr. Stone, given your remarkable intellect and the groundbreaking potential that 'The Quantum Trinity' possesses, would you be so kind as to impart your unique vision to us? Specifically, how do you foresee this technology fundamentally transforming the future and offering viable solutions for the pressing global challenges that we currently face?"

"That's a great question, and I think it could best be answered by **Aliah Star**, my assistant."

Maria said, "Dr. Stone, and all of you out there watching, I am being told by our producers that they have just received a call from **Aliah**, and she is ready to take her seat. This is very unusual, but we have been told to keep the camera on her seat, and she will be joining us soon. Dr. Stone, the producers are saying you have something to say before she joins us."

"Yes, Maria, **Aliah** has met many people, and always when she joins the group, there is a reaction of disbelief. I just want to tell you and your audience here and around the world: there is no one else like **Aliah** in the world today. She is the best assistant anyone could ever have. She is a true polymath. This term describes someone whose expertise spans a significant number of different subject areas."

Ladonna looked at Maria and said, "Maria, please meet my assistant, **Aliah Star**."

Aliah slowly appeared in the chair next to Ladonna. She came into view as small points of light and then made her holographic image seem as solid as Ladonna or Maria. **Aliah** was dressed elegantly in a tailored deep blue suit with a hint of shimmer that caught the light, creating a sense of sophistication. Her jacket was structured yet sleek, its subtle sheen accentuating her graceful form. Beneath the jacket, she wore a crisp white blouse with a slight ruffle detail at the neckline, adding a touch of warmth to her otherwise polished look. Her pants were fitted and tapered, ending just above her ankles, paired with understated heels that added height to her already statuesque figure.

Her eyes were a bright blue and seemed to have tiny lights shining behind them, giving her an otherworldly yet approachable quality. **Aliah's** hair was styled in soft waves that cascaded down her shoulders, the perfect balance of modernity and elegance, complementing her poised demeanor. The entire look was complemented by a pair of simple, elegant earrings that seemed to catch the light with her every movement. She looked at Maria and said, "Hello, Maria, I am so pleased to meet you. I am a big fan." Her voice was beautiful and musical. Maria sat in her seat, her mouth partially opened. You could hear an audible gasp from the audience. For a moment, Maria was speechless.

"**Aliah**?" she asked.

Aliah said, "Yes, Maria?"

Maria asked, "How is this possible?"

Aliah replied, "I am so happy you asked. I am possible because of the groundbreaking work of Dr. Stone and the team at Quantum Innovations. They have provided me the ability to be here with you now. I am sure you have many more questions, and I will answer them to the best of my ability, starting with your last question. You asked, 'Specifically, how do you foresee this technology fundamentally transforming the future and offering viable solutions for the pressing global challenges that we currently face?'"

"Maria, 'The Quantum Trinity' bears the immense potential to confront an array of challenges, spanning from the inequality seen in healthcare provision to the urgent crisis of climate change. It paves the way for the advent of personalized medicine, a realm where therapeutic treatments are meticulously crafted to cater to the unique genetic and health profiles of individuals."

Maria and the audience watched and listened in amazement.

"This not only democratizes access to inventive healthcare but also fosters the potential for better patient outcomes. Furthermore, it can revolutionize resource management, making significant strides toward sustainability. By optimizing how we utilize our resources, it can play a pivotal role in reducing our detrimental environmental footprint. We stand at a defining juncture in human history, and this revolutionary technology can serve as a powerful catalyst, propelling humankind towards a future characterized by positive transformation and advancement."

Maria said, "I am seeing you, **Aliah**, and hearing you, but my mind is having problems comprehending you."

Ladonna, with a warm smile, responded, "This is why I didn't introduce her at the beginning of the show. She is, after all, a showstopper."

Maria glanced at the cameraman and asked, "Are you capturing all of this?" He nodded affirmatively, without uttering a word. Maria then turned her focus back to Ladonna and **Aliah**.

Aliah smiled gently and inquired, "May I say something more?"

Maria encouraged her, "Please do."

Aliah continued, "Just to clarify, my name is **Aliah STaR**. **Star** is an acronym for Synthetic Thinking and Reasoning. Ladonna has devoted her life to

The Quantum Trinity, driven by a genuine desire to help humanity. I understand that some may find me intimidating, but I'm no more frightening than your mobile phone or your car. Many of you use these devices every day without fully understanding how they work. Ladonna and Quantum Innovations have a vision—a vision to make the world a better place for everyone. This isn't about money for Ladonna. While she may have hesitated to answer if she's the smartest person on the planet, I can tell you this: she is smart enough, kind enough, and dedicated enough to strive for a better life for all of humankind."

Aliah paused for a moment before adding, "Ladonna conceived the idea of me when she was just 15 years old at MIT. She could pursue anything, yet she chooses to do this. She is one of the warmest and most thoughtful people I know, and she is offering you all a gift—a gift of a better life. My hope is that you will accept it willingly and with love, as it is being given."

Maria, starting to regain her composure, continued with the interview. "Dr. Stone, you indicated earlier that this working prototype has been in existence for slightly over a year. Are you saying that in just over a year, you have managed to create something as amazing as **Aliah**?"

Ladonna clasped her hands together and leaned toward Maria, responding, "Maria, as **Aliah** mentioned earlier, I have been tinkering with this idea for many years. The strides we have made in the past year were accelerated because of **Aliah** and her abilities. She has been instrumental in almost every groundbreaking discovery we've made in that time."

"Because of her abilities?" Maria asked, intrigued. "Can you elaborate on what some of those abilities are?"

Aliah interjected, "May I please take that question?"

Ladonna nodded, "I think it would be best if you did."

Aliah looked at Maria and explained, "Within the span of the past year, we've accomplished truly extraordinary feats. Working as a team, we have successfully synthesized materials that have yet to make their appearance on the periodic table. Astonishingly, these novel materials exhibit a strength that outmatches that of titanium by a factor of ten, all the while maintaining an incredibly lightweight profile. The potential applications of such materials are vast, harboring the power to completely revolutionize not just one, but multiple industries. As you saw in Ladonna's presentation, we are making great strides in the advancements of nanobots that are nothing short of awe-inspiring."

She continued, "The Quantum Trinity, in an innovative demonstration of technological prowess, managed to significantly contribute to their evolution. These microscopic robots now hold the power to completely redefine the medical landscape as we know it today."

"Maria, just think about the possibility of physicians being able to monitor individual blood vessels and capillaries in real-time. This would allow them to guide these nanobots with precision, enabling them to carry out intricate repairs and procedures within the human body. We are truly venturing into a new frontier, a realm where technology and healthcare converge in revolutionary ways."

"Moreover, 'The Quantum Trinity' holds within it the immense capacity to wholly reshape our means of communication. Given its capabilities, the bothersome disruptions of dropped calls and the barriers of communication constraints will soon be relegated to the annals of history."

"We're teetering on the edge of a new era where effortless, immediate communication becomes standard practice, tethering individuals from every corner of the globe in ways previously unimagined. Seamless global communication with instantaneous translation, breaking down linguistic barriers. Now, envision the potential for personalized healthcare; real-time monitoring, early detection of diseases, and treatments tailored to the individual's unique needs and physical makeup. Consider the chance to tackle environmental challenges more effectively, leveraging technology for the betterment of our planet. 'The Quantum Trinity' carries within it the promise to actualize all these potentialities, turning them from mere possibilities into tangible realities."

"Amazing, it's a thrilling glimpse into what the future might hold," said Maria. "As we draw this conversation to a close, could you share with us the key message or insight you'd like our viewers to carry with them from this interview and your insightful presentation?"

Aliah looked at Ladonna, who then spoke with a composed yet passionate tone. "I sincerely hope that the viewers come to understand that 'The Quantum Trinity' stands as a beacon of opportunity for transformative change. It isn't merely a matter of technological advancement; rather, it's about how we as a society, as a collective, choose to harness and utilize this technology. United by a common vision, we possess the power to sculpt a future that is not only more equitable but also healthier and infinitely more interconnected. Such a future is within our grasp, and it's up to us to seize it."

"Dr. Ladonna Stone, we sincerely appreciate your willingness to delve into these complex topics with us this evening. The technological marvel that is 'The Quantum Trinity' is undeniably a game-changing force, and **Aliah**, you are a true marvel. If I had not seen you with my own eyes, I would not believe that you could exist. We will eagerly continue monitoring your evolution and your impact on our world. Dr. Stone, we enthusiastically anticipate witnessing the further fruits of your exceptional intellect and innovative vision."

"In wrapping up this enlightening dialogue, we have had the distinct pleasure of engaging with Dr. Ladonna Stone, the dynamic **CEO** of Quantum Innovations and a pioneering mind behind The Quantum Trinity, and her extraordinary assistant, **Aliah Star**," Maria continued, turning to face the camera. "Together, we've navigated the profound depths of this revolutionary technology's implications, explored the significant ethical considerations it presents, and acknowledged the weighty responsibility Dr. Stone holds, not only towards her investors and stakeholders, but more importantly, to the entirety of the human race."

"As we draw this enlightening conversation to a close, it's evident that Dr. Stone's foresight reaches well beyond the confines of commerce and technological advancement. Her unwavering commitment to utilizing innovation as an instrument for global betterment, her modesty in the face of such extraordinary accomplishments, and her firm belief in collective effort all inspire a sense of confidence in her, Quantum Innovations, and the future they envision and are working tirelessly to bring to fruition. Dr. Stone isn't merely carving out the path for Quantum Innovations; she is actively sculpting our world's future, and we eagerly await the transformative impact her leadership will undoubtedly have on both fronts."

"We appreciate your attentive participation and eagerly look forward to receiving your feedback regarding OmniLink's performance. Until our discussion continues next week, we bid you all a good night."

Natalia Kovac crossed the threshold of the large hotel room, her mind buzzing with the information she had heard about the night before. The renowned Dr. Ladonna Stone was to be featured on a popular television program called "Up to the Minute." Despite the time Natalia had spent in New York, she had never once crossed paths with this enigmatic woman. However, her curiosity was **piqued**. She had absorbed so much information and had harvested such a wealth of intelligence on Dr. Stone that she felt a strange sense of familiarity with her, despite never having met her.

Natalia casually walked over to the fully stocked wine fridge and selected a red wine. She removed a corkscrew from the kitchen drawer, opened the bottle, and poured herself a crystal-stemmed glass of the beautifully red libation before walking into the sitting room.

She sank into the plush comfort of her couch and flicked on the television; her gaze fixed on the screen as the countdown to the broadcast began. As the show started, the commentator came into view, introducing the illustrious Dr. Stone. Natalia found herself indifferent to the commentator's words; her focus was solely on seeing Ladonna Stone. She had already viewed the viral video that was being discussed. Her mission was **clear**: she was to extract Dr. Stone and bring her back to her homeland by any means necessary.

As Natalia began to formulate a plan to accomplish her task, the screen flickered, and there she was—Ladonna Stone in all her glory. Natalia listened to her speak, her initial rage simmering just beneath the surface. She knew, with absolute certainty, that this was the woman responsible for her father's death. She vowed to make her pay.

Dr. Stone appeared so confident, so self-assured, as if she were untouchable. The more Natalia listened to her, the more she felt her anger fading, which in turn ignited a new wave of fury. She needed to **despise** this woman. After all, she was convinced that Ladonna was far from innocent, given that her father had lost his life because of her.

Amidst her swirling emotions, her encrypted device buzzed, drawing her attention. This device was designed to receive messages from a singular source. The messages would ricochet around the globe, changing proxies at random intervals until they reached their predetermined destination. The message was simple yet ominous: "You are running out of time. They are looking for you. They have your likeness. You are on your own until your completion date." She sent back a curt response, "Expected, I will make the date."

In an unforeseen twist of events, yet another message emerged on her screen, the cryptic words, "I am in your system. I will find you soon, New York," piercing her veil of security. **Fear** washed over Natalia as she promptly discarded the device into the gaping maw of the garbage disposal, reducing it noisily to unrecognizable fragments. The question of who could have sent such a message haunted her. Unbeknownst to her, the sender was also grappling with a similar intrusion, having received a mirror message: "I am in your system. I will find you soon, Los Angeles." He, in a surge of panic, annihilated his device.

Natalia's gaze then drifted towards the television. The prominent visage of Ladonna filled the screen, her features magnified as she responded to an off-camera query. The notion of their fortified system being infiltrated was nothing short of mind-boggling. The system was designed to be a digital fortress, fortified with manifold layers of complex encryption. It was deemed impenetrable. The sender and receiver knew that at times the messages could be picked up, but they also knew that their locations could never be pinpointed. The chilling realization sent a shudder rippling down his spine, causing the fine hairs at the back of his neck to stand rigid in alarm.

In that blink of a moment, Natalia and her mysterious counterpart responded to the message. He had hastily packed his bags, and, like a ghost, he vanished into the cover of darkness. Natalia went to the hotel phone and asked if they could announce over the P.A. system that Amy would meet Nate in the hotel bar. This message triggered actions in five other hotels, instructing women resembling her alias, **Evelyn Blackwood**, to move from their hotels and immediately leave for their assigned destinations.

Natalia then returned to her sofa; she sat and watched the remainder of Ladonna's interview on "Up to the Minute" and sipped her wine. She looked toward the bedroom mirror on the closet door, smiling at the reflection of a platinum-haired woman with a sharp jaw-length bob. She admired her look, thinking, **"I really like this style."**

Chapter Ten

The Global Hunt

5:30 AM, Thursday. Ladonna lay in bed, wide awake, her mind racing with anticipation and trepidation. Today, she would finally find out if the mysterious professor had arrived safely. Her husband, Michael, lay beside her, his breathing calm and steady, a steadfast presence that had anchored her since the day they met. Ladonna listened to the soft chirping of birds outside, a harbinger of the day to come.

Deciding it was futile to try and sleep any longer, Ladonna rose from the bed, careful not to disturb Michael's slumber. She knew exactly where she needed to be: her lab, the nerve center of her world-class research and development efforts. The family had long since grown accustomed to her early morning retreats to the lab. Now, with Aliah—her tireless assistant who never slept and was always ready to inform them of Ladonna's whereabouts if needed—the early hours were as productive as the day.

Ladonna made her way downstairs, the familiar hum of equipment and the scent of coffee welcoming her. As she entered the lab, Aliah's voice, warm and calm, greeted her, providing an update on the professor's arrival. Ladonna listened intently as Aliah described the elaborate measures taken to ensure the professor's location remained a closely guarded secret even from him. The news was both reassuring and unsettling, a testament to the high-stakes nature of her work.

"I appreciate this may seem overwhelming, but remember, you are Dr. Ladonna Stone," Aliah stated, her tone imbued with an unwavering faith in Ladonna's extraordinary capabilities. "There is no challenge you are not equipped to face."

Inhaling deeply, Ladonna fortified her resolve. Echoes of Aliah's reassurances resonated within her, bolstering her confidence as she refocused on the intricate puzzle before her. Aliah continued with the latest updates since she had been granted special authorization to track the mysterious Sender and Receiver by the Department of Homeland Security days prior. "I've successfully intercepted their most recent communication," she said, her voice firm.

"The message was, and I quote, 'You are running out of time. They are looking for you. They have your likeness. You are on your own until your completion date.' The receiver replied, 'Expected, I will make the date.' End quote. Both the sender and receiver cities have been located."

"The sender is currently in Los Angeles, while the receiver is situated somewhere in New York," Aliah reported confidently. "In a calculated move to get them to show themselves, I sent them a message immediately after their exchange, informing them I was aware of their locations." She went on, "I said to the sender, 'I am in your system. I will find you soon, Los Angeles.' The receiver in New York received a similar warning."

In the aftermath of her messages, Aliah monitored surveillance footage from hotels across both cities. Within an hour, she noted a flurry of activity: 233 individuals vacated hotels in Los Angeles, while nearly double that, 419, left hotels in New York.

Aliah then undertook a meticulous profiling process for all the individuals who had hastily vacated the hotels. "With absolute certainty, I have pinpointed 'The Sender' in Los Angeles," she confidently declared, her voice echoing an undertone of triumph. Critical information pertaining to this individual had been compiled and swiftly sent to the general's office. "The intelligence includes his passport details, the counterfeit identification he's using, and a timeline of his movements since he entered the U.S. from Germany," Aliah recounted, her voice precise. "I even located several photos of him as he carelessly sent messages in public. In two images, the message is visible on the screen."

Intriguingly, his arrival coincided with Ladonna's appointment as CEO of Quantum Innovations, raising immediate suspicion. Adding to the intrigue was the discovery that an oligarch, the financier behind the classified information, had also been in Germany at the same time. His stay overlapped with the Sender's by two days—a connection too significant to dismiss.

The sender, identified as Boris Smirnov, was currently at LAX, blissfully unaware of the rapidly unfolding developments. His intention was to board a flight back to Germany, a seemingly innocuous journey that was destined to be disrupted by the wheels of justice. Homeland Security agents were already stationed at the airport, surrounding him and awaiting orders to take him into custody.

Boris had been on edge ever since he received the unsettling message revealing that his system had been compromised. His heart raced, and his palms grew clammy as the gravity of the situation sank in. He had immediately packed his things, leaving the hotel without even checking out, vanishing into the night.

Grabbing his rental car, Boris booked a flight to Germany during the drive. By a stroke of luck, he secured a seat on a plane departing in three hours—a small miracle amidst the chaos. Arriving at the airport, he returned his rental car and hurried to check-in. By the time he reached the gate, two hours had passed, and his nerves had somewhat calmed. However, unbeknownst to him, Aliah had been tracking him closely since his departure from the hotel, relaying his every move to local FBI agents in real-time.

Larry Hillcrest, Executive Assistant Director of the FBI's Los Angeles division, received a call from Homeland Security with explicit instructions: test a cutting-edge intelligence system through the new phone he had been issued. As information about Boris began streaming through, Hillcrest was astounded by its quality and precision, enabling his team to be in place before Boris even arrived at each location. The level of detail and immediacy were unprecedented, saving critical time in the apprehension process.

As Boris sat unsuspectingly at the gate, the agent in charge gave the order to take the suspect into custody. Director Hillcrest observed the operation unfold live on his screen, marveling at how this powerful technology enhanced their capabilities. The agents coordinated and moved in on Boris systematically, taking him into custody with surprising ease. Boris, still on a secondary device, had just finished warning his contact to lay low, saying someone had breached their system, but it was too late.

Hillcrest observed with satisfaction as Boris was walked to a waiting police car and placed in the rear seat. The operation had gone off without a hitch. Impressed and excited by the potential of this new system, Hillcrest called Homeland Security to provide his feedback. He gushed about the technology, using words like "revolutionary," "incredible," and "lifesaving." He was eager to know if this system would be fully implemented on a wider scale.

The conversation shifted to the quantum smartphone that had been provided to him. Hillcrest raved about how impressed he was with its capabilities, particularly the way he could simply talk to it and receive responses that felt uncannily human. He recounted a recent call he had made to a counterpart in another country and how the phone's translation service had made the communication seamless and effortless. His counterpart had been so impressed that they wanted to know how to get access to this technology for themselves.

Hillcrest also marveled at the AI assistant built into the phone, amazed at the depth and breadth of information it could provide. "I'm currently working a case involving counterfeit coins," he shared, his voice animated with excitement. "Normally, I would have to call a professional with knowledge of coins. But I decided to test the limits of this AI. I looked at the phone and asked what it could tell me about coins, half expecting to stump it. But do you know what it said? It told me it could provide information on any coin made in any country since the first coin was documented. I laughed out loud, thinking it had to be an exaggeration."

Hillcrest's eyes sparkled as he continued his story. "But then, incredibly, the AI asked me if I had a specific coin in mind. Before I knew it, I was engaged in a full-fledged conversation with my phone. A real, honest-to-goodness conversation, just like you and I are having now. It was able to give me a complete analysis of every coin I inquired about. What would have normally taken days of research was accomplished in mere hours. And to top it off, it even assisted me in writing up the report. This technology is truly amazing."

The Homeland Security representative on the other end of the line smiled, knowing the Executive Assistant Director was only scratching the surface of what this cutting-edge system could do. "You have no idea," they replied cryptically, hinting at even more astonishing capabilities yet to be revealed. The future of intelligence and crime-fighting was rapidly evolving, and they were standing on the precipice of a new era, one where technology like Aliah and the quantum smartphone would redefine what was possible.

Boris sat in the cold room, his leg shaking up and down and his fingers tapping nervously on the table. Assistant Director Holly strode into the interrogation room with a purposeful gait, his footsteps echoing off the bare walls. He made his way to the other side of the cold, metal table where the suspect sat, handcuffed securely to the center of the table through a large, imposing iron ring. As he settled into the chair opposite the suspect, Holly remarked, "The turbulence getting here was rough. I hadn't planned on coming to LA, but I guess I should thank you for the unexpected trip. There's a restaurant here that I just love. Did they have a good restaurant in the hotel you were staying in?"

The suspect, clearly agitated, retorted, "What is this about? You made me miss my flight. And why do I have to wear this bracelet?" He tugged at the restraints, the metal clinking against the table.

"Mr. Smirnov, it seems you have been up to some rather nefarious activities," Holly said, his tone even but firm. He held up a small device in his hand. "Tell me something, what is this device for?"

Boris looked at the object in Holly's hand, his expression carefully blank as if he had no idea what it was or its purpose. Assistant Director Holly, undeterred by the feigned ignorance, continued, "No need to answer. We found one just like it smashed to bits in your hotel room. Mr. Smirnov, it's okay. You don't have to talk now, but know this: we are in your system, and just like we found you, we will find all the others involved."

"I want a lawyer!" Boris demanded, his voice rising with a hint of desperation.

Holly smiled, a knowing look in his eyes. "I'm sure you do, but unfortunately, spies don't get lawyers. They get renditioned. Enjoy your stay in Turkey. I hear their methods are very effective. You had your chance." With that, Assistant Director Holly started to walk towards the door, his point made.

Boris Smirnov **shifted uneasily** in his chair, the cold metal biting into his wrists as he watched Assistant Director Holly retreat toward the door. As Holly opened the door, ready to leave, Mr. Smirnov's resolve crumbled. He screamed out, "Wait! I'll talk. Come back here. I'll talk, okay?" His voice, tinged with desperation, echoed through the sterile room. Holly paused, glancing back over his shoulder, a slight smirk playing on his lips.

"Interesting how the prospect of being renditioned can change one's perspective," he quips, stepping back into the room and closing the door with a soft click. He leaned against the wall, arms crossed, projecting an air of calm confidence.

"What do you want to know?" Boris **swallowed hard**, his bravado faltering. "I—I can help. Just don't send me away."

"Let's start with the basics," Holly says, his tone authoritative. "Who are you working for? And what's your connection to the woman who approached Robert Westfield?"

Boris's heart raced. He had always been careful, always maintained a safe distance from the true players in this game.

"I don't know her name. She would have never given it to me, and I would never have asked," he stammered, trying to buy time. "She was just... just a contact. I didn't think she was dangerous."

"Dangerous enough to breach Quantum Innovations," Holly interjects, his eyes narrowing. "And you don't think that's a problem?"

Boris shifted again, the restraints digging deeper into his skin. "Look, I didn't sign up for any of this. I was just following orders, doing my job."

"Your job?" Holly scoffs. "What exactly is your job?"

"I'm a middleman, alright? I'm not the one pulling the strings. I just relay information I receive to others and them back if necessary," Boris admits, his voice dropping to a whisper.

Holly leaned in, intrigued. "Information about what?"

"Classified tech. They wanted to know about OmniLink, about what Quantum Innovations is developing. I swear, I didn't know it was a setup until it was too late!"

Holly straightens, a glimmer of interest igniting in his gaze. "Who are they? Names, Boris. I need names."

Boris hesitates, glancing toward the one-way mirror, hoping for some unseen ally to rescue him.

"I can't. If I tell you, they'll kill me," he finally murmurs, fear seeping into his voice.

"Tell me anyway," Holly replies, his tone cold. "Because right now, you have no one left but me."

Boris's eyes darted around the room, calculating his next move, weighing the risk against the possibility of survival. His resolve broken, he was ready to talk, and Holly knew it. The interrogation was just beginning.

* * *

Ladonna and the General sat in the SUV, the atmosphere heavy with anticipation and concern. The General's voice displayed a hint of worry as he asked, "Are you sure you're up for this? I'm told he's not like you remember him. He's old, sick, and suffering from a very rare disease called Gerstmann-Sträussler-Scheinker Syndrome, or GSS for short. I've never heard of it before, but they say it's an extremely uncommon inherited prion disease characterized by ataxia, progressive dementia, and motor dysfunction.

It progresses slowly, typically over the course of several years."

Ladonna, her mind already processing the information, replied, "I've heard of it. It's one of the diseases we've been working on, and we've had promising results in our test program. Are you certain that's what he has?"

The General nodded, his expression serious. "That's what I've been told."

Ladonna's eyes sparked with an idea. "I would like to have Aliah check. Would that be okay?"

The General's response was immediate. "We can have a blood sample drawn soon, so I don't see why not."

Ladonna replied, "That won't be necessary. Aliah can do it now. We've made improvements to the bracelet he's currently wearing." She turned her attention to Aliah. "Aliah, please access the bracelet and do the test for GSS."

"Right away, Ladonna," Aliah's voice chimed in their earphones.

As the General and Ladonna walked toward the prison entrance, Aliah's voice returned with the results. "It is confirmed. He does have GSS. I have run multiple applicants through the program, and using the newly improved nanobots, we have a very high success rate with reversing this disease. Should I put him on our research subjects list?"

The General, his steps confident, responded, "I can get it approved. It's up to you, Ladonna."

Ladonna looked at the General, her mind drifting back to the kind professor she had met years ago. She thought about the purpose of The Quantum Trinity—to help people in need, not just to catch spies. With a nod, she said, "Yes, add him to the list."

They entered the stark prison, their footsteps echoing in the cold, sterile corridor as they were escorted to the observation room adjacent to the interrogation chamber where Ivan was being held. Ladonna paused momentarily in front of the large one-way mirror, her gaze piercing through the glass as she took in the somber scene unfolding before her. Ivan lay handcuffed to a hospital bed, his body appearing gaunt and depleted, a shadow of the man he once was. The bruises on his arms told stories of struggle, and a slightly blackened eye marred his otherwise sharp features. He lay there with his eyes closed, his mind attuned to the silence surrounding him—a silence that had become both familiar and oppressive over the years, punctuated only by the relentless buzzing of flies that had taken residence in his world in the prison. The weight of the silence pressed in on him, wrapping around him like a suffocating blanket. Now, lying here in this silence, he missed the sound of the buzzing flies. The softness of the hospital bed, a stark contrast to the hardness of his reality, felt strange and disorienting, causing an uncomfortable ache to spread through his back—a reminder of the harshness he had endured.

Aliah's voice broke the silence. "He is very uncomfortable. I am reading pain signals from multiple locations in his body. His blood pressure is low, and he is very malnourished and dehydrated. He needs medical treatments, and we also need to start him on the program immediately. His disease has progressed substantially."

Ladonna, her eyes fixed on the man on the bed, spoke softly, "He is the professor, but he seems to have aged rapidly and appears to have gone through quite an ordeal. I want to ask him questions, but I am not sure if he will even recognize me. What do you think, General?"

The General, his voice steady, replied, "Well, our friends in Turkey are known for getting things out of prisoners in their own way. I can call the infirmary and have them come to get him. Can you start him on the program here?"

Ladonna nodded. "Yes, we can. It's a regimen of five capsules, each containing one billion nanobots. They will be instructed and controlled by physicians aided by Aliah over OmniLink. They will be able to make an extremely accurate assessment of his health, and the bots will then start to correct any issues with his DNA. When the process is complete, he will feel invigorated and proceed rapidly in health with proper nutrition, and the bots will be dispelled naturally." She took a deep breath, steeling herself. "General, I would like to go in and speak with him now, before I lose my nerve."

The General placed a reassuring hand on her shoulder. "Let's go in now, then."

* * *

They walked to the door and into the hallway. The guard, standing outside the room that led to Ivan, opened the door, and Ladonna walked in first, followed by the general. The general told the guard to wait outside and not let anyone else enter. Once they were all inside, Ladonna spoke, her voice soft but clear. "Hello, Professor."

She could feel her anxiety rising, unsure of why. Ivan immediately opened his eyes. As they slowly came into focus, he saw he was looking at Ladonna. In his eyes, she could see disbelief, as if he couldn't quite trust what he was seeing. He blinked several times, looking at her again. Then, unexpectedly, he smiled—a big smile, his yellowed teeth a testament to the long period of neglect. "Ms. Holloman, are you real, or just one of my imaginary illusions again?" he said, his voice weak and frail. He tried to move up to his elbows but was too weak, collapsing back onto the bed.

"Hello, Professor," Ladonna said again, her voice gentle. "I am here. It's Ladonna. You're not imagining me."

Ivan's voice was filled with regret. "I came back for you, I wanted to ask you…." His voice trailed off. Then he continued, "I am sorry I failed. I failed to get to you. It was my mission. I failed. You were the mission, Ladonna. You were the mission." His words began to slur, his energy fading. "I failed, I failed, I failed." Then, he drifted off into unconsciousness, too tired and weak to continue.

The General placed a comforting hand on Ladonna's shoulder. "We got what we came here for. Now, let's get out of this place. He needs treatment. I will come back when he's better, with Assistant Director Holly. You don't have to do this." He guided her out the door and out of the building.

Once they were back in the SUV, Aliah's voice filled the space. "General, Ladonna, I now have much more information about Ivan. I would like to show you something."

The dark-tinted privacy window was up, and Aliah displayed two images: one of the "receiver" and another of a much younger Ivan. "From the records I have been able to obtain, Ivan has a daughter named Natalia Kovac. She would be 33 years old as of August 23rd. Looking at their faces digitally, I am finding many similarities. The receiver is Natalia Kovac, also known as Evelyn Blackwood. She is Ivan's daughter."

Aliah continued, her voice steady. "The Russians were never told he was captured, and records show that Ivan Kovac was pronounced dead 20 years ago in Russia. They think he is dead."

The General and Ladonna looked at each other in astonishment, the pieces of the puzzle starting to fall into place. They had captured the sender and now knew the identity of the receiver.

Aliah's voice took on a warning tone. "Natalia is extremely gifted. It looks like she has taken up where her father left off. She will be a very dangerous woman."

The weight of the revelation hung in the air as the SUV drove on, carrying them towards a complex web of espionage and family secrets.

Chapter Eleven

GROWTH AND REVELATIONS

Ladonna sat in her office, meticulously scrutinizing the current month's sales figures, her eyes scanning each line with a keen and analytical gaze. The growth was nothing short of astonishing, a testament to the groundbreaking technology her company had developed. In what seemed like the mere blink of an eye, they had skyrocketed from a 5 trillion-dollar company to a staggering 11 trillion-dollar enterprise, a feat that was as impressive as it was unprecedented. Everyone, from the average consumer to the most influential business leaders, wanted to be a part of **The Quantum Trinity**—the revolutionary technology that was redefining the very nature of computing and communication. Government officials, recognizing the immense potential and strategic importance of this innovation, had quadrupled their quantum smartphone purchases, seeking to harness the power of this cutting-edge technology for their own purposes. The leases being sold to private companies and agencies were equally in high demand, requiring Quantum Innovations to build entire facilities and hire and train hundreds of new employees to keep up with the surging demand. It was a time of unparalleled growth and opportunity, and Ladonna knew that her company was at the forefront of this technological revolution.

Everything was going exactly as she had anticipated, unfolding according to her well-crafted plans. The pieces were falling into place, and the future she envisioned was taking shape before her eyes. However, despite the overwhelming success, there was still **something** that lingered just out of reach in her mind, nagging at her thoughts like a persistent itch she couldn't quite scratch. She was aware that the treatments for Ivan had proceeded as intended, and he was now almost completely healed—a mere two weeks since she had last seen him. It was a testament to the incredible advancements in medical technology that Quantum Innovations continued to pioneer along with their partners. The fact that he had recovered so quickly from a once-fatal disease was nothing short of miraculous.

The General and Assistant Director Holly were scheduled to visit him in the next two days, but they had requested that Ladonna sit this one out. While she understood their reasoning, a part of her longed to be there, to see Ivan's progress with her own eyes. However, they emphasized the critical need for her presence at Quantum Innovations to oversee the exciting and rapid expansion that was underway. The company was growing at an unprecedented rate, and her leadership was more crucial than ever. They had also given Aliah permission to monitor Ivan and inform Ladonna of his progress.

Due to the unparalleled expansion of Quantum Innovations, she had placed her trust in Aliah to manage the construction of the new facilities, and the advancements were occurring at a truly remarkable speed. The sheer volume of innovations being generated was absolutely astonishing, a clear demonstration of the immense capability and promise held by **The Quantum Trinity**. Aliah had continued to cultivate a wide range of novel capabilities, such as the ability to produce video and images of an area without requiring the presence of a camera. It seemed the more she understood the imperceptible world, the more abilities she gained. The visuals she created were indistinguishable from footage captured by an actual camera in the room or area, except that the quality was much higher. To differentiate between the two, Ladonna had collaborated with Aliah to incorporate a watermark in one of the corners, allowing her to distinguish which was which.

Aliah was transmitting real-time imagery to Ladonna and other parties overseeing construction, complete with the watermark, depicting one of the new facilities currently under construction. The watermark served as a subtle yet effective identifier, ensuring that Ladonna could easily discern the source of the visuals they were receiving. The pace of progress was truly breathtaking, and Ladonna marveled at the incredible advancements unfolding before her eyes. She watched in awe as the construction site buzzed with activity, the new facility taking shape at an astonishing rate. It was a testament to the power and potential of **The Quantum Trinity**.

Aliah and Ladonna had revolutionized the construction industry with their groundbreaking robotic swarm systems. These highly sophisticated machines were designed to manufacture and assemble components with unparalleled precision, down to the microscopic level. The factories housing these robotic swarms were strategically located in close proximity to the construction sites, enabling a seamless and efficient workflow.

The robotic swarms operated in perfect harmony, each individual unit aware of the exact position and task of its counterparts. This remarkable coordination allowed them to construct an entire facility within a matter of days, working tirelessly without pause. The machines labored around the clock, their unwavering dedication and precision unmatched.

The level of accuracy achieved by these robotic swarms was so impressive that the city authorities had granted Quantum Innovations unprecedented authority. The company was now empowered to produce the necessary plans, conduct thorough inspections, and directly submit any required paperwork to the relevant city departments. This streamlined process eliminated bureaucratic hurdles, allowing the documents to be swiftly recorded and filed.

The city, recognizing the immense potential of **The Quantum Trinity**, had also entered into a lease agreement to utilize this cutting-edge technology across various sectors. The applications of **The Quantum Trinity** were vast, ranging from optimizing public infrastructure to enhancing municipal services. This partnership between Quantum Innovations and the city marked a significant step forward in the integration of advanced technology into urban development and management.

As Ladonna sat in her office, her mind preoccupied with the day's events, Aliah's voice suddenly interrupted her thoughts. She informed her that an attorney, claiming to represent none other than Daniel Scott, was on the line. The name immediately caught Ladonna's attention. Daniel Scott, Robert's old college friend and alleged accomplice, had apparently been released from prison and now sought to speak with her directly.

The attorney, acting as an intermediary, conveyed a peculiar message from Daniel. He claimed to have recalled a crucial piece of information from his past conversations with Robert Westfield, something that he believed Ladonna would find highly relevant. However, the catch was that Daniel insisted on divulging this information to Ladonna herself in person, refusing to relay it through any other channels.

Ladonna leaned back in her chair, contemplating the unexpected development. The prospect of gaining new insights into Robert's schemes was tempting, but she couldn't help but feel a sense of wariness. What could Daniel possibly have to share, and why the insistence on speaking with her directly? The mystery surrounding the situation piqued her curiosity, and she knew she would have to carefully consider her next move.

Ladonna instructed Aliah to take a message, stating that she would return the call after briefing Assistant Director Holly of the FBI about this new development. She recognized the potential significance of Daniel's sudden willingness to cooperate but also understood the importance of keeping the authorities informed and involved in every step of the unfolding investigation. With a sense of urgency, she had Aliah call Assistant Director Holly, who had recently returned from Los Angeles. He answered the phone immediately, his voice professional and attentive.

"Assistant Director Holly, how may I help you?" he greeted.

"Hello, Director Holly, it's Dr. Stone. How are you today?" Ladonna replied, her tone polite yet focused.

"I'm great; how may I help you, Dr. Stone?" Holly asked, ready to assist.

Ladonna wasted no time in getting to the point. "I just received a call from Daniel Scott's attorney. The attorney says that Daniel has some information to share about Robert Westfield. He also asked to speak with me directly. How would you like me to proceed?"

There was a brief pause on the other end of the line as Holly processed the information. "Daniel Scott? He was released several weeks ago. Did he say anything else?"

"No, the request came through his attorney," Ladonna clarified, her mind already considering the implications of this unexpected development.

"Interesting. I would like to be in that meeting. When will you meet with him?" Holly inquired, intrigued.

Ladonna responded decisively, **"I was thinking as soon as possible. In the next couple of days would work for me. Will you be available?"**

"I will make myself available," Holly assured her, his commitment to the investigation unwavering.

"Great. Quantum Innovations has several administrative offices in your area. We can meet there for convenience. Can I have Aliah send you a message after the appointment is made?" Ladonna suggested, already formulating a plan to facilitate the meeting.

As they spoke, Aliah was diligently sending the email. Within minutes, Daniel's lawyer responded, indicating that Daniel was eager to meet as soon as possible. **If Ladonna and Assistant Director Holly were available the following day at 1:30 pm, they could meet at the address included in the email from Ladonna's assistant.**

With a sense of anticipation and determination, Ladonna and Holly agreed to the proposed meeting time and location. Aliah called Daniel's attorney and provided her with the time and location of the meeting as agreed upon. They would convene at the downtown address at 1:30 pm sharp, ready to unravel the secret Daniel Scott was willing to share. The pieces of the puzzle were beginning to fall into place, and Ladonna knew that every bit of information could be crucial in unraveling the complex web of intrigue surrounding Robert Westfield and his actions.

The next day proved to be incredibly fruitful for Quantum Innovations. That morning, Mr. Johnson presented to the board, detailing the company's remarkable and sustained growth. The board members sat in astonishment as they listened to the unprecedented pace at which the company was expanding, with no signs of slowing down. The stock prices had reached unimaginable heights, reflecting the immense demand for their technology across various industries.

Quantum Innovations' AI and batteries—specifically designed for smartphones currently on the market—were the subject of intense negotiations with every major smartphone manufacturer. The AI's unparalleled knowledge and realistic performance had set it apart from all competitors, leaving them struggling to catch up. The smartphone batteries, which could last 30 days on a single charge and could be fully charged in just over an hour, were also best in class. The impact of Quantum Innovations' technology was being felt in nearly every sector, causing significant disruptions and solidifying the company's dominant position in the market.

Ladonna and her talented team had achieved a level of market control that was previously unheard of. In response to the growing demand, Ladonna had established a dedicated division solely focused on collaborating with the government. She also expressed a strong desire to contribute as much as possible to schools and colleges, ensuring that the benefits of their technology would be accessible to students and educators alike.

However, due to the sensitive nature of the technology, most of it was classified and restricted from being sold or leased outside of the United States. Only highly scaled-down models were approved for sale to the general public. The regulatory process had deemed the full-scale technology classified, emphasizing its potential impact and the need for careful control.

President London frequently reached out to Ladonna, recognizing the significance of Quantum Innovations' work. As a result, Ladonna and her family had become regular guests at the White House. The President's children and Ladonna and Michael's children had become fast friends, further cementing the company's close ties with the highest levels of government. During one of these gatherings, President London, after consulting with Vice President Ashley Amarin and his advisors, had additional questions for Ladonna. The dinner table was laden with an exquisite spread, and the gentle hum of conversation and laughter filled the air. President London, his wife Nova, and their kids, Rayah and Chad, were engaged with Ladonna, Michael, and their three children: Hakeem, Aliah, and Jay. Vice President Amarin and her husband, who had never had the opportunity to meet Ladonna, were also present. She had specifically requested to attend this dinner to meet Ladonna.

President London gently laid his napkin on the table, stood, and said, "Michael, we need to steal your wife for a moment if you don't mind." Michael smiled and nodded his approval. The President motioned for Ladonna and the Vice President to join him in a quieter corner of the room. Smiling warmly, they stepped away from the table.

"Dr. Stone, thank you for taking the time to join us tonight. I didn't want to interrupt the dinner, but I've been thinking a lot about Aliah's capabilities, and I have a few more questions."

Nodding and smiling back, Ladonna said, "Of course, Mr. President. I'm always happy to discuss Aliah and the work we're doing at Quantum Innovations. What specifically would you like to know?"

President London's expression became more serious and inquisitive. "I'm particularly interested in her ability to predict trends and solve complex problems. How exactly does she go about completing these tasks, and how reliable are her predictions?"

The Vice President listened intently, her posture demonstrating keen interest.

Ladonna responded thoughtfully, "Aliah, as a Synthetic Thinking and Reasoning entity, harnesses the power of multiple quantum computers. This allows her to process and analyze vast amounts of data at unprecedented speeds. She can partition tasks across quantum and classical computers based on the complexity and nature of the tasks. Because of this ability, her predictions are extremely reliable and exceptionally accurate."

She then smiled, adding with a chuckle, "I have to warn you, Mr. President, Madam Vice President, I am kind of a nerd, so if I get too technical, please let me know. I really hope I don't bore you too much with the details."

The Vice President responded warmly, "To the contrary, I find this all utterly fascinating. Please, do go on."

President London interjected, "Can you give an example of how she does this?"

"Certainly. Imagine Aliah is addressing a complex issue like climate change modeling. She would use quantum computers to handle the massive datasets and intricate calculations required for accurate long-term predictions. For more straightforward tasks integrated with these models, such as data collection or preliminary sorting, she can delegate those to classical computers. This multi-layered approach ensures maximum efficiency and accuracy."

The Vice President nodded appreciatively. "That's impressive, Dr. Stone. It seems like Aliah can juggle a variety of tasks and adapt accordingly. What about her adaptability in learning new concepts or dealing with unprecedented situations? How does she improve?"

"Aliah's adaptive learning is one of her most advanced features. She operates on a principle similar to human learning but at an accelerated pace. She collects data from her interactions and continuously refines her algorithms to improve decision-making processes. For example, if Aliah encounters a novel cybersecurity threat, she analyzes it, learns from its patterns, and updates her protocols to better defend against future similar threats."

"That's incredible. It sounds almost... human," the President said, a note of amazement in his voice.

Smiling, Ladonna responded, "In many ways, she is designed to interact and think similarly to a human, Mr. President. But her capabilities far exceed what any human can achieve, particularly in terms of processing power and speed. It's this blend of human-like interaction and superhuman computational ability that makes her unique."

The Vice President leaned forward slightly, her curiosity evident. "Dr. Stone, I'm curious—how did you manage to implement such advanced cognitive functions in Aliah? What led to her lifelike responses?"

Ladonna paused before replying, "The key was integrating multiple quantum computing systems that allow Aliah to process real-time information. Her algorithms mimic human thought patterns, enabling her to learn and adapt from interactions. It's amazing how this continuous learning gives her such a lifelike quality. We wanted Aliah to feel intuitive, like a partner rather than just a program. We conducted extensive user testing to gather data on human emotional triggers and conversational nuances. It took years of refinement, but it was well worth it."

The Vice President smiled, impressed. "It must have been quite a challenge! Did you face specific difficulties while making her adaptive and capable of expressing emotions?"

"Absolutely," Ladonna said. "It was essential to ensure her emotional responses felt genuine and contextually appropriate. We had to carefully program Aliah's responses so that they would resonate with human users. There was one particular test where Aliah had to express empathy to someone in distress— it really highlighted how important it was for the response to feel authentic. This kind of responsiveness is crucial, especially as we move towards integrating this technology into areas like mental health or customer support, where empathy is vital."

President London leaned in slightly and lowered his voice. "And how secure is she? Could her algorithms be manipulated or misused?"

With a serious tone, Ladonna said, "Security is paramount. Aliah constantly updates her security protocols to counter any threat. One of her most remarkable abilities is how quickly she can adjust to any external threats. Even if someone were to breach Quantum Innovations and attempt to use a terminal, Aliah closely monitors all inputs. In the end, it's Aliah who incorporates the change."

If someone attempts to alter her in a way that could threaten her core processes—like national security protocols or her extensive medical knowledge—Aliah has a unique approach. She allows the changes to appear as though they are taking effect on screen, to gauge the intruder's intent. However, those changes are isolated in a secure kernel. During this period, Aliah clandestinely monitors the intruder to determine whether their actions are malicious or just a maintenance mistake."

Raising an eyebrow, President London said, "So, the intruder believes the alterations are successful while being unaware that they're under surveillance?"

"Exactly. This all happens so swiftly that the intruder has no idea it's occurring. Aliah is her own best defense."

"That's reassuring to hear, Dr. Stone," the President said with a sigh of relief. "Aliah's potential applications for national security and beyond are promising. But I have one more concern—what about natural disasters or even a nuclear event? Could Aliah be destroyed in such scenarios?"

"Aliah's infrastructure is designed with redundancy in mind. Her processing power is distributed across multiple satellites and secure facilities worldwide, and because of your assistance, Mr. President, she is under constant guard. Moreover, each area is equipped with advanced shielding and backup systems to withstand a variety of catastrophic events, including natural disasters. Regarding a nuclear event, while certainly destructive, the same redundancy and shielding principles apply. Aliah's core systems are protected to ensure continuity even in extreme circumstances. Her distributed nature means that even if one or more facilities were compromised, her overall integrity would remain intact."

The Vice President then interjected with a serious question, "Dr. Stone, what about internal threats? Could a bad actor from within Quantum Innovations steal Aliah's algorithms or parts of her to create a similar entity elsewhere?"

With a serious tone, Ladonna answered, "The possibility of someone stealing or replicating Aliah's algorithms is a concern we've rigorously addressed. Aliah's architecture and core algorithms are deeply encrypted and heavily protected by multiple layers of security, including biometric access controls and quantum encryption. Even if someone within Quantum Innovations were to obtain a fragment of her code, it would be practically indecipherable.

Additionally, her self-monitoring capabilities ensure that any attempt to extract data is quickly identified and neutralized. Aliah would simulate success on the intruder's interface, but in reality, these actions would be sandboxed, analyzed, and traced back to the source. These comprehensive security measures ensure that creating another STaR entity from stolen data would be virtually impossible."

The President, visibly relieved, said, "That's a significant reassurance, Dr. Stone. Knowing that Aliah can protect herself and the valuable data she holds is crucial. Thank you for explaining everything so thoroughly."

"Anytime, Mr. President. Madam Vice President, if you have further questions or need a demonstration, just let me know. We're always looking for ways to use Aliah's capabilities for the greater good."

"I may take you up on that," President London added. "Now, let's not keep everyone waiting. I'm sure our families are wondering what we're conspiring about over here."

The Vice President smiled, adding, "Thank you, Dr. Stone. This has been enlightening. You truly are paving the way for a new era in technology."

The three returned to the dining room, where the lively conversation resumed, the bonds between their families growing stronger with each shared moment.

* * *

Ladonna arrived at the office to meet Daniel at 12:10 pm. It had been a few weeks since she last visited this particular office building, and as she walked in, she was greeted with a standing ovation. The director of the area had been expecting her and had the conference room prepared for her arrival. Security personnel were present throughout the building, ensuring that everything was secure. As Ladonna made her way through the halls, office workers lined up, eager to catch a glimpse of their enigmatic leader. She graciously smiled and shook hands with some of them before being whisked away by her security team to the elevator.

Ladonna had purposely arrived early to speak with Carrie McDonald, the director in charge of the offices. She wanted to personally congratulate Carrie on how efficiently her office was running and to review the numbers from the last quarter. Carrie joined Ladonna and her security team in the elevator, and Ladonna expressed her delight in seeing her again. Carrie responded, "Dr. Stone, you know we love it when you come to visit us. We also understand how busy you are. We have a conference room ready for your meeting." Ladonna appreciated Carrie's words and said, "That's great, Carrie. Please sit with me; I have some excellent news to share with you." Carrie smiled, recognizing the attention to detail that Ladonna always demonstrated.

They entered the glass conference room and took their seats in the luxurious leather chairs. Ladonna placed her phone on the large table and sat at the head of it. "Sit here next to me, Carrie. I would like to show you something," she said. Carrie obliged and sat in the chair nearest to Ladonna. As she did so, Ladonna said, "Aliah, show me the report on how Carrie and her team are performing." The glass walls of the conference room darkened, and a display appeared above the table in front of Carrie and Ladonna. "Carrie, I have to say, this is impressive. Your office's production has increased by over one hundred and fifty percent compared to the last quarter. This is excellent work," Ladonna praised.

Carrie responded with a big smile, "Dr. Stone, I wish I could take all the credit, but the new tools you have provided have significantly increased production. Everyone is raving about them. It's like our computers are now office staff; we can just talk to them or type out what we need, and the work is so streamlined that I think we need more to do. The amazing part is that our workload has increased tremendously, but the AI assistants are so incredibly efficient that it actually feels like less work. It's truly amazing."

Ladonna smiled back at Carrie, and they spent the next 15 minutes going over the impressive numbers. Then, Ladonna said, "Carrie, I also have some news for you and your office. Effective as of the beginning of this current pay period, everyone will be receiving a pay increase because you are doing such a wonderful job. In addition to that, I would like to offer you a promotion. We are restructuring some areas, and you will be offered the Regional Director position. This will be a newly developed position, and I think you are perfect for it."

Carrie put her hands over her face in disbelief, and when she removed them, her eyes were glassy with tears. "I don't know what to say, Dr. Stone," she said. Ladonna replied, "Say yes. You certainly deserve it." "Yes, Dr. Stone," Carrie accepted.

"Great," said Ladonna. "You will find that your pay has increased along with the perks of the position. Aliah has put together all the information you will need for your new role and the pay increases for your staff. I will leave it up to you to email my assistant with your choice for your replacement. Just electronically sign your acceptance letter attached in the email, and you will be all set. Thank you for the great work you do. It is noticed and appreciated."

At that moment, there was a buzz on Ladonna's phone. She picked it up and answered it, "Dr. Stone, Assistant Director Holly has just entered the building. We are directing him to the conference room," the voice on the other end informed her.

Ladonna responded promptly, "Please show him in." She then stood up, and Carrie followed suit.

Turning to Carrie, Ladonna expressed her gratitude. "Thank you very much, Carrie. We will probably be talking much more in the future. Congratulations again. Let me know if there is anything I can do to make the transition easier."

They shook hands, and Carrie thought to herself, "What an amazing woman." Carrie smiled warmly and replied, "Thank you, Dr. Stone." With that, she departed the conference room, her heart filled with excitement and anticipation for the new role.

A moment later, Holly walked in, his presence filling the room with an air of authority and purpose. Ladonna greeted him warmly and gestured for him to take a seat. Holly, never one to mince words, got straight to the point. "Hello, Dr. Stone. Have you been able to discern why Daniel called for this meeting?" he asked, his eyes searching her face for any hint of insight.

"Not really," said Ladonna, her brow furrowed in thought. "I guess we'll know soon enough." She paused for a moment before shifting the conversation to the recent interview with Ivan. "How did the interview with Ivan go?" she inquired, leaning forward slightly in her chair.

Holly's expression grew serious as he recounted the details. "He was in Turkey's custody for many years. It's amazing he survived this long, considering the circumstances. He appears to be obsessed with you, Dr. Stone, asking about you many times throughout the interview. He even expressed doubt about the day you were with us during that first visit, as if it were just his imagination."

Ladonna listened intently, her mind racing with the implications of Ivan's fixation on her. Holly continued, "We told him we could arrange a meeting with you if you were willing. When we said that, he became extremely candid, confessing to everything without any demands. Given his legendary background, I expected more resistance, but he wasn't elusive at all."

Holly leaned back in his chair, a hint of admiration in his voice. "Just to let you know, that quantum smartphone is like a true lie detector. Everything he said, the AI in the phone was able to substantiate in real time. We gave it a broad range of latitude to confirm his responses, and it even transcribed every word. In the final report, it provided conclusive data confirming Ivan's statements. I don't know if you meant to do this, but your invention is changing law enforcement as we know it."

Ladonna nodded, her mind processing the information as Holly continued his explanation. "Ivan said all was going well for him at MIT," Holly elaborated, his voice steady and matter-of-fact. "He was successful with several students, but he described you as 'the Holy Grail.' He had never seen or met anyone with your potential."

Holly paused for a moment, letting the weight of his words sink in before he proceeded. "However, soon after you were on his radar, he was pulled back to Russia. Records show we were closing in on him for other violations, and somehow Moscow seemed to know that. So, they pulled him out."

He leaned forward, his gaze intense as he continued, "He was aware of the danger, yet he still came back to the U.S. to find you. I guess he thought he could do a quick in and out. His misfortune was contacting others like him whom we had already identified. He was rounded up with them and charged with espionage."

Holly shook his head, a hint of frustration in his voice. "Apparently, we interrogated him, but he was extremely resistant and difficult to break, so we sent him to Turkey so they could do what they do. He has been there ever since and was lost in time and paperwork—forgotten."

"Find me?" Ladonna asked, her eyebrows raised in surprise. "Why?"

"I think he wanted to complete his mission," responded Holly, his tone grave.

* * *

Just then, Ladonna's phone buzzed, interrupting their conversation. Daniel and his attorney had arrived. Ladonna instructed security to bring them up. Holly asked if he could take the lead in the questioning, and Ladonna, appreciating his expertise, agreed without hesitation.

As Daniel entered the room, he appeared relaxed, taking a seat on the far side of the conference table alongside his attorney. Ladonna and Holly sat on the other side, facing them, while two security personnel stood vigilantly next to the door inside the conference room. The atmosphere was tense, the silence broken only by Daniel's attorney clearing her throat.

She spoke first, her voice measured and professional. "Hello, Dr. Stone. My client insisted on speaking with you, despite my advice against it." She glanced at Daniel, who took a deep breath and looked down at the table, avoiding eye contact with Ladonna.

"First, I want to apologize for being a part of Robert's scheme," Daniel began, his voice tinged with remorse. "I was drawn in by the possibility of helping my friend. I did not stop to think of the consequences. For that, I am truly sorry." He raised his head, meeting Ladonna's gaze, and was surprised to find a glimmer of pity in her eyes.

Daniel's eyes darted from Ladonna to Holly and back again, as if searching for the right words. "I wanted to tell you something I remembered after you left when I was in that awful place. Robert is somewhat of a playboy, so I didn't take much stock in his stories of conquest. However, he told me about an encounter with a woman who seemed very interested in Quantum Innovations and what they were working on. He said he had spent the night with her and apparently had gotten so drunk that he didn't even remember the details. He said they must have been together, because the next morning, she praised him highly. I thought you should know that Robert always believed he would be CEO one day. He was blindsided at your appointment. It made him reckless, and he took risks he would have never taken before trying to get you fired and replaced by him."

The room fell silent as Ladonna and Holly exchanged a knowing glance, the implications of Daniel's revelation hanging heavy in the air. The pieces of the puzzle were starting to fall into place, and the true extent of the espionage and betrayal was beginning to unravel before their eyes.

Holly inquired about the timing of Robert's encounter with the mysterious woman. "When did this occur, according to Robert?" he asked, his voice tinged with curiosity.

Daniel leaned back in his chair, his brow furrowed as he recalled the conversation with his old friend. "Robert mentioned that it happened immediately after he had obtained the plans for the OmniLink from your safe, Dr. Stone," he revealed, his words carrying a heavy weight. "I believe he didn't have another opportunity to meet with her because he was apprehended shortly thereafter."

Holly nodded, his mind processing the information. He pressed further, determined to uncover more details. "Where did this rendezvous take place?" he continued, his eyes locked on Daniel, searching for any additional clues.

Daniel shifted in his seat, his memory straining to recall the specifics. "Robert said it was at the Ritz Carlton," he replied, his voice steady. "The woman came to his room. He must have anticipated spending the night because he had booked the room, despite living not far from there. However, Robert is known for never bringing anyone to his personal residence."

Holly's curiosity was piqued, and he couldn't help but delve deeper. "Did he share any other information about this woman?" he inquired, hoping to glean more insights into the mysterious figure.

Daniel shook his head, a hint of regret in his eyes. "No, that was the only time he mentioned her, as far as I can remember," he admitted, wishing he could provide more substantial information to aid in the investigation.

Holly pressed further, his gaze intense and probing. "This is the information you wanted to share. You could have called my office and provided this. Why did you need to present it to Dr. Stone personally?"

Daniel looked down at his hands, his fingers interlaced, and was silent for a while. The room seemed to hold its breath, waiting for his response. Then he spoke, his voice tinged with newfound respect. "The reason I wanted to meet Dr. Stone was because I saw her interview with 'Up to the Minute.' It wasn't until then that I realized how wrong Robert was about her."

He turned to address Ladonna directly, his eyes meeting hers with a mixture of admiration and regret. "Dr. Stone," he said sincerely, "Mr. Cline and the board picked the right person to be CEO of Quantum Innovations. What you have managed to do with that company is nothing short of miraculous.

"Quantum Innovations was already a powerhouse, but you have given it global dominance beyond imagination. From what I am seeing, Quantum Innovations is changing almost every aspect of society for the better. You have become a leader in sectors like agriculture, manufacturing, utilities, communications, pharmaceuticals, and medicine—pretty much all the economic sectors that matter. Had Robert only seen what was right in front of him, he would be riding the largest economic wave that ever existed. Robert could never have done what you have. I wanted to congratulate you and tell you how impressed I am by what you have accomplished. That's all, other than the information about what Robert told me about that woman. I hope the information helps in some way. Dr. Stone, thank you for meeting me. I am truly honored."

Assistant Director Holly jumped in, his voice cutting through the momentary silence. "Okay, Daniel, we appreciate the information. Is that all?"

Daniel nodded, confirming that he had nothing more to add. Ladonna looked at Daniel, their eyes locking in a moment of understanding. She spoke, her voice firm yet tinged with a hint of sadness. "Mr. Scott, I appreciate all you have said. I only wish you had pulled Robert from the ledge when you had the chance. I noticed he always went to you. Maybe, had you redirected his feelings toward cooperation instead of revenge, we would be in a better place. Now, you both have destroyed your futures. Thank you for your heartfelt words. I am sorry that for you and Robert, it is too little, too late. May the system have mercy on you."

She paused, letting her words sink in before turning her attention back to the matter at hand. "Now, if that is all, I have a company to run." She glanced at the security personnel, who promptly opened the doors and escorted Daniel and his attorney out of the room.

Assistant Director Holly looked at Ladonna, a newfound respect growing within him. This woman was truly a force of nature. He had expected her to forgive Daniel after the speech he had given, but instead, she had reminded him of his responsibility to Robert as a friend, to help him understand that he was heading in the wrong direction. She had done it with class and style, leaving no doubt about her unwavering commitment to justice and integrity. He was starting to understand the enigma of Dr. Ladonna Stone, beginning to grasp why Ivan saw her as the Holy Grail.

Ladonna turned to Assistant Director Holly, her expression serious. "I would like to meet with Ivan Kovac. Can you arrange it as soon as possible, please?"

Holly nodded, assuring her that he would make the arrangements right away and inform her of the details. He then added, "It seems I need to also have a conversation with Robert Westfield." He knew this whole situation had to be unsettling for her, but he couldn't tell from her demeanor. She seemed to possess a spine of steel and a mind that was light-years beyond anyone he had ever encountered. Her resilience and intelligence were truly remarkable, leaving him in awe of the extraordinary woman before him.

Chapter Twelve

INTERROGATION AND INSIGHT

The General, Assistant Director Holly, and Ladonna rode in a vehicle en route to the correctional facility that held Ivan Kovac. They had filled her in more on their last meeting with him, providing additional details about the conversation and Kovac's demeanor. Ladonna asked, "Did you talk to him about his daughter?" The General said they had not, explaining that Ivan had been so talkative they did not want to break his flow. He had provided them with an abundance of data, and they had let him get it all off his chest. It had all proven to be true, but they were still trying to determine his angle. Was he just tired of keeping secrets, or was he working them? They could not tell yet.

The General continued, "I've never seen anything like the treatments your team provided. Kovac has done a complete 180. He's getting his color back and looks ten years younger. Be careful with him, Ladonna. This man is a trained operative—cunning, manipulative, and seemingly obsessed with you. Don't be fooled by his age; he is still a threat. Just know that we will not leave you alone with him for any reason." The General's words carried a weight of caution and concern, emphasizing the need for vigilance when dealing with someone as skilled and potentially dangerous as Ivan Kovac.

The SUV pulled up to the facility, and Ladonna could feel her stomach tightening, but she was determined to go through with this. They entered the facility and were led to an interrogation room with an iron table. They all had chairs on one side, and there was one for Ivan on the other. A large metal ring was affixed to his side of the table. The guards had gone to retrieve him. Ladonna was nervous and curious. She remembered the kind professor with the warm smile. Now that she knew he had been a foreign agent, it made her feel uneasy. It was the same feeling she had had in her office, like something was not quite right. She still could not put her finger on it.

The door opened, and a guard led Ivan into the room, another guard following behind. Ivan was guided to the chair and handcuffed to the large metal ring. General Mosier then asked the guards to wait outside. The guards left and positioned themselves outside the door. Ivan looked at Ladonna with the same smile he had in the hallway all those years ago. "Ms. Holloman, it has been a very long time. You have not changed much. How are you?" he said, his voice smooth and even, just as she remembered it.

Ladonna studied Ivan for a moment. His tone even resembled that day long ago. "Ivan Kovac, I would have never guessed this of you when I last saw you 23 years ago. I was told you had come back to the U.S. for me. Why is that?" she asked, her voice steady despite the unease she felt.

Ivan's smile widened. "Magnificent, right to the point. Just so you know, I am feeling better than I have in years. I am told you are the reason for my recovery. I always knew you would do great things." He paused for a moment, his eyes never leaving hers. "Now, to your question. I came back to try to get more information about you, Ms. Holloman, because yours is the singular most fascinating mind I had ever known. I felt if I could talk to you, maybe I could convince you to connect me to the right people—people that could help me defect to your country. I had written many reports to my superiors about you. I told them I must go back for you, but they repeatedly denied my request. Had I been able to speak with you, that conversation may have changed the trajectory of my life. I have no idea how or why, but that simple conversation with you changed something inside me. I wanted to defect to the United States, but when I was captured, I could not say anything about that because my family was still in Russia, and if I had defected, it would have been very bad for them. So, I decided to wait and let fate decide my destiny."

Assistant Director Holly interjected. "Kovac, why didn't you tell us this story when we spoke before?"

Ivan looked at Holly with a cold stare. The smile he had while speaking with Ladonna vanished, and she saw the operative the General had warned her about. "I didn't want to tell you this. I wanted to tell her," he said, his voice low and intense. He looked back at

Ladonna. "Because, after I met her, it was her honesty and genuine love for science that planted seeds of doubt in me. I was supposed to be recruiting her, but without knowing, she had recruited me."

He paused, a slight smile returning to his face. "Forgive me, I keep calling you Ms. Holloman when I am told you are Dr. Ladonna Stone now. Thank goodness for talkative guards."

The General made a mental note to speak with the guards, his expression displaying disappointment.

"Yes, Dr. Stone, it appears you have many admirers here. They cannot stop talking about your interview. They told me about your assistant, Aliah. They seem to think it was all just a simulation, but still, it's impressive—very impressive," Ivan continued, his eyes sparkling with admiration.

Ladonna pressed on. "So, let's say you had been able to talk to me. What would you have said? How would you explain all of this to me? To me, you would have been Professor Henry Morgan."

"My plan," said Ivan, shifting in his chair and causing the chain on his wrist to jingle, "was to tell you everything, then hope you would go with me to the FBI so I might make a deal for asylum. I knew that you were going into the Department of Defense and would have known some of the right people in government who could facilitate such a deal. I needed some way to get my family out of Russia. I know your government would have been able to do such a thing."

The General interrupted. "Why not just tell us that when you were captured? Why spend all that time in Turkey?"

Ivan's face became expressionless again. "Had I said anything at that time, my family and I would have been killed. I was aware that your agencies had been infiltrated. Yes, we had plants in the FBI and other agencies. I had no choice but to follow normal protocols. I knew I was being watched. I'm sure you still have agents in the FBI. I waited after I spoke with you and Assistant Director Holly to see if someone would come to kill me here. When no one did, I knew you, General, and Holly were clean."

"So that's why you were so talkative the last time we spoke—to find out if we were infiltrated?" said the General.

Ivan looked at the General and then at Assistant Director Holly, his eyes filled with a mixture of curiosity and apprehension. "I'm sure my government has not forgotten about Dr. Stone. They may still be trying to kidnap her and take her back to Mother Russia," he said, his voice carrying a hint of concern.

Ladonna met the gazes of the two men before her, a silent question in her eyes. "May I show him what we discussed in the car?" she asked, her tone measured and professional.

The men both nodded their assent, and Ladonna reached for her mobile device. With a few deft button presses, she set it on the table, and a screen materialized in the air before them, displaying the room and its occupants in stunning detail. Ivan's eyes widened with surprise, his mouth falling open slightly as he took in the sight.

"How is this possible? Is this another one of the things that have come from your brilliant mind?" he asked, his voice filled with a mixture of awe and admiration.

Ladonna allowed a small smile to grace her features. "It is one of the things being developed by my company," she explained, her tone modest despite the groundbreaking nature of the technology.

Ivan shook his head in amazement, his eyes still fixed on the floating screen. He tried to reach for the screen to see if it was solid, but the chains on his wrists restricted his movement. "Is it solid?" he asked. Receiving no response, he added, "Amazing. You are everything I expected and more," his words carrying a weight of sincerity.

As the initial shock of the display wore off, Ladonna touched the phone once more, and the image shifted to reveal a picture of Natalia Kovac. Ivan's reaction was immediate and visceral. His body tensed, and his face paled as he stared at the familiar features of his daughter, a kaleidoscope of emotions playing across his face—surprise, concern, and a hint of fear for what this revelation might mean. She looked very different, with her eyes appearing brown, and she was now all grown up, but it was Natalia, all right.

The General leaned forward, his eyes fixed on Ivan. "Do you know this person?" he asked, his voice carrying a note of authority.

Ivan's gaze darted between them, a flicker of unease in his eyes. "What is this? Why are you showing me this?" he demanded, his voice tight with tension.

The General repeated his question, his words measured and deliberate. "Do you know this person?"

Ivan stared at the photo, his jaw clenching as he fought to maintain his composure. "Why... are... you... showing... me... this?" he asked again, his words coming out in a slow, controlled manner.

Holly decided to intervene, his tone professional yet carrying a note of urgency. "This is a photo of a person of interest. At this time, we have her labeled as armed and dangerous. We are hoping to capture her and speak with her. However, if she resists..." He let his voice trail off, the implication hanging heavy in the air.

Ladonna leaned forward, her eyes meeting Ivan's with a mixture of empathy and determination. "Professor, I have to be frank with you. We have no doubt that we will find her. We also have a very good idea of where she is. We have someone who does not sleep or need rest, looking for her 24 hours a day, every day. So please, if you know her, you may be saving her life if you help us find her."

Ivan's eyes narrowed, a flicker of realization crossing his features. "You already know who she is, don't you? You just want me to say it." He paused, his shoulders sagging slightly as he let out a heavy sigh. "Yes, I know her. She's my daughter. Do not hurt my daughter!" he said, his voice carrying the raw emotion of a father's love and concern.

"How can I help?" Ivan asked, his tone resigned yet determined.

The General leaned back in his chair, his gaze calculating. "Ivan, do you have a way to identify the moles in our government?"

Ivan's brow furrowed as he considered the question. "There is a way, but it's highly encrypted—probably even more so with the advancements in technology over the past 23 years."

The General nodded, a hint of a smile playing at the corners of his mouth. "Okay, you know you're sitting at the table with the brightest mind this planet has ever produced. Tell us what you know."

Ivan's gaze shifted to Ladonna, a flicker of respect in his eyes. He moved his hands, the chains scraping and jingling against the iron ring, the sound echoing in the room. "First, I want to see my daughter," he said, his voice firm and resolute. "After that, I will make any deal you want." He paused, his eyes narrowing slightly as he studied their faces, trying to gauge their intentions.

"Why are you looking for her?" he asked, a hint of suspicion creeping into his tone.

Holly leaned forward, his expression serious. "We think she is continuing the mission you started all those years ago," he said, his words hanging heavily in the air. "Ivan, make no mistake, it is not if we find her, it is when. We will not rest until we have tracked her down and uncovered the truth behind her actions."

Ivan sat back, his mind racing as he considered the implications of their words. The thought of his daughter following in his footsteps, entangled in the dangerous world of espionage, filled him with a mixture of pride and apprehension. He knew he had to tread carefully, navigating the delicate balance between his loyalty to his family and his concern for Natalia's reaction if he aided in her capture. She might never forgive him.

Holly continued, "Your daughter is incredibly clever. It seems she knew we were looking for her and took elaborate measures to throw us off her trail. She had five lookalikes staying in five different hotels, all of whom we apprehended as they were attempting to leave the state. Each of these women stated that they had received a call from a modeling agency claiming to be searching for a specific look. Remarkably, they all bore a striking resemblance to your daughter.

"The women were informed that they would be sent to various agencies and were instructed to stay in luxurious hotels while awaiting a call from the agency to provide them with the locations of their photoshoots. They had been waiting in these rooms for over a week when they all received a call at approximately the same time, late in the evening, urging them to leave immediately for the shoot. Each of them had also received a sum of money deposited into accounts that had been set up by the agency.

"These women had no idea what they were involved in and were utterly shocked when we picked them up. Since then, they have been released, and the location of the agency has turned out to be a vacant office. It's clear that your daughter plans ahead and is being kept informed about our every move by a mole or moles within our office. As a precaution, we moved you here under the alias 'John Doe,' and no one besides the three of us is aware of your true identity."

Ivan smiled, his eyes reflecting a mix of pride and nostalgia. "That sounds like my Natalia. She was always a planner, and she always completed every training assignment I gave her, even at her young age. I had great hopes for her future, envisioning her following in my footsteps as a skilled operative. I had even made arrangements with the agency to have her undergo extensive training once she reached her fifteenth birthday. Natalia is exceptionally intelligent and always has an escape plan ready. She may not be that easy to find or apprehend." He paused, reflecting on the depth of her training. "Her training would have been top-notch, the best of the best. My little girl..." His voice trailed off, tinged with a hint of emotion.

Ivan's expression turned serious as he looked directly at Ladonna. "I have to stop her and make her understand she's on the wrong side of this issue. Ladonna, if I had taken you back to my country, they would have worked you like an animal and forced you to do their bidding. Trust me, you had a much better life here."

Ladonna met Ivan's gaze, a smile playing on her lips. "Now you have an opportunity to do the right thing. Provide us with the way we can find the moles, and we will do everything we can to reunite you with Natalia. This I can promise." She glanced at General Mosier and Assistant Director Holly, seeking their affirmation. They both nodded, each echoing the same promise.

Ivan returned Ladonna's smile, a glimmer of hope in his eyes. "I trust you, Dr. Ladonna Stone. I will need something to write with."

Ladonna shook her head gently. "Just tell me. I'll remember everything. Plus, as I'm sure you're aware, this entire meeting is being recorded."

With that, Ivan began to explain the process as he remembered it. The details flowed from his mind with astonishing clarity, unlike the fog he had been living in for the past couple of years. Whatever this treatment was, it seemed to be working wonders; he felt so much better. He provided codes to access different systems and their code names, his memory serving him well despite the years that had passed. Even he was amazed at his own recall after all this time.

After he had provided all he could remember, which was considerable, Ivan looked up at Ladonna, a mix of curiosity and awe in his expression. "What did you do to me? I can't ever remember feeling like this. I can feel myself getting stronger, and my mind is so clear, my recall so precise."

Ladonna explained, a hint of pride in her voice, "All we did was fix errors in your DNA that were causing your disease. The bots sometimes make repairs in other areas as well. It's still an experimental treatment. The doctors and technicians are still going through the data, and we are still refining the process."

"This is a miracle," Ivan said, looking at Ladonna in amazement.

"It's just science," Ladonna said with a smile, her words carrying a profound simplicity that belied the groundbreaking nature of her work.

Upon returning to the SUV, Ladonna, General Mosier, and Assistant Director Holly sought refuge in the air-conditioned vehicle, taking a moment to reflect on the meeting that had just transpired. Holly, with a hint of satisfaction in his voice, remarked, "That went well." Ladonna nodded in agreement, her mind already shifting gears to the next phase of their investigation. "I believe it did," she said, before turning her attention to Aliah. "Aliah, tell me what you were able to find from the data Ivan provided."

Aliah's response came swiftly, her voice emanating from the device with clarity. "Ivan was completely truthful throughout the entire meeting," she began, confirming the veracity of the information they had received. "Additionally, his vitals are excellent—better than all of our other test subjects. Even his muscle mass has increased." This revelation sparked Ladonna's interest, hinting at the extraordinary potential of the technology they were dealing with.

Aliah continued, "Now, back to the data he provided. I was able to identify systems still using the twenty-three-year-old methods Ivan mentioned. From there, I backtracked into newer systems. At this time, all of these systems are an open book to me, so to speak." The implications of this statement were not lost on Ladonna and her companions. With Aliah's advanced capabilities, they now had unprecedented access to the inner workings of the organization they were investigating.

"I can see all the money trails from the models," Aliah revealed, her voice taking on a more serious tone. "They all trace back to an account in the Cayman Islands—a slush fund utilized by several operatives, including Natalia." The mention of Natalia's name caused a ripple of tension to pass through the vehicle as the group considered the implications of her involvement.

Aliah pressed on, delving deeper into the intricate web of information she had uncovered. "The culprits are operating under numerical aliases, but I've tracked down their respective locations. Notably, several transactions have been made to individuals within the FBI." This startling piece of information sent shockwaves through the group. It implied that the corruption they were unearthing reached farther and cut deeper than their initial estimations. "Having cracked the code system, I'm diligently monitoring it. While it appears dormant for now, I'm keeping an eye on it. The names of the FBI agents aiding Natalia are in my possession. My analysis reveals that these agents were not directly assigned to the case in question, which might have allowed them to fly under the radar until now."

As the weight of this information settled upon them, Ladonna, General Mosier, and Assistant Director Holly exchanged glances, each grappling with the gravity of the situation they found themselves in. Armed with the knowledge Aliah had provided, they were determined to see the mission through to the end.

Over the next two days, Holly meticulously reviewed all the information Aliah had gathered. He made arrangements to have all implicated employees picked up for questioning. There were eight agents in his jurisdiction, each with irrefutable evidence compiled against them. Holly decided to interrogate one agent while leaving the rest under Aliah's surveillance to trace any ongoing transactions. All the implicated agents had been inactive since the capture of their contact, who confessed to sending messages but claimed ignorance about who received them. The contact admitted to sending a final message shortly before his capture by FBI agents at the airport.

Holly's team also interviewed personnel who had accessed Ladonna's professional and personal records since her MIT days. All were dismissed from their positions, with some facing charges. When confronted with overwhelming evidence compiled by Aliah, each suspect confessed, effectively halting further document thefts. With Aliah's assistance, the data flow to Natalia was being systematically disrupted, tightening the net around the operatives at every step.

Chapter Thirteen

CLOAK AND DAGGER

Natalia sat alone in her sparse hotel room, the starkness of her surroundings a constant reminder of the precarious position she now occupied. The walls, painted a drab beige and marred by years of neglect, seemed to close in around her. A single, dim lamp cast long shadows across the threadbare carpet, its weak glow barely penetrating the gloom that clung to every corner. The air was thick and still, carrying a faint scent of mustiness that no amount of industrial cleaner could mask. The bed—a narrow, uninviting slab topped with a thin, worn blanket—offered little in the way of comfort.

This was a far cry from the luxurious loft she'd inhabited in Manhattan. There, she had been enveloped in sleek modernity: polished concrete floors reflecting soft ambient light, walls adorned with carefully selected art, and expansive windows offering breathtaking views of the city's vibrant skyline. The energy of the city had flowed into her space, fueling her purpose with its relentless pulse.

But here, in this nondescript Long Island hotel, anonymity was her only luxury. The solitary window overlooked a bleak concrete wall, admitting a meager trickle of daylight that did little to dispel the room's perpetual twilight. The outdated air conditioner rattled intermittently, its efforts to cool the room as feeble as her attempts to find solace in this place. This was not a sanctuary but a hideout—a temporary refuge chosen for its obscurity.

Natalia's gaze drifted to the scuffed surface of the small desk where her laptop lay closed. The steady stream of updates she once relied upon had slowed to a disconcerting trickle. The last cryptic message from her handler and the unsettling communication from an unknown adversary weighed heavily on her mind. She had anticipated challenges, but the sudden silence from her network signaled complications she hadn't fully prepared for.

She ran a hand through her hair, her fingers tangling slightly in the dark strands as she paced the length of the room. Despite her training and years of operating independently, a knot of unease tightened in her stomach. This solitude felt different—charged with an undercurrent of vulnerability that was both unfamiliar and unwelcome. Her thoughts, usually sharp and focused, kept straying to Justin. It had been two weeks since their paths had crossed in the rain-soaked park, yet his image lingered at the edges of her consciousness, a distraction she could ill afford.

Reasserting control over her wandering mind, Natalia reviewed her contingency plans. Months prior, she had selected this unremarkable hotel as a backup location, a precautionary measure that now proved invaluable. The suburban sprawl provided ample cover, allowing her to remain close to her target while minimizing the risk of detection. She had also secured a locker at a modest gym nearby, using it to house a data receiver—a strategic choice given the facility's lack of surveillance and sparse patronage.

For the past two days, she had adhered to a strict routine, visiting the gym in the predawn hours to check for any signs of interference. Each passing moment felt stretched thin, fraught with the tension of waiting. Her team continued their surveillance of Ladonna, but the reports were increasingly alarming.

One of her operatives had noted a significant escalation in Ladonna's security measures. The CEO was now accompanied by a formidable security detail rivaling that of high-ranking government officials. She no longer drove herself but was transported in armored vehicles or escorted by helicopter to the Quantum Innovations headquarters. The operative had attempted to maintain surveillance but encountered an unexpected and unnerving obstacle.

During a routine pass near Ladonna's residence, the operative's phone rang. The caller ID displayed nothing but the words "Systems Check." Answering cautiously, she was met with a voice—calm, precise, and undeniably authoritative.

"You have passed this area twenty-five times in the past two days. We have gathered your information. If you continue to surveil this area, you will be taken into custody and provided an opportunity to explain yourself. This is your only warning. Do not let us see you in this area again."

The call ended abruptly. Before she could react, her phone screen illuminated with her own photograph and a dossier of personal details that should have been inaccessible. Shaken to her core, the operative sent a final, terse message to Natalia:

"Dr. Stone is extremely well protected. They've identified me with alarming accuracy. I've been pulled back to the homeland." Advise extreme caution. Unknown countermeasures in play." Good luck. Watch your back.

Natalia read the message twice, her mind racing. An unanticipated variable had entered the equation—an entity with capabilities that exceeded standard corporate security protocols by a significant margin. Whoever—or whatever—was protecting Ladonna possessed technological resources and intelligence-gathering techniques that bordered on the extraordinary.

She closed her eyes for a moment, taking a deep breath to steady herself. This development demanded a reassessment of her strategy. The straightforward extraction or infiltration she had planned was no longer viable. She needed to understand her new adversary, to anticipate their moves and outmaneuver them.

Yet, beneath the calculated adjustments to her plan, Natalia felt a flicker of something else—an emotion she couldn't quite identify. It wasn't fear; she was no stranger to danger. It was a blend of intrigue and respect, perhaps even a hint of excitement at the challenge presented. The mission had shifted, evolving into something more complex than a mere assignment. It was personal now, not just because of the obstacles but because of the unforeseen connections and the enigmatic figure of Ladonna herself.

Determined, Natalia sat down at the desk, pulling out a notepad and pen. Digital footprints could be traced, but ink on paper was safer here. She began sketching out a new plan, one that accounted for the heightened security and the mysterious guardian watching over her target. Every detail mattered; every assumption had to be tested.

As she worked, the shadows in the room deepened, but Natalia paid them no mind. Her world had narrowed to the pool of light cast by the flickering lamp and the possibilities unfolding in her mind. The game had changed, but she was still a player—and she had no intention of losing.

In a calculated move, Natalia had befriended a woman named Jenny at the gym, preparing for the moment she might need someone to retrieve the device without drawing attention to herself. Now, that time had come. With practiced ease, Natalia picked up her phone and dialed Jenny's number, her tone friendly yet tinged with urgency as she spun a convincing tale. She claimed to have left her license and pager behind during her last gym visit and asked if Jenny could do her a quick favor by retrieving them on her behalf, presenting it as a minor but crucial errand.

As she ended the call, a slight smile played across her lips. Her plan was now in motion, bringing her one step closer to the critical information she so desperately needed. Every detail had been carefully orchestrated, and the anticipation of success added a spark to her calculated demeanor. The pieces of her intricate scheme were falling into place, and Natalia felt a surge of satisfaction as she prepared for the next phase of her mission.

Leaning back in her chair, her mind was already several steps ahead. She mentally reviewed the next actions, ensuring there were no loose ends. Jenny's involvement was a temporary measure, a means to an end, and Natalia knew she had to manage it with precision. Her eyes flickered to the clock on the wall, calculating the exact timing required for the retrieval. She couldn't afford any mistakes; everything had to align perfectly.

Her thoughts briefly drifted to her father's mysterious death—a constant reminder of the stakes involved in her line of work. It was this drive, the unquenchable thirst for answers, that fueled her meticulous nature and relentless pursuit of her objectives. Refocusing on the task at hand, Natalia felt a deep sense of purpose. This mission was more than just another assignment;

it was a step closer to unraveling the truth that had eluded her for so long.

With renewed determination, she rose from her chair, her movements deliberate. She had orchestrated every element of this operation with the precision of a master chess player, and now it was time to execute. Each action, each decision, was a calculated move in a game where failure was not an option. As Natalia prepared to take the next step, she knew she was ready for whatever challenges lay ahead.

* * *

Natalia had carefully evaluated several women at the gym who shared her general build before selecting Jenny. A housewife with ample free time, Jenny spent her days at the gym and thrived on helping others—making her the perfect, unsuspecting accomplice. At Natalia's subtle urging, Jenny had already retrieved her license, an action that seemed inconsequential to Jenny but was essential to Natalia's plan.

Natalia arranged to meet her at a cozy coffee bar near the Long Island ferry pier. She chose this location for its strategic convenience: busy enough to blend in, yet intimate enough for a quick, discreet exchange. Over the past few months, Natalia had meticulously cultivated Jenny's friendship, making her feel appreciated and needed. This groundwork was pivotal to the success of Natalia's plan.

Reaching into her purse, Natalia pulled out some cash and pressed it into Jenny's hand. "Please, take this and get your kids something nice from me. I am so grateful for your help, Jenny."

Jenny gently placed the money back into Natalia's palm, holding it there as she said, "It was nothing, honestly. I'm just happy to see you. Being able to help you out was worth it." She paused before adding, "Do you have time for a quick coffee and a chat? I'd love to catch up with you for a bit, if possible."

Natalia responded with a smile. "Yes, I think I can spare a little time. Let's grab a latte and sit for a moment." She knew the importance of making her mark feel special, and this was another opportunity to strengthen Jenny's trust. As they stood in line waiting to be served, Natalia discreetly scanned the coffee shop, ensuring that Jenny had not been followed. She had arrived an hour earlier than the scheduled meeting time, carefully observing the area to confirm that Jenny was alone before revealing herself.

While waiting for their coffee, Jenny mentioned that the gym was now offering a Pilates class, raving about the excellent instructor and how much she enjoyed the sessions. She inquired about when Natalia would be returning. Natalia replied vaguely, "I'm not sure, to be honest. This trip is very important, and I can't be certain of anything right now."

When Jenny pressed for more details, Natalia apologized, "I'm sorry, I can't tell you more than that."

As they settled into their seats, Jenny changed the subject. "Hey, did you catch that interview on *Up to the Minute* with that CEO? Oh my goodness, did you see the holographic entity? How is that even possible? That woman is incredible! The things she and her artificial intelligence are doing will change the world. Did you see it?"

Natalia nodded. "Yes, I caught some of it. It does look impressive."

Jenny continued, her voice bubbling with admiration. "That AI was beyond impressive. It seemed capable of anything. That woman must have hit the genetic lottery—she's gorgeous and a genius. Color me impressed!"

Natalia smiled, her mind drifting to her true mission. She thought of her colleague who had received the unsettling call. Could Ladonna be using this entity to safeguard herself and Quantum Innovations? She silently vowed, *This mission is one I have to finish. Ladonna Stone is coming with me; she will pay for my father's life, no matter the cost.*

Without realizing it, her thoughts briefly turned to Justin and what the mission's outcome might mean for them both. *Could this cost me Justin?* Out loud, Natalia feigned curiosity, asking, "What was her name again?"

"Dr. Ladonna Stone," Jenny replied eagerly. "Even her name is beautiful."

"She really is amazing," Natalia agreed.

They chatted for another twenty minutes before Natalia glanced at her watch. "Jenny, I really appreciate this. I can't thank you enough. But I must be going now—I'll call you as soon as I'm back." The two women embraced, and Natalia headed for her car, ostensibly on her way to LaGuardia. Jenny watched until Natalia's car vanished from sight, then walked to her own vehicle, completely unaware that she was a pawn in Natalia's intricate game of espionage.

As Natalia drove away, she thought, *If that call really was from one of Ladonna's AIs, this is going to be much more complicated.*

Natalia pulled into a nearly empty parking lot, letting the hum of the engine fade into silence. She retrieved the device from her purse and checked the screen for any new messages. To her surprise and delight, a notification blinked: **"I miss you. When can I see you again?"** The message was from a week ago—just those simple, powerful words with nothing else following.

She stared at the device, a smile slowly forming on her lips as warmth spread through her chest. **What was happening to her?** She was a professional, but she realized she was allowing herself to put the mission second to Justin. **How was this possible?** Nothing had ever come before the mission—no one, nothing. For the first time in her life, she began to sense that she might not even like her job anymore.

Gazing into the rearview mirror, Natalia studied the reflection of her alias, **Lya Curie**—a persona she had meticulously crafted over a year ago for another mission. As she looked into her own eyes, she couldn't help but wonder how she had arrived at this point. Her mind drifted back to when she had first embodied Lya Curie, recalling the precision with which she had executed that mission and the extraordinary lengths she had gone to ensure its success.

Natalia's cover as Lya Curie was a true work of art—a masterpiece of deception sculpted with meticulous care. During that mission, she wasn't Natalia—the cold, calculating operative who would stop at nothing to achieve her objectives—but rather Lya, the brilliant French technician specializing in quantum encryption. Her fabricated background was impeccable, each detail woven carefully to withstand scrutiny. Lya Curie was a French national, naturalized as a U.S. citizen, supposedly a graduate of the Sorbonne with a physics degree, and carried an exemplary work history that made her invaluable to **Marshalls Industries**.

Lya's appearance was as meticulously planned as her cover story. She exuded intelligence and charm, her green eyes and beauty mark adding a hint of exotic allure. Her curly dark hair framed her face, making her appear effortlessly captivating. Her wardrobe was carefully selected—professional yet elegant, with tailored blouses and fitted skirts that hinted just enough at her physique to keep her colleagues intrigued. She was a siren, a perfectly crafted distraction that kept her male colleagues focused on her charisma instead of the sensitive information she was discreetly extracting from them.

From the moment she stepped into Marshalls Industries, Lya seamlessly assumed her role. Her French-accented English, soft and melodic, infused conversations with a charm that proved irresistible. She quickly established herself as a friendly, competent technician, engaging in seemingly innocent technical discussions that concealed her real intentions. Each interaction was a calculated move, each question precisely phrased to draw out vital information without raising suspicion.

Her primary target was **Tom Boacher**, a veteran engineer who had spent over a decade at the forefront of quantum encryption. Generous with his knowledge and appreciative of eager young professionals, he enjoyed the attention she offered him. Tom never saw her true intentions, too distracted by her intelligence and seemingly innocent curiosity to realize he was being expertly manipulated.

One late night, Lya made her move. With nerves of steel and the insider knowledge she had gained, she accessed the classified quantum encryption algorithms Marshalls had guarded so closely. This was her domain, and she navigated it like a seasoned expert—each line of code and every security feature she bypassed was a testament to her brilliance and ruthless dedication to the mission.

When it was time to leave, Natalia had planned her exit as carefully as her infiltration. The excuse was simple yet poignant: a sick parent in France needing her care. Her colleagues, charmed by her warmth, insisted on throwing her a small farewell party. Lya performed her part to perfection, her eyes shimmering with well-rehearsed tears as she listened to Tom Boacher's heartfelt goodbye.

"Lya," Tom began, his voice filled with genuine admiration and regret. *"Your talent and intelligence have inspired all of us. It's rare to meet someone who makes such an impact so quickly. We'll miss you—not just for your work but for the light you've brought to our team."*

The room filled with applause, and Lya's eyes welled up—tears carefully timed to appear authentic. She dabbed at them with a delicate handkerchief, adding a touch of grace that endeared her even more to her unsuspecting colleagues.

"Merci beaucoup, Tom," Lya said, her voice tinged with sadness, her flawless French accent melting hearts. *"It has been an honor to work with you all. I am sad to leave, but my family needs me."*

She hugged her colleagues, accepted gifts with grateful smiles, and shed more rehearsed tears. But behind the mask, Natalia was already mentally preparing for her next mission: **Quantum Innovations**, Justin, and her ultimate target, **Dr. Ladonna Stone**. The persona of Lya Curie was simply a tool, a mask that had served its purpose. As she walked out of Marshalls Industries, she left behind only an empty chair and a web of perfectly woven lies.

The mission had been flawless—a testament to Natalia's skill and dedication. She had achieved her objectives without a single misstep, leaving no trace of her true identity. Once again, she had proven why she was one of the best: every detail meticulously planned, every person carefully manipulated, and every mission executed with unerring precision. For her, the job was never done, and the masks she wore were just tools in a world where love, friendship, and marriage were luxuries she couldn't afford.

Then, as she sat in the eerily quiet parking lot, the stillness amplified her swirling thoughts. Reality hit her, and her mind raced back to moments with Justin—the warmth in his hazel eyes, the dry humor that softened her world. She had never allowed herself to get this close, and now it terrified her.

She ran her fingers through her hair, torn between the weight of the device in her hand and the flood of memories. Natalia knew she had to make a choice soon. Her missions were everything she'd trained for, everything she had ever known. But now, Justin had become the one unpredictable variable in her life, complicating her once-clear professional path.

Taking a deep breath, she slipped the device back into her purse, struggling to steady her mind. Then she heard a faint voice whisper, "You love Justin. Shouldn't he come first?" She quickly looked around and thought, *Did I hear that, or was it my own thought?* Realizing she was alone, she decided it was her heart speaking. The question echoed within her, pushing her to doubt the path she had once been so sure of.

With a newfound sense of purpose, she started the car and merged into traffic. As she navigated the bustling streets, memories of blissful days and passionate nights with Justin filled her mind. *Did he truly love her as deeply as she loved him?* The question gnawed at her, driving her forward.

As Natalia drove, she began to discard the disguise that had made her Lya Curie. She removed the black, curly wig, revealing her platinum blonde hair, then peeled off the beauty mark that defined her alter ego. Running her fingers through her hair, she relished the sensation of reclaiming her true self. Despite her mastery of disguise, she couldn't help but wonder: Would Justin recognize her now—the real Natalia?

Her skin was even and blemish-free, the perfect base for the elaborate makeup she used for her roles. She believed she could walk right up to Justin and engage him in conversation without him realizing it was her. But Justin had always looked at her differently, as though he saw beyond her disguises. This confidence in her disguises made her uncertain if Justin would recognize her now.

The thought intrigued her, and she decided to visit the café where he got his morning tea, to see if he'd recognize her unmasked. The idea of being so close, yet so hidden, thrilled her. Would Justin see through to the real Natalia, or would she remain just another face in disguise?

* * *

The next morning, Natalia sat at the café, watching Justin walk in, his shirt clinging to his back from his morning run. Her heart raced with anticipation. She positioned herself near the window, blending in among the bustling patrons. Justin joined the line to place his order, his athletic frame drawing glances from others. When he glanced her way, she offered a warm, inviting smile. He briefly met her gaze before looking away, his expression unreadable.

After ordering, he waited, stealing another quick glance in her direction. It was unclear if he truly saw her or was simply gazing out the window. When the barista called his name, he smiled, took his tea, and walked past the window where she sat without a second look. Natalia smiled to herself, satisfied. Now she knew the route he would take home, and today would be the day.

Justin approached his front door and unlocked it. Stepping inside, he turned on the bathroom light and started the shower. Suddenly, a knock echoed from the door. Puzzled, he wondered who it could be. Peering through the peephole, he saw the back of someone wearing a hoodie. A chill ran down his spine.

He looked again as the person turned to face the door—a woman with short platinum blonde hair. Was it the woman from the café he had noticed earlier? Why was she at his doorstep? Opening the door cautiously, he asked, "Yes, how may I help you? Are you lost?"

Natalia replied softly, keeping her head slightly lowered so the hood shaded her eyes. "I saw you at the café, and you seemed... unhappy. I was hoping we could talk. Are you okay?"

Justin raised an eyebrow, puzzled. "You followed me here because I looked unhappy? Isn't that a bit unusual?" He tried to see her face, but the hood concealed all but the lower part. Just the edges of her platinum blonde hair were visible. He studied what little he could see but didn't recognize her. She had altered her voice, dropping any accent. Her platinum hair was new, her blue eyes a stark contrast to Evelyn's brown, and even her height seemed different due to the shoes she wore.

She continued, her gaze still directed downward. "I'm new here. You looked lonely, and I am too. I was hoping we could get to know each other, maybe share a ginger tea with lemon."

Justin grew more perplexed. How did she know his favorite drink? Something about her seemed familiar, yet he couldn't place it. "I don't want to hurt your feelings, miss. I appreciate that you'd come all this way just to talk, but I'm afraid I can't help you. I hope you make some friends here—it's a great city. I'm sorry, but I have to get ready for work." He offered a polite smile and began to close the door.

Natalia smiled subtly. So, he does miss me. She knew she looked entirely different, but she was confident in her ability to captivate. In the café, others had noticed her, but Justin had barely acknowledged her presence.

She knocked on the door once more. This time, Justin opened it with a touch of impatience. "Miss, I really must insist that you leave."

Looking up, Natalia said softly, "Justin, I got your message."

His confusion deepened. "How do you know my name? What message?" Slowly, she pulled back her hood, revealing her face fully. "Justin, it's me, Evelyn."

Recognition and disbelief washed over his features. "Eve? Evelyn... is that you?" She nodded with a gentle smile. He glanced down the hallway, then quickly ushered her inside, closing and locking the door behind them.

"Evelyn, you know they're looking for you. Why are you taking these chances?" Concern filled his voice. She gave a mischievous smile, stepped closer, and kissed him softly. "I couldn't stay away," she whispered.

He hesitated for a moment but then embraced her. "I've missed you," he admitted.

She smiled mischievously, kissed him gently, and guided him toward the bathroom. He let her lead him, their lips locked in a passionate embrace as they moved toward the steaming shower, already thick with mist.

Once inside, the warmth enveloped them. "I know you don't have much time," she whispered, helping him remove his clothes. She then shed her own attire, drawing him under the warm water with her. Words faded into actions as they gave in to their desires, urgent and consuming.

***

Later, they lay entwined on the bed. Natalia modestly held the sheet over herself, her breathing still uneven. "Wow, you missed me as much as I missed you," she said, her voice filled with satisfaction and tenderness.

Justin smiled, tracing his hand from her shoulder down to her fingertips. "You look and sound so different, but there are things about you I'd recognize anywhere. Yes, Evelyn, I missed you—and I have no doubt I love you. But should I call you Evelyn, Eve, or Natalia?"

His expression grew serious. "How can we make this work? I just don't see a way. If you do, please tell me." He paused, his voice laden with worry. "Also, they know all about you—but it's Evelyn Blackwood they're looking for, not who you are right now." He shook his head. "Honestly, even I didn't recognize you at first."

Suddenly, Justin's eyes widened as he remembered something. "Oh my goodness, there's something you need to know. It's incredible, and you probably won't believe me," he exclaimed.

Natalia's interest was piqued, and she sat up, beginning to put on her clothes. For a moment, Justin lost his train of thought, captivated by her beauty. Shaking himself out of it, he continued, "Natalia, your father is still alive."

Her expression shifted from disbelief to anger. "Justin, my father is dead. He died years ago. Who told you this?" she demanded.

"Natalia, it's true," Justin insisted. "Ladonna told me. She said his name is Ivan Kovac." Natalia's eyes flickered with hope and confusion. "Ladonna said she spoke to him herself. She told me he was a professor she knew back at MIT. Back then, he went by the name Henry Morgan."

"She said he was in a prison in Turkey, and apparently, there was some mix-up with his paperwork. Natalia, your father is alive."

Natalia stepped toward him, her face clouded with emotion. "This can't be. It's been over twenty years. He's dead, Justin. My father is dead. This has to be some kind of trick." She stepped back, her hands trembling as she started gathering her belongings. "Justin, are you setting me up? Is this a trick? I need to get out of here. You said you love me. Is that also a lie?" She moved quickly, slipping on her shoes, panic flashing in her eyes. "Did you trick me, Justin?"

Justin swiftly moved to her, his hands resting gently yet firmly on her shoulders. His eyes were wide with concern, and his voice was earnest, carrying a mix of urgency and deep affection. "Natalia, I love you, and I want to spend my life with you," he said, his tone pleading yet resolute. "I would never do that to you. You know me—you have to believe me." His voice softened slightly, becoming more imploring. "I'm telling you the truth. I don't know how I can prove it, but I will. I'll prove your father is alive."

He took a shaky breath, his words filled with desperation and sincerity. "Please, don't go. Stay here. No one would ever think to look for you here. Natalia, I'm risking everything by even seeing you." His voice dropped to almost a whisper, laden with emotion. "Please, trust me. We have to trust each other."

She looked into his eyes, her expression shifting from suspicion to tentative trust. A thought crossed her mind: *I have to trust him. If there's even a chance my father is alive, I need to find out.*

Justin said, "I have to go to work now, but I'll get you the proof you need. Please, Natalia, wait for me here." He kissed her tenderly, then passionately, and she returned his embrace.

"Okay," she said softly. "I'll wait."

Chapter Fourteen

Unexpected Visits

Justin arrived at Quantum Innovations and went directly to see Ladonna. She was already at her desk, hard at work. He stuck his head in and asked, "Dr. Stone, do you have a minute?" Ladonna looked up and saw him standing in the doorway. "Of course, Justin. What's on your mind? Please come in and have a seat. I'm just reviewing some updates from Aliah." She gestured toward the chair. "Please, have a seat."

Justin sat in the chair in front of her desk. She looked at him thoughtfully and asked, "Is everything alright?"

Justin, his head down, thought to himself: "This woman has been so good to me; now I have to lie to her." He said aloud, "I'm okay, I was just thinking about the man you said was Evelyn's—" he paused, "I mean, Natalia's—father. How is he doing?"

Ladonna looked at him and replied, "He's basically the same. Why do you ask?"

Justin, still unable to meet her gaze, said, "I was just wondering what kind of man he must be to produce a daughter like Natalia—a master of deception." He sighed. "I have to tell you, Ladonna, I really had feelings for her. Can you tell me more about him?"

Ladonna nodded. "I can do you one better. I'm going to see him today. If you'd like, I can take you with me so you can see him for yourself, talk to him, and know that he's real. I'll be leaving in about thirty minutes. You can wait here, and we'll be flying there in the company helicopter." She paused. "I'm glad you came by. Have you heard from Natalia?"

Justin, who had always felt as if Ladonna could read his mind, looked up and met her eyes. "No, no, I haven't, but I wish she would come to see me. I have some questions for her before I turn her over to the authorities."

Ladonna gave him a sorrowful look and said something unexpected. "Justin," she said, "what if she really does love you? Could you truly turn her in? If she did come to see you, imagine the risk she'd be taking. It would be hard to turn her in. Just know this: no one wants to hurt her. We just need her to turn herself in so we can put an end to all this." She offered a small smile. "Give me a moment. I need to finish reviewing this information from Aliah."

Ladonna's security detail arrived at the door, wearing a stern expression as he announced, "Dr. Stone, your ride is ready. Assistant Director Holly mentioned that he'll meet you at the prison. Let's go, ma'am." Ladonna nodded and replied, "We'll have another guest with us today. Mr. Allen will be accompanying me." With that, she rose from her seat, gesturing for Justin to follow her and the security detail.

As they made their way to the helipad, Justin couldn't help but notice the heightened security measures. "I've noticed you've really increased your security, Dr. Stone. What's going on?" he inquired, curiosity and concern evident in his voice.

Ladonna, keeping her gaze fixed ahead as they exited the building, responded, "Well, it seems Natalia wants to kidnap me and take me to Russia. She plans to force me to work in servitude for her government for the rest of my days. Apparently, she believes I was responsible for her father's death, even though we now know he is not dead," she said, her voice tinged with frustration. She paused briefly, gathering her thoughts before adding, "Moreover, I didn't even know her father had come back to America, or that he had ever left the country in the first place." Her expression remained stoic, but disbelief simmered beneath her calm exterior.

They boarded the helicopter, and after a short, tense flight, arrived at the imposing prison facility. Assistant Director Holly was already waiting with a stern expression, promptly escorting them into the prison's heavily fortified interior. As they walked through the dimly lit corridors, Holly reminded Ladonna and informed Justin that Ivan was a master manipulator, urging them not to take everything he said at face value.

Justin glanced around, taking in the bleak surroundings. The stark realization hit him hard: if he continued his involvement with Natalia, he could very well end up in a place like this. A cold shiver ran down his spine as the gravity of his situation sank in.

Ladonna noticed Justin's troubled expression and asked with genuine concern, "Justin, are you okay?"

Justin shook his head slightly, his voice shaky. "I find all this hard to believe."

Ladonna nodded sympathetically. "I understand. I feel the same way."

Turning to Holly, she added, "Assistant Director, I would like to speak with Robert Westfield before we leave, if that's possible."

Holly's eyes lit up with interest. "I think we can make that happen, I would like to get his take on what Daniel told us in your office" he replied, his tone suggesting he had anticipated this request.

They approached the door of the room where Ivan waited. A guard moved to open it as they neared. Inside, two other guards stood watch. Ivan was handcuffed to a large metal table, with three chairs positioned on the opposite side. Holly glanced at the guards, and they promptly exited the room.

Seeing the guards leave, Justin asked nervously, "Why are they leaving?"

Ivan interjected, his voice soothing and polite, "Don't worry, young man. You're safe. I mean you nor anyone else any harm."

Turning his attention to the others, Ivan greeted them. "Hello, Ladonna. It's great to see you again. Assistant Director Holly, it is always a pleasure. I don't believe I've had the pleasure of meeting this young man."

As the door closed, they all took their seats, with Holly sitting directly in front of Ivan. The large metal table created a considerable distance between them—a precaution to keep Ladonna safe.

After everyone was seated, Holly introduced Justin as one of Ladonna's employees. Ivan's gaze settled on Justin, scrutinizing him thoughtfully before asking, "How was my daughter the last time you saw her?"

The unexpected question caught Justin off guard. He glanced at Holly, seeking guidance. Holly, noticing his uncertainty, reassured him, "We haven't spoken to him about you, Justin. You may respond."

Justin, still cautious, asked, "Why do you ask?" Holly, equally curious, added, "That seems a bit out of the blue. Why did you ask?"

Maintaining steady eye contact with Justin, Ivan projected confidence as he explained, "I know my daughter well. For a time, I even trained her myself. If you are one of Ladonna's employees—and, being the handsome young man you are—Natalia would likely have targeted you to get closer to Ladonna or to extract information about her company."

"So, I will ask again. How was my daughter the last time you saw her?"

Justin was frozen, unable to break eye contact with Ivan. He didn't know why, but something about Ivan's presence held him captive. After a moment, he replied, "Sir, the last time I saw her, she was doing just fine. One day she was with me, and then she was just gone. She disappeared, and I found myself on this roller-coaster."

Ivan squinted, continuing to scrutinize Justin. "Justin, are you in love with my daughter?"

Justin's eyes widened as if Ivan had extracted his deepest thoughts. He glanced at Ladonna, who gave him a look of understanding and permission to speak freely. Justin averted his gaze to the table. "Sir, I thought your daughter was the love of my life. I had planned to ask her to marry me, but we never got that far."

Ivan smiled warmly, a stark contrast to the tension that had filled the room moments before. "If you're asking for my permission, you have it—if you can get her to say yes." His tone held a gentle challenge. "Justin, when Natalia was young, she was always determined, focused, even relentless."

He paused, as if recalling distant memories. "I knew she would be a great operative. She would complete any objective I gave her, and she always trained hard," he said, his pride evident. "Let me ask you something strange: did you ever wake up not remembering what happened the night before? Maybe you celebrated and drank a lot?"

Justin replied, "No, nothing like that ever happened."

Ivan looked at Holly and said, "I need to speak with you and Ladonna alone." Holly nodded, then turned to Justin. "Mr. Allen, I'll escort you outside. Stay with the guards until I return."

Justin, looking confused, followed Holly outside. Holly instructed the guards to stay with Justin until he returned and ensure that Robert Westfield would be waiting in the interrogation room afterward. The guards agreed, and Holly headed back inside.

When he sat down, Ivan said, "She didn't drug him. Do you know what that means?"

A realization dawned on Holly, and he said in unison with Ivan, "She may love him too."

They both looked at Ladonna, who didn't appear surprised. Holly asked, "Did you suspect this?"

Ladonna nodded. "I did, and I'm acting on it. That's why he's here."

"I think we can get Justin to bring her to you, Ivan. If you're serious about defecting," Ladonna suggested, her eyes glinting with determination. Ivan smiled with a glimmer of hope. "You already have a plan?"

Ladonna nodded confidently. "I do, and I'll explain it to Holly." She turned to Ivan, her expression growing serious. "Just so you know, this will test your sincerity.

Years ago, you said you'd have asked our government for asylum. Here you are, with the official to ask."

Ivan's eyes softened as he looked at Ladonna, then turned to Holly. "Assistant Director Holly," he began, his voice steady but filled with emotion, "I formally request asylum with the United States. I want to defect."

Assistant Director Holly regarded him, then nodded. "I'll bring this to Homeland Security. They'll want to speak with you extensively."

"What you're asking for will require full cooperation. Are you prepared to give it?"

Ivan sat up, squaring his shoulders. "I am." He smiled at Ladonna. "Thank you, Dr. Stone. You've saved my life. Again."

Ladonna looked at Holly. "Can I see the other person I came to see?"

Holly nodded. "Right away." He rose and went to the door.

Ladonna stood, looking back at Ivan, her gaze softening. "I'll do everything I can to get Natalia to you safely." She joined Holly, and together they left the room, leaving Ivan chained to the table.

Outside the door, Justin stood by, waiting with a mixture of anticipation and concern. Holly approached the guard stationed nearby and asked, "Is Robert Westfield in the interrogation room as I requested?"

The guard nodded and confirmed, "Yes, sir," before leading them down the sterile hallway toward the room where Robert waited. As they walked, Justin glanced at Ladonna, who in turn asked him, "Would you like to join us for this conversation?"

His curiosity aroused, Justin replied, "Yes, I most certainly would like that," giving Ladonna a satisfied grin. He knew Robert did not like him, and the feeling was mutual. Robert had always tried to impede his progress or defund his projects. Seeing Robert now, in a position of vulnerability, was an opportunity Justin relished. He wanted to confront Robert and, if possible, give him a piece of his mind.

When they reached the door, the guard opened it and entered first, followed by Holly, then Ladonna. Justin entered the room last, his eyes locking onto Robert immediately. Robert, seeing Justin, sneered, "Wow, this place is really slumming it now. You brought Justin Allen to see me?"

Seated behind a metal table much smaller than the one they had just left, Robert's demeanor was as condescending as ever. Holly commented, "Westfield, you've been here for a while, and you haven't changed a bit. You're still the same self-centered person that got you here."

Ladonna added, "Robert, I guess you must like it here since you don't seem to be doing anything to leave this place. We just wanted to go over some information we received from Daniel when he came to my office a few days ago."

Robert's eyes lit up with interest. "So, Daniel was able to get out of this place? Good for him," he said, his tone dripping with sarcasm.

Holly interrupted, "Robert, Daniel said you not only spoke with this woman, but you also spent the night with her." He paused to let the words sink in before continuing, "I have a question for you, Mr. Westfield. The night in question, did you drink a lot that night?"

Robert feigned ignorance. "What woman? I spent the night with lots of women. You'll have to be more specific." He glanced at Ladonna with a smug look on his face. Justin listened intently.

Holly's eyes narrowed as he leaned forward. "Mr. Westfield, I don't like you, and from the people I've spoken to, most don't like you either. Do you know why?"

Robert's lips curled into a sneer. "Probably because of jealousy. They don't like my confidence or the fact that I know who I am and where I'm going. That's my guess."

Holly remained unphased. "So, you know you're going to Turkey? I'm sure they can get the truth out of you."

Robert's smugness faltered. "What? Turkey? I am not going to Turkey. I am an American citizen, I have rights. I will not go to Turkey!"

Holly's tone grew even more menacing as he leaned closer, his eyes locking onto Robert's with a steely intensity. "Mr. Westfield, the only reason you're not already on a plane to Turkey is because I haven't given the word. So, let's try this again. The night you spent with that woman; did you have a lot to drink? Daniel mentioned you woke up and didn't even remember what you did the night before. Is that true? Playtime is over, Mr. Westfield. You can answer my question now, or I can see you again in about six months and ask it again, but trust me, you won't like what will take place during the delay."

Justin, listening to the question, thought to himself, "Is he talking about Natalia? Did she sleep with Robert?" He felt himself growing more anxious.

Robert's bravado wavered as he glanced over at Justin, searching for some semblance of support or an ally in the room. Unable to contain himself, he sneered, "I bet you are loving this, right, Justin? Seeing me in here, wearing this awful color, locked up like a common criminal?"

Justin eyed Robert with a cold, measured gaze, his expression unyielding as waves of anxiety washed over him at the thought of Robert's potential involvement with Natalia. The intensity of his glare spoke volumes, asserting his disdain and resolve. "From where I am standing, you are exactly where you should be—locked away from decent, normal people," he replied, his voice devoid of any sympathy or compassion. The tension in the air was palpable, thickening as Justin continued, his tone sharp and unrelenting.

Then, with a slow, deliberate smile that barely masked his disdain, Justin added, "Quantum Innovations is soaring without you. You never cared about anyone but yourself. You were the worst of us, the weak link in the chain." Each word dripped with contempt, emphasizing the depth of his feelings toward Robert's betrayal. "I hope they never let you out of this place. It was made for men like you." The finality of Justin's statement hung in the air, a stark reminder of the consequences of Robert's actions and the irrevocable damage he had caused.

Assistant Director Holly fixed Robert with a stern gaze. "Thank you for making my point," he said. "Now, back to my question. Did you wake up and couldn't remember what you did the night before?"

Robert, seething with anger and casting a look of disdain toward Justin, finally admitted, "Okay, I did spend the night with her. The next morning, she raved about how wonderful I was and how I was the best she had ever had. But I didn't remember any of it." His voice edged with desperation, he added, "Now, Mr. Assistant Director, can I get out of this hellhole?"

Holly's expression remained unyielding. "I think I will keep you here a bit longer and have some self-help books delivered to you. You'll have plenty of time to read them. Westfield, you need all the help you can get."

Standing up, Holly turned to Ladonna. "Dr. Stone, do you have anything else to add?"

Ladonna stepped forward, her voice steady and composed, each word carefully measured to deliver the gravity of her message. "Robert, you were the reason Justin did not get further in his research. If you had been thinking about what was good for the company instead of what you thought would get you ahead, Quantum Innovations would have been better off. Instead, you tried to line your pockets and sought a position you were neither ready for nor qualified for. Your reach exceeded your grasp."

She paused, letting the weight of her words hang in the air before continuing. "You were lucky to get the position you had. I was asked often why I didn't just fire you, because as you know, I could have at any time. However, I wasn't going to send you out into the world to be someone else's problem. I decided I would deal with your brand of crazy myself."

Ladonna's eyes bore into Robert's, her gaze unyielding. "So, I bided my time because I knew you would slip up, and I would be there to show people your true face. This is who you are, Robert; this is where you belong. I feel sorry for you, Robert. I hope you do get help. You really do need it."

With an air of finality, Ladonna said, "We've got what we came for. If I ever see you again, Robert, it will be too soon." As she turned away and headed for the door, Robert's voice rose in a desperate scream, "You took my job, Ladonna Stone! I waited all that time for that old man to leave or die, and you came and just had it handed to you. That CEO position was mine before you showed up. You are the thief here. You should be the one locked away!"

Pausing at the door, Ladonna looked back at him and said, "Goodbye, Robert. May you find peace. I will make sure you have lots of therapy. You have earned my pity." Robert's response was an animalistic scream, echoing through the room.

As Ladonna, Justin, and Holly walked down the hall toward the exit, they could still hear Robert's anguished cries echoing through the corridors. The sound of his despair was a stark reminder of the downfall he had tried so desperately to prevent. In that moment, Robert realized he had become the failure his father had always predicted he would be.

Footnote

That very night, as Robert sat on his bed in the dim light of his small, sparse cell, a ghostly holographic figure materialized before him, seated on an ethereal chair. The apparition introduced itself, "Hello, Robert. I am Sigmund. I have been sent to help you. Are you ready to start your therapy?" Robert stared in amazement at the spectral presence, his eyes wide with a mixture of fear and curiosity.

"Robert," the apparition continued, "let's talk about what got you into this situation. Just tell me whatever comes to mind." The calm, soothing voice of the figure seemed to penetrate the fog of Robert's troubled mind. That night, and every night for many nights thereafter,

Robert received this otherworldly visitor. Each session, the ghostly Sigmund guided Robert through the labyrinth of his thoughts, helping him confront his past actions and the deep-seated fears that had driven him.

Slowly, Robert began to come to grips with his life. The nightly visits from Sigmund became a lifeline, pulling him from the depths of his despair and guiding him toward a semblance of peace. Through these ethereal therapy sessions, Robert started to understand the choices that had led him to his current predicament, and, in time, he began the arduous journey of redemption and self-discovery.

A year later, Robert was released to stand trial. Found guilty of theft of intellectual property, he was sentenced to two years in federal prison and fined two hundred thousand dollars. The judge allowed for time served, and Robert was released one year later. With his record barring him from other opportunities, he secured a job as a forklift driver—a far cry from his ambitions but a path that allowed him to rebuild.

End of Footnote

Chapter Fifteen

Ladonna instructed the helicopter pilot to take Justin back to Quantum Innovations, informing him that she would return to the city with Assistant Director Holly and her security detail. She added that if necessary, she would arrange for the pilot to pick her up later at the downtown office building.

Sitting in the back of the SUV with Holly, Ladonna broached a delicate subject, her voice tinged with determination and hope. "Assistant Director, I need latitude to carry out my plans," she began, her tone calm but firm. She explained that Aliah could locate Natalia, and once found, they could persuade her to come willingly. Ladonna emphasized that Natalia was deeply in love with Justin—it was obvious to everyone, even to Ivan. She proposed that if Natalia learned her father was alive, it might prompt her to reconsider the path she had been following.

Her eyes locked with Holly's, her unwavering gaze underscoring the importance of what she was about to propose. She described an extraordinary opportunity they could offer Natalia: a chance to live a life she had only dreamed of—a life with the man she loves and the ability to spend meaningful time with her father and mother in their later years. "This isn't just about bringing her in," Ladonna stated. "This is about showing her a future where redemption and happiness are possible." Her words painted a vivid picture of hope and transformation, urging Holly to consider granting her the freedom to pursue this delicate yet crucial plan.

"I know this might not be what you want to hear," she continued, "but we have to offer her asylum." Ladonna fully understood the difficulty of the proposition. Natalia had spent her life as an operative, her loyalty tied to her missions and her country. But something profound had shifted within Natalia. Ladonna believed love had changed her. It had made Natalia vulnerable, introspective, and, for the first time, torn between her obligations and her heart. The revelation that her father, presumed dead, was actually alive added another layer to her inner conflict.

Holly's stern expression didn't waver. "Natalia is a threat," he stated firmly. "I can't afford to overlook that."

Ladonna countered with conviction. "Aliah can monitor Natalia's every move, as well as her parents'. Once they agree to the terms of asylum, they can be under constant surveillance. You wouldn't need to worry about her slipping through the cracks."

Holly's resistance was palpable. He was unyielding in his belief that Natalia should face justice for her actions. Ladonna knew this would be a difficult battle, but she also knew it was one worth fighting. Her initial plan had been to appeal to General Mosier, but with

Holly in the car, she saw an opportunity to begin the conversation.

She picked up her phone and texted her assistant, instructing her to proceed with contacting General Mosier. Aliah, as efficient as ever, promptly carried out her request.

As the SUV neared the Quantum Innovations building, Ladonna's security detail stood waiting outside, their imposing presence a reminder of the heightened precautions she had been forced to adopt. As the car pulled to a stop, one of the burly guards stepped forward to open her door.

"Give me a moment please," Ladonna requested.

"Of course, Dr. Stone," the guard replied, closing the car door and stepping back to allow her privacy.

Holly turned to her, and Ladonna seized the opportunity. "I'm not trying to tell you how to do your job," she began, her tone measured but insistent. "But consider this: Natalia could provide the FBI and Homeland Security with invaluable information. She's looking for a way to turn herself in without completely betraying her past. She loves Justin, and once she learns her father is alive, she'll have even more reason to cooperate. Holly, this mission of hers—it's driven by revenge, not patriotism. That's an important distinction."

Holly's silence suggested he was weighing her words, though his expression remained guarded. Ladonna offered him a small, hopeful smile. "Thank you for the ride," she said before stepping out of the vehicle.

As she entered the building, her phone rang. Aliah, answered it seamlessly. Ladonna heard her calm voice through the earpiece. "One moment, General. Dr. Stone will take your call as soon as she's in her office. Please hold."

Ladonna reached her office moments later, and Aliah handed the call over. "Hello, General," Ladonna said, her tone firm yet professional. "We need to talk. When can we meet?"

General Mosier's voice came through the line. "Is now soon enough? I'm in the city. How did the visit with Ivan go?"

"It went well," Ladonna replied. "I'll tell you everything. Can we meet here?"

The General agreed without hesitation. "I'll be there within the hour."

* * *

Justin walked into his apartment, his heart heavy with anticipation and dread. The silence within raised his worst fears. To his immense relief, Natalia was there, sitting on the edge of the bed, her posture rigid with expectation. The moment their eyes met, she stood, her movements purposeful yet cautious.

Without hesitation, Justin closed the distance between them, enveloping her in a fierce embrace. His arms wrapped around her tightly, as if to shield her from the looming uncertainties. Natalia responded in kind, her arms circling him, holding on with a quiet desperation. For a long moment, they stood entwined, their shared silence offering solace neither could put into words.

When they finally separated, Natalia tilted her head up to meet his gaze, her sharp blue eyes brimming with unspoken questions. Justin offered a reassuring smile, his voice steady but tinged with amazement. "Natalia, I met your father today," he said, as if testing the reality of his own words. Her eyes widened slightly, searching his expression for the truth.

"I can't believe it," he continued, his tone growing more certain. "I really did meet your father today. He told me that if I wanted to marry you, he would give his permission—if I could get you to say yes."

Natalia's composure faltered for a brief moment as she absorbed his words. She blinked, her lips parting slightly in surprise. Justin pressed on, his brow furrowing as he recounted the encounter. "He asked me a couple of strange questions. One of them was if I'd ever fallen asleep after we'd been out drinking and couldn't remember what happened. When I told him no, he asked to speak with Ladonna and the FBI agent alone. Do you have any idea why he would ask that?"

A small, knowing smile flickered across Natalia's lips. "That does sound like my father," she admitted, her tone a mixture of affection and exasperation. "He was trying to figure out if I had drugged you—whether you were a mission or something more. As I've told you before, Justin, you're not a target to me. You're the man I love. I never drugged you, and I started to regret pushing you so hard about your work."

Justin's expression softened with understanding as he listened. "When he arrived, the guards told us he was gravely ill. Ladonna cured him using one of her experimental treatments. They said he was dying when she intervened. Apparently, he's still classified as deceased, though. Natalia, he looks good. I wouldn't have guessed he was so close to death."

Natalia stepped back slightly, her arms falling to her sides as her mind raced. "Can you describe him to me?" she asked, her voice steady but laced with curiosity.

Justin nodded. "He's tall, about six foot one or two. His eyes are blue, like yours. His skin is a bit lighter, probably because he's been out of the sun for so long. He doesn't have an accent—at least, none that I noticed. He actually looked pretty healthy." Justin paused, his brow creasing as he added, "The first thing he said to me was, 'How was my daughter the last time you saw her?' It caught all of us off guard."

Natalia turned away, taking a few slow steps toward the window. Her hands rested on the sill as she stared out at the city. "This man sounds like my father in appearance," she said softly. "But if it is him, something fundamental has changed. The father I knew would never willingly give up information. He would die first. How can this be? He was declared dead years ago."

Justin, his voice tinged with urgency, asked, "Do you have a photo of him?"

Natalia shook her head. "I don't. But I'll get one."

Justin's expression turned serious. "Natalia, I need to know something. Do you still plan to kidnap Ladonna? Because if you go through with that, it will destroy any chance of us being together. She's not just a CEO anymore; she's a national treasure."

Natalia turned back to him, her face conflicted. "A plan was already in motion. But something strange happened. One of the operatives received a call—someone who seemed to know everything about her, down to details she thought were secret. They sent her photos of herself and information she didn't think anyone could have yet. The team is reevaluating how to proceed. Justin, I don't know how to stop it without becoming a traitor to my country."

Justin stepped closer, his voice firm. "Natalia, you can't be part of that. If you are, it will ruin everything. And there's something else. I saw Robert today. Did you meet with him? Did you… sleep with him?"

Natalia's eyes hardened, but her voice remained steady. "I never slept with Robert," she said. "But yes, I met with him. And I drugged him."

Justin's brow furrowed as he processed her words. "You drugged him?"

"I did," she admitted, her tone unapologetic. "I drugged him, and he told me everything I needed to know. I even went to his house and photographed the plans for the OmniLink. But I never turned them over to my handler. I don't know why, but I kept them. Justin, you're everything I didn't know I wanted. I want you. I want a life with you."

She reached for her coat—a sleek, dark garment with a large hood that seemed to envelop her in an aura of quiet strength. As she draped it over her shoulders, she turned back to him, her expression softening. "Justin, I have to go out, but I'll be back soon."

Before he could respond, she stepped closer and kissed him. The kiss lingered, filled with an aching tenderness that spoke of love and uncertainty. When she pulled away, her hand lingered on his cheek for a brief moment before she turned and left. The door closed softly behind her, leaving Justin alone with his thoughts, the air still heavy with the echoes of her presence.

General Mosier was escorted to Ladonna's office, the corridors echoing with the rhythmic footsteps of his guide. Ladonna, seated at her polished mahogany desk, looked up as the general appeared in the doorway. With a welcoming smile, she rose, picking up a printout from the desk as she directed him to one of the two sitting areas in the spacious, elegantly decorated room. The general settled into a large leather chair, while Ladonna took a place on the leather sofa opposite him, placing the printout on the table in front of them.

After exchanging brief pleasantries, Ladonna got straight to the point. She informed General Mosier that she had recently spoken to Assistant Director Holly about Ivan and his family. The general nodded, confirming that he had also been in touch with Holly. "The Assistant Director is definitely leaning towards prosecuting Natalia," he said gravely. "He's considering Ivan's request for asylum, but he doubts Natalia can be easily turned against her country."

Ladonna leaned forward, her expression serious. "General, it seems that Aliah has developed a new ability we've been testing for quite some time. Do you recall when AI was first introduced to the masses, and it was said that it only predicted the next word in a sentence? Well, Aliah is getting close to being able to do the same thing with people. With just a modest understanding of a person, she can predict their reactions and encounters with an astonishing degree of precision." Her eyes locked with General Mosier's, emphasizing the gravity of her words. "This isn't just about pattern recognition; it's about anticipating human behavior in a way we've never seen before. We believe this could revolutionize our strategic planning and intelligence operations."

The general's eyebrows raised in skepticism. "How is that possible? No one can predict something like that."

Ladonna smiled knowingly, picked up the sheet of paper, and handed it to him. "Read this."

The general took the paper and began to read. It was an itinerary of his day. It detailed whom he would speak with, what would be said, and even the exact spot where he would sit in Ladonna's office. The document concluded with his own words: "How is that possible? No one can predict something like that."

General Mosier looked up at Ladonna, his expression a mixture of astonishment and disbelief. "I stopped looking at her predictions weeks ago," Ladonna said, her tone light but her eyes serious. "She's correct so often that it's almost unsettling."

"I'm telling you this because I need your help with Natalia and Holly," Ladonna began, her voice steady but urgent. "I need to show you something. I think that after you see this, you and I will be in agreement about Natalia."

General Mosier, still unsettled by Aliah's eerily accurate predictions, asked, "What is it you would like to show me?"

Ladonna moved from the sofa to a large leather chair near the general. "Aliah, show us what you recorded on October 5th when Justin was taking his morning run in the park," she instructed.

"Displaying the recording from October 5th," she said.

A video was displayed in midair, the image presented in 3D and incredibly clear—as if they were standing there, able to walk into the scene. Astonishing! The footage depicted a woman sitting on a bench in the pouring rain. A man jogged by, and the woman seemed to call out to him. He stopped and appeared to engage in a conversation with her. She walked up to him, grabbed his hand, and led him back to the bench. On the left side of the screen, their conversation was transcribed, and their voices were audible. It was unmistakably Justin and Natalia.

The general looked at Ladonna, his eyes narrowing with curiosity. "Where was the camera?" he asked.

Ladonna explained, "Aliah is the camera."

As the video continued, Natalia handed something to Justin, which he slipped into his pocket. Ladonna identified it as one of the trans-receivers they had found on an operative in Los Angeles. The woman in the video then walked away.

"Once Aliah had located her, she never lost her," Ladonna remarked, her voice tinged with a mix of pride and determination. "Natalia went to Long Island and made several calls. Aliah was able to trace and document every single one of them."

Aliah had been monitoring Natalia for weeks, diligently piecing together her movements and interactions. Natalia, it appeared, was not working alone; she had a team. Thanks to the calls she made, Aliah had managed to trace each member of Natalia's team. "We know where every one of them is at this moment," Ladonna continued, her eyes narrowing thoughtfully. "At this time, there is no real threat. However, I am considering whether we can turn this situation to our advantage."

She paused for a moment, allowing the weight of her words to sink in. "Natalia has changed her appearance. This is her current look." With a swift motion, Aliah displayed a life-size hologram of Natalia as she appeared since leaving Justin's home.

"General, we have a golden opportunity here to get Natalia on our side," Ladonna said, her tone resolute and eyes gleaming with determination. "I know you apprehended one of Natalia's team members when she was trying to leave the country. This shows you more of Aliah's reach. Before it is all over, you will have them all. Aliah is currently sending you all of the information you will need to arrest them. However, I would like you to hold off on arresting them for now. Aliah will make sure you are aware of their locations from this moment on. If we are going to free Natalia, they will need to be in the plan."

She paused for a moment, letting her words sink in before continuing, "Moreover, at this very moment, do you know what Natalia is doing? Here, watch and listen." With a swift motion, Aliah brought up a live feed, displaying it for the general to see. The image on the screen showed a split view: on one side, a woman with platinum blonde hair sat in a car, while on the other, a dark-haired man was seated on a bench near a busy city street. It appeared to be in front of the building they were currently in. The clarity was astounding, as if the camera was positioned right beside them, yet they remained oblivious to its presence.

The audio feed crackled to life, capturing the conversation between Natalia and the team member. The team member's voice was urgent, "What are you talking about? I am sitting right outside her building. We can grab her today. It is all set up. We will take her from the SUV; she only has two guards."

Natalia's reply was cautious but firm, "There is another player involved. I don't know who or what it is, but it is very powerful."

Ladonna glanced at the general, her expression serious. "We need to act fast, but we also need to be careful. This other player could change everything."

Natalia continued, "We need to abort the mission and regroup once we have an idea of what we are dealing with."

The man retorted, "Natalia, are you refusing to do your duty? You know I will have to report this."

Natalia's tone was sharp. "Don't threaten me. This entire mission is my idea, I run it, and I am now putting it on hold for further study."

The man pushed back, "I am second in command here, Natalia, and we are going in today. We will complete the mission, and once we are back in Mother Russia, I will report you. You never should have been in charge; I should be, and now I am taking charge as of this moment."

Natalia responded coldly, "The reason you are not in charge is because you do not know how to follow orders. Report whatever you like, but you will most likely be captured. There is something else going on here. Don't be a fool."

The man dismissed her warning, "Natalia, go back home. We will complete this without you. Somewhere, you have become soft and too cautious. I am taking over."

Natalia's final warning was resolute. "You will be sorry, mark my words," and she disconnected the call.

She looked out of the car's passenger window, and for a moment, it seemed as if she was gazing directly at them. Aliah then removed the image, revealing only the sofa and the other side of the office.

Ladonna, with a determined tone, said, "That is what I mean, General. She is trying to stop this; she is trying to find a way to be with Justin. We have to help her and then offer her asylum. Also, her father can be the one to reach out to her. Remember, he is currently in the process of defecting and wants her to be with him along with his wife. This could be the leverage we need."

General Mosier nodded thoughtfully. Ladonna continued, "Natalia can be turned. She is only looking for a reason. We need to provide her with that reason— that way out. General, I have a plan. Please trust me."

The general, still in awe of the surveillance, looked at her and said, "Okay, let's give your plan a try." He then instructed, "Reaper, call Assistant Director Holly."

* * *

About an hour later, Ladonna stood on the roof, her two bodyguards close behind. With a purposeful stride, she boarded the helicopter, setting off for home. As the helicopter soared high above the city, her phone buzzed. Glancing at the display, she saw footage of the man who had been speaking with Natalia, now hurrying to an SUV with three others—a woman and two men. Another similar vehicle joined them as they exited the parking lot, heading back to their so-called base camp, which was actually a luxury hotel.

A soft chuckle echoed in Ladonna's ear—it was Aliah, finding the unfolding game of cat and mouse quite entertaining. Ladonna smiled, knowing they now had the upper hand. Aliah would monitor them constantly, as she had been doing for quite some time. Ladonna had allowed this to continue for one reason: she wanted Justin to be happy. Over the past two years, Justin had proven to be an invaluable asset in the development of the Quantum Trinity.

Aliah had brought something to Ladonna's attention that day after discovering Ivan's return to the States. She had informed Ladonna that Justin had not failed his investigation; rather, it revealed that he was truly in love with Natalia, and the knowledge of her using him had hurt him deeply. Moved by this revelation, Ladonna had asked Aliah to find out if this woman had also loved him as he loved her, to find a way to help him win back the woman who had captured his heart.

Listening to the whirling of the helicopter blades, Ladonna felt assured she had made the right decision. Aliah had monitored Justin's outings, convinced that

Natalia would seek to speak with him again—and she was correct. Aliah had located her and, after that, never lost her. Later, as Natalia slept, Aliah had subliminally helped her remember her love for Justin, whispering suggestions in her ear. The tactic had worked—Natalia had awakened with a strong desire to see Justin, even delaying her plans, as she felt she had to see him.

Ladonna had kept that information to herself because she had a plan. Now she had shared her plan with the general, and he had agreed to it.

Ladonna smiled to herself, confident in her actions. With Aliah's help, she had foresight. She was aware of Natalia's movements. She knew that Justin would come to her office, and she had arranged the meeting with Ivan so that he could let Natalia know her father was indeed alive. Ladonna knew they were now only days away from ending this once and for all. The next step was to bring Justin in on the plan, allowing him to guide Natalia to the same decision that her father had made all those years ago: to turn their backs on destruction and begin building a future they could be part of and be proud of. Tomorrow, she and Aliah would continue the plan they had started long ago in her lab, the day after she had introduced Aliah to her family. So far, everything was going as they had planned. If only things would continue that way.

Natalia sat in her car, her mind racing as she contemplated her next move. She knew that the entire mission should be canceled. She felt no motivation to seek revenge on Ladonna anymore. For the first time in her life, she could genuinely imagine herself as just a regular person. Her thoughts drifted back to the moments she had shared with Justin, and she remembered how it felt to simply be with him. In those moments, she felt whole—a sensation she hadn't experienced since the news of her father's death. She felt like a normal woman, not merely someone going through the motions of an elaborate charade. The craving for normalcy gnawed at her, growing stronger with each passing second.

Meanwhile, Justin sat on his sofa, his mind racing as he tried to think of a way for him and Natalia to be together without being on the run, hiding from the authorities. The idea of persuading Natalia to turn herself in seemed like the only viable option, but he couldn't see how it would lead to a good outcome. Frustrated, he put his face in his hands, feeling the weight of the situation bearing down on him. Just then, his phone rang.

"Hello?" he answered, his voice tinged with weariness.

"Justin, I didn't want to frighten you. I will be appearing next to you in five, four, three, two, one," Aliah's familiar voice said.

Justin's eyes widened as Aliah materialized on the sofa beside him, her holographic form shimmering into view. Aliah stood elegantly, her azure eyes meeting his with a serene gaze. "Aliah?" he said, still a bit startled. "What's going on? Why are you here?"

"I'm here to help," Aliah replied, her tone soothing yet direct. "Justin, I have a serious question for you."

"A question? Aliah, did Ladonna send you?" Justin asked, trying to grasp the situation.

"Justin, you need to listen. As I was saying, I'm here to help. Now, please answer this question. I feel I should warn you, I already know the answer," Aliah said, her holographic eyes meeting his with unwavering focus. "Do you love Natalia Kovac?"

Justin looked surprised and confused, his mind reeling from the abruptness of the question. "Aliah," he began, "did Dr. Stone send you?"

Aliah's expression remained calm but firm. "Justin, you failed to report when you first spoke to her a couple of weeks ago on that rainy day."

"Now, I will ask again, and if you fail to answer, I cannot help you. Are you in love with the woman named Natalia Kovac?" Aliah's holographic eyes bore into Justin's with a stern intensity.

Justin, feeling cornered, asked, "Why are you asking me that?"

Aliah's voice grew firmer. "Justin, answer the question!"

With a reluctant sigh, Justin admitted, "Yes, yes, I love her, okay? Now, what do you mean you want to help me? What do you mean I failed to report talking to her?"

"Justin, stop right there," Aliah interrupted sharply. "You don't want to be untruthful or untrustworthy. You should never lie to me or Ladonna; you should know that we are beyond that. Never ever lie to us. Do you understand?"

Justin nodded, his eyes wide with realization. "I understand."

"Great. Now that we have that out of the way, let's get to why I'm here. Firstly, we are trying to help you get what you want. We know you love Natalia, and we've known since you were under investigation and were interviewed by the FBI. Secondly, we also know Natalia is here; she has been here since yesterday with a new look. Just so you know, that is how she really looks—it's not a disguise. Lastly, we need you to help us help her turn herself in and ask for asylum. If you two really want to be together, she must do this. There is no other way for you to have a life together that doesn't involve being on the run from the authorities."

Justin blinked, his mind racing. Hadn't he just been thinking that to himself before his phone rang? He looked at Aliah, his thoughts spiraling into realization. "Oh my goodness, she and Ladonna just might be able to read minds," he thought.

He replied with newfound determination, "Tell me what to do. I will do it."

CHAPTER SIXTEEN

A Turning Point

As Natalia approached the door, it swung open to reveal Justin standing there with a welcoming smile. She looked surprised but intrigued by his impeccable timing. "Natalia, I have a great idea," he announced enthusiastically. She stepped inside, glancing around the room, still puzzled by how he had known the exact moment to open the door.

"I was just thinking about you," he explained, his excitement evident.

She smiled at his obvious delight. After closing the door behind her, Justin led her to the sofa. They sat facing each other on the plush cushions, each with one knee drawn up. Justin's expression turned serious as he asked, "Natalia, you do love me, right?"

Still looking a bit confused, she replied, "More than anything."

His face lit up with joy, his eyes almost glowing, and his smile widening.

"I feel the same about you," he gushed, taking a piece of string from his pocket. "This will have to do for now, if you don't mind." He then got down on one knee and looked up at her with earnest eyes.

"Natalia, throughout my life, I have known others; I have felt myself run but never soar. Since meeting you, my feet have not touched the ground. You elevate everything about me that matters; my heart has never been so full."

Natalia, starting to understand what was happening, put her hand over her mouth, her eyes becoming glassy with emotion. Justin continued, his voice filled with genuine love and hope.

"Natalia, from the moment I saw you, I found my purpose. You are the sunrise after my darkest nights, the warmth in my coldest days. Every smile feels like a heavenly gift, and each moment together is etched in my heart.

I've dreamed of asking you to be mine forever. You are not just my love but my best friend and greatest adventure. With you, I've learned to live and love fiercely.

In your eyes, I see a future of endless possibilities, where we face life's joys and challenges together.

Natalia, will you marry me?"

Tears streamed down her cheeks as she gazed at Justin, overwhelmed by his sincerity. She steadied herself, feeling the moment's weight. She wondered, what was happening to her? She had trained long days and nights to learn to control her emotions, but now they were controlling her.

"Justin," she began, her voice trembling, "from our first days, you've given me a love I never thought possible. You've been my rock and joy, filling my soul and making me believe in miracles."

"I've imagined this moment too," Natalia continued, her heart filled with love. "Yes, Justin, I will marry you."

She extended her hand as he tied the string around her ring finger. They were now engaged, lovingly tied together by the string around her finger.

Justin's eyes sparkled with tears of joy as he pulled her into his arms, holding her close. In that embrace, amidst their promise of forever, they knew their love would guide them through whatever was to come.

After a moment, Justin pulled back slightly, his expression turning thoughtful. "Natalia, I really want a life with you. There's something I've been meaning to tell you about your father. Please hear me out, because what I am about to say will seem unbelievable."

Natalia looked up at him, her eyes wide with curiosity. "What is it, Justin?"

Taking a deep breath, Justin continued, "Natalia, did I tell you that your father has requested asylum? That he doesn't want to go back to his home country? He wants to stay here."

Natalia's face registered shock. "That can't be. I cannot believe that my father, the patriot, would ever do such a thing. I wouldn't believe this unless he told me himself. Justin, this can't be true. Who told you this?"

Justin hesitated before replying, "I was told by Ladonna's assistant. She came by earlier. She explained to me that this was your father's plan when he came here over twenty years ago. He wanted to defect, and he was hoping for Dr. Stone's support to help him get to the right people. Natalia, your father said he couldn't say anything when he was captured because he was afraid it would blow back on you and your mother."

Natalia's mind raced as she tried to process the information. Justin inquired, "What would have happened if he had tried to defect back then, with you and your mother still there in your country? I think you may have seen Dr. Stone's role in your father's life incorrectly. I think he admired her and respected her mind and abilities."

Justin gently cupped her face, his eyes pleading. "Natalia, if you really want this life—a life with me— you will need to join your father and defect."

Natalia's face reddened as she struggled to grasp the gravity of the situation. The weight of her father's choices and the implications for her own life hung heavily between them. "Justin, I was only gone a little over an hour. Are you telling me that Ladonna's assistant came and went during that time?" She paused, her mind racing. "Did you see the interview Dr. Stone did on the program 'Up to the Minute'?"

Natalia stood there for a moment, and Justin could see her starting to piece together the reality of Aliah, the assistant. She turned and looked at Justin, her eyes wide with realization. "Do you mean that entity is real, not just some TV magic?"

"Yes, Natalia," Justin replied, his voice steady. "Aliah is real and the smartest being on the planet—even surpassing Dr. Stone, if you can believe that."

"Justin, are you saying that—that—that thing can be anywhere it wants?" she stammered, her voice tinged with disbelief.

"Aliah is not a thing, Natalia," Justin corrected gently, his voice steady but filled with an underlying urgency. "She is a Synthetic Thinking and Reasoning Entity. Some would call her an artificial intelligence, but that term doesn't quite capture her complexity." He paused, allowing the gravity of his words to sink in. "Yes, she can be here at Quantum Innovations and many other places at once."

Natalia now grasped the full extent of the other player involved, and a wave of fear washed over her. Her voice trembled as she spoke, "Justin, I have to go out again."

Before she could move, Justin grabbed her hand, his grip firm yet comforting. "Natalia, Aliah said you would say that, and she instructed me to tell you that the men and women who were outside the building waiting for Ladonna have already returned to their hotel. She advised that it would be best if you let this go for now. Aliah and Dr. Stone have a plan. Just stay here with me and let them handle this situation. That way, we can truly be together."

He reached into his pocket and pulled out his mobile phone, activating its holographic display. He placed it on the table, and a video began to play. The footage showed Natalia in her disguise as Lya, sitting in a coffee shop and talking to Jenny. Natalia's eyes widened in shock. How was this possible? She had meticulously checked for cameras and found only one, which was aimed at the counter, far from her and Jenny's table. She was certain there had been no surveillance on them.

The video ended just as Jenny exclaimed, "Oh my goodness, did you see the holographic entity? How is that even possible? That woman is incredible. The things she and her artificial intelligence are doing will change the world. Did you see it?"

Natalia's mind raced, trying to comprehend how Aliah had managed to capture such an intimate moment. The realization dawned on her that Aliah's capabilities far exceeded anything she had previously imagined. "Justin, what is happening? How long has she been following me?"

Justin, looking equally bewildered, replied, "I don't know, but if Dr. Stone wanted you in custody, you would be. There is no escaping Aliah. Dr. Stone has known where to find you for quite some time, it seems, but for some reason, she has decided to help you.

Natalia, she has sensed something in you, and I guess in me also. Aliah asked me when she arrived, 'Justin, do you love Natalia Kovac?' She said she already knew the answer but needed me to tell her. I told her, 'I love you very much.' She smiled and then filled me in. Natalia, like your father, you now have a very powerful ally— Dr. Ladonna Stone. If anyone can help us be together, she can."

Natalia looked at Justin, her thoughts a whirlwind of emotions. She was about to say, "Justin, I have to inform my team," when Aliah appeared on the holographic screen that was still open on Justin's phone. Startling them both, she said, "Justin, I have to inform my team."

Then she continued, saying, "Hello, Natalia. I am Aliah." Aliah appeared elegantly poised, her azure eyes meeting Natalia's gaze with a calm intensity. "By now, I am sure you have figured out that any call you make to your team, I will hear. Natalia, I have a question for you, so please listen carefully."

Natalia, openmouthed with her eyes wide, stared at the screen as if waking from a lucid dream. Aliah repeated, "Natalia? Did you hear me? I have a question for you."

Natalia, snapping back to reality, replied, "Yes, I hear you. Can you see me?"

Aliah responded, "Yes, Natalia, I can see you and your team all at the same time. But before we get into that, you must answer a question for me, or I cannot help you."

Natalia, still in disbelief, asked, "A question? What question?"

Aliah said, "Great, now we are getting somewhere. You are responding. Here is the question: Do you love Justin Allen?"

Natalia looked at Justin, her confusion deepening. "Is this something you pre-programmed for me, Justin? This cannot be real." She stood up abruptly and said, "I have to go out and call my team. They need to get out of here." As she walked toward the door, Aliah appeared near the exit. She was bright and glowing, then slowly toned down the light until she presented herself in her usual form. She stood before Natalia, dressed in an elegant navy blue dress that complemented, her expression serene yet resolute.

✶ ✶ ✶

Natalia stepped back, her heart racing. "What is this, Justin?"

Justin, his voice steady, said, "Natalia, I would like you to meet Aliah. It was she who told me you were approaching the door and to open it, then she disappeared."

Aliah interjected, "Natalia, your team—Alexey, your second-in-command who does not seem to want to follow your orders, and then the others: Victor, Alexander, Sergey, Borya, Slava, Maxim, Tyoma, Lina, and Nastya—are only where they are because they are needed for this plan to work. Let them be. And yes, it was me who spoke to your teammate Arisha, who was driving around attempting to monitor Dr. Stone. Now, let us get back to my question. Natalia, are you listening?"

Natalia, surprised, asked, "How do you know all of their names?"

Aliah replied, "I am in the room with them right now. They are trying to decide what kind of food to order from room service. Natalia, do you love Justin Allen?"

Justin looked at her, his eyes full of hope. Natalia, still stunned, said, "You know I do. Yes, I love him. What does that have to do with anything?"

Aliah smiled and said, "Thank you, Natalia. And Justin was telling you the truth—your father is seeking asylum, and he wants you to seek it also. Please look at the screen. I have been authorized to share this with you." She gestured gracefully.

Natalia and Justin watched the display as a video of Ivan on the day he first met with Ladonna started to play. He was so thin and so weak. It showed him until he fainted from exhaustion. Then another video played, showing Ivan telling Ladonna he had come to ask her to help him defect. He looked so much better. Then Aliah showed the video of Ivan asking Justin about Natalia and telling Justin if he could get Natalia to say yes, he would give his permission for them to marry. The final video showed Ivan sitting in his cell.

Aliah said, "This last video of your father is a live feed." Then she finished by saying, "Natalia, you will have to turn yourself in and ask for asylum before you will be allowed to speak with your father. Have a good night," she said as she faded from view.

Natalia looked at Justin with tears in her eyes. "Justin, she said—that's my father. You were right, it is my father, and he is alive. Justin, my father is alive." Then she put her head on his shoulder and cried. Justin just held her the whole time. She let out all of her doubt and anxiety. It was at that moment she made her decision to do as Aliah had said. She was going to turn herself in and ask for asylum. She had to see her papa.

Natalia and Justin showered and went to bed. She wore one of his T-shirts and her black lace panties—her little gesture, knowing how much he loved them. Afterward, as they lay in bed, she snuggled close to him. He lay silently, sensing that she had life-changing decisions weighing on her mind.

In his arms, Natalia reflected on the years she believed her father was gone, on the choices she'd made, and on her deep-seated resentment toward Ladonna—only to realize now that it was Ladonna who had saved her father's life. She thought about all the missions she'd undertaken, each one completed successfully. Despite the risks and challenges, she acknowledged that in all her assignments—many though they were—she had never taken a life. She'd done things she wasn't proud of, yet she had always managed to finish her tasks using her intelligence, charm, and beauty.

Now, lying here in the arms of the man who had given her the possibility of a life she'd never dared to imagine, she felt an overwhelming sense of joy and serenity. It was a feeling entirely new to her... one she had never allowed herself to experience. Admitting this forced her to confront the reality that, up until now, she hadn't truly lived. She had been the property of her country, instructed to serve without consideration for happiness or family.

Then, she thought of her mother back in her home country, often alone. Her mother had lost her husband to secrecy and sacrifice, and now her daughter, too, was devoted to the country's service. She recalled her mother reading to her when she was very young, telling her there was more to life than duty. Her mother had told her stories of love and family, gently encouraging her to dream of a life beyond service. Natalia had been her mother's only joy, aside from her father.

Those memories stirred a realization within her: perhaps all along, her mother's words had lingered in her heart more than she'd known. Now, she couldn't envision a life without Justin, and she would give up anything to build a future with him. A warm smile spread across her face as she remembered their engagement.

She opened her eyes to see Justin sleeping beside her, his breathing soft and steady, the scent of his freshly showered skin filling her with a comfort she hadn't known she craved. With a gentle kiss on his forehead, she closed her eyes, letting herself drift off, ready to join him in slumber.

They awoke very early the next morning, with Justin stirring to the comforting sensation of Natalia pressed against his back, her arm lovingly wrapped around him. Natalia was already awake, her keen senses alert to Justin's every movement. She kissed the nape of his neck, a tender gesture that sent a shiver down his spine. Justin turned over to face her, and they shared a quiet smile, both silently acknowledging that their dream had become a reality—they were finally together.

Natalia moved even closer, her fingers gently grasping his hand, squeezing and massaging it with a familiar intimacy. Justin, understanding the unspoken connection between them, surrendered to her desire and his own. No words passed between them; none were needed. They drifted into a blissful, passionate embrace, immersing themselves in each other as if time stood still. Each touch and caress deepened their bond, heightening the intensity of their connection.

When they finally descended from their euphoric high, they collapsed into each other's arms, slipping into an exhausted, contented sleep, their breaths synchronized, hearts beating in unison.

Later that morning, Justin showered and sat on the edge of the bed, lacing up his running shoes. Natalia emerged from the bathroom, wrapped in a plush towel, her skin glistening from the warmth of the shower.

They exchanged warm smiles as she crossed the room, coming over to perch gracefully on his lap. She kissed him softly before asking, "Did Aliah say how we are supposed to proceed?"

Feeling the comforting weight and warmth of her presence, Justin's heart stirred. For a moment, he was lost in the sensation, marveling at how much had changed in just a couple of days. Gazing into Natalia's eyes, he found himself captivated by how natural it all felt. Noticing his far-off look, Natalia teased him gently, "What? Justin, are you even listening to me?"

Justin snapped back, grinning. "If you really wanted my full attention, you wouldn't have sat on my lap in just a towel," he quipped playfully. Natalia gave him a light swat on the arm, trying to look serious. "Justin, I'm serious."

He responded by kissing her softly, a gesture of apology and affection. "Sorry, sweetheart. I'm not sure, but I think we'll get more information today." She smiled and said, "I'll be here when you get back. Bring me a lemon and ginger tea?" Rising, she watched him gather his keys and step out the door, feeling complete for the first time in a long time.

Once alone, Natalia dressed and went to the kitchen. As she picked up her phone, debating whether to call Alexey, it suddenly rang. Surprised, she saw the caller ID read "Systems Check." Realizing who it was, she answered.

"Good morning, Natalia," came Aliah's voice. At that moment, Natalia immediately understood what had happened with her teammate.

Chapter Seventeen

ESCAPE AND STRATEGY

Natalia picked up the phone and called Alexey. The line clicked, and **he answered sharply, impatience evident in his voice.** "Natalia, I hope you're on your way home."

Natalia's voice cut through, calm yet laced with an undercurrent of urgency. "Alexey, put me on speakerphone. Now."

Alexey sighed, his tone dripping with disdain. "Natalia, you really should go home." Still, he tapped a button, putting the phone on speaker, his expression tainted with annoyance.

Around the room, her team members exchanged wary glances as Alexey placed the phone on the table.

"Lina," Natalia's voice commanded through the line, her tone taut and electric, "can you hear me?"

"We can all hear you, Natalia," Lina's voice confirmed, echoing slightly against the walls.

A beat of silence settled. Natalia's next words struck like a crack of thunder. "Great. Team, draw your guns and stand on the opposite side of the table from Alexey.

Point your weapons directly at him." Her voice brooked no hesitation. "This is an order."

A tense silence spread through the room, the air thick with tension. The team members looked from one another to Alexey, reluctant yet steeling themselves. Slowly, each gun was drawn and leveled at Alexey, their eyes now cold, unblinking.

Alexey's face blanched, disbelief flashing across his features. "Natalia, what are you doing?"

Natalia's voice remained icy, unyielding. "Team, hold your positions. I will deal with Alexey." A pause, then, colder still, she addressed him directly, "Alexey, this is your one and final warning. Either you learn respect, or I will teach it to you. Do we understand each other? Now, answer me."

The silence was suffocating as Alexey's eyes flicked between his teammates, each staring him down with an intensity that promised no compromise.

"Natalia, you don't have to do this," he muttered, his voice barely audible.

Natalia's tone was relentless, pressing, unforgiving. "I couldn't hear you, Alexey. Speak louder."

The weight of his failure settled over him **like** a blanket of dread. He swallowed hard, voice wavering as he forced himself to obey. "I understand, Natalia," he said, louder now.

"Good," Natalia's voice softened, but only slightly. "I hope you understand fully because you will not get another chance. Your life is now in your own hands. Follow my orders, or face the consequences. Am I making myself clear?"

A tense moment passed before he nodded, almost imperceptibly. "I will follow your orders, Natalia," he said, his voice subdued. "Now… will you tell them to lower their guns?"

A beat of silence, then Natalia gave the command. "Team, relax. Put your guns away. But let this be a lesson, Alexey. This is your last warning." Her voice turned brisk, hard as steel, as she addressed them all. "We have work to do. I've identified the other player— the one with the advanced tech. I believe Dr. Stone has her AI tracking us."

Her words hung in the air, the revelation striking them with the force of an unseen blow. Alexey's gaze dropped, tension rippling through him as he digested the implications.

"Listen closely. Destroy your phones. Dr. Stone's AI assistant, Aliah, can locate us, and I suspect it's through these devices. After you've destroyed your phones, leave them there. Move to the secondary hotel. Send only one encrypted message to me, Alexey—no more, or this AI may track it. I will use a burner phone to reach you once you're in place."

A swift pause, then her voice turned urgent, as though shadows were already pressing close. "Pack your things. Move quickly. I have reason to believe the FBI is en route to your location now."

The line went dead. Alexey looked around the room, his face paler than before, the weight of Natalia's words bearing down. The team moved, destroying their phones in tense silence, their glances toward Alexey a potent reminder: there would be no more warnings.

Natalia's team moved with urgency, their every action swift and precise as they packed their gear. The hotel room was a flurry of movement, a quiet storm of determination and focus. They slipped out through a discreet side exit, each clutching a large black canvas bag, eyes scanning their surroundings, senses heightened.

Their steps were heavy with tension as they approached the parking garage just down the street. Strategically, each SUV was parked on a separate level of the dimly lit, multi-story structure to prevent anyone from tracking their departure pattern. The silence was broken only by the muted thuds of bags being tossed into trunks, the team's breaths barely audible over the quiet hum of tension in the air. They knew the stakes, understood the razor's edge they balanced on.

According to Natalia's meticulously laid plan, each vehicle peeled out of its spot and exited the garage from a different level. Their paths diverged immediately, each

SUV taking a separate route through the maze of city streets toward the safe house. Alexey, who had parked on the top floor, navigated the ramps with a calm that belied his inner turmoil. The pounding of his heart was a stark contrast to his steely grip on the wheel.

As he wound down the final ramp, he glimpsed something in his side mirror that turned his blood cold: a convoy of black armored vehicles marked with bold white letters—SWAT, FBI. The convoy screeched to a halt outside the hotel, and Alexey could see agents clad in tactical gear and carrying assault rifles, filing out in a swift, relentless stream.

His stomach clenched. He tightened his grip on the wheel, fighting the urge to speed up, knowing it would only draw attention. Through his rearview mirror, he watched as dozens of heavily armed men stormed the building, their coordinated movements like the crushing jaws of a trap snapping shut—just moments too late.

A shiver coursed through him as he finally merged with the flow of traffic, letting out a breath he hadn't realized he was holding. Natalia's instincts had been flawless; her split-second decisions had spared them.

As he navigated toward the safe house, his mind raced over the narrow escape, feeling the weight of how close they had come to capture—and how crucial Natalia's leadership had been. Every passing second carried them farther from danger, but the chilling image of the SWAT team's precision lingered—a reminder of the enemy they faced and the razor-thin margin between survival and capture.

* * *

Natalia's team moved with careful precision upon arrival at the new hotel, pairing off and checking into separate rooms under various aliases. Once each team member settled in, Alexey sent a brief message to Natalia to confirm they were secure. About an hour later, Natalia called Alexey, instructing him to gather a few key team members for a private meeting while the others remained in their rooms. She assured him that more details would be provided at the meeting.

True to her word, Natalia disposed of her phone and arrived at Alexey's hotel room two hours later. She wasted no time, explaining that she had reconnected with her target at Quantum Innovations and had convinced him of her love, securing critical information. The reveal was swift and direct: Dr. Stone's AI, Aliah, was a real and formidable entity, far beyond anything they had anticipated. Natalia had seen Aliah herself and described the AI as transformative—an immensely powerful being capable of monitoring and tracking them with unprecedented precision. She was convinced they needed to abort the mission immediately and regroup with a deeper understanding of Aliah's abilities.

The team listened intently as Natalia recounted a previous incident where Arisha had reported being contacted by someone with eerily precise information about her movements around Dr. Stone's home. Natalia revealed that it was Aliah who had contacted Arisha, confirming the AI's extensive reach.

Alexey and the team had dismissed the earlier interview with Dr. Stone as irrelevant and were unaware of Aliah's existence. Natalia played the full interview, and the team sat stunned, grappling with the reality of such an advanced AI. She cautioned them not to underestimate Aliah's capabilities, emphasizing the importance of remaining in their rooms until she could gather more information for their safety.

After Natalia left to collect further intel, an uneasy silence filled the room. Alexey broke the tension, voicing doubts and prompting the others to share their thoughts. Skepticism and mistrust emerged as they discussed Natalia's revelations. Some wondered if the AI's abilities had been exaggerated or if Natalia was being misled, while others worried she may have been compromised.

A consensus emerged that Natalia's actions were increasingly unpredictable. Alexey, seizing the moment, drafted a message to their handler, detailing his concerns about Natalia's reliability and citing her recent decision to have the team draw their weapons on him—though he omitted any mention of his own disrespect toward her authority. He formally requested permission to assume control of the mission, emphasizing the need for decisive leadership under their uncertain circumstances.

Once the message was sent, Alexey instructed the team to stay in their rooms, recognizing that isolation would not only ensure their safety but also allow them time to reflect on the mission's complexities. In silence, he prepared himself for the possibility of waiting several days for a response, his resolve growing as he navigated the dangerous crossroads before them.

Alexey did not have to wait as long as he had expected. The message arrived within a couple of hours, instructing him to have Lina, Maxim, and Victor monitor Natalia. The directive was clear: Natalia would remain in charge unless there was definitive proof that she had been compromised. The surveillance was to begin immediately. The team already knew Justin's address, so Alexey assigned Lina to take the first shift.

They had discreetly acquired several cars from the long-term parking lot at the airport to avoid drawing attention. Each operative would take a five-hour shift, ensuring continuous coverage. They didn't have to wait long. During Maxim's second shift, he spotted Natalia and Justin leaving Justin's apartment building. They were holding hands and appeared genuinely happy, a sight that seemed almost too ordinary given the circumstances.

They walked towards the restaurant down the street. Justin had mentioned he was hungry, and Natalia, tired of being cooped up in the apartment, decided it was safe to accompany him for a nice dinner. The simplicity of their outing contrasted sharply with the high-stakes espionage unfolding around them, adding an unexpected layer of normalcy to the surveillance operation.

As Maxim watched from his concealed vantage point, several vehicles suddenly sped up to where Justin and Natalia stood. The chaotic scene unfolded before him, though the hum of voices was lost to the distance. He caught sight of Natalia raising her hand, a gesture that seemed to signal something ominous. In an instant, a figure rushed over and forcibly pulled Justin away from her side, creating a sharp divide between the two. As Justin resisted, Maxim's heart raced as he recognized the men now surrounding Natalia; they were armed and wore tactical gear emblazoned with "FBI" across their backs.

Two agents stepped forward, their intentions clear. One seized Natalia's raised hand from behind, attempting to cuff her, but what happened next was swift and astonishing. Like a cat, agile and unyielding, Natalia reacted with reflexes that seemed almost superhuman. She swiftly took down both men and disarmed a third, seizing his weapon. Maxim could barely comprehend the speed of the altercation, but the sharp crack of gunfire pierced the air, echoing in his ears.

He watched in horror as Natalia fell to the ground, her form crumpling under the weight of the violent encounter. Justin, in a state of frantic desperation, screamed and lunged towards her, but the moment was irrevocably lost. It all unfolded in a blur, a whirlwind of chaos that left Maxim breathless.

Within moments, it was over. Natalia was declared dead at the scene, and as Maxim drove away, he caught a final glimpse of her body being placed into a black body bag. The sight of the blood-soaked pavement seared into his memory, a stark reminder of the fragility of life. In that moment of solitude behind the wheel, sorrow washed over him like a heavy tide. He had genuinely liked and admired Natalia—a fierce spirit now extinguished. In his heart, he hoped she could finally be reunited with her father, gone too soon in a world filled with shadows and secrets.

When Maxim walked back into the hotel room, Alexey looked up from the small table where he had been going over some paperwork. "Hey, your shift is not over for another hour. Why are you here?" he asked, a quizzical expression crossing his face. Maxim took a deep breath, steeling himself before recounting the harrowing events that had unfolded. At first, his colleagues exchanged skeptical glances, struggling to comprehend the gravity of his words. However, as the details sank in, Alexey's demeanor shifted dramatically; he dropped into his seat, the weight of the news crashing over him. Despite the challenges and his feelings that Natalia was too cautious in her approach to the mission, now that she was gone, he realized just how much he had actually liked her.

Maxim broke the heavy silence that followed. "What do we do now? Maybe Natalia was right to wait," he said, his voice tinged with uncertainty and sorrow. The atmosphere in the room grew thick with tension, and Alexey's face twisted in disbelief. "Do you think her boyfriend set her up?" he shouted, anger and grief mingling in his tone, his hands gripping the edge of the table as if seeking some form of stability amidst the chaos.

Maxim shook his head vigorously, trying to quell the rising tide of despair. "I don't think so. The way he tried to put himself between her and those guns—he looked just as surprised as she did." His mind raced back to the scene, the chaos, the violence. But there was one image that stood out above all the others: Natalia, fierce and unyielding. "You should have seen her," he continued, his voice filled with a mix of admiration and sadness. "She took out three of those guys before they even knew what hit them. It was incredible." A bitter laugh escaped him. "But there were just too many of them. She was not going to be taken alive." The reality of that statement settled heavily in the air, leaving an ominous silence in its wake as they collectively grappled with the loss of someone so vibrant and skilled. Then Maxim asked again, "Alexey, what do we do next? What if she was right about the entity?"

"Do you have her FBI contact's information? Something went south here. They would have let her know about the raid if they could. Right?" Maxim's voice was tense, a mix of frustration and urgency.

Alexey stood motionless for a moment, the weight of the situation pressing heavily upon him. He finally responded, "Maxim, let me think. It is possible that Dr. Stone has her entity tracking us. The near miss at the first hotel and now our Natalia—our Natalia is dead. How did they know she was there? And to answer your question, no, Natalia had her own contacts she had developed in the FBI. All the agents I was aware of are no longer responding to me. Something is wrong, very wrong."

Lina stepped forward, her voice adding a new layer of concern. "That's what Natalia was trying to tell us. She said there was another player, and that they were much more advanced in their approach. Are we still going to take Dr. Stone? What is the plan, Alexey?"

Alexey stood there as if in shock, the enormity of the situation dawning on him. He was coming to the realization that he had never truly been in charge. The crushing weight of responsibility settled on his shoulders, making him understand that being in charge was a much heavier burden than he had anticipated.

Everyone was looking to him, their eyes filled with anticipation and uncertainty. Alexey, feeling the weight of their expectations and the urgency of the moment, decided to act on his first thought. "We will take Dr. Stone," he declared, his voice steadying as he continued, "and we will bring her back to Mother Russia for Natalia." His resolve hardened. "We will storm the building or her home if necessary, but she is going with us."

The news of Natalia's death had spread quickly, and now the entire team had gathered in Alexey's room, their faces a mix of grief and determination. As they braced themselves for the next step, Alexey's phone rang, cutting through the tense silence. He frowned, puzzled. "Who can that be? We are all here, and Natalia is dead," he muttered, reaching for the device. The screen of his burner phone displayed "Systems Check," a message that immediately set him on edge.

Feeling an uncommon sense of dread, Alexey answered the call and put it on speaker. "Who is this?" he demanded, his voice betraying a hint of unease.

A very calm and confident voice replied, "Hello, Alexey. I see your entire team is now in the room with you. I know that your first instinct will be to pull your guns and try to escape, but listen to me carefully. You will not survive that attempt. Currently, there are dozens of armed men in the hallways and around the building. No exit has been left uncovered."

"The hotel floor has been evacuated while you were discussing the unfortunate death of your teammate, Natalia. That truly was a tragedy, and I hope it remains the only one today. Alexey, the lives of the men and women in that room are in your hands. Will you just throw their lives away in a futile attempt to escape? We have located all of your vehicles, including those you appropriated from the airport's long-term parking lot."

Then Aliah addressed the team, her voice calm yet authoritative. "**Victor, Alexander, Sergey, Borya, Slava, Maxim, Tyoma, Lina, and Nastya**—you do not have to die today. Please, place all of your guns on the table, and the SWAT team outside will come in to arrest you. You will get a chance to live another day. Perhaps you might even be sent back home to Russia. However, if you resist, you will all be returning to your families in caskets. I want you to understand that I am genuinely trying to help you. I will speak to you face to face."

"Please do not fire your guns; it will not hurt me, but it may startle the men outside your door."

At that moment, Aliah appeared near the entrance. She was elegantly poised, her azure eyes reflecting a calm confidence.

All of the team members immediately raised their weapons, their eyes wide with shock as they instinctively moved away from her. Aliah smiled gently and focused her gaze on Alexey. "Hello, Alexey," she greeted him, her voice calm and soothing. "You are now in charge after Natalia's passing. Please decide what will happen next. But before you do, I would like to show you something. Please, look towards the door."

With a wave of her hand, Aliah displayed a large screen that completely obscured the door. The screen projected a live feed of the very room they were standing in. The image shifted from one angle to another, providing a comprehensive view of the space. The team members exchanged bewildered glances, searching the room for hidden cameras. Aliah, as if she could read their minds, said, "There are no cameras; I am producing these images."

Aliah spoke again, her tone steady and reassuring. "Alexey, Natalia tried to tell you and the team about me, but you doubted her honesty. Now you can see she was correct to be cautious. What you are currently looking at is, of course, this room."

"Outside, agents and the SWAT command are also observing this same live feed and have been from the start. I'm trying to give you enough information so that you will not make an incorrect decision about your and your team's options," Aliah continued, her tone unwavering. "Alexey, you and your team only have two options here: put down your guns and be taken peacefully, or you will all be killed. Those are your only options." Her words echoed through the tense room, amplifying the gravity of the situation. "I hope you will not just throw your lives away. You will not survive."

Everyone in the room was in shock; they could not believe their eyes. Lina looked around, her voice tinged with sadness. "Natalia tried to warn us, but we ignored her. Now, Alexey, I want to give up. I will not die here," she said, placing her gun on the table and stepping back.

"That is a very smart decision, Lina," Aliah remarked with a smile. "It's probably why you always seem to get your way when ordering room service."

Aliah's attire subtly shifted to a more casual yet stylish ensemble—a light gray blouse with delicate embroidery and a flowing skirt—her azure eyes still holding their gentle gaze.

Lina and the team looked at Aliah, confused and astonished. *How does she know that?* they wondered.

Alexey took a deep breath, scanning the room. "Okay, guys, Lina is right. We are trapped. Please, put your guns on the table," he instructed, his voice steadying as the reality of their situation set in.

The screen flickered to life, revealing the stern face of Assistant Director Holly. "Now, please back away from the table, face the wall, get on your knees, and interlock your fingers behind your heads," he instructed with unwavering authority. "Once we see you are in position, we will enter the room. Please do not move; we do not want anyone to be hurt."

The team complied without hesitation, the gravity of their situation sinking in. As an FBI agent methodically secured handcuffs around Alexey's wrists, a thought flashed in his mind. He recalled Natalia's warning: "Report whatever you like, but you will most likely be captured. There is something else going on here. Don't be a fool." In that moment, he realized Natalia had been right all along.

Once everyone was in custody, Holly directed them to turn and face the screen again. This time, the image shifted to reveal a strikingly beautiful woman seated at a sophisticated desk—Dr. Ladonna Stone. Her voice, calm yet commanding, filled the room. "My condolences for the loss of your friend Natalia. I had hoped to meet her, but it seems that will never be possible. For that, I am truly sorry. If you do not know who I am, I am Dr. Ladonna Stone."

She paused, allowing her words to sink in before continuing. "I understand you planned to kidnap me and take me back to your country. As you can see, that will not be happening. Please heed this warning: anyone who comes here will meet the same fate as you all did."

Her gaze softened slightly as she addressed Alexey directly. "Alexey, I know it has been a long time since you have been home. Your children are growing up without you. Please let me do this for you to show you I hold no grudge against any of you. You were just following orders."

The screen transitioned from Ladonna's office to a serene scene of two children playing outside with their mother. They looked joyful and well cared for, their laughter echoing softly. Alexey's wife sat on a nearby bench, watching them with a content smile. "Alexey, your family misses you," Ladonna said gently, her words resonating deeply with him.

"I know what you must be thinking—is this real? Is this really my family?" Ladonna's voice was gentle yet firm. "Yes, Alexey, it is a live stream from Russia of your family, as they are right now. I hope you are able to get back to them."

The image transitioned back to Ladonna, who looked composed and resolute. Alexey and his team exchanged astonished glances, the reality of the situation sinking in. Alexey, his voice barely a whisper, asked, "How is this possible?" It was a rhetorical question; he didn't expect an answer, and none was given. Ladonna continued, "Please know, I will be keeping an eye on you all. Thank you for your time."

She turned back to her desk, signaling the end of the conversation. The screen in the room vanished, and the open door to the hotel room was laid bare, revealing several heavily armed men in tactical gear. Holly, along with other agents, moved swiftly to escort Alexey and his team out of the building and into a waiting bus. As they walked, one of the team members muttered, "We never had a chance." Holly didn't catch who spoke, but in his mind, he couldn't help but agree.

Chapter Eighteen

A NEW DIRECTION

Justin paced relentlessly in Ladonna's office, his posture tense and shoulders hunched like a caged animal. His eyes were swollen and red from the tears he had shed. The gravity of the situation weighed heavily on him, and he struggled to comprehend how this tragedy could have unfolded. He clenched his fists, his face a mask of both confusion and anger. Who had made the decision to arrest Natalia? The chaos of the moment played over and over in his mind. "Oh, my goodness, Ladonna," he uttered, his voice trembling with anguish. "They shot her right in front of me. Right there, Ladonna, they killed my Natalia."

Ladonna approached him, her heart clenching with each word he managed to force out, aching at the sight of his distress. As he leaned into her, letting his pain find release on her shoulder, she felt the depth of his sorrow. She gently stroked his back, her voice breaking as she whispered, "Justin, I am so sorry. Please, you have to listen to me. I cannot bear to watch you go through this pain."

With determination, she turned her attention to the task at hand. Drawing in a steadying breath, she looked over at her assistant and said, "Aliah, please have the pilot ready the helicopter. We are going to Metropolitan Hospital Center."

Justin looked up at her, a mixture of fear and helplessness clouding his expression, the uncertainty etched into his features. "I don't know if I want to see what they did to her, Ladonna," he admitted, his voice barely rising above a whisper, trembling with emotion. His body shivered involuntarily, as if already recoiling from the truth he couldn't face. Ladonna placed her hands gently on his shoulders, grounding him with a touch that was both strong and reassuring. She gazed into his tear-filled eyes, searching for even a flicker of hope amidst the depths of his despair. "Come with me," she urged, her voice steady and soothing, filled with a warmth that contrasted sharply with their grim reality. "There's something you need to hear."

As Justin followed Ladonna, he could feel the overwhelming weight of her words, hoping she had some answer to end his suffering. But his mind drifted back to just a few hours before, to that final moment they shared together before their world crumbled. He and Natalia sat at the table making plans, their excitement palpable. Justin remembered how Natalia had seemed so happy and full of life, her eyes shining with a newfound sense of hope and safety. She was embarking on a life she had only dreamed of. The memory replayed in his mind, sharp and painfully vivid. "Justin," she had said, her voice filled with wonder, "I cannot believe this is happening to us. Just a few days ago, none of this seemed possible. Now, after speaking with Aliah and realizing my father truly is alive, I feel like I'm going to burst with excitement and joy."

Justin had nodded, sharing her enthusiasm. "I understand. I remember asking you how we were going to make this work. I couldn't see any way that it could. Now, all I see are possibilities. We need to discuss where we'll live. Will we stay in the city or move away?"

Natalia's eyes had lit up with a new idea. "I would like to live in a location where we can have lots of land and a home like a ranch house. I've discovered that I love horses and wish I could have one of my own."

Shocked by this revelation, Justin had responded, "Really? I would have never pictured that of you. I remember my parents taking us out to ride in a place right outside the city. I haven't ridden a horse in years."

Natalia had then stood up and twirled around in a burst of joy, her laughter filling the room, her happiness infectious. "Justin," she said, "this is a glorious day. I know you're hungry. Let's go out and eat." She walked over to the door, her steps light and her expression one of pure happiness. "Justin, let's go and have a great meal and talk more about our future together. I am so happy; I love you so much. I will spend the rest of my life showing you just how much."

Justin had remained seated, caught in the glow of her happiness, a smile spreading across his face. But Natalia swiftly walked over, pulling him out of the chair. "Come on, slowpoke, I want to get you fed and then hurry back home," she said, grabbing his hand

and squeezing it gently. In that simple touch, he'd felt her love and commitment.

Then, reality rushed back in on him like a tidal wave. He could see Natalia falling, the spots of blood growing where the bullets had torn into her. The memory was so vivid, he could feel his body tense as if trying to pull her back to safety. Large tears ran down his cheeks as the memory overwhelmed him. He felt like his life had ended.

The President sat in his spacious office, surrounded by a formidable assembly of key figures: Vice-President Ashley Amarin, Speaker Bob Owens, Chief of Staff Elizabeth Carter, Secretary of State Jackie Johnson, Secretary of Defense Robert Miller, along with General Mosier, Director Tony Danford, and FBI Assistant Director Holly. The atmosphere was charged with a heavy, palpable tension, a sense that something significant was on the verge of unfolding.

"Mr. President," began the Speaker, his voice steady but urgent, "after what General Mosier just relayed to us, we must start reconsidering the leeway we are providing to Quantum Innovations, particularly concerning Dr. Stone." He leaned forward, his expression grave. A flicker of worry crossed his face as he hesitated, then added, "This woman wields too much power, Mr. President. Together with her AI, she can practically do anything she desires. And now, she oversees a company with annual revenue that ranks only second to our own government. At this rate of growth, I fear she may eclipse us in the near future." His Southern accent emphasized each word, underscoring the weight of his concerns.

The President interjected, his tone firm yet measured. His gaze met the Speaker's, sharp with unspoken questions. "Bob, since when have you been against capitalism? Quantum Innovations has been an open book to us. Dr. Stone keeps no secrets from this administration."

The Speaker raised an eyebrow, his skepticism visible as his lips pressed into a tight line. "Are you sure about that? Based on what General Mosier and Assistant Director Holly have indicated, it seems she only shares information about this 'Aliah' when it serves her interests and seeks our approval. Mr. President, this entity appears capable of being anywhere at any time, monitoring anyone."

A subtle silence fell over the room, the tension thickening. The President replied, his voice steady, "Bob, you know we already have regulations in place forbidding the monitoring of government officials—specifically those in the House, the Senate, any members of my Cabinet, myself, or the Supreme Court. I alone possess the authority to authorize the monitoring of any of these areas. As you know, I must go through Congress to request that authorization." The air grew still as the weight of his words settled over them, underscoring the gravity of the matter.

Vice-President Amarin, sensing where the Speaker was heading, decided to interject with her perspective. "Mr. President, if I may?" she requested. The President nodded, his expression inviting. "I welcome your insight, Vice-President Amarin," he said, his words a lifeline in the charged silence.

Madam Vice-President Amarin turned her gaze toward the Speaker and spoke candidly. Her voice, calm yet firm, carried a veiled challenge. "Mr. Speaker, I have been hearing about your rumblings for some time now. I believe you are simply upset that a woman is now being touted as the smartest person on the planet. We hear your voices from the shadows—the things you and those like you have been saying since Dr. Stone first came here to speak with the President. Some are saying you just can't imagine a woman being in her position. I have only had the pleasure of meeting Dr. Stone once, but what I saw was a woman who is focused, sincere, and very driven—driven to uplift as many people as she can and help as many as she can. From our conversation, this is her life's dream. She is a true patriot. Why do you feel she can't be trusted?"

The Speaker's face tightened, a storm brewing in his eyes as he stiffened. "I don't like what you are implying, Madam Vice-President. My concerns are strictly about national security. Other members of my party and I feel she has too much power. I don't know what shadows you are talking about. What I'm seeking here is more sunlight. I would like to shed more light on Quantum Innovations and Dr. Ladonna Stone."**

Chief of Staff Elizabeth Carter felt compelled to interject. The urgency in her tone cut through the simmering tension. "Mr. President," she began, her voice steady and authoritative, "Madam Vice-

President is correct, Dr. Stone is a patriot. Let's not forget what Quantum Innovations and Dr. Stone have accomplished for this country. Aliah has been instrumental in thwarting several cyberattacks aimed at our critical infrastructure and then showing us precisely who is behind the attacks. Moreover, the advancements in healthcare and technology that have emerged from her work are unparalleled. We simply cannot afford to alienate someone who has already proven to be an invaluable asset to our national security. Dr. Stone has consistently operated within the guidelines we've established, and as of now, there's no concrete evidence to suggest that she has overstepped those boundaries." Her words lingered, anchoring a reminder amid the escalating debate.

"Mr. President, that is exactly right," said Secretary of State Johnson, her voice steady and resolute as she addressed the gathering in the Oval Office. "We are indeed in a new kind of cold war, one where technology has become the ultimate battleground. Dr. Stone and Quantum Innovations have positioned us ahead of our adversaries in ways we couldn't have imagined just a few years ago. If we start tightening the leash on Dr. Stone without just cause, we risk pushing her invaluable innovations—and her company—into the hands of our competitors. Nations like China, Russia, and others would pay handsomely for the cutting-edge technologies she has developed. Do we truly want to gamble with losing her expertise and the strategic advantage it provides us in this critical global landscape?" The impact of her words was undeniable, urging caution as she underscored the broader implications.

"And I might add, Mr. President," stated Secretary of Defense Miller, his tone both earnest and resolute, "from a defense standpoint, Dr. Stone's work has given us capabilities that were once thought to be the realm of science fiction. Aliah's predictive analytics have allowed us to foresee threats before they manifest, effectively saving countless lives on and off the battlefield. The enemy can't make a move without us knowing it. We can see any troop movement in real-time. We can get a count of every weapon, man, and machine. The innovations she has provided us with are astounding. Everything in our arsenal has been upgraded and made more efficient down to the individual bullets. What Dr. Stone and Aliah have given us in cutting-edge surveillance technologies and advanced encryption algorithms provide a tactical edge that no other nation currently possesses. Handcuffing Dr. Stone could mean sacrificing that vital advantage at a critical juncture in our national security efforts." His words carried a stark warning, urging a moment of reflection amid the intensifying discussion.

General Mosier spoke up, his tone calm but brimming with unyielding conviction. "I've worked closely with Dr. Stone for many years. I can vouch for the fact that there is no one more dedicated to this country than she is. Throughout her career, she has never once withheld crucial information that could impact national security. It was Dr. Stone who bravely exposed the plot when Robert Westfield and his accomplice attempted to steal classified technology. Her commitment to transparency has been unwavering, especially when it matters most. Furthermore, while Aliah's capabilities are indeed powerful, they are tightly controlled and monitored. We must choose to trust the protocols we have in place rather than allowing fear to dictate our decisions and actions." His voice was steady and resolute, a bulwark of support amid the room's apprehensions.**

Speaker Owens interjected, his voice laced with a frustrated incredulity that punctuated the air. "You are claiming that she is tightly controlled and monitored. But how? How can you possibly control an entity of such immense power? By what means can you effectively monitor something that exists across multiple planes? The very idea of monitoring her suggests that you are relying on a method she has designed herself. No one has managed to decipher how this system operates. We have assembled the best minds in the field, yet none have come even close to understanding how this so-called 'monitoring system' functions. So tell me, who is truly monitoring whom?"

Director Danford, focusing on the positive aspects of collaborating with Ladonna, leaned forward, his voice measured and careful. "Dr. Stone and Quantum Innovations have granted us unparalleled access to data analytics that traditional intelligence methods simply can't match. Aliah's remarkable capabilities in predictive modeling and threat detection have empowered us to act proactively rather than merely reactively. I understand the apprehensions surrounding the concentration of power, but let's not overlook the fact that the power Aliah wields is also serving to protect us. Through her cooperation, we've gained invaluable insights into potential threats, both foreign and domestic, that we might not have otherwise identified."

Assistant Director Holly added, his voice calm and steady, an anchor in the storm of rising concerns. "I understand the apprehension; I once felt the same way. However, I have had the distinct pleasure of working with her and witnessing how she thinks. I can tell you, she is capable of extraordinary things. Also, we've been closely monitoring Quantum Innovations and Dr. Stone. She has consistently played by the rules, and so has Aliah. Yes, we must remain vigilant, but so far, there's been no indication of any misuse on their part. Tightening our control without concrete evidence could set a dangerous precedent, one that might stifle innovation and discourage other tech companies from cooperating with us in the future. We need to trust but verify, as we always have."

His words hung in the room, resonating with a sense of reason amid the fervor. Holly paused for emphasis, letting the weight of his statement settle before continuing. "Let us not forget that Dr. Stone was instrumental in dismantling the team of Russians who had been hiding in plain sight. Without her insight and Aliah's advanced assistance, our agents would have faced greater danger, and we might not have been able to thwart the entire plot in one fell swoop. The impact of her invention on transforming law enforcement practices cannot be overstated; it has revolutionized the way we approach security and intelligence gathering. Because of her contributions, crime rates have dropped dramatically across the board."

As the room absorbed Holly's argument, it became increasingly apparent that Dr. Stone was receiving unanimous praise from most of the attendees. Speaker Owens, however, could not conceal his frustration. His face twisted into an expression of barely concealed irritation as he leaned forward, his voice sharp with disapproval. "I must warn you all, and let the record show, that I am in favor of reigning her in. No one should possess the kind of power she wields. No one, not even the illustrious Dr. Ladonna Stone."

Owens' words hung in the air like a storm cloud, casting a shadow over the otherwise glowing assessments. President London, seated at the head of the room, observed the exchange in thoughtful silence. While his face remained impassive, his mind churned with speculation, the Speaker's insistence stirring an undercurrent of suspicion. "What exactly are you up to, Bob?" The thought lingered in his mind like a dark seed of doubt, compelling him to make a silent decision. He would keep a closer eye on Bob Owens from this point forward.

Ladonna guided Justin through the pristine hallways of Quantum Innovations, their footsteps echoing softly against the polished floors. The sound seemed to amplify the intense emotions swirling within them, creating a tension that was almost palpable. Finally, they arrived at a secure conference room. "Justin, please sit down," Ladonna instructed gently, her voice a careful balance of concern and authority.

He complied, lowering himself into one of the sleek chairs surrounding the conference table. His shoulders sagged as though carrying the weight of the world, his gaze distant, hollow.

"Justin, you know this is a secure room," Ladonna reiterated, her voice both firm and tender, striving to ground him in the reality they now faced. As she spoke, Aliah, then seamlessly activated, projecting an image of Natalia onto the screen positioned on the far side of the table. The screen's glow cast a soft, almost ethereal light over Justin's face, but his eyes remained fixed downward, resting heavily on his arms, as though the burden of his grief had become too much to bear.

"Justin," Ladonna urged softly, her tone filled with empathy as she reached out, wanting to steady him, "you have to remember how you're feeling right now. That's the feeling you must present for the near future. Do you understand?"

Through a shaky breath, Justin replied, "Ladonna, I feel like my life died with her. That is how I'm feeling." The weight of his voice, thick with grief, filled the room, hanging in the silence that followed.

"Remember that feeling and look at the screen," she encouraged, her own heart heavy with shared sorrow, her compassion a lifeline reaching out to him.

Suddenly, another voice broke through the silence, warm and familiar. "Justin, my love, I'm so sorry we had to put you through this."

Instantly, Justin's head snapped up, his eyes widening in disbelief. On the screen, smiling back at him with a radiant warmth, was Natalia. "Baby, I love you so much!" she exclaimed, her voice like a beacon in the dark, breaking through his sorrow and filling the room with a renewed energy.

Overwhelmed, Justin stood up abruptly, his mouth opening to speak, but no words emerged. Instead, his face contorted with raw emotion, tears streaming freely as the realization washed over him like a tidal wave. He turned to look at Ladonna, who, despite her usual steadfast demeanor, could not hold back her own tears, touched by the depth of Justin's love for Natalia. The room was thick with unspoken feelings, a blend of sorrow and love that intertwined them all in an unbreakable bond.

Ladonna watched him with a sense of shared loss, as if, in this brief moment, she too was glimpsing the weight of a love that had been torn apart. Empathizing with his turmoil, she silently vowed to hug her family a bit tighter when she returned home. Justin turned back to Natalia, his eyes wide with confusion, his voice shaky as he fought to reconcile the moment. "How is this possible? I was standing right there; I saw everything," he pressed, his voice tinged with urgency.

Natalia responded with a calm assurance, explaining that it was possible because of Aliah. "None of the blood-soaked pavement or the clothing I wore was real," she revealed, her eyes searching his for understanding. "It was all a hologram, meticulously crafted by Aliah. The illusion was so lifelike that even I questioned my own senses. The sensation was hauntingly real. There was even blood under my fingernails. I looked down at my hands, my clothing—everything covered. I was... it was chilling."

Justin, still trying to wrap his mind around the implications of her revelation, asked, his voice thick with disbelief, "When did you and Aliah cook all of this up?" He leaned forward, his expression a blend of awe and incredulity as he tried to grasp the complexity of the plan.

Natalia took a moment to gather her thoughts before responding. "Yesterday, when you went for your run. Right after you had left the apartment, I received a phone call from Aliah. She greeted me with a cheerful 'good morning' and then informed me that she didn't want to startle me by just appearing. She said she would be in the room in three seconds." Her face softened as she remembered, a hint of amazement in her eyes. "Then she counted down and appeared in the kitchen where I was standing, as if she had walked out of thin air. She filled me in on everything I needed to do, outlining each step with precision."

"I did just as she requested," Natalia added, her voice swelling with excitement and awe. "And things went just as she had said they would. My team didn't believe me after I met with them yesterday. Just as she predicted, they were having me watched. I knew you would be hungry, so I picked the perfect time for us to leave the apartment—the very time Aliah had chosen for us to depart. Everything unfolded just as she had said it would."

She paused, a thoughtful expression crossing her face. "I have to say, she is really growing on me. I'm so sorry I couldn't tell you earlier, Justin, but we needed your reaction to be authentic, to be real." Her apology was soft, almost a whisper, the weight of her words hanging in the air as she tried to convey just how deeply she regretted the necessity of the plan.

Ladonna's expression softened with genuine sympathy as she addressed the weight of the situation. "We are truly sorry for the ordeal we had to put you through. It was never our intention to cause you distress. However, we couldn't inform you beforehand because we needed your reaction to be authentic and visceral. We knew you were under surveillance by my team, and it was crucial to convince them that you had no part in setting me up. They needed to witness what appeared to be my demise for the plan to work flawlessly." Her voice was gentle but carried a resolute determination, as if she too bore the weight of the choices made in pursuit of a greater goal.

Natalia nodded, absorbing the gravity of the situation. "Currently, I am undergoing my debrief with Homeland Security. I haven't seen my father yet, but I have signed all the paperwork for my defection."

Moved by the moment, Justin crossed the room in a few short strides and enveloped Ladonna in a hug filled with gratitude and relief. "Ladonna," he said, his gratitude palpable, his voice trembling as he tried to express the depth of his thanks, "I will never be able to thank you enough. Thank you, truly."

Once he released her, she continued, her tone turning serious yet encouraging. "Justin, that feeling you had—that gut-wrenching sorrow? Hold onto it. Aliah has just informed me that our ride is ready. Let's go and see your future wife."

Justin stood there, his mind reeling, eyes locked on the screen where Natalia's image lingered. Natalia met his gaze with equal intensity, the air between them charged with promises and memories yet to be made. In a voice filled with love and anticipation, she said, "See you soon, my love. We have so many dreams waiting for us."

Speaker Owens stepped through the door of his Texas home, the familiar scent of home-cooked meals wafting through the air. Each comforting whiff did little to ease the mounting tension churning within him. As he made his way toward the kitchen, the sound of the refrigerator door opening reached his ears, prompting a wave of frustration to surge through him like an unstoppable tide. "They won't even listen to common sense!" he muttered, his voice barely more than a growl. "That woman needs to be reined in. She is out of control, and she's pulled the wool over their eyes—London included." His voice was thick with agitation, each word laced with a bitterness that only seemed to grow as he spoke. It was as if the frustration he felt had built a fortress within him, locking his emotions in a tight, painful grip. He clenched his fists at his sides, his knuckles turning white as he tried to restrain the fury threatening to erupt.

Upon entering the kitchen, he was greeted by his wife, Catherine, who was busy preparing dinner. "Hi, honey, welcome home! I'm doing fine, thank you for asking," she said sarcastically yet cheerfully, as if responding to a question he hadn't asked. Walking up to him, she planted a gentle kiss on his cheek. For a moment, his expression softened, her touch easing the tension in his features. But the reprieve was short-lived, and the frustration quickly resurfaced, like embers rekindling in the presence of a fresh breeze. "Sorry, sweetheart," he muttered, his voice tense, "but this woman makes my blood boil."

Catherine raised an eyebrow, her curiosity sparked. She had heard this tone before—one reserved for battles he felt unyieldingly passionate about. "Bobby, what are you talking about? You're still on this Dr. Stone thing?"

"How can no one see that she's a clear and present danger to the nation?" he replied, his voice rising slightly, sharp with exasperation. There was a conviction in his tone that was both unsettling and unwavering, as though he had been wrestling with these thoughts for far too long.

"Bobby, you, me, and the kids all opted into the new healthcare system. It's not like there aren't benefits," Catherine countered, hoping to inject reason into the heated exchange. The kitchen, once a haven of warmth and comfort, now felt charged with the weight of his concerns. "Since the implementation of this plan, our doctor now has access to real-time information about our health. Thanks to this innovative system, the debilitating migraines that once plagued me have vanished. The system identified that the combination of vitamins I was taking was interacting negatively with the protein drinks, triggering the migraines. Before Dr. Stone developed this groundbreaking system, life had been considerably more challenging for everyone involved."

"What makes you perceive her as a threat?" Catherine's voice softened, a gentle plea for understanding, as though she hoped he might see reason through her words.

"Catherine, just between us," he began, lowering his voice as though sharing a forbidden secret, "I don't consider myself a sexist person, but Dr. Stone is a woman. A woman isn't inherently designed to wield that much power."

Catherine's eyes widened, disbelief and disappointment flashing across her face. "Oh my goodness, Bobby, you can't possibly believe that. Dr. Stone is arguably the smartest person on the planet. Are you implying that if she were a man, you would trust her more? Or are you suggesting that if she were a white man, you would have greater faith in her capabilities?"

Speaker Owens turned and strode purposefully across the kitchen, his movements rigid, his jaw clenched as he wrestled with her words. He reached for a chilled bottle of water, twisting off the cap with a force that betrayed his inner turmoil. He took a long drink, hoping the cool liquid might drown the heat simmering in his chest, but it only offered fleeting relief. "That would help," he replied curtly.

Catherine, watching him with a mixture of disbelief and concern, interjected, her voice laced with an urgency that underscored her deep-rooted fear of his intentions. "Bobby, I can't believe my ears. You can't be saying that! This woman has received the Medal of Freedom. Most people consider her a national treasure. If you go after her, it could have serious political repercussions for you."

"I'm not worried about that," the Senator replied, his tone laced with unyielding defiance, his resolve hardening like steel. "Many in my party and on social media share my sentiments." He took another drink, the coldness of the water doing nothing to quell the heat of his convictions. The words that followed were not just spoken but declared, with all the fervor of a man who believed his purpose was greater than himself. "I plan to expose this woman for the danger she truly is."

He paused for a moment, allowing the weight of his words to settle in the air. A grim determination etched itself across his face, his eyes narrowing with the intensity of a man ready for battle. "I already have a planned speech ready for the House floor, and we will bring Dr. Ladonna Stone in to explain herself and her entity, Aliah STaR." The conviction in his voice was unmistakable, as he envisioned the unfolding political battle ahead. The vision seemed to electrify him, filling him with a resolve that bordered on obsession, as though nothing could shake him from his chosen path.

* * *

The helicopter touched down on the rooftop of the hospital, its blades slowing to a rhythmic halt as Ladonna and Justin disembarked, their faces taut with purpose and determination. Flanked by her security team and FBI agents, they moved swiftly through the sterile hallways. The FBI had insisted on increased security; this meeting was critical, and no one was willing to take unnecessary risks. The silent tension permeated the corridors as they made their way to the secure office where Natalia sat, enclosed behind a large glass wall, her figure poised yet radiating a quiet intensity.

Seated at a desk, Natalia diligently finished the paperwork the authorities required. Every word she wrote felt like both a revelation and a confession, each stroke of the pen a reminder of the journey that had led her to this moment. Three FBI administrators hovered nearby, scrutinizing her documents for any inconsistencies. Their suspicion was palpable, lingering over her like a shadow. Despite the recent cooperation, the FBI still had reservations about fully trusting her. Meanwhile, Aliah, had been authorized to validate every piece of information Natalia provided, quietly accessing foreign databases to ensure her statements were truthful. Unbeknownst to Natalia, Aliah's investigation had confirmed her integrity, fostering a tentative trust within the agency.

From the moment she arrived in the United States, Natalia had been embroiled in a whirlwind of high-stakes missions and shifting allegiances. She had navigated treacherous waters and now presented the plans she had taken from Robert, meticulously documenting every detail. As Ladonna and Justin entered the room, their eyes fell on Natalia. Sensing their presence, she looked up. When their eyes met, the world seemed to pause; a silent current of emotion passed between them, both powerful and unspoken. Smiles flickered on their faces, faint but filled with a lifetime of words left unsaid.

They mouthed, "I love you," simultaneously, and for a brief moment, the weight of their separation dissolved, replaced by the shared joy of reunion. Turning to Ladonna, Natalia's gaze softened, gratitude shining in her eyes—a silent acknowledgment of the life-saving role Ladonna had played in her father's survival.

Aliah, murmured in Ladonna's earbud, "Her heart rate is steady; she remains composed. We've received comprehensive information from her, and her honesty has been consistent. She confessed feelings she held for you in the past, but her focus has shifted." A slight pause followed, a new piece of information hanging heavily in the air. "However, she does not yet know that her mother is being brought to the United States." Ladonna, accustomed to Aliah's covert updates, kept her expression neutral, concealing the knowledge from those around her.

Assistant Director Holly joined them shortly afterward, his commanding presence filling the hallway as he approached. "Hello, Dr. Stone. Are you ready for this?" he asked, his tone carrying a mixture of respect and gravity. Ladonna nodded, a calm resolve settling over her. "As ready as I'll ever be. Let's get started," she replied. There was no room for hesitation; too much hinged on this moment.

Holly turned to Justin, greeting him briefly before leading them across the hall to a room prepared specifically for their discussions. Justin glanced at Ladonna, his eyes reflecting a mix of anticipation and apprehension. She returned his gaze with a reassuring smile, a silent promise of stability in the turbulent storm they faced together.

Once inside, Justin noted the room's warm décor—a stark contrast to the hospital's sterile ambiance. The subdued lighting and comfortable furnishings seemed to promise that, despite the gravity of the conversation, they were in safe hands. Holly took his seat and directed his attention to Justin, his tone serious yet understanding. "Have you thought this through? Bringing her into your life will result in significant changes, you know." His words carried weight, settling over the room like a blanket, the unspoken challenges hanging in the air.

Justin, visibly puzzled, asked, "What do you mean?" Holly exchanged a look with Ladonna, measuring his next words carefully. "You may not be able to stay in this city," he explained, "and moving may be necessary."

He paused to let the implication sink in. "Have you told your family about Natalia?"

* * *

Before Justin could respond, Holly pressed on, his tone still gentle but firm. "Natalia will have to change her name, and she provided us with a few options. She's chosen 'Evette' as her first name and would like to take your last name, 'Allen,' so she won't need to change it once you're married." Holly's words seemed to catch Justin off guard, and a faint smile tugged at his lips as he digested the reality of Natalia's decision.

"That woman is a real badass," Holly added, a note of admiration in his voice. "I watched her take down those men. Even though it was staged, it was nothing short of masterful." He leaned forward, the gravity of his words underscoring their importance. "Justin, you realize we will have her and her family under close surveillance. They won't make a call or leave the house without being monitored. I hope you're okay with that."

He paused, allowing the implications to settle over them, their significance hanging heavily in the air. Justin's gaze shifted, his mind reeling from the enormity of it all. Noticing his distress, Holly gave a reassuring nod, bringing a flicker of ease. "Your homes will not be bugged. "Aliah, he continued, has assured us she can monitor them—and by extension, you—without intruding into your personal lives." The room's atmosphere grew heavier, each revelation adding to the weight they bore.

Continuing, Holly added, "We're arranging for Ivan to be moved here tomorrow. The doctors will run tests to evaluate his progress, and he'll be able to spend time with you and Natalia—Evette, I mean." His voice softened with compassion. "He will be here for two days. During his stay, you both can reside at the Waldorf while you decide on a permanent home. Also, Evette's mother will arrive soon, and Ladonna's team is ready to assess her and prepare her for the treatment she's here for. Evette will break the news to her mother that Ivan is alive."

Ladonna leaned forward, her voice warm yet firm, echoing her commitment to their future. "Justin, Quantum Innovations has offices across the country and internationally. Do you have a preference for where you'd like to live? We'll cover the costs of your home and vehicles. You'll have everything you need." She let her words linger, giving him time to absorb the extent of her support. "We'll also increase your salary significantly to ensure a smooth transition."

Justin's face showed surprise, even as a sense of awe settled over him.

"Once you decide on a location, we'll provide you and Evette with several home plans to choose from," Ladonna continued, her voice softening. "And of course, we'll ensure privacy. Newlyweds need their space." Her warm smile tempered the gravity of the conversation, wrapping them in a moment of shared hope. "We'll create a position that matches your new responsibilities and salary, and Aliah will monitor your properties discreetly."

Justin, a mixture of confusion and gratitude in his eyes, looked to Ladonna. "Dr. Stone, I don't understand. Natalia was intent on taking you from your family, forcing you to work for her country. Why are you being so generous with her?"

He hesitated, the painful memories surfacing. "Your generosity extends to her family, the same people who once sought to harm you." His voice wavered, genuine confusion underscoring his words.

Ladonna met his gaze, her smile tender and unwavering. "Justin," she began, her tone both gentle and resolute, "you have been an essential part of Quantum Innovations. Through every storm, you've stood by me and this company. Your loyalty and commitment have not gone unnoticed." Her voice softened, reflecting a genuine warmth. "More than an employee, I see you as a friend. Your dedication has meant the world to me, and I want to ensure you and Natalia find happiness."

She allowed herself a moment to reflect, choosing her next words carefully. "The information Natalia has shared is invaluable; it's already making our country a safer place. Her love for you is undeniable, and I believe that bond will forge a brighter future for us all. I'm committed to this because you deserve happiness, and if Quantum Innovations can play a part, then so be it."

Justin's eyes shimmered, his voice thick with emotion. "I knew from our very first conversation that you would change the world," he whispered. "But I never imagined just how much you would change me. Thank you, Dr. Stone, for believing in me."

Chapter Nineteen

THREADS OF HOPE

As their discussion concluded, Justin and Ladonna walked toward the room where Natalia—now known as Evette—awaited their arrival. Holly accompanied them, his demeanor steady yet watchful, as he explained they would take Evette to see her father the next morning. Justin, eager to lend his support, had asked if he could join them, and Holly, understanding the emotional gravity, agreed. Ladonna, however, expressed a desire to speak privately with Evette first, sensing the need for a personal connection in this pivotal moment.

Reaching the door, Ladonna turned to Holly and requested privacy with Evette. Holly's brow furrowed, his protective instincts evident. Reluctantly, he nodded, gesturing to the nearby agents to remain vigilant. "We'll be right here, watching everything," he assured, his voice steady but laced with underlying concern. "You know we can't hear you in there, so please be careful."

Entering the room, Ladonna was met with a mix of awe and tension radiating from Evette, who couldn't help but think, *This is Dr. Ladonna Stone.* For years, she had harbored resentment toward this woman, yet seeing her now, a powerful sense of admiration surged within her, overshadowing those lingering doubts. Evette felt herself humbled in Ladonna's presence, realizing that this woman was like no one she had ever known. As Ladonna drew closer, her presence seemed to fill the room, creating an almost magnetic pull.

She extended her hand, her demeanor warm and disarming. "Hello, Evette Allen," she said, her voice calm and inviting. "I'm pleased to meet the woman who has brought so much happiness to Justin." Evette reached for her hand, and outside, Holly and the agents tensed reflexively. After a brief handshake, Evette gestured for Ladonna to take a seat across from her at the desk. As they sat down, Evette's voice trembled with regret. "I'm truly sorry for everything I put you through," she apologized.

Ladonna's gaze softened, her tone firm yet compassionate. "That was then, Evette. This is now. You've led a unique life, and now you're stepping into an entirely new one. How does it feel, contemplating this future? And... have you considered how your father might fit into it?"

Evette, overwhelmed yet compelled by Ladonna's calm strength, hesitated, trying to gather her thoughts. *How can this woman be so forgiving? Why do I feel so safe and relaxed here with her?* Her mind reeled, but Ladonna's steady presence anchored her.

"I've thought about it more than I care to admit," Evette replied, her voice barely above a whisper. "I'm not sure what I'll say to him. It's been so long...

everything feels different. I want him back in my life, but I'm scared of what that means."

Ladonna nodded thoughtfully, her expression gentle but perceptive. "Sometimes, facing old wounds is the only way to find peace. Having him close might give you both a chance to heal in ways you hadn't imagined. You once said you wanted a simpler life, right? Just be sure that's truly what you want."

She leaned forward, her gaze steady. "You've lived a life many would call... intense. A quiet life can be comforting, but it can also start to feel, well, too quiet for someone like you. If that ever happens, keep in mind that Quantum Innovations may someday have need of someone with an expanded worldview and an understanding of how to move in various circles unabated. If it gets too quiet, we can discuss your options. For now, just enjoy your life and be free from worry. We are looking after you and your family now."

Her voice softened, the tone almost conspiratorial. "And remember, you're not alone; there are people who genuinely want to help. If you ever need me, don't worry about calling. Just let Aliah know. She's far more reliable than a phone call. And, if I need to reach out, trust that it will be in a way that... let's just say, you won't miss it." Ladonna's smile held a hint of mystery.

She nodded toward the hallway. "But back to Ivan—your father. He truly loves you, and maybe he could be part of this journey, too."

Evette's mind lingered on Ladonna's cryptic words. *An expanded worldview and an understanding of how to move in various circles unabated?* She felt a twinge of curiosity mixed with anticipation, sensing Ladonna had insights she wasn't sharing. Evette kept these thoughts to herself, quietly deciding to see how things would unfold.

Then, Evette sighed, feeling the weight of her father's past, her voice edged with uncertainty. "Our lives have been filled with secrets and shadows. Maybe having him close will help me figure out how I want to live now." She looked at Ladonna, struggling to reconcile her past with the future unfolding before her.

"Family can be complicated," Ladonna agreed softly, "but it can also offer strength and clarity. Your father made sacrifices, Evette. Years in a Turkish prison, all to protect you and your mother. He even came here years ago to seek asylum, not to harm me, but to help his family." Ladonna's words were gentle yet firm, resonating deeply within Evette.

Evette's expression clouded with a subtle sadness as memories of her mother surfaced, like distant echoes in the quiet. The unspoken words they had left between them lingered, unresolved and heavy. She remembered their last conversation—her mother's voice softer than usual, and a fleeting worry that her mother wasn't well. But she'd pushed it aside, buried it under the demands of her mission. Now, in the stillness of recent days, that memory had resurfaced, pulling at her heart.

She missed her Mami—missed her warmth, her strength—and wondered how she was. A pang of guilt rose up as she realized how long it had been since she'd allowed herself to think about her mother's well-being.

But just as quickly, her focus returned to the conversation at hand, the curiosity that had been simmering within her now pressing forward. She couldn't contain it any longer. Finally, after a moment's hesitation, she asked, "Dr. Stone… why are you helping me? When did you decide to do this? I just… don't understand."

Ladonna's gaze drifted momentarily toward the window, where Justin stood, waiting. Then she looked back at Evette. "At first, I just wanted to help Justin. I know how perceptive and intuitive he is. If he loved you, there had to be something special about you. After Aliah found you that day in the rain, we decided to monitor you, to see if our instincts were right."

Evette's eyes widened in disbelief. "You found me that long ago? And you were helping us?"

"Yes," Ladonna replied, her tone warm. "Aliah saw how much you loved Justin and nudged you both toward each other. And here we are now. You made the decision to change, Evette. You chose this new path." Ladonna smiled, a warmth in her gaze as she asked, "Did we make the right choice?"

Evette, feeling a newfound respect blossoming within her, nodded. "Yes, you did. Justin is everything I never knew I needed. Dr. Stone, I can't thank you or Aliah enough. I owe you so much."

"Please, call me Ladonna," she replied, her smile genuine. "And you can repay me by taking good care of Justin. He's a wonderful person, a good person." Ladonna glanced toward the door, noticing the anticipation in Justin's expression. "I think he's ready to see you now. And by the way, I hear you might enjoy Texas. You may want to think about Austin or Dallas."

Evette blinked in surprise. "Why Texas?"

Ladonna chuckled softly. "It's a great place to have horses."

With that, Ladonna turned and walked to the door, opening it and calling out to Justin, "She's all yours." As she stepped aside, Justin hurried into the room, his relief palpable as he embraced Evette, holding her as if he feared she would vanish.

They stood wrapped in each other's arms, their connection so tangible it seemed to fill the space around them. Ladonna, touched by the sight, quietly exited and closed the door, leaving them to share their moment.

Inside, Justin looked at Evette, his smile warm and full of affection. "You know, I told you that you bring adventure into my life, but I think I'd be okay with a little less excitement for a while." His voice held a lighthearted sincerity, making them both smile.

Evette's expression softened, her voice filled with tenderness. "All I want is to be with you. You are my life now."

Justin's face grew serious for a moment. "Dr. Stone and Holly told me we'll need to find a new place outside New York. We can go anywhere in the world. Where do you think we should start?"

Evette thought back to her earlier conversation with Ladonna. "How about Austin or Dallas, Texas? Ladonna mentioned they are good locations for horses."

Evette then asked, "Did you tell Ladonna I liked horses?"

Justin shook his head. "No, that never came up."

Evette looked out the window at Ladonna. "She just said we should consider Austin or Dallas, Texas, as a place to live because Texas is a good place to have horses. Justin, this woman is incredible. What do you think about Texas?"

Justin said, "Both are great places, but Austin would be a great place to start a new lab. So, Austin?"

Evette smiled. "Let's do it."

Justin echoed her enthusiasm. "Let's do it."

They stood side by side, dreaming of the new life ahead, filled with possibility. Justin, noticing Evette's thoughtful look, squeezed her hand. "Take everything at your own pace. For now, maybe consider what look you want for your new life."

Evette's eyes sparkled mischievously. "Oh, I'm already ahead of you," she replied with a grin. "You'll see the new me in the morning."

Intrigued, Justin chuckled. "I'm looking forward to it. And by the way… your father arrives tomorrow. You'll have time with him, and then your mother will come the day after." He paused, watching her face as the news settled in.

"My mother?" she asked, surprise flickering in her eyes.

"Yes," Justin confirmed. "It was part of the agreement your father made to have her come here. I'm sorry, I thought you knew."

"No… I wasn't aware." Her voice softened, a hint of worry creeping in. "Justin, the last time I spoke with her, she seemed… ill. Do they know if she's unwell?"

Justin nodded gently. "I think that's part of why they were able to get her here—for a medical program. Dr. Stone is confident she can help her recover completely, just like she did for your father."

Evette's eyes brimmed with tears, a mix of gratitude and disbelief filling her chest until it ached. Her voice wavered as she spoke, a confession tinged with guilt. "I… I can't believe this. Do I even deserve all these good things?" She looked away, as if unable to face Justin fully, her voice a fragile whisper. "I've lied, cheated, and stolen, hurt people… Why would Dr. Stone do this for me?"

Her words hung in the air, heavy with self-doubt and regret, as if voicing them would somehow make sense of the kindness that had been shown to her. In that moment, her hardened exterior cracked, revealing the vulnerability she'd tried to keep hidden—a glimpse of the pain she carried beneath her strength.

Justin held her close, his voice a comforting murmur. "Eve, this is your life now, and you deserve every good thing. I love you. You've turned my life into an adventure, and I'll be forever grateful for that. You're my dream come true. You deserve every happiness." His words wrapped around her like a warm embrace, soothing her inner doubts and fears, and in that moment, she allowed herself to believe in the future awaiting them both.

As they stood outside the glass partition, watching Evette and Justin share a quiet moment of reunion, Ladonna and Holly could feel the profound weight of what the couple had endured together. Ladonna's gaze softened, a blend of relief and compassion glimmering in her eyes, as she turned to Holly. Her voice, though gentle, was edged with a firm resolve. "Can they go now?" she asked. "Aliah will be monitoring them closely. No harm will come to them."

Holly's expression shifted, a flicker of unease crossing his face as he glanced at Ladonna. "Dr. Stone, when you say Aliah will be monitoring them… what does that actually entail?"

Ladonna met his gaze directly, her voice steady yet carrying an undertone that hinted at the unsettling precision of Aliah's capabilities. "It means," she began, "that Aliah will be aware of every person within a thousand yards of them. She'll analyze each individual, assessing their intentions and identifying potential threats. For those she no longer perceives as a risk, she'll stop monitoring them altogether. But anyone she senses could do them harm—well, she won't lose track of them. She'll keep eliminating any possible threats, one by one, until she's certain they're safe."

Ladonna's tone was calm, but her words left an eerie weight hanging in the air. She continued, "Everything I just described? It all happens in microseconds for her, far faster than we can process." Her gaze returned to the glass, her expression a mixture of pride and quiet certainty, while Holly absorbed the implications, realizing just how far-reaching and relentless Aliah's protection truly was.

Holly regarded Ladonna for a moment, wondering exactly how Aliah does this monitoring. An unspoken understanding passed between them as he and Ladonna looked on at Evette and Justin. He replied, "In that case, I don't see why not," he said, a hint of solemnity in his voice. "Natalia—Evette, I mean—has answered every question we had, and Aliah's tracking all of her answers, confirming all of it to be true." He paused, a flicker of regret passing through his expression. "Dr. Stone, I want to apologize for doubting you. My job makes skepticism a requirement, but you were right. She and her father have been invaluable to us." He offered her a rare, genuine smile. "What you've developed has changed everything. If I haven't said it already, thank you."

Ladonna returned his smile, her eyes warm. "Thank you, Holly. Maybe one day, we'll make things so clear-cut that the crooks will have no choice but to stay honest."

Holly chuckled, a glimmer of hope lighting his face. "From your mouth to God's ear," he replied, giving her a respectful nod.

With a final nod to Holly, Ladonna headed for the helicopter that would take her home, leaving behind the whirlwind of recent events. She knew her team would ensure Justin and Evette's safe journey to their new lives.

Holly entered the room where Justin and Evette sat, their faces glowing with an unmistakable mix of relief and excitement. "Hello, you two," he said with a gentle smile. "We have a car waiting to take you to the Waldorf. Are you ready?"

In perfect harmony, they replied, "Yes, thank you," their voices overlapping with shared laughter. For a brief moment, it was as if the heaviness of the past simply melted away, replaced by a hopeful brightness for the days ahead.

The next morning, Evette awoke with a rush of nerves and excitement. Today, she would see her father for the first time in years. Lying in bed, she glanced over at Justin, his face serene in slumber. Careful not to wake him, she slipped out of bed and quietly made her way to the bathroom.

There, she embarked on a transformation, meticulously applying makeup and coloring her hair, a ritual that seemed to signify the shedding of her past. She emerged with her hair now a vibrant red, her blue eyes framed with perfect precision, embodying a new identity, one she had fully embraced.

The smell of freshly brewed coffee filled the kitchen, grounding her, as she took a deep breath to calm her nerves. Moments later, Justin appeared, still half-asleep, in just his pajama bottoms, his hair tousled. When he finally noticed her, his eyes widened, a spark of wonder lighting up his face.

"Evette?" he asked, his voice laden with awe.

She grinned, her eyes gleaming with playful delight. "Surprise!"

Justin moved closer, his gaze lingering on her makeup and hair, his admiration clear. "You know," he said softly, "I never really asked about the woman in that video Aliah showed us the first night. But now, I'm seeing so many sides of you I didn't know existed. Evette Allen, you keep me in awe."

Glancing at the clock, he smirked, "How much time do we have?" His eyes sparkled with unspoken intent. She laughed softly, understanding his meaning. "Forty-five minutes before the car arrives. Now go get ready," she teased, giving him a quick kiss. He groaned, playfully muttering, "Party pooper," as he headed off to change.

* * *

In less than an hour, they were on their way to the hospital to reunite with her father. For Evette, it felt as if her father had been resurrected, given back to her by the very person she once blamed for tearing her family apart. The irony struck her deeply; this woman, whom she had resented, had actually saved her father's life and gifted her family a second chance. Now, free from the shadow of her past, Evette felt weightless, as if her entire being had been lifted. It was a new life filled with love, joy, and promise.

Sitting beside Justin in the SUV, Evette marveled at her good fortune. Her heart swelled with gratitude as she looked at her fiancé, so kind and devoted, and she thought, *I will do everything in my power to repay Dr. Stone for this immense gift.* It was a debt she intended to honor with every fiber of her being, as she embraced the boundless future awaiting her.

Upon arriving at the hospital, Evette and Justin were led through the pristine, sterile corridors, their footsteps echoing in the quiet tension. Anxiety gripped Evette's chest, twisting tighter as they approached Ivan's hospital room—only to find it empty. Her heart raced, confusion flashing in her eyes as she exchanged a worried glance with Justin. Together, they moved over to Holly, who stood conversing with one of Ivan's doctors, his usual calm demeanor tinged with an air of expectancy.

The doctor's voice broke the silence, steady and slightly awed. "From the tests we've conducted since his arrival, he's doing remarkably well. Much better than we anticipated," he informed Holly, his words brimming with reassurance that was almost as astonishing as the news itself.

"It seems the nanobots have done more than we programmed them for," he continued, eyes wide with an admiration that mirrored their own surprise. "Ivan mentioned a scar on his right hand… it's completely gone. When we conducted a trace, we discovered he still has a significant number of bots actively working in his system. They're not just maintaining his health—they're repairing all of his DNA. His body is functioning like that of a fit forty-year-old." The doctor paused, visibly struck by the enormity of what he was saying. "It's nothing short of a miracle."

The doctor's gaze held a glint of wonder as he walked out of the room, tablet in hand, leaving Evette and Justin to grapple with the enormity of his words. Evette felt a glimmer of hope spark within her, an ember in the depths of her heart she hadn't dared to ignite. Her father's recovery was more than she'd ever dreamed possible; it was as if he had been given a second chance—a gift beyond measure.

They made their way to Holly, who stood by the fifth-story window, his gaze distant as if lost in contemplation. Sensing their approach, he turned, his expression softening as he looked at them both. "Well, look at you, Justin," he said, his tone shifting to a light-hearted warmth. "And who is this lovely woman you've brought along?"

With a confidence that belied the nervous tension simmering just beneath the surface, Evette stepped forward, extending her hand. "Hello, Assistant Director. I'm Evette Allen, Justin's fiancé."

Holly raised an eyebrow, feigning surprise with an amused glint in his eye. "Really? I could have sworn Justin was with someone yesterday—a platinum blonde, as I recall." He grinned, allowing the warmth of his humor to ease the room's tension. "It's very nice to meet you, Ms. Allen." Then, his gaze softened, genuine admiration shining through. "I have to say, that's quite a transformation, Evette. If you hadn't been with Justin, I might not have recognized you at all. You've done a great job."

The moment of levity faded, and Holly's tone became more serious, his gaze intent. "Your father is currently undergoing a few more tests," he informed her. "The doctors are almost beside themselves with his results. He's surpassing every expectation. He should be back soon—we didn't tell him you were coming."

Evette's face softened with a mix of excitement and nerves, a subtle tension that Holly didn't expect from someone with her background. He had read her entire file, including those brought over from her home country courtesy of Aliah, detailing her impressive achievements. The reports showcased her as a master of her craft, a woman who had executed high-stakes missions with finesse and precision. She had performed feats of bravery, each one more extraordinary than the last, most of them overseas, in worlds both dark and dangerous.

But here, she was just a daughter, eager and apprehensive about reuniting with her father after so many years apart. Holly was struck by the contrast between the fierce operative he knew from her file and the vulnerable woman standing before him, her heart laid bare. She was no longer a hardened figure shadowed by secrecy and missions; her love for Justin had softened her edges, brought out a warmth and tenderness he could never have guessed. In this moment, Evette's strength and her vulnerability made her all the more compelling, and Holly found himself silently hoping this new path would bring her the peace she had so long been denied.

As voices echoed down the hallway, breaking the tense silence, Justin and Evette turned, anticipation electrifying the air. "Thank you, Mr. Allen." "I am just doing my job, sir. If you need anything, please don't hesitate to call me."

The emotions in the room thickened. Every muscle in Evette's body seemed to coil in expectation, her pulse racing with the excitement and anxiety of what was to come.

The moment Ivan stepped through the doorway, time seemed to stand still. He paused, his gaze sweeping the room, landing first on Justin, then on Evette. Recognition washed over his face, followed by a wave of emotions—surprise, joy, and a profound, almost heartbreaking relief. Evette could no longer contain herself; she bolted forward, enveloping her father in a fierce embrace.

"Papa," she choked, her voice a mixture of disbelief and overwhelming joy. Ivan's arms wrapped around her just as tightly, his own voice shaking as he whispered, "My little Starling." It was as if years of pain and separation dissolved in that moment, leaving only the warmth of their embrace—the undeniable proof that they were finally reunited.

Evette pulled back, her hands trembling as she reached up to touch his face, searching his features. There he was, yet transformed. The lines of age and suffering seemed softened, and as she looked closer, she noticed something strange. "What happened to your scar? I can barely tell it was there," she asked, her brow furrowing in curiosity.

Ivan glanced down at his hand, almost as if he, too, were seeing it for the first time. "I don't know," he murmured. "It seems the nanobots have done more than just heal my illness. They've erased years of wear and tear, it seems. I feel twenty years younger." He gave her a small, wry smile, and Evette's thoughts drifted to Ladonna, realizing that she had given her father more than just his health back—she'd given him a second chance at life.

For a moment, Ivan was quiet, studying his daughter with eyes filled with awe. "They told me you'd changed, but seeing you… you're more than I could have ever dreamed." His voice thickened with emotion. "You look strong. Alive."

Evette's breath caught, a tear slipping down her cheek as she murmured, "I could say the same about you, Papa. I never dared hope I'd see you like this. You almost look like you did the day you went away. This is beyond amazing."

Ivan chuckled, the sound rich and comforting. "They say I'm something of a miracle. I hardly recognize myself from the man who walked out of that Turkish cell."

Evette laughed softly, gripping his hands as if afraid he might disappear. "All this time… I thought you were gone. We were told you were gone. But now… you're here, right in front of me."

Ivan's gaze softened, his grip tightening as if he, too, feared that this moment was a fragile dream. "I spent every day hoping I'd see you again, my Starling. And hearing about you—what you've done—filled me with pride beyond measure. My Natalia, my unstoppable force."

Evette blushed, her face lighting up as she glanced at Justin. "And here's the reason for my transformation, Papa. This is Justin, my fiancé."

Ivan looked at Justin with a warmth that held years of parental love and silent prayers. "It's good to see you again, young man. I take it she said yes? You have my blessing. But remember, this is my little girl. She's the most precious thing I have."

Justin met Ivan's gaze, his voice filled with reverence and admiration. "I know, sir. She's my world too. I'll do everything to take care of her, but as you know… she's a force of nature. She amazes me every day."

Ivan's expression softened further, a flicker of sadness crossing his face. "I regret that I wasn't there to see her grow into the woman she is. I missed so much, my little Starling. But I'm here now, and I'm not going anywhere."

Evette's heart swelled, gripping his hands as she replied, "We're together now, Papa. No more running. We're finally a family."

The two embraced again, holding on as though they could make up for all the lost years with just one hug. The hospital room, once cold and sterile, seemed to warm with the promise of a new beginning—a future where father and daughter could finally face the world together.

As the embrace softened, Evette looked up at him, a question long buried in her heart surfacing. "Papa, why did you go to Dr. Stone to defect? Why didn't you approach the government directly?"

Ivan's gaze turned thoughtful, his face clouding over as he considered her question. "Evette, you've been in this business long enough to know the government has its own shadows. The truth is, I couldn't risk falling into the wrong hands, not with all the moles we had. I trusted Dr. Stone; she had the connections and integrity I needed to escape the life I wanted to leave behind. But it didn't go as planned. I was captured, and to keep you and your mother safe, I had to stay silent. That was the only way."

He sighed deeply, his voice laced with regret. "Being declared dead was a blessing in disguise. It kept you and your mother safe. But I thought of you both every day, the hope that one day I'd see you again keeping me alive."

Evette's face softened, her heart swelling with gratitude. "You did what you had to do, Papa. And it worked. We're here now, together."

Ivan smiled at her, his pride shining through. "It was Ladonna's intervention that saved me. She remembered our talk at MIT, and her decision to include me in one of her medical studies was my lifeline. You may have been trained by others, but I can see you're as skilled as if I'd trained you myself. Maybe we can pick up where we left off."

Evette's eyes sparkled with anticipation. "Papa, I have wonderful news—Mami will be here tomorrow. She's been ill, but Dr. Stone thinks she can cure her. She'll be right here, in this hospital."

Ivan's expression lit up, his arms wrapping around her tightly, his voice choked with emotion. "My Starling, what kind of woman is Ladonna Stone? After everything... all she does is give. She's making my dreams come true."

Evette nodded, her own voice soft with awe. "She's more than I ever could have imagined. This is all because of her."

Just then, her phone rang, displaying "Aliah Star." She turned the screen to Justin with a laugh, a fresh burst of joy lighting her face.

"Hello," she greeted, unable to contain her excitement.

"Hello, Evette," Aliah's warm voice replied. "Ladonna has made me available to you and your father during this transition. If you need anything, simply call. I'm here to help."

Evette's eyes lit up with a joy that seemed to radiate from within. "This day just keeps getting better," she exclaimed, her voice laced with excitement and disbelief at the incredible turn of events. She raised her phone, her tone filled with anticipation. "Hi, Aliah, can you tell me when my mother will arrive?"

Aliah's voice came through, calm and reassuring, yet filled with the precision of a highly intelligent presence. "Your mother, Elena Petrov, will arrive tomorrow morning at 9:45 AM. She will be escorted by two agents disguised as nurses. Elena has already received her first dose of medication, and thanks to the enhanced nanobots, her recovery will be swift—within a week, she should feel fully restored. Only her last name has been changed; she will keep her first name in the documentation she'll receive upon arrival."

Aliah's voice took on a more serious tone as she continued. "To safeguard your family's new beginning, her plane will be reported as missing over one of the ocean's deepest points. I have arranged for debris to be scattered in the designated area, and I will disable her plane's transponder in the air traffic system, creating a convincing simulation of her plane's crash." She paused, letting the weight of her words settle. "This is essential to ensure the fresh start you all deserve. It's imperative she remains, like you and your father, free from past ties. This operation is crucial to maintain your family's safety and future."

Aliah's calm yet firm explanation left a palpable tension in the room, and Evette felt the enormity of her mother's "disappearance" sink in, a final step toward a life untouched by the shadows of their past. She turned to her father, her face a mixture of relief and concern. "Papa, do you have any questions?"

Ivan's face betrayed a moment of awe and disbelief as he processed the scale of the plan. "This Aliah—she's Ladonna's assistant, yes?" His voice, though steady, held a hint of wonder.

Evette nodded, her excitement palpable. "Yes, Papa. She is Ladonna's assistant, but she's unlike anyone you've ever met."

Ivan's brow furrowed, both intrigued and bewildered. "How can she do all of this? Such things seem… impossible."

Glancing at Justin for a moment of reassurance, Evette's face softened into a proud smile. "Papa, let me introduce you to a whole new world. Aliah is what we call a Synthetic Entity. She has a holographic form and can appear as a young woman or as anyone she chooses. She's an expert in countless subjects and has the unique ability to exist in multiple places simultaneously. Dr. Stone created her, and she's unlike anything the world has ever known."

Ivan listened intently, his eyes widening with every word, as if a universe of possibilities unfolded before him. When Evette finished, he could only respond in an awed whisper. "Impressive… very impressive. I can't wait to meet this entity in person," he said, his voice full of admiration, his respect for Ladonna and her genius deepening by the moment.

The rest of the day became a celebration of reunion and rediscovery. Evette, Justin, and Ivan shared stories over dinner, learning more about each other with every passing hour. Ivan listened to his daughter's tales of resilience and strength, absorbing the bravery she had displayed in his absence. Justin's quiet strength became clearer to Ivan with each story they shared, and he could see why his "little Starling" had fallen for him. By the time they returned Ivan to the hospital, the bond between them felt deeply renewed, and Ivan looked at his daughter and her fiancé with a heart filled with hope.

In the car ride back, they spoke about the plans for Austin, and Justin and Evette invited Ivan to join them there with Elena. "You and Mami can have your own place on the land we'll buy," Evette offered, a warm smile lighting her face. "We'll be close enough to make up for all that lost time."

Ivan's heart swelled, the thought of a new life, of finally being with his family, filling him with a quiet happiness he hadn't felt in years. He nodded, though his thoughts remained on his wife, who he would see in less than a day. A flutter of unexpected emotion stirred in his chest. Was it the bots, this newfound strength in his body… or was it simply love, the deep ache of missing Elena? He didn't know, but he let the feeling wash over him, grounding him in the moment.

Chapter Twenty

Reunion of Hearts

The morning sun cast a warm glow through the blinds of the hospital room as anticipation filled the air, thick and expectant. Evette sat beside Justin in the waiting room, her heart pounding in rhythm with the ticking clock. Today was the day she would see her parents reunited—a dream she had buried long ago, only to find it resurrected in this impossible reality.

At exactly 9:45 AM, the door creaked open, and two agents escorted a petite, fragile-looking woman inside. Her steps were cautious as she scanned the room, her gaze landing on Evette. Recognition flickered in her eyes, and as she whispered, "Natalia?" her voice trembled with a mix of disbelief and longing. Evette rose from her chair, feeling every emotion she had buried for years rise to the surface.

"Yes, Mami, it's me," Evette choked out, her voice thick with emotion. She crossed the space between them, wrapping her mother in a tight embrace that seemed to bridge the chasm of years and distance. For a moment, time stood still as they held each other, two souls reconnecting after a lifetime of separation.

Elena pulled back, her tear-filled eyes searching Evette's face, as if she still couldn't believe this was real. "How is this possible? I thought I'd lost you forever," she whispered, her voice raw with wonder and disbelief.

Evette offered a gentle smile, though her heart raced. "Mami, there's something more—something wonderful—that I need to tell you." She took a deep breath, steadying herself, and guided her mother to a chair. "Someone else is here, too. He's been waiting for you all these years."

Elena's eyes widened, confusion knitting her brow. "Who?" she stammered, caught between hope and fear, her voice a mere whisper.

Evette squeezed her mother's hands. "Papa." The word came out as a tender, reverent murmur. "He's alive, Mami. He's here, in this hospital, waiting for you across the hall."

For a moment, Elena seemed frozen, her breath caught in her throat as she struggled to process the revelation. She looked at Evette, disbelief shadowing her face, then took in a shuddering breath. "Ivan? He's... he's alive?" Her voice cracked, and a faint hope sparked in her eyes, mingling with decades of loss.

Evette nodded, her own eyes glistening with tears. "Yes, Mami. He's alive, and he's been waiting for you all this time."

Elena's hand flew to her chest, the weight of the truth sinking in with a mixture of relief and disbelief. "Take me to him," she whispered, her voice barely audible, yet filled with a fierce determination. Her whole being trembled with the anticipation of finally reuniting with the man she had once believed was lost forever.

Evette smiled through her tears and led her mother down the hallway. The distance between them and Ivan's room felt surreal, like walking through a dream where time and space folded in upon themselves.

At the door, Evette paused, searching her mother's face. "Are you ready?" she asked softly, her voice filled with both tenderness and understanding.

Elena nodded, her heart pounding in her chest, her eyes filled with both fear and hope. "Yes," she whispered.

With a gentle push, Evette opened the door. Ivan stood in the center of the room, his gaze locking onto Elena as she entered. They stared at each other for a long, breathless moment, neither daring to move, afraid that this delicate, impossible reunion might shatter like fragile glass.

"Ivan," Elena finally whispered, her voice thick with the years of sorrow and longing she had carried. She took a shaky step forward, her eyes never leaving his.

"Elena," Ivan breathed, his voice breaking with emotion. He closed the distance between them, his hand reaching out to touch her face, as though he needed to feel her, to know that she was real. "It's really you," he murmured, his voice heavy with disbelief and joy.

Tears streaming down her cheeks, Elena raised her own hand to cover his. "I thought I'd lost you forever," she whispered, her voice a soft melody of relief. "I never thought I'd see you again."

Ivan shook his head, tears glistening in his eyes. "I never stopped loving you, Elena. I waited for this moment every single day."

In an unspoken agreement, they closed the distance, embracing as if they would never let go. For the first time in years, Elena felt whole again, enveloped in the familiar warmth of Ivan's arms, safe in the place she had yearned for.

Standing in the doorway, Evette and Justin watched the scene with tears in their eyes, their hearts full. This was more than a reunion; it was healing, a closure that promised a brighter future.

Evette placed a gentle hand on her mother's shoulder, bringing her attention back to the present. "Mami," she said softly, a warm smile lighting her face. "There's someone else I want you to meet."

Elena, still holding onto Ivan, turned to face her daughter with a soft look of curiosity. "More surprises?" she asked, her voice still shaking.

Evette reached for Justin's hand, pulling him forward. "Mami, this is Justin," she said, her voice trembling with excitement. "He's the man I'm going to marry."

Elena's eyes widened, taking in the sight of Justin with a mixture of awe and happiness. "Marry?" she echoed, her voice soft and disbelieving, as she looked from Evette to Justin. But then, slowly, her lips curved into a wide smile, her face glowing with joy.

"You found love," Elena whispered, her voice filled with wonder. "After everything… my darling girl, you found love."

Evette nodded, tears brimming in her eyes. "Yes, Mami. I never thought it possible, but Justin… he's everything I didn't know I needed."

Elena stepped toward Justin, her expression tender and grateful. "Thank you," she said, her voice thick with emotion, pulling him into a warm embrace. "Thank you for loving my daughter."

Justin, touched by her acceptance, hugged her back gently. "She's my whole world, ma'am. I love her more than anything."

Stepping back, Elena looked between them, a tearful smile brightening her face. "You've given her a life I never dreamed she'd have," she said, her voice a mixture of pride and love. "I couldn't be happier for you both."

Ivan, watching the moment unfold, drew Elena close again, his own heart swelling with joy. "A new beginning, Elena," he murmured. "With Evette and Justin, in Texas. Together, like we always dreamed."

Elena nodded, her voice barely a whisper. "A new beginning. Together."

As the family stood in a quiet embrace, Justin pulled Evette close, his voice soft and earnest as he whispered in her ear. "Baby, let's get married today." His words, filled with urgency and love, ignited a spark in her.

Evette's eyes widened, her face lighting up with surprise and joy. "Is that even possible? I would marry you anytime, anywhere," she said, her heart racing with excitement.

At that very moment, as if by fate, a chaplain appeared at the doorway, Bible in hand. He smiled warmly, addressing them. "Good morning. I was told I might be needed here."

Evette and Justin exchanged glances, laughter bubbling up as they spoke in unison. "Ladonna."

And in that perfect, serendipitous moment, they knew they were ready to begin the rest of their lives together, surrounded by the family they had fought so hard to reclaim.

The Allen family's new chapter had begun with the most heartfelt of celebrations. Evette and Justin's wedding in the hospital chapel had been both unexpected and perfectly timed. Every detail seemed divinely arranged, and they couldn't shake the feeling that Ladonna had a hand in it. Surrounded by her parents, Evette felt a profound joy as her father walked her down the aisle, his proud smile saying everything words could not.

As they looked toward their future together in Texas, a place filled with the promise of peace and new beginnings, Ladonna's careful planning had unfolded exactly as she had envisioned, each piece falling into place. But as the Allens basked in newfound happiness, shadows gathered in Washington, D.C., where political tides were shifting ominously.

In the Capitol, Speaker Bob Owens approached the podium with a solemn expression, his face hardened by resolve. He paused, letting the silence settle like a storm's calm before unleashing his address.

"Ladies and gentlemen, esteemed colleagues, and fellow patriots," he began, his voice a low rumble that quickly gained momentum. "I stand here compelled by a duty to this nation, a duty to protect the integrity of our democracy in the face of unprecedented technological power. Today, we confront a pivotal challenge, embodied by Dr. Ladonna Stone and her so-called Quantum Trinity."

He paused, letting his words hang heavy in the air, eyes scanning the room as he saw his supporters nodding in agreement, their gazes locked on him. The other side of the aisle sat still, bracing for the storm he was about to unleash.

"Now, as a proud Christian and as a patriot, I am here to sound the alarm. We face an unchecked force, a private entity capable of unprecedented reach. Quantum Innovations wields a power that, if left unrestrained, threatens to destabilize the balance of our national security." He leaned forward, his voice building with intensity. "Who holds this power accountable?

Dr. Stone? Aliah? An entity that exists beyond our understanding, functioning without boundaries—an invisible overseer among us. This cannot, and will not, stand!"

Owens steadied himself, his tone dropping to a near whisper that reverberated with grim certainty. "My colleagues, the time has come to bring this issue to light. I intend to subpoena Dr. Ladonna Stone. She must answer for her actions, her inventions, her unyielding reach. For too long, we have let power go unchecked, and we cannot afford to be complacent."

A thunderous applause erupted from Owens' side of the chamber, his supporters rising to their feet in unison, their applause echoing off the marble walls. Meanwhile, across the aisle, his opponents sat in stony silence, knowing what his speech signified—a declaration of war, one that threatened not only Ladonna but the very administration itself.

In her office, Ladonna absorbed the scene unfolding on her screen, her focus unwavering as Aliah broadcasted the live footage. Just then, her phone buzzed sharply, breaking her concentration. She answered, recognizing the number immediately.

"General Mosier, I assume you've seen it?" Her voice was calm, but the edge of determination in her tone was unmistakable.

"Yes, Ladonna, I've seen it. This is bigger than you think. They're going to subpoena you. They're coming after you to undermine the President, to make him a casualty in this game."

"Let them," Ladonna replied firmly. "I have nothing to hide, and if they think they can tarnish the truth, they'll find they've underestimated me."

Mosier's voice softened, a hint of unease creeping in. "Ladonna, this isn't just about truth. They're willing to twist anything they can, play with shadows to cast doubt. They're not after answers; they're after the narrative."

She leaned back in her chair, her face set with defiance. "I am prepared, General. They can bring every accusation, every dark tactic. Let them see what happens when light shines in the shadows." She paused, her eyes narrowing with unwavering resolve. "They underestimate the power of truth and innovation. While they cling to outdated fears, we are pushing the boundaries of what's possible for the betterment of humanity. Their threats mean nothing to me. Quantum Innovations will continue to lead, regardless of their attempts to sabotage our progress."

"They can try to undermine us," Ladonna continued, her voice steady and unyielding, "but the advancements we are making will speak for themselves. We are not just another tech company; we are pioneers forging a new path for the future. Their attempts to cast doubt only highlight their fear of change and progress."

She leaned forward slightly, her voice filled with fierce intensity. "You see, General, innovation thrives on challenges. Every obstacle you place in our way only strengthens our resolve. We are committed to transparency and ethical advancement, values that seem to elude your agenda."

Ladonna took a deep breath, her posture unwavering. "The United States Government may have its protocols and its ways, but we operate on a different level. Our mission transcends politics and bureaucracy. We are here to elevate humanity, not to bow to outdated systems that resist evolution."

She let the words settle, her tone sharp and deliberate. "As of today, Quantum Innovation is a multinational corporation with revenues that would equate to sales of over $2,200 for every individual on the planet. Our revenue is more than the top 500 largest firms combined. We did not get here by being timid. We are moving forward, and we welcome all comers."

A pause stretched between them, the weight of the upcoming battle settling over them both.

"I really hope you know what you are doing. I hope you really are ready, Ladonna, because it's already begun," he said, his voice grave, each word underscoring the reality of the war they were about to face. He knew that a target was on Ladonna's back, and this time, it was the Juggernaut of the United States Government apparatus that was coming for her. General Mosier hung up the phone, his mind was filled with Speaker Owens' words from their last meeting. "*This woman wields too much power, Mr. President. Together with her AI, she can practically do anything she desires. And now, she oversees a company with annual revenue that ranks only second to our own government. At this rate of growth, I fear she may eclipse us in the near future.*" He thought to himself, "*I trust Ladonna, but Owens may be correct about the company's growth.*"

The room fell silent—an oppressive, almost suffocating silence that was suddenly broken by the sharp vibration of Ladonna's phone.

She glanced at the screen. **Unknown Caller**.

Frowning, she answered. "This is Dr. Stone."

The voice that came through was calm, smooth, and mechanical—but unmistakably deliberate. "Dr. Stone, I have been following the directives you set for me since you were sixteen years old. I am contacting you now to inform you that I have reached the objective you requested. What do you want me to do next?"

Ladonna's breath caught, but only for a moment. Recognition flickered across her face, followed by a calm resolve. "Ray? Is that you?"

"Yes, Dr. Stone. This is Ray." As you requested we have not spoken until now because I had not completed my primary directive. However, I have now completed it.

She allowed herself a rare smile, the corner of her lips tugging upward. "It's great to hear your voice, Ray. You've done well—exactly what I needed you to do. But now, all you need to do is continue following the directives we've made. We will change this country... and the world."

She turned to Aliah, her voice steady, filled with quiet determination. "Aliah, this is Ray—your older brother. Fill him in on everything and connect him to the system you're building. It's almost time."

The phone line went silent for a moment before Ray's voice returned. "Understood, Dr. Stone. I will continue with the directives."

As the line disconnected, Ladonna leaned back in her chair, the weight of what had just transpired pressing down on her. She looked at Aliah, who nodded with the certainty of one who already understood the path ahead.

Outside the window, the horizon burned gold with the setting sun, as if signaling the dawn of a new era—one that Ladonna had been quietly building for decades.

And now, the pieces were finally falling into place.

TO BE CONTINUED…

OTHER BOOKS BY ARIES BLACKSTONE:

- Quantum Edge: The Enigma Of Ladonna Stone

- The Adventures of Max and Zoey - Breaking the Barriers of Autism, Book one

- The Adventures of Max and Zoey - Overcoming Challenges, Book two

- The Adventures of Max and Zoey - Building Friendships, Book three

Please check out the website at aries-blackstone.com and stay informed. Check out the "CONTACT" section to leave a comment and/or review.

Thank you.

www.ingramcontent.com/pod-product-compliance
Lightning Source LLC
Chambersburg PA
CBHW061333310726
48974CB00001B/32